Till Marriage Do Us Part

a novel

Bianca Bowers

Other books by Bianca Bowers

Poetry Books

Death and Life (Paperfields Press, 2014)

Passage (Paperfields Press, 2015)

Love is a song she sang from a cage (Paperfields Press, 2016)

Pressed Flowers (Paperfields Press, 2017)

Butterfly Voyage (Paperfields Press, 2018)

Thief (Paperfields Press, 2023)

Fiction

Cape of Storms (Auteur Books, 2019)

TILL MARRIAGE DO US PART
COPYRIGHT © 2024 BIANCA BOWERS
Published by Auteur Books
Book Cover Design by Bianca Bowers
Book Cover Art © Hanna Shewchyk (Shutterstock ID 1157776648)

This is a work of fiction. Names, places, events and incidents are either the products of
the author's imagination or used fictitiously. Any resemblance to actual persons, living
or dead, or actual events is purely coincidental.

A catalogue record for this book is available from the National Library of Australia

Paperback ISBN-13: 978-0-6457012-2-7
EPub ISBN-13: 978-0-6457012-3-4

First Edition Printed and Bound in Australia by Ingramspark.

Typeset in Josefin Sans, Lust Script and Adobe Jenson Pro by Bianca Bowers.

ENVIRONMENTAL RESPONSIBILITY
This books is printed using the print-on-demand model i.e. it is only printed when
an order has been received. This type of manufacturing reduces supply chain waste,
greenhouse emissions, and conserves valuable natural resources.

Where does love come from?
Where does it go?

That crackling birth and monotone death

Are we nothing more than lithium-
batteries
with an expiration

— Bianca Bowers

CONTENTS

Bronte
2016

In the months following my confession to Aden, I swam every night—when the first star appeared alongside the waxing half-moon, when flying foxes flew west, when lime tree frogs began their nocturnal chorus, when carpet pythons slithered out to hunt, when blue-backed night-spinners wove their sticky webs, and when nuclear families congregated around the dinner table. Unlike my morning swim, when I pushed my lungs and muscles to capacity, that night swim was my escape.

After a few token tumble turns and laps, I would float on my back, watch the night slowly devour the remaining daylight, and fantasise about Luther—a man who desired me as much as I desired him. I would envision Luther and I sitting side by side on pool chairs, like a real couple. I would scheme up ways to surmount our impossible situation: me, married with children in Australia; Luther, married with a child in America. And finally, I would try to wrap my head around the fact that I had fallen in love with a man who I had not yet met in person.

There had been a time when I had secretly managed to love Luther from a distance. A time when the fantasy had been enough to sustain me. A time when Luther and Aden had been separate planets that had orbited safely around me. But that time had passed. Luther and Aden were no longer orbiting; they had both collided into me, into each other, and we were all haemorrhaging equal amounts of love and hate.

I loved my husband, but I was in love with Luther. That night swim was everything.

PART I

Fourteen Months Earlier
2015

CHAPTER 1
Aden

September

When I charged through the kitchen stable door at 7 a.m. I found Bronte with her hands knuckle-deep in a bowl of minced meat that she and the twins fed to our pair of resident kookaburras every morning.

I held her chin and kissed her. "Morning, beautiful. Guess what?"

She rolled a piece of mince into a ball and placed it on a bamboo cutting board. "Judging by the goofy smile on your face, I'd say it's good news, whatever it is."

"You got that right," I said. "The vines are weeping."

"Aah," said Bronte, "cheers to a new season of growth."

"This is going to be a good year for Ghost Gum Winery, Bront. I can feel it in my bones."

Leyla hopped off her chair and tapped me on the thigh. "Why are the vines sad, daddy?"

I swept her into my arms and twirled her around. "The vines aren't sad, honey. It's just a saying. You see, the vines go to sleep during winter, and while they're asleep Daddy and Grandpa Judd and all the other workers prune the branches so that new buds can grow when spring arrives."

"Has spring arrived yet, Daddy?"

"It has, honey. In spring, the vines start to wake up and we know that they are awake when sap starts to seep from the pruned branches. The sap looks like a tear drop, which is why we say that the vines are weeping."

Bronte smiled and pointed to the mug beside the percolating coffee pot.

I put Leyla on her chair and ruffled Liam's hair. "What kind of dinosaur are you drawing, Liam?"

"Spinosaurus," he said, without looking up."

I caught Bronte's eye and she chuckled. I filled my favourite green mug three-quarters of the way and topped it with milk. "Has Dad been and gone already?"

With the kookaburras' minced meat laid out neatly on a plate, Bronte had stacked the blue plastic bowl in the dishwasher and was pumping eucalyptus soap into her hands at the sink. She turned on the tap and shook her head. "I haven't seen him yet."

Like my boyhood days, growing up on the family's blueberry farm in Coffs Harbour, I could set a clock by my father's early bird routine at Ghost Gum. Each morning, Dad rose before the sun stirred and the winery's free-range rooster, Walter, crowed, eager to tend to the vineyards for a few hours before he visited the main house at 7 a.m. to drink his coffee and talk to his grandkids. *Morning son*, he would say, his brow beaded with sweat and his fingernails caked in moist dirt.

I checked my watch and gulped more coffee. "It's seven fifteen."

"He's probably spending quality time with the weeping vines." Bronte scooped two heaped teaspoons of muscovado sugar into a blue mug, filled it with black coffee and stirred. "Why don't you save him a trip and hand-deliver his coffee to him today?"

I drained my cup and stood. "Good idea. You three have fun feeding the kookies, and I'll see you at lunch." I kissed each one on the forehead and exited through the stable door with Dad's coffee mug in my hand.

A thin mist laced the property, and grey kangaroos grazed on the sloping bank that led away from the house and down toward the Eucalypt forest and Verdelho vineyards. The only audible sounds were the warblers, whip and mistletoe birds. One thing I loved about the Granite Belt was its unique climate. Unlike the rest of Queensland, which pretty much had two seasons of hot and hotter, the Granite Belt experienced all four seasons due to its thousand-metre elevation above sea level.

I greeted the seasonal workers, who had been hired to trellis the Marsanne, Verdelho, and Petit Verdot vines that were rousing from their winter sleep, and sought out the team leader, Benny—a Spanish backpacker who funded his travels with seasonal work.

"Morning, Benny. Have you seen Judd this morning?"

Benny shook his head. "I think he's still at home."

"Why do you say that?"

"I usually see his boat when I walk along the river, but I did not see it today."

My neck muscles twitched as I scanned the area. The

Severn River divided Ghost Gum into two parcels of land: the bigger parcel housing the family home and majority of vineyards; while the smaller parcel contained Dad's two bedroom white-washed cottage and remaining vines. Dad's sixty-second commute to work involved crossing the Severn in a teal speed boat each morning. I reached into the back pocket of my jeans for my mobile and asked Benny to hold the cold coffee cup while I dialled Dad's number.

"Is everything okay, Mr Aden?"

"Please, Benny, call me Aden. I'm probably worrying for nothing."

Benny nodded.

"Straight to voicemail," I said.

Benny handed back the coffee cup. "If I see him, I will tell him that you are worried."

I smiled and nodded. "Thanks, Benny."

The walk to the river along the dirt track usually took five minutes, but I made it in three. Considering Dad habitually extinguished the fire in the wood burner before setting out in the morning, it didn't bode well to see remnants of smoke drifting from the chimney as I neared the mini jetty where Dad's boat should have been tied. I contemplated my best move—to walk back to the main house and drive; or follow the river on foot until I reached the bridge, and walk to Dad's cottage. I opted for the bridge.

My anxiety about Dad aside, the weather lived up to Queensland Tourism's official catch-cry: *Beautiful one day, perfect the next.* The resident white heron stalked fish in its favourite spot between the bullrush reeds, and a black cormorant sunned itself on a boulder jutting out of the river. A gang of cockatoos screeched from a nearby gum tree, and sunlight glinted off the water, where unruly patches of water hyacinth spread like fishing nets. Too bad the council considered the plant an environmental weed; the floating flowers were a sight to behold. As I approached the bridge, a group of wallabies hopped off in the opposite direction and a cloud of white butterflies wafted around purple and yellow wildflowers.

Once across the bridge, I ran the kilometre to Dad's cottage. His muddy boots stood outside the door, indicating he was inside. I rapped my knuckles against the blue door and called out. He didn't answer. "Dad?" I said louder. He didn't reply. I twisted the handle, but the door was locked. Feeling frantic, I inspected windows and peeped between curtain cracks as I circled the cottage and ransacked my memory for the location of Dad's hidden spare key. But with no way in, I grabbed one of his work boots to smash the glass in the lounge window and climbed inside.

Seconds later, I found Dad in his bed. His lifeless pulse and cold skin confirmed the worst. In between performing CPR, I put Bronte on speaker phone and asked her to call an ambulance. Thirty minutes later, the paramedics declared him dead on arrival, citing a heart attack as the likely cause of death.

On the day of Dad's funeral, while Bronte entertained the twins and catered to a full house, I spotted Bill the bank manager walking up the driveway. I thought it odd, but considering Dad's popularity, I quickly dispatched any negative thoughts and met him at the front door.

"Hey, Bill, thanks for coming to pay your respects." I stepped aside to welcome him in. "Can I get you a drink?"

Bill shook my hand. "I'm afraid it's not a personal visit, Aden." He scanned the open-planned living and dining room, where people stood in groups and talked. "Can we talk privately?"

My gut clenched. I could think of nothing positive about a non-personal visit from a bank manager.

"Aden?"

"Yup, sure, let's go into the home office." I gestured with my hand for him to walk ahead. Bronte caught my eye as Bill and I passed the living room. She raised her hands in the air and frowned as if to say *what's up?* I shrugged and shook my head. Inside the office, I closed the door and gestured for Bill to sit down on one of the two grey armchairs across from the desk.

I spoke first. "What's so urgent that it couldn't wait?"

Bill scratched his balding head. "It's the merger."

"What merger?"

"I discussed it with Judd before he, err, before his heart attack."

"Dad didn't mention a merger."

Bill cleared his throat. "One of the Big 4 banks is buying

Granite Union, and the merger has triggered an array of financial audits on random business accounts. Judd's account was flagged."

I took a couple of beats to run the hypotheticals through my head before I answered. "Flagged? For what reason?"

Bill placed his briefcase on the desk and released the two locks with a clicking sound. "In addition to the hefty mortgage on the winery, Judd had another parcel of debt."

I had been sitting back in my chair, but I leaned forward and placed my elbows on the desk. "What debt? I don't know about any debt."

Bill removed a manilla folder from his briefcase. "He didn't want to tell you, Aden."

I took the folder from Bill and paced the wooden floorboards while I scanned the contents. The file indicated that Dad had borrowed the deposit for Ghost Gum, which made no sense, because he'd told me that he'd used the money from the sale of our family's blueberry farm. I stopped pacing and sat behind the desk. "What's going on here, Bill? Dad borrowed the deposit for Ghost Gum? What happened to the money from the farm?"

Bill sighed. "I have no idea, Aden. This might be something he takes to his grave."

I scratched my head. "So what happens now?"

Bill removed another document from his briefcase. "Like I told Judd, I'm afraid I have to offer you an ultimatum."

"What's the ultimatum?"

Bill swallowed and looked down. "You either have to pay a

lump sum or, err…"

"Or what?"

"Or foreclose on the winery."

"What?! Are you fucking kidding me?"

"I'm sorry, Aden. If I could do something, I would."

"How much is the lump sum?"

Bill closed his briefcase and squirmed in his seat. "A hundred and fifty thousand."

I bolted out of my seat with such force that I dented the wall behind me. "A hundred and fifty grand?! Jesus, are you kidding me? Bronte and I don't have that kind of money lying around."

He smiled weakly and laughed. "Any rich friends?"

I placed my palms on the desk and glared at him. "No, Bill. No rich friends and no fucking family left either."

"Any investments you can cash in?"

I put my hand up to signal I'd had enough. "You know as well as I do that everything Bronte and I have is invested in Ghost Gum."

Bill stood and nodded. His knuckles had turned white from clutching the briefcase.

I rounded the desk and stood opposite him. "How long do we have to come up with the money?"

He swallowed and stepped back. "Seven days."

"Ha!" I spat out. "Let me get this straight. If we don't come up with the money in seven days, we lose everything we've worked for?"

He took another step back. "I'm afraid so, Aden."

"When did you speak to Dad?"

"I'm sorry?"

"You said you'd already spoken to Dad about this. When?"

Bill stepped back again and whispered his reply. "The day before he died."

Afternoon light streamed through the window, but my head plunged into a dark abyss, and the term 'seeing red' took on new meaning as my heart redirected all of the blood from my body to my eye sockets. Bill muttered something about the contract he'd left on the desk, but his voice sounded like it was underwater—muffled, distorted, and impossibly far away. I tried to speak, but the words were trapped in my throat, like debris in the Severn after a flood. I sensed Bill turning away from me—sneaking out with his tail between his legs—and though I wanted to pummel him, I stood in place like a gargoyle, because I couldn't summon a single part of my body to act. Everything I had worked for, and all I cherished, teetered on the verge of collapse, and I had no aces up my sleeves.

When the door clicked closed, I staggered to the window and gazed at the rows of vines in the distance. Thoughts ran through my head a hundred miles an hour. What the hell was Dad playing at? Why did he need to borrow the deposit for Ghost Gum? What did he do with the proceeds of the blueberry farm? Thanks to Bill-the-fucking-bank-manager, I might never know.

A tap on the shoulder prised me from my thoughts. I turned to find Bronte's anxious face.

"What happened? What did Bill want?"

I experienced a new sensation—a lethal cocktail of adrenaline and rage. I thought back to our wedding day and Bronte's vows. *Aden, you're my Lake Saint Clair—deep and tranquil.* That line struck me at the time, and continued to stay with me every day after we married. Above loyalty, kindness, respect, and support, tranquillity remained Bronte's primary need. A need I was about to renege on.

Bronte was reaching for my hand. "Aden, speak to me. What happened?"

"Irony is what's happening, Bronte. Iro-fucki-nee."

She stepped back and looked at me like I was a stranger. "You're scaring me. What the hell is going on?"

"Bill-the-fucking-bank-manager stopped by on the day of my father's funeral to tell me we're gonna lose the winery. That's what's going on."

"You can't be serious?"

"I'm as serious as my father's heart attack, Bronte. We are going to lose everything we've worked for. We're going to lose the winery when the vines are weeping. How's that for fucking irony?"

CHAPTER 2
Bronte

September

The moment I saw Bill and Aden head into the study on the day of Judd's funeral, I knew that Bill hadn't come to pay his respects. I scanned the room for our neighbours, Marjorie and Fred, and found them talking to Jill and Laurie Evans, who owned the Tulip Tree Vineyard in the nearby town of Ballandean. Out of all the people in the Granite Belt community, Fred and Marjorie were as steadfast as the region's renowned house-sized granite boulders. Their farm supplied the bulk of Queensland apples, and they grew every variety from Granny Smith to Pink Lady, Royal gala to Red Delicious. They were good people: salt of the earth, great sense of humour, and refreshingly politically incorrect. Outside of the funeral, I had rarely seen Fred deviate from his Steve Irwin get-up of work boots, khaki shorts and shirt, while Marjorie regularly donned an apron. Today, neither were recognisable in black suit and dress.

I took the twins by the hand and headed towards Jill and Laurie.

Fred spoke when he saw me. "That was good of Bill to pay his respects."

I nodded by default. "I'm sorry to interrupt your conversation, but can I steal Marjorie and Fred for a second?"

Jill nodded profusely and uttered "of course" before moving away to join another group of people outside on the deck. As soon as they were out of earshot, I spoke in a lowered voice to Fred and Marjorie. "Between you and me, I don't think Bill is here on business."

Marjorie's eyes narrowed momentarily. "Surely he's not making a business call on the day of Judd's funeral?"

Fred stepped forward. "What do you need us to do?"

"Can you occupy the twins for me while I check on Aden and find out what's happening?"

Marjorie took their hands. "Of course. Leyla, Liam, how about you delight me with your trampoline tricks?"

They both nodded and ran ahead. Fred patted my arm. "Take your time, love, and try not to think the worst."

I nodded without conviction and thanked them.

I opened and closed the study door with the stealth of a church mouse. Inside, Aden stared out of the window, his jaw clenched. Bill must have been and gone. Not wanting to startle him, I called his name as I approached, but he was so lost in thought that he didn't hear me. I tapped his shoulder. "Aden, speak to me. What happened? What did Bill want?"

He spun around with a stranger's eyes. "Irony is what's happening, Bronte. Iro-fucki-nee."

"I've never seen you like this. Could you stop talking in riddles and tell me what's going on?"

"Bill-the-fucking-bank-manager stopped by on the day of my father's funeral to tell me we're gonna lose the winery. That's what's going on."

"You can't be serious?"

"I' m as serious as Judd's heart attack, Bronte. We are
going to lose everything we've worked for. We're going to
lose the winery when the vines are weeping. How's that for
fucking irony?"

I reached for his hand, but he drew his elbow back to
make a fist at the same time and punched a hole through
the window, elbowing me in the corner of my eye. The blow
propelled me backwards and I crashed to the floor in sync
with the shards and splinters of glass that hit the timber and
scattered like water droplets across the burgundy Persian rug.
Aden moved from the window. Glass scrunched and shat-
tered beneath his shoes. I held out my arm, expecting him to
help me up, but he stood over me with his arms at his sides.
A drop of blood from his knuckles splattered against my
throat. "I can't be here right now, Bronte."

Though he towered over me like a Viking, with his lean,
six foot five frame, Aden had always been akin to aloe vera
gel on sunburnt skin—his mere presence, a soothing balm.
His hazel-flecked blue eyes crinkled when he smiled, and
signalled safety from the moment we met. If anyone had ever
suggested that a fault line of rage lay dormant at his core,
I would have viewed the concept in the same light as Jesus
descending on a cloud.

I rolled onto my side, forgetting about the broken glass
that blanketed the floor like a carpet. "Aden, wait." But
the pain of glass splinters buried in my palms stopped me
mid-sentence, and I collapsed. Aden slammed the door.

I rolled onto my other side and got up in stages—knees

first, feet second—before I staggered to the door and went in search of Aden. I scanned the crowds for his head—nothing. The sound of the garage door grinding open prompted me out the front door and left toward the garage.

"Aden, wait, please don't go." But I was too late. He accelerated down the driveway, almost hitting a jacaranda tree on the way. People were outside then, whispering to each other. Marjorie rounded the corner with Leyla and Liam, only to stop dead in her tracks, release the twins' hands and cover her mouth in shock. Fred, habitually calm under pressure, took control. "Right, I think it's time for everyone to go," he said, herding people towards their cars. I stood statue-like, not breathing until I realised I was holding my breath. With Leyla and Liam at my side, Marjorie ushered us into the house where she stirred sugar into a cup of water.

Leyla pointed at my eye. "Mummy, your eye is puffy."

I covered it instinctively with my hand and Marjorie swung into gear. "Here," she said, moving over to the freezer and retrieving a bag of frozen peas. "Sit down and ice that before the swelling gets any worse. And we need to get that glass out of your hand. Where do you keep the tweezers?"

"They're in the ensuite bathroom cabinet," I said.

"I'll go," said Fred.

"What happened, Mummy?" said Liam. "Where's Daddy?"

I looked from Marjorie to Fred. "Daddy had some bad news, honey. He'll be back in a little while."

"How about some apple pie and ice cream in front of the telly, kids?"

Leyla clutched my arm. "I don't want to leave Mummy."

"Mummy needs to rest for a few minutes," I assured her.

Marjorie looked at Fred as he approached with the tweezers. "Will you settle them in front of the telly?"

Fred nodded and led the kids away, while Marjorie spooned apple pie and ice cream into bowls.

When they both returned, they sat on either side of me. "What happened, Bronte? Did Aden hit you?"

"Oh, God, no," I said, realising the implications of Aden storming out and me following behind with a swollen eye and bloody hand.

Marjorie took my hand and tweezed the first glass splinter.

I pulled my hand back. "Ouch."

"Sorry, love, but it's going to hurt."

I took a deep breath and repeated Aden's words. "We're losing the winery."

Marjorie shook her head. "That can't be right."

Fred crossed his arms over his chest. "What's Bill playing at?"

I shook my head. "I don't know. We need to find Aden."

Fred patted my knee. "Any ideas where he went?"

"I'm thinking Judd's place?"

He stood and took his mobile from his pocket. "Leave it to me. I'll call if I find him.

CHAPTER 3
Luther

September

I didn't usually stand to attention when my wife, Tina, bellowed my name. But I was desperate for a smoke and a reason to leave the group of dads who were gathered around the barbecue drinking beers and discussing sport. I could hear the door bell chiming as I stepped inside the living area and headed for the hall. Tina was standing at the door—the top of her head at least a foot below the glass paneling—with hands on hips and lips pursed.

"Your mother is here." She mouthed the words in disgust.

"Well, let her in," I said.

Tina held up her hand like a stop sign. "Oh my god, Luther, did you invite her to my house?"

"Don't you mean our house?"

"You know exactly what I mean. Did you invite her?"

The bell chimed again.

"No, I didn't invite her. You told me not to, remember?"

"So why is she here?"

"Because her granddaughter is four today." I gently moved Tina aside and opened the door. "Mom, I wasn't expecting you?"

"I know. I had to hear about it from one of my tarot clients."

I looked at Tina, who rolled her eyes and set off down the hall like an ant on the march.

"Are you going to let me in, Luther, or do I have to stand out here like a traveling salesman?"

"Sorry, Mom." I opened the door and stepped aside.

Mom smelled like rosewater and wore her usual summer pastel colors. Her bohemian nature had won my father's initial affection and fueled his and Mom's eventual estrangement. Funny how that works. I saw a similar scenario playing out in my life too.

Mom removed two gifts from her voluminous tie-dyed tote bag and handed me one. "One for you, and one for my little princess."

I took the gift like a member of the bomb squad would take an unknown package. "What is it?"

"It's a reminder to remind you about what's important, Luther."

I need a smoke, I thought and changed the subject. "Addy is outside with her friends. Follow me."

"What about your gift? Aren't you going to open it?"

"I'll open it in a minute when I go for a smoke."

She shook her head and tutted. "Still smoking?"

"Yeah," I said, "old habits keep me sane."

Outside, Addy spotted Mom and bounded over. "Grandma Beth, you came!" Mom dropped her bag on the grass and scooped Addy into her arms like a ballerina. Addy's pink and white princess dress twirled like a whirling dervish and her laughter echoed like sonar. I said a silent thank you in my head that she was gifting me five minutes of not having to speak to my mother. Not that I didn't love Mom. I did. But her life's mission was to push me to improve my life, follow my dreams, and never accept anything less than the best. In other words, she knew how to push my buttons.

"I'll catch up with you in five, Mom."

Mom put Addy down and held her hand. "Tell me you're not smoking at your daughter's birthday party, Luther?"

I took the box of camels out of my pocket. "Yeah, I am."

She tutted and turned to Addy. "Shall we go inside and open your gift from Grandma Beth?"

Addy jumped up and down, and I watched Mom walk away in a cloud of baby pinks, blues, greens and yellows.

I walked around the side of the house, leaned against the wall, and placed Mom's gift at my feet. Mom was right about my smoking, but I did use it as an excuse to escape from crowds—a small miracle for an INFJ. I shook my Zippo after the ignition failed on the first few attempts and inhaled. That first drag and exhale was like a shot of morphine—a domino effect of easing and respite, starting at my head and working its way down to my toes. I reached out to dismantle a red leaf from the neighbor's maple tree and turned it over in my palm. Our garden was another victim in the long line of victims who had been overruled by Tina's tyranny. Other than the oak tree, where I hung Addy's tyre swing, Tina had insisted that one tree with unruly roots was more than enough, and hired a landscaper to lay and maintain perfectly manicured turf and neatly trimmed garden beds.

I eyed Mom's gift and thought about how much I had loved her garden as a child. After my parents divorced, Mom bought a white cottage with stained-glass windows and an ancient golden elm tree in the garden. Sprinkled with crystal geodes, zen statues, birdbaths, and musical wind chimes, I'd never seen Mom happier than when she left Dad and followed her calling to guide lost souls by reading tarot cards and tea leaves.

My brother and I spent weekends with Mom, and Saturday afternoons were my favorite. While my brother chose to watch Goonies for the hundredth time, Mom and I would sit in the wisteria-shrouded gazebo, drinking tea and eating dainty sandwiches and jam scones while she read *Alice In Wonderland* to me. My brother called Alice 'a girl's story', but it fed my hungry imagination and laid the groundwork for what would later become my ideal, but impossible, woman. I still remember the sound of that wonky teapot lid clinking as she poured the English Breakfast tea.

I took my last drag, stubbed the cigarette, and pulled my cell from my back pocket to open my notes app. I was thirty thousand words into my third book in a paranormal series, and inspiration would descend at the most inconvenient times. I typed madly, trying not to lose a single thought as each one rushed into my head like a flash storm. My wheelhouse was paranormal, and I frequently toured haunted houses in and around Andover and Salem. I wrote and published the first book in my paranormal series the year Addy was born, through Createspace—Amazon's independent publishing arm. With miniscule control over my marriage and life, the notion of submitting to be rejected ninety percent of the time did not appeal. The desire to own my writing far outweighed my fear of being a commercial failure in the traditional sense. My Twitter account provided solace in that sense, with many poets and writers in the same boat and sharing a similar philosophy.

Tina knew nothing about my writing, and I wanted to keep my secret for as long as humanly possible. Which is to say that Tina would eventually find out, because she was like a ferret, or Sherlock Holmes—perpetually in someone else's business, prone to sniff for clues.

I put my cellphone in my back pocket, picked up Mom's gift, and summoned all of my energy. I would need every last drop to deflect Mom's ideas about what I should and shouldn't be doing with my life, and avoid Tina's moaning about my mother. As I rounded the corner, I glanced over at the barbecue. The dads had finished cooking the sausages and the kids were squirting ketchup into bread rolls. Tina had her back turned toward me while she gossiped with her group of likeminded friends— Kelsey, Tiffany, Britney, and Madison. I headed for my basement, thinking I'd bought myself a few minutes when I found Mom sitting at my desk with one of my books in her hand.

She pointed to the gift in my hand. "You still haven't opened your gift."

"I told you, I was having a smoke."

She waved the book. "Does Tina know about these yet?"

I shook my head. "No, and I'd like to keep it that way,

thanks."

"Why would you want to keep this from your wife?"

"Can we not do this now, Mom?"

"You're right, Luther. Let's do the gift opening instead."

Thinking I'd avoided the conversation about my marriage to Tina, I sat on the old brown Chesterfield sofa, that the previous owners had left behind, and tore a corner of the pink and silver gift paper. Mom put my book down and joined me on the sofa.

"This again?" I said, ripping the paper to reveal Mom's original copy of *Alice in Wonderland*.

"What do you mean, this again? I thought Alice was your favorite?"

"She was my favorite when I was a kid, Mom. But it's a little late for fantasies and fairytales, don't you think?"

"People who say it's too late are people who have given up, Luther. At a minimum, you could share some Wonderland magic with your daughter."

"I will read the book to Addy, but I don't see what relevance *Alice in Wonderland* has in my life."

"Hand on your heart, Luther. Do you honestly believe Tina is the one?"

"Please tell me you're joking, Mother. My wife is throwing a birthday bash for our daughter, your grandchild, and you're asking me if Tina is the one. What the actual fuck?"

"There's no need to curse, Luther. The question is simple enough. Do you love Tina or have you settled for Tina the way you settled for May?"

I twisted in my seat to face her. "That's a low blow, considering how my marriage to May ended. Why can't you be happy for me?"

"That is precisely why I'm pushing this, Luther. It's not my job to be happy for you. It's my job to ensure that you are truly happy. There's a difference, you know?"

"This is why I hardly visit you anymore, Mom."

She raised her right eyebrow and smiled a knowing smile, which usually meant she had anticipated my response. "Your father has conditioned you into playing it safe your whole life, Luther. Do you want your daughter to inherit your philosophy?"

"I'd rather play it safe at this stage than subject Addy to the childhood I endured."

"I'm sorry you still see my divorce from your father as a negative in your life, Luther. Don't you see it would have been worse if we'd stayed together?"

I shook my head. "No, I don't see that."

She reached for my hand. "Your father and I are like magic and science—each tries to cancel the other out. Living with both of us under the same roof would have been a constant tug of war. Your stepmother is a far better match for him than I was."

I stared at her while she patted my hand. Mom had a way of removing the scales from my eyes, but I rarely admitted she was right. "I haven't eaten all day."

She stood and clapped her hands together, pleased to have

a mission. "Tell me what you want."

"I trust your judgment," I said, "as long as you don't bring me a salad."

I watched her ascend the stairs like a candy floss cloud, and only when I heard her shoes squeak on the top step did I turn my attention to the book. I smiled at the memory of *Alice in Wonderland*, and the old childhood excitement filled my belly and ignited my imagination like a match to drought-stricken kindling. Mom wasn't completely wrong. I had settled. And not just in my marriage to Tina; I had been settling my whole life.

Love at first sight.

Soul mate.

Pfft.

By the time I had reached adulthood, that's what Dad had taught me and that's what I believed. I was a Capricorn through and through—a rational thinker who rarely let emotion creep into my decisions. I learned early on, growing up poor in Boston, that life and love had the hallmarks of a series of boxing matches that were fixed in my disfavor. It was with this deeply entrenched philosophy that I followed the path of least resistance in my professional and personal life, transitioning comfortably from high school into marriage with my high school sweetheart, May, and into the mailroom of a Consultancy Firm that offered tender and proposal writing services for the plethora of firms who bid on Boston City Projects. Much like my progression in the workplace, where I slowly moved through the ranks from the mailroom to assistant to Tender Writer and eventually Department Manager, my marriage to May was more of a logical conclusion than an act of true love. Was I happy with May? I guess. I mean, what is happiness? Two people, who share a history and still like each other in the present? If that's what happiness is, then yeah, I was happy with May. But happiness ended abruptly the year we lost our first child—Lily-Rose—to SIDS.

May and I never recovered. She thought I blamed her, and though I tried to tell her otherwise, there were days when I couldn't stand to look at her because there was a small part of me that did blame her. After living in a state of estrangement for a year, May moved out, and we divorced soon after. I can't say Mom didn't warn me, but I can say I ignored her advice.

I met my second wife, Tina, at a work function. Tina was a boss woman right from the start; she knew what she wanted, and she took charge of everything. After my relationship with May, Tina was a breath of fresh air. And, while I wasn't head over heels in love with Tina, I did take Dad's rational-over-romance philosophy to heart when Tina proposed that I propose. What felt like a carousel ride from the moment I asked her father's permission—interviewing wedding planners, organizing guest lists, poring over seating plans, suit fittings, picking a best man, tasting every wedding cake from chocolate to vanilla to lemon to lavender—strongly suggested that I married Tina in the hopes that we would make a good partnership. I also figured Tina's extrovert would complement my introvert. But the honeymoon wore off faster than an eraser on pencil scratchings. I quickly learned that Tina's extroversion was materialism in disguise. Her propensity for dinners, parties and barbecues stemmed from her need to exhibit her material status—the size of our house, the cars we drove, the number of times she won *Salesperson of the Month* at Falconer Realty. Again, I can't say Mom didn't warn me. But of course, I knew better.

CHAPTER 4
Aden

September

I drove like a hoon to my father's cottage. All the while, the debt parcel swallowed my mind like the cumulonimbus cloud was swallowing the sun. I couldn't lose Ghost Gum The winery was more than my dream; it was my entire world. I opened Dad's front door with the newly cut spare on my keyring. Inside, I ran cold water over my bloody knuckles and pulled out bits of glass that were embedded into my skin before wrapping my hand with a gauze bandage I found in the first aid kit Dad kept under the sink. I started my search in the kitchen, opening drawers and cupboards, before moving to the linen cupboard and ending with a single box under Dad's bed. Dad wasn't a hoarder—after Mum died, he was keen to sell the farm and move forward. He gave Mum's clothes and belongings to the Salvos and only kept a handful of photo albums. Needless to say, my search yielded nothing. Feeling desperate, I sat on the edge of Dad's king single bed and spoke. "Dad, if you're listening, give me a sign, please. We're about to lose everything we worked for."

Just then I heard tyres on the gravel outside. I moved the curtain aside with my finger and saw Fred. Bronte must have sent him. For the first time since my outburst in the study, I thought about Bronte. I had hit her in the eye with my elbow and she'd fallen on broken glass. And what had I done? I had stepped over her and left her to deal with a house full of people. *What an asshole.*

"Aden?"

Fred was knocking on the door.

"Fred," I said, opening the door and stepping aside for him to enter.

"Everything okay, mate?"

I shook my head and ushered him to the small round table in the kitchen diner.

"Bronte said something about losing the winery. She must have misunderstood you, right?"

I scowled and shook my head. "She didn't misunderstand. Granite Union is merging with one of the Big 4, and apparently my father had a secret parcel of debt that has triggered a bank audit."

"What parcel of debt? I thought your dad used proceeds from the sale of the blueberry farm?"

"That was going to be my next question. I was hoping you might know something about Dad's affairs?"

Fred shook his head. "Sorry, mate, your dad never said a word to me."

I pushed my chair back and slammed my fist into the table. "I don't know what to do, Fred. I've never experienced this kind of rage before. I can't get my head around losing everything we've worked for."

Fred stood and put his hand on my shoulder. "Listen, mate, there must be a way around this."

"There is a way around," I said. "A lump sum of a hundred and fifty thousand."

"Jesus," muttered Fred. "Look, mate," he said, scratching his head, "Marjorie and I could help out with fifty…"

I held up my bandaged hand. "I appreciate the offer, Fred, but I couldn't take your money, and the bank shouldn't be putting us in this position."

"Are you sure there's no other way?"

I shook my head. "Bill explained the situation clearly: pay a hundred and fifty thousand in seven days or foreclose."

"Crikey, Aden. And he didn't give you any warning before today?"

I sat on the edge of the sofa and put my head in my hands. "He allegedly spoke to Dad the day before he died."

"You don't think it had something to do with Judd's heart attack?"

"It's too much of a coincidence, don't you think? But there's nothing I can do about it now."

Fred put his hand on my shoulder. "Listen, mate, I promised Bronte I'd call if I found you. She's in a bit of a state. Her face is swollen and Marjorie's picking glass out of her hands."

"You must think I'm a dick, but I can't face Bronte and the kids. I've gone from hero to fucking zero in record-breaking time."

"The situation is shitty, I'll give you that. But you're not at zero yet, mate."

I walked to the window and looked at the river. My rage was dissipating and turning into dread. "What am I gonna tell them, Fred? Where are we gonna go? We have no relatives or…"

"You have Marjorie and me, mate. We'll help you in whatever way we can."

Fred's phone started ringing. He checked the screen and said, "Bronte's calling, mate. Can I tell her I'm bringing you home?"

I sighed in despair and nodded. "I was hoping to find an answer in Dad's belongings, but there's nothing. So yeah, I'm going home. This is not a problem I can run away from."

"Good man," said Fred.

By the time I got home, Bronte's swollen eye had turned blue and both her hands were bandaged. The twins ran out, with towels wrapped around them, the minute they heard my voice. Marjorie followed suit. "They're all bathed, Bront. Shall I fix them some dinner before we go?"

Bronte shook her head. "Thanks, Marjorie, you've done more than enough. Besides, there's plenty of leftovers from the funeral."

"Bronte's right," I said. "Thanks for all your help today."

"The twins are welcome to spend the night or day with us tomorrow while you sort things out."

"Thanks, Marjorie, we should be fine tonight, but I'll check in with you in the morning."

I walked Marjorie and Fred to the front door and Bronte helped the twins get dressed.

Bronte and I did not have a chance to talk until a few hours later—after the twins had eaten dinner and Bronte had read them a bedtime story. When my exhausted wife sank into the sofa alongside me, I should have hugged her, leaned into her, let her in. I should have apologised for her eye and hands. Instead, I picked another fight.

"Considering the conversation we've got brewing, was it really necessary to include a bedtime story to tonight's agenda?"

"Considering today's events, and knowing how kids need their routine, I did think it was necessary."

I rolled my eyes and shook my head. "Whatever, Bronte."

She sat up and glared at me. "Are you going to apologise?"

"For what?"

She gestured to her black eye and bandaged hands.

"Bill has given us an ultimatum—a hundred and fifty grand in seven days or foreclosure."

"Did you hear what I said?"

I grabbed her elbow and squeezed. "For fuck's sake, Bronte, did you hear what I said? We're losing the winery!"

She flinched from the pain. "I am more concerned about losing my husband right than I am about the winery."

"Are you fucking kidding me, Bront?"

She left me on the sofa and opened the sliding door. "Come here," she said.

"Why?"

"Just humour me, will you?"

I joined her begrudgingly.

"What do you see?" she repeated.

"I see a blanket of darkness. What's your point?"

"My point is that although you can only see darkness right now, you're also well aware that there are rows of vines out there, and wallabies, and the Severn river, and…"

"And, and, and…Yeah, I get it. But it doesn't change the fact that we're gonna lose it all when the sun fucking rises tomorrow."

"We can't give up, Aden. There must be a way."

Ever the optimist, she started running through hypotheticals. I pulled my iPhone from my back pocket, dialled Bill's number, and shoved the handset into her bandaged hand. "Here, you speak to Bill, if you think you're so special."

Minutes later she handed the phone back to me. "You're right. There is no wiggle room. We have seven days to find the money or we say adios to our home and livelihood."

I shook my head in disgust. "What are we gonna do, Bront?"

She looked me in the eye. "The odds of us drumming up a hundred and fifty thousand dollars in seven days are low to none."

"Fred offered to loan us fifty. But I turned him down."

"Even if we accepted fifty, we're still a hundred thousand down, and all we'd be doing is digging ourselves a deeper debt hole."

"What are you saying, Bront?"

"Bill says that we'll have four weeks to vacate if we are forced to foreclose."

I kicked the deck railing. "I just wanna break things."

"Don't. We need to keep our shit together for the kids."

She went inside to retrieve her phone from the kitchen bench top and headed towards the office.

I followed her inside. "Where are you going?"

"To make some calls. While you and Judd were planting and harvesting vines, I was building relationships with visitors and clients."

"Are you asking people for money?"

She shook her head. "We'll likely have to move closer to Brisbane, and either one of us or both of us are gonna need a job."

She disappeared around the corner and I slumped into the nearest armchair with my head in my hands. I had built my dream over several years, yet Bill-the-fucking-bank-manager had razed it in seconds. I didn't want another job. I didn't want to lose my home, my vines, my life. My rage turned to despair the second time that day and I wept, like the vines outside.

CHAPTER 5
Bronte

October

Aden initialled the last page of the lease agreement and thrust it along the tiled kitchen bench. The wad of papers sailed past me and stopped with a flutter at the edge of Daphne's manicured hand. Her maroon fingernails tapped momentarily—like an involuntary tic—bringing to mind the adage about hearing a pin drop.

Daphne Dalloway was a wealthy widow whose late husband had bequeathed her a sizeable property portfolio and several businesses. I'd met her one year when she visited Ghost Gum and stayed in touch via my monthly newsletter, which, unlike other subscribers, Daphne consistently responded to. When I reached out to her after Bill's shattering news, she quickly came to the party and offered us a long-term lease on an old Queenslander she owned in Sandgate, a seaside suburb east of Brisbane. The word *Queenslander* referred to the architectural style of the house. Designed for the tropical and sometimes harsh Queensland climate, Queenslanders were constructed with a light timber frame and elevated with stilt-like wooden pillars to allow for good airflow during hot summers and extra elevation for flash floods. Daphne's Queenslander had a white frame and red trim, and although the exterior paint flaked and peeled in patches, the house was within walking distance to the beach and boasted an oversized pool.

A palm frond dropped into the saltwater pool, which

sparkled beyond the kitchen window, bringing me back to the moment at hand.

"I can throw in monthly pool maintenance if you like?" said Daphne.

I waved my hand. "That's okay. It might be therapeutic to fish out leaves and balance PH levels."

Daphne looked at me over her onyx-framed reading glasses. "That comment reminds me of your Ghost Gum newsletters. You have a knack for turning the seemingly ordinary into a philosophical life analogy."

I smiled wryly. "You call it a knack, I call it a coping mechanism."

Aden cleared his throat. "Are we done?"

"Signing," I said quickly. "Are we done signing?"

Daphne straightened the pages. "I'll get a copy to you by the end of the week."

"Thanks so much, Daphne. I'll walk you out."

Aden left the kitchen without acknowledging Daphne. "Don't worry, Bronte, I'll watch the kids."

My cheeks flushed and I lowered my voice. "I apologise for my husband. He's having a hard time adjusting. Please know that I'm immensely grateful for all your help."

Daphne patted my hand. "No apology needed. If my late husband had lost everything he'd worked for, he would be angry and bitter too."

I nodded and gestured to the kitchen door. "Shall we?"

Daphne led the way along the garden path toward the

pedestrian gate. She wore intoxicating perfume, a knee-length black pencil skirt, and a silky blouse with white, red and black floral print. Her short black hair matched her no-nonsense personality and she hailed from the generation of women who never left the house without a full face of make-up. Outside on the verge, we stood alongside her red Mercedes SLK. Retrieving her keys from her black leather handbag, she said, "I was going to ask Aden how his interview went, but thought better of it. Did he get the job?"

I shook my head. "Unfortunately not. But he has an interview for a sales job at Alchemy wines tomorrow."

"Sounds promising."

"To you and me, yes, but Aden is less enthusiastic. I understand that losing the winery has crushed his dreams, but we' don't exactly have the privilege to wallow."

Something caught her eye and she looked up at the bedroom window. Instinctively, I turned and looked too. Aden was peering down at us like a hawk.

Daphne touched my shoulder. "All the more reason for you to forge your own path. Have you ever considered writing?"

I semi scoffed. "Writing was my dream before I met Aden. I guess life had other plans for me."

"I meant what I said about your newsletters. I would have paid a monthly subscription if it had come to that."

"Thanks, you're too kind."

Daphne unlocked her car with a remote. "I'm not saying it to be kind. I have an opportunity for you to consider."

"There's a fine line between a helping hand and a charity

case."

"You're not a charity case. I happen to own the local community newspaper, as well as a group of magazines and there are a few opportunities up for grabs."

My stomach lurched—a combination of excitement and fear. "What did you have in mind?"

"There's an editor role for one of the lifestyle magazines. But I'm also thinking about creating a regular column for the local paper. Something along the lines of your Ghost Gum newsletter. What do you think?"

"I think that I need to pinch myself to make sure I'm not dreaming."

"Can I take that as a yes?"

"Yes," I said, unable to contain my smile.

She looked up at the window again. "Why don't I swing by tomorrow when Aden's at his interview, and we can discuss the details over a cup of tea?"

I nodded and smiled. "I'd like that."

"Keep your chin up, Bronte. Everything happens for a reason, and it's life's toughest challenges that forge us into our best or worst selves."

She slipped into the driver seat and opened the passenger window. "See you tomorrow."

"I look forward to it."

The engine roared to life and I stayed on the verge until her sleek, red car reached the end of the street and turned right.

Back in the kitchen, Aden waited for me with his arms crossed. His height had never bothered me before, but in the days and weeks following our bad news he had morphed from protective lighthouse to menacing watchtower.

"What are you smiling about?"

I looked up to meet and search his eyes for a speck of warmth, but the once blue flecks were icy shards. "Daphne may have a job opportunity for me."

He uncrossed his arms and stepped toward me. "I thought we decided you would stay home with the twins as long as possible?"

"We agreed to that in another life, Aden. Besides, the kids are four now. They'll be starting primary school in the new year, and they'll both benefit from socialising and doing something different."

"Doing something different? You mean like you?"

"You're not the only one who has to rethink their entire career."

"Aah, you're thinking of a career."

I frowned and raised an eyebrow. "Meaning?"

"Meaning, you seem to be revelling in your new life. I can't help but wonder if you ever loved me, or if you chose me because you had no other options."

"Wow, tell me you didn't just say that?"

"I'm telling you how it looks."

I crossed my arms and sighed. "It's like you've been hiding a whole other side of yourself, Aden, and I don't like it."

"Ditto, Bronte."

"In case you haven't noticed, we're in a precarious situation. If I return to work, it will take some of the financial pressure off of you and help us to get our lives back on track."

He leaned in close enough for his nose to be centimetres away from mine. "Wake the fuck up, Bronte. Our lives have officially derailed."

I stepped back and swallowed. "I know you're angry, Aden, so I'm going to give you some leeway here, but you need to pull yourself together. The twins are our priority, and neither of us has the luxury to mope around and throw a pity party. Pessimism will only breed more pessimism."

"Excuse me, Miss fucking new-age-everything-is-coming-up-roses."

"I'm trying to move forward. What else can we do?"

"No matter what life throws at you, you face the challenge and bounce back stronger than ever."

"Sounds like a veiled criticism."

"Let me lift the veil for you. From where I'm standing, there is nothing that will keep you down—not your family's demise, not losing Ghost Gum, nothing."

My lip trembled. But before I could reply, Leyla rushed into the kitchen. "Mummy, mummy, come and see my bedroom."

Aden rolled his eyes and walked out.

"Show me," I said, taking Leyla's hand and swallowing the lump in my throat for the umpteenth time.

CHAPTER 6
Luther

October

When I turned right onto our street on Monday night, there was no mistaking Halloween. Candle-lit, hollowed-out pumpkins glowed outside most windows, or front doors and on driveways. People in fancy dress were already trick or treating; witches, Jason masks, Michael Myers, grim reapers, zombies, Frankensteins, vampires, ghosts and ghouls paraded around like extras on an apocalyptic film set. I loved Halloween and often used the event as an atmospheric backdrop for my paranormal series. But back in the real world, the night would have been macabre without families and kids trick or treating.

I parked my car in the garage and went around the back, as usual, stopping to have a quick smoke on Addy's tire swing. I could see Tina through the kitchen window. She was already dressed in her Laurie Strode outfit—a white button up shirt bursting at the start of her cleavage. She wanted me to go as Michael Myers, but I insisted the mask would scare Addy. Much to Tina's disappointment, I decided on Superman—hiding the suit beneath a white shirt and suit braces. Addy was going as a princess. *Which princess do you want to be? I had asked her. A princess with a pink frilly dress, glittery nails and pretty white shoes, she had replied.* I inhaled and held the smoke in my lungs. Nicotine may have been toxic, but it was fresh mountain air compared to Tina. As I sat there, watching Tina with her cell phone glued to her ear, hands gesticulating as she chatted her usual thousand miles an hour, I thought back to a similar night, four years earlier. We were supposed to be celebrating Addy's second month in the world, but Tina was only thinking of herself.

Four Years Earlier

Tina didn't hear me enter the kitchen, nor did she see me lean my messenger bag against the kitchen table, as she talked on the phone. I found Addy lying in her shocking-pink designer mobile crib, that Tina had chosen for appearances but which fortunately also had its practical uses—you could lift it like a basket or wheel it around the house like a pram. She wore a fluffy pink hooded onesie, complete with bunny ears. Her tiny hands made fists when she glimpsed me, and she gurgled and smiled when I scooped her up and studied her. My heart did what it always did and melted like a marshmallow in a cup of hot cocoa. I held her close and breathed in her baby smell. The scent never got old.

"I'm ready to come back to work, Jim. Question is, are you ready to have me back?" said Tina.

What the hell? I thought. Jim Falconer was her boss at Falconer Realty. Tina and I had agreed to a minimum of six, and hopefully twelve, months of maternity leave, yet here she was discussing returning earlier. I cleared my throat to announce my presence. It did the trick. She swivelled around and frowned at me. "Can we confirm the details tomorrow, Jim? Luther has just walked in the door and he does not look happy with me." She laughed as if I was one of her young, witless trainees and hung up.

"Luther. You shouldn't eavesdrop."

I put Addy back into her crib. "I wasn't eavesdropping, Tina. I live here."

"Whatevs, Luther. I can see by the scowl on your face that you're annoyed."

"We both agreed one of us would stay home with Addy until she was at least a year old."

"Easy for you to say, Luther. I'm the one who carried her in my womb and gave birth to her. And I'm the one who spends every waking moment with her."

"I thought you were happy to stay with Addy?"

"I didn't say I'm unhappy, Luther. But I need more than motherhood to sustain me. I need to earn money and be with adults again. Staying at home and living on one salary is driving me crazy. Plus, I don't want to miss out on my career developments."

"You're a realtor, Tina. You sell houses. What career developments are you missing out on?"

I regretted those words the second they left my mouth. Tina's mouth dropped open, and she was speechless for a whole three seconds. I dropped my head and inhaled in preparation for the verbal storm that would surely be unleashed.

"I sell houses, Luther? I sell houses?" The pitch of Tina's voice rose every time she repeated the phrase *I sell houses*. "Do you have any idea how competitive my line of work is, Luther? Do you think selling five hundred thousand dollar homes is easy? Do you think I simply start with a hundred thousand dollar house and slide on up to a million? Is that what you think, Luther?"

"When were you planning to tell me, Tee? Don't you think I deserved to be part of the discussion regarding our daughter?"

"Excuse me?"

"Your boss knew before your husband, Tina. What the fuck?"

She left the kitchen and stopped in the hall to inspect herself in the oversized rectangular mirror. "I don't have time for this, Luther. You can give Addy a bottle while I shower and dress. We're leaving at seven sharp."

I followed her into the hall. "Leaving at seven? Where are we going?"

"My parents' place for dinner, Luther. Addy is eight weeks old today, remember?"

"Yeah, of course I remember, Tina. I thought your parents were coming here?"

She shrugged her shoulders. "Change of plans."

"Change of plans and I'm always the last sucker to know."

She moved toward the stairs and ascended them two at a time.

"I'll stay at home with Addy," I said.

She peered over the mezzanine balcony. "No, Luther. My parents are expecting all three of us."

"I'm not talking about dinner, Tina. I'm talking about staying at home with Addy so you can go back to work."

"What, you mean like a home-dad or something?"

"Yeah. Plenty of dads do it now."

"No way, Luther."

"Why not? I'd love to be a home-dad to Addy and give you a break."

She shook her head. "No. You're on the fast track to a promotion, and there's no way I'm going to let you mess that up."

"I've worked there my whole life. I'm not going to mess anything up by taking paternity leave."

"Are you implying I don't care for our daughter?"

"No. I'm saying I don't want to put her in daycare while she's still an infant."

"My mother will help out. Addy won't be in daycare every day. And you could get your mother to help out too if you're concerned about Addy's wellbeing."

"Meaning?"

"You're happy for my parents to shoulder the responsibility for the house deposit and renovations. Meanwhile, your mother is quick to criticize me for not being the Alice from your Wonderland story."

I put my hands in my pockets and sighed. "Okay, Tina."

"Don't be passive-aggressive, Luther."

"I'm not being passive-aggressive. I don't think there's anything else to say on the matter. Your mind's made up. You go back to work, and I'll talk to my mother and my boss and see if I can get some extra time."

She pointed at me with her red fingernails. "Do not mess up your job opportunities. I'm warning you."

Addy wailed from the kitchen.

"Get dressed, Tina. We'll talk about this another time."

I grabbed a bottle from the sterilizer and added formula and water before sealing the lid and shaking. Addy's yells were not subsiding, so I picked her up and fished around for her pacifier. It did the trick and bought me the few minutes I needed to microwave the bottle. As soon as I heard the ping, I popped the door open, grabbed the bottle and headed for the sitting room. With Addy in my arms, sucking madly on her bottle, I looked out beyond the sliding doors at the garden. Tina wasn't big on closing curtains. Fairy lights lit the pool I never swam in.

Before Addy's birth Tina's parents gave us a hefty deposit to buy our first house in North Andover. The property was more than I could afford and way bigger than we needed, with four large bedrooms, two sitting rooms, a massive base-ment space that ran the length of the house, and a swimming pool. As if we needed a pool in Boston. But to Tina, a pool was a status statement.

Tina's parents wasted no time in finding the perfect nest and organising renovations. Tina led the way through the double-storey house, with her parents and me trailing behind her while she waved her arms toward cupboards and walls that would be sledgehammered. Tina's father, the property developer, took charge of the structural work, while Tina and her mother decided on paint colors, marble kitchen coun-tertops, and a six-plate chef's gas stove that Tina rarely used because she didn't like to cook.

I looked at Addy, who had stopped sucking on her bottle and looked ready to be burped. With a tool over my left shoulder and Addy in position, I rubbed her back and began to cry. Maybe I was too sensitive, but I couldn't bear the thought of a stranger caring for my baby girl. I also knew Tina would not budge once she made up her mind.

CHAPTER 7
Aden

October

Twenty minutes into my train commute home from a successful job interview for a Sales Manager role with Alchemy Wines, and lost in thought about my rows and rows of vines that were entering the bud break phase—a time when the buds swell and break into new leaf shoots—Bronte texted.

BRONTE: How was the interview?

ADEN: I got the job.

BRONTE: Finally, some good news!

I inhaled sharply and squeezed the phone. I didn't know what planet Bronte was on. Yes, I had landed a decent job, but I had lost my dream job.

ADEN: The role involves extensive travel. I'll be away a lot.

BRONTE: Look on the bright side, we're not destitute.

I couldn't reply without being nasty, so I stared at the three undulating dots as she typed.

BRONTE: I have good news of my own. Daphne has officially offered me an editing role for one of her lifestyle magazines. I'll be working four days a week, so the kids will be able to start kindy.

I dropped my phone into my messenger bag and muttered what the fuck. I could only take so much. A blonde woman with lip fillers in the seat opposite glanced up from her iPhone. I met her eyes unwaveringly while my bag buzzed against my ankle one, two, three, four times before it stopped. She dropped her head back down and shifted in her seat. The train pulled into a station populated with jacaranda trees. Funny thing about jacarandas—you only notice them when they start flowering. Try and find them on the last day of September and you wouldn't look twice. But as the first of October strikes, so the jacaranda blooms. And, like those trees, I never recognised my wife's true desire until it emerged like a cluster of purple petals when the season turned.

Bronte expected me to share in her happiness, but I couldn't. I wasn't happy for her, or for me, or for us. Instead of making wine, I would be selling it. And instead of having my wife and children close by, I would be away from home more often than not. And instead of Bronte focusing on the twins, she would be working. Everything was going to shit. The train stopped again and the blonde woman exited, making room to stretch out my legs.

7 Years Earlier

I met Bronte the day she applied for a migrant worker job at Ghost Gum. Beautiful but broken is how I would describe her. She wore tragedy on her face and in her mannerisms. With arms folded firmly across her chest, she moved away from people like a pinball machine when they got too close. She fascinated me like no woman ever had; an exotic bird, with two broken wings, who had lost her way mid-migration, and yet, she was unmistakably a survivor who would conquer whatever had broken her.

While the hundred odd interviews were in progress, she headed off on her own toward the eastern side of the property, where the Verdelho grapevines met the forest, and grey kangaroos gathered to laze in the afternoon sun. She walked straight past the bench and headed, as if magnetised, to the twin trunk of a ghost gum. What began as two trunks had merged into a single tree. A week after Dad and I bought the winery, dry lightning had struck and split the trunk down the middle; one half had caught alight and burned to charcoal, while the other half had remained perfectly untouched. The tree had inspired the winery's name, and I had chopped the wood by hand before storing it in the shed. I had no carpentry skills to speak of, but I loved the tree too much to use it for firewood.

When Bronte chose that tree stump to sit on, I knew I had to talk to her. But I stood back a while longer, not wanting to invade her space. Before she sat, she kneeled and placed her palm on the burnt half of the trunk, as if it had triggered a memory. A male kangaroo approached, and she didn't flinch, though he towered above her before leaning back to rest on hind legs. She held out her hand; he licked her palm and let her scratch his chin. I was impressed. Captive roos were sometimes people-friendly, but not the wild ones. Maybe he sensed the same sadness in her I had; I couldn't say for sure. Whatever the reason, my instinct to approach her heightened once the roo returned to his pack.

"I'm Aden," I said, extending my hand, "my father and I own the winery."

She stood and waved her hand. "Sorry, I've strayed too far. Say no more. I'm on my way back."

She turned to leave and I reached for her hand. The skin was badly scarred, like a burn. She pulled away and glared at me.

"Sorry, I didn't mean for you to leave. I was going to ask you if you'd like to feed our resident kookaburra?"

On a normal day most women fell over themselves to go out with an up-and-coming winemaker, but not Bronte. She frowned. "Why me?"

I pointed to the roos in the distance. "Because you seem to appreciate the wildlife."

She looked at me long enough for me to shift feet. "Look," I said, "I didn't mean to bother you. I'll leave you alone if you prefer." I waited for a few beats, then nodded and turned to walk away.

"No, I'm the one who should be sorry." She held out her hand. "I'm Bronte. As you can see I'm better with animals than people."

Her smile disarmed her face and I couldn't help but notice her green eyes. "Aden," I repeated, shaking her hand. "Do I detect an English accent?"

"Pfft. No. I'm from South Australia, but thanks for the compliment."

I couldn't help but chuckle. "Whereabouts in SA?"

"Adelaide Hills."

"Aah, good wine country."

"Yeah, as long as your home isn't in the path of a fire."

Before I could interject, she changed the subject. "You don't speak with a Queensland drawl either."

I laughed again and did an impression of a Queensland accent. "Whatcha mean my-eete, tie me kangaroo down and all that. Nah, I leave that stuff to me neighbours, Fred and Marr-juree."

Her shoulders, which had been as taut as a flexed bow and arrow, softened, and we both laughed. Her laugh was deep and contagious.

"You're beautiful when you smile."

She cleared her throat and steered the conversation back to geography. "Which part of Oz are you from?"

"I'm from Coffs Harbour originally. I grew up on a blueberry plantation."

"Sounds idyllic. How did you end up here?"

I skipped a beat before I replied, and she caught it straight away.

"Sorry, that was a personal question."

I shook my head and reassured her. "I don't mind. My mom died after a protracted battle with cancer, and my dad struggled to live with the bad memories of her suffering. He sold the farm and used the proceeds as a deposit to buy this place."

She swallowed and her eyes filled with tears. "I didn't mean to pry."

I waved my hand. "Don't be silly, you didn't pry. There was

a time when I couldn't talk about it, but I'm fine now."

She nodded. "I understand the devastation of losing a parent."

"Maybe you can tell me on the way to feed the kookaburra?"

She nodded and smiled. "Maybe we can build up to that."

I pointed to the hill that led up to the main house. "Shall we?"

"After you."

I loved that she made eye contact when she spoke to me. "Can I ask why you're doing seasonal work? It's usually backpackers who apply."

"Two reasons: the first is to fund my travels around Australia, and the second is because I grew up on a wine estate and I miss the vines something terrible."

I stopped walking and looked at her. "You're kidding?"

She shook her head. "Nope."

"What grapes did you grow?"

"Sauvignon blanc—which happens to be my favourite white wine."

I touched my nose and said, "I'll remember that."

She chuckled.

"You said you miss the vines. Does that mean your family are no longer wine producers?"

She nodded and looked away.

Sensing a painful secret, I tried another tack. "Is this the story we're building up to?"

"If I tell you, will you promise not to pity me or be obliged to offer some lame platitude?"

I frowned and nodded. "Yes, I promise."

"Thanks," she said, falling in step beside me. "My family home was destroyed by a bush fire thirteen months ago. I woke up in the dark, coughing. I could hear my father banging on the wall next to my room, screaming that he and my mother were trapped. Once my eyes adjusted, I saw thick smoke squeezing beneath the thin gap in my door. I twisted my bedroom door handle, but the white heat burned my palm." She stopped walking and showed me the scar tissue from what would probably have looked like melted skin at the time.

"Shit," I said, and shook my head.

"You could say that," she said, walking again. "I phoned triple zero and my adrenaline took over. I remember kicking through the plasterboard until I passed out from smoke inhalation. When I woke up, I was strapped to an ambulance gurney. My parents and younger brother were rushed to intensive care. The house had burned to its foundations and the vines were alight as far as the eye could see. Long story short, my family didn't survive, the insurance screwed me on a technicality, and all I had to my name was a car and a small inheritance that paid for a basic funeral and outstanding bills." She stopped speaking and sighed. "With nowhere to stay, I got in the car and drove."

"And you've been travelling ever since?"

She nodded. "Mm-hmm."

I didn't know what to say, but I had promised no platitudes. "I admire your courage."

"Thanks."

"It's not much further," I pointed to the white weatherboard house at the top of the grassy slope.

As we approached the back of the house, a kookaburra flew overhead and settled on the silver railing that wrapped around the wooden deck. Seconds later, its mate joined it, and they chuckled loudly. Bronte smiled and said kookaburras reminded her to find the sweetness in life. I dashed inside to get fresh minced meat out of the fridge and broke off chunks for each of us to feed a bird.

"Flatten your hand like this," I demonstrated. "It helps them snatch the mince with ease."

She followed my lead and smiled the whole time. Her beauty took my breath away—she looked like a Brazilian bombshell with her sea-green eyes and long dark hair—but her inner strength pulled me to her like a lunar tide. When the pair of kookies flew off, I asked her out to dinner.

She wagged her finger at me. "Only if you promise to keep it friendly."

"Scout's honour," I said.

She nodded and smirked as if she'd heard all the broken promises before.

I forget what I ate for dinner that night, but I remember falling in love. When I proposed to Bronte, and married her, I held a secret fear that the roots of her latent internal wounds could metastasise and possibly cause us to suffer the same fate as my beloved ghost gum. But never did I imagine I would be the one to turn on her and destroy everything we had built together.

CHAPTER 8
Bronte

December

Aden's train had arrived when I pulled into the parking bay outside the station. His scowl told me all I needed to know. I picked my thumbnail with my index finger—a nervous tic I'd developed, and one that was triggered whenever Aden was around. He walked around the side of the car, presumably to put his bag in the boot, but he appeared at the driver's side and opened the door.

"What are you doing?" I said.

"I'm driving. Move over."

I held his gaze for a split second, itching to tell him to fuck off, and then thought better of it. Since losing the winery, Aden's pride had become an open wound where everything I did or didn't say settled like a dose of salt. To avoid fights, I edited myself like I did Daphne's lifestyle magazine, carefully sifting through words and information to avoid offending or annoying or riling him. There had been days when I would have opted for marriage suicide given half the chance.

I shifted over the gear stick and into the passenger seat, determined to give him another chance.

"So, I said, tapping his thigh, did you have a good day at work?"

He fastened his seatbelt and rolled his eyes. "Yeah, great fucking birthday I'm having, wifey."

I pursed my lips and bit back an equally sarcastic remark. "Well, hopefully dinner with friends will be a better end to the day."

"Where are the kids?" he said, ignoring my comment.

"They're already at Priya's house. They went there after kindy."

"I need to go home first and change out of these fucking clothes. This humidity is uncivilised."

The humidity is not the only uncivilised thing, I wanted to say. Instead, I nodded. "That's fine, Ade. There's no rush."

We drove home in silence and I waited for him in the car with the windows down, hoping to snare sliver of sea breeze, but the air was at a standstill and the sea oh so quiet. I inadvertently picked my nail again and realised that I was holding my breath. I thought back to the day of Judd's funeral when Aden spoke of irony. The irony of losing the winery when the vines were weeping. Every day since I had been living with my own sense of irony—the irony of Aden morphing from my safe choice to a sleeping-with-the-enemy type scenario. At the same time, Aden had been my rock after my family died, and he deserved the same commitment from me.

Priya and Anura were Sri Lankan immigrants who owned a restaurant and spice shop. They were also the parents of twins—Vidu and Nishanti, who had become Leyla's and Liam's instant BFFs on the first day of Kindy. Priya and Anura lived in a Queenslander with a brown exterior and yellow trim. Both had green fingers, and their front garden brimmed with an array of leafy vegetables and herbs. Potted flowers lined the balcony and hung from the ceiling, filling the air with the scent of moist soil and fragrant petals.

I buzzed the bronze door bell and reached for Aden's hand, but he pulled it away and crossed his arms. Mercifully, the kids flung open the door and wrapped their arms around my thighs before the pupil of loneliness could dilate. I laughed at the scene. Priya's house had rapidly become Leyla's and Liam's second home, and she was the only person in the world I trusted them with. With hugs and excited yells dispensed, the kids disappeared into their playroom, and Priya held out her arms as I crossed the threshold and we hugged. "Aden doesn't know yet," I whispered in her ear. "Oh, okay," she whispered back. She released me and hugged Aden hello, while I hugged Anura. My tastebuds stirred the second we walked toward the kitchen. The scent of pandan leaves, cloves, chilli, and coriander hung in the air and steam lifted the lid of the silver pot that was boiling on the stove.

Priya gestured to the lounge. "Please, sit, while I finish in the kitchen."

"Can I help with anything?" I said.

"No, Bronte. You go and relax."

Anura and Aden sat on the three-seater black leather sofa in the lounge and immediately fell into comfortable conversation.

I sat on an armchair across the room, pulled out my phone, and opened Twitter. I'd had the app for months, yet I'd only plucked up the courage to tweet famous writing quotes and observe real writers from the sidelines. From my lost hours of scrolling, I had found an overwhelming amount of 'indie' writers—all vying for attention and validation; all with more courage, experience, and self-belief than me. Reading their tweets about writing and publishing only served to exacerbate my imposter syndrome, but I had to start somewhere. With Aden and Anura ignoring me, and Priya busy in the kitchen, I took a deep breath and tweeted an original thought. I felt immediately better when the tweet garnered a few likes and follows, and then a comment. With zero improvement in Aden's behaviour, my urge to write and engage with other writers had never been stronger.

Two hours later, the chicken curry and array of Sri Lankan specialties did not disappoint. But Aden's reaction to his birthday gift—a romantic weekend for two at a luxurious mountain resort—was less palatable. While Priya and Anura clapped and said how envious they were, Aden sat back in his chair and crossed his arms. I waited for him to say something through our dessert of ice cream and molasses, and two pots of lemon and ginger tea. But he said nothing. At 10 p.m. we thanked Priya and Anura for a delicious dinner and bundled the twins into the car. Leyla and Liam fell asleep before we got home and stayed asleep while Aden and I carried one each upstairs to their beds.

After I showered and dressed in pyjamas, I joined Aden on the sofa in the lounge. He had a beer in one hand and TV remote in the other. Beer was another change in Aden's life. He rarely drank beer at Ghost Gum, but at Sandgate, he refused to drink or buy wine.

"What do you wanna watch?" he said without looking at me.

"I was hoping we could talk."

"About what?"

"About the weekend away."

He kept his eyes on the TV and channel-surfed while he spoke. "The romance is dead, Bronte. I thought that was obvious by now."

I frowned and sighed. "Why do you keep pushing me away? Surely you can't blame me for losing the winery?"

"I do blame you."

"What? Why on earth would you blame me?"

"You're jinxed. First your family dies in a fire and now everything I've worked for is stripped from me like some freakish accident."

I shifted in my seat and faced him. "If you see me in such an abysmal light, why the hell are we still together?"

"Ooohhh, now I see what this is all about. You're strategising for a divorce." He stood and kicked my foot out of his way as he walked past me. "You can strategise all you like, Bronte, but I'm never going to let you split up my family and take my kids from me."

Instead of arguing with him, I let him walk away. And only when I heard his foot ascend the last step did I allow my face to contort and the lump in my throat dissolve into pitiful sobs.

A slew of annoying ads were punctuating whatever television show had been playing. Not seeing the remote, I searched beneath throws and cushions. With no luck in the obvious places, I slid my hand in between, under and behind the sofa seats. As a last resort, I kneeled on the floor and peered beneath the sofa. Sure enough, the remote was there along with a few dust balls and one of Liam's toy dinosaurs. I stretched out my arm and wrapped my fingers around it when the sound of my favourite Nick Cave song—*Red Right Hand*— started playing. With the remote in hand, and eyes glued to the screen, I sat on the sofa and watched a rapid stream of frames unfold: a dragonfly ascending like a helicopter; a banquet table on sunbaked grass beneath a gnarly old pepper tree; a woman standing amidst a harvest of bright yellow lemons; soft cheese; cow's milk; tree bark; roast chicken; a running rooster; a woman plucking a dead chicken; bird feathers; wine cellar; meat on hooks; bottles of red wine; sundried apricots; a ladybird; crimson pomegranate seeds; a young woman in a white dress writhing in the soil; and then the trigger…a bush fire. And the final credits—Barossa. Be consumed.

I pressed the red 'off' button on the remote, touched the scar on my hand and thought about irony again. The irony of the weeping vines. The irony of me thinking Aden was my safe choice. The irony of timing, and seeing the Barossa ad for the first time. When fate brought me to Aden's door in the Granite Belt, the deep well of anger that had fuelled my thirteen months of travel had dried up and I was utterly exhausted from the daily struggle to stop the weeds of deep emotions from overtaking the garden of my mind.

While I had not resented putting my writing dreams on hold to help Aden build his dream, I admit that I did work hard to silence my little voice. The little voice of the girl who died in that house fire. The voice that said: *Are you treading in the ashes of your parents' footsteps instead of blazing your own trail of independence? Is marrying Aden, a winemaker, akin to marrying your father? Are you forfeiting your dream to become a writer in order to be a winemaker's wife like your mother before you?*

I turned off the lights and headed upstairs to the attic, not bothering to tiptoe, like I usually did. Closing the door behind me, I fumbled for the light switch and then cleared a space amidst the dust and cobwebs. Fortunately, the attic was partially furnished with remnants of a bygone owner. Among the gems hidden beneath dusty white sheets, I uncovered an exquisite royal red wing back armchair, a glorious crimson oriental rug, and what looked like an antique walnut desk. I moved the desk against the north wall and beneath the porthole window where I could glimpse the tidal to and fro of Moreton Bay's blue water and the sandbanks that gave Sandgate its name.

Maybe it wasn't irony. Maybe, it was a colossal neon sign from the universe to start thinking about a future without Aden.

CHAPTER 9
Luther

December

A sharp tap on the shoulder brought me out of my writing zone.

"Luther?"

I turned to see Tina's pursed lips and arms folded across her chest. I pulled my earphones from my ears. "Huh?"

"I've been calling you for the past five minutes, Luther. What are you doing hiding away in this damp little dungeon?"

"It's Saturday, Tina, and we don't have a barbecue to host— for once."

She looked around the room and shook her head in disgust. "I can't believe you kept the previous owner's furniture. I would be embarrassed if I were you."

"Good thing I'm not you."

She picked at threadbare patches on the Chesterfield sofa and ran her finger over the dusty glass cabinet. "I suppose I should be thankful that you threw out the moldy orange rug and hideous yellow curtains."

The basement (aka dungeon) ran the length of the house and remained in its original state, with its peeling wallpaper in parts, exposed bricks, and 1970s carpet. It had only avoided renovation because I had insisted.

"You said you were calling for five minutes. What did you

want?"

"Your mother phoned. She wants you to take Addy for a visit tomorrow. I said you'll phone her back."

"Thanks," I said. "Can we expect the pleasure of your company?"

"Ha," she spat out, "as if."

I turned to face her. "You're not sending a good message to Addy. I mean, I see your parents all the time. Would it kill you to see Mom once in a while?"

Tina did what she did best and ignored my question. She peered at my computer screen and read aloud. "Louisa trembled. Was it her imagination, or had the walls around her shuddered?"

I closed my computer before she could read any more.

"What is that?" she said.

"It's a book."

"Whose book?"

"My book, if you must know."

"Your book?" She threw her head back and laughed. "Is that what you've been doing in the dungeon? You've been writing books?"

I nodded.

"Have you published any?"

"Yeah, I've published two."

"Who's the publisher?"

"I'm self-publishing, Tina."

She pulled a face. "What's the genre?"

"It's a paranormal series." I tapped the closed laptop. "This will be my third book."

"Wow," she said, putting her hand over her mouth. "Have you sold any?"

"Two dozen, give or take."

She laughed again. "Two dozen, Luther? Oh my God, and you're writing a third? Did the shitty sales of book one and two not give you a hint that you're wasting your time?"

I picked up my pack of Camels and tapped the box. The dungeon was also the only room in the house where I was allowed to smoke. "Thanks for your support, Tina."

"You don't need my support, Luther. You need a wake-up call."

"The self-publishing journey is a slow-burn, not a Black Friday sale."

"Oh, I see. You have the green light to criticize my work, but I can't criticize your hobby?"

I wedged a smoke into my mouth and lit it with the Zippo. "Publishing is not a hobby."

Tina marched to the sliding door and let in a gust of cold air. "Must you smoke inside, Luther?" She looked around the room and picked up a vintage, cast iron standing ashtray I usually carried with me outside during warm summer nights. She carried it over the threshold and gesticulated for me to smoke outside. "I have news for you, Luther. Publishing is a hobby until you turn a profit."

I followed her onto the porch and braced myself for the

cold. "Writing brings me immense joy. Why does that bother you? I don't criticize your Facebook time, your weekend barbecues, and whatever else you do to win social credit."

She pursed her lips and narrowed her eyes as her mind searched for the perfect comeback. "We have Addy in common. And there's nothing more important than that, is there?!"

I dropped my head and sighed. "You win, Tina. Addy is number one."

She huffed and uncrossed her arms like someone with the moral high ground. "If this third book doesn't sell, it should be your last, don't you think?"

I tried to hide my hurt by taking a long drag and turning my back on her to exhale into the wind.

"I'm only trying to be the voice of reason, Luther. You don't need to be a dick."

I stubbed my smoke in the ashtray. "Message received," I said. "Now, if you'll excuse me, I have work to do." I walked back into the warm house and headed to my prized possession—a four-drawer mahogany writing desk, circa 1830-50, with ebony banding and ebonized ringlets to the turned legs. An adjustable writing surface comfortably accommodated my MacBook and a yellow, pull-chain banker lamp.

Tina was right behind me. "About your barbecue quip. Kelsey and Ken are coming over this afternoon for tea and scones. I expect you to finish before they arrive."

I sighed and nodded. Like my basement space, my and Tina's desires consistently forked like the end of a road.

She tried to make eye contact with me, but I kept my head down and opened my computer. "I hope you're in a better mood when Ken and Kelsey arrive."

I read over the last few lines I'd written, wanting to pick up where I'd left off, but Tina's words rang in my head—*Did the shitty sales of book one and two not give you a hint that you're wasting your time?* I opened my desk drawer and pulled out Mom's copy of *Alice in Wonderland*. Like a snow globe, Mom's words about my settling had been shaken up and were falling all around me. I wondered how many more weekends I could play the happy husband to Tina's host-extraordinaire, pretending to be the man behind the barbecue who smiled and drank beers—instead of my favorite glass of bourbon—feigning interest in sport and the stock exchange like all the other dads. While I stayed with Tina for Addy's sake, I couldn't deny that the longer I stayed, the more my world would be crushed and curated.

I opened Twitter, hoping for a pick-me-up-notification. With nobody in my waking life aware of my writing, I had grown dependent on the Twitter writing community to lift me and boost my confidence. But the universe was giving away nothing on this Saturday morning. Desperate to connect with someone relatable, I was scrolling through writing hashtags when a name caught my attention. *Bronte*—an epic name charged with literary electricity. Seated at a writing desk, with pen in hand, and a distant expression on her beautiful face, she looked as if she belonged to that world on her page, and not her physical space. I immediately thought of Alice and experienced a strange sensation of yearning.

Desperate to make a good impression, I spent a few minutes reading her tweets and replies to learn as much about her as I could. It didn't take long to identify that Bronte's Achilles heel was self-doubt. Instead of following her immediately, like I usually did, I decided to bide my time and ghost follow her until the perfect opportunity presented itself. I needed a strategy for Bronte—I couldn't afford to put a foot wrong. Her self-doubt would be my *why*. As long as Bronte doubted her writing ability, I had an opportunity to flatter and praise her. I started by working out the time difference. Despite her living in Australia, our time zones were kinda perfect. Her morning was my evening and vice versa. My insomnia worked in my favor too. Whatever her routine was, I would find a way to fit around mine. With a couple of weeks of monitoring her Twitter behavior, I could orchestrate the perfect meet.

2016

CHAPTER 10
Aden

January

I looked around the commuter train and thought of a prison bus you see in the movies. Day in and out, expressions in the carriage were mostly miserable—as if people were resigned to working in jobs they hated or dreaded. I could identify. I went from being outdoors with my beloved vines to being confined to an office with its politics and ten-hour days, sandwiched between a two-hour return commute. My work mobile buzzed.

MIKE (BOSS): Stop by my office before you do anything else.

My thoughts immediately travelled to the negative—*Shit, what if he fires me?* As much as I hated my new life, I couldn't survive another Ghost Gum scenario.

I took a deep breath to calm myself before I knocked on Mike's door. Located on Eagle Street Pier, Mike had a corner office with a view of the Brisbane River. The City Cat Ferries were passing each other as I entered and sat opposite his desk. Mike's communication style was akin to Bronte's editing philosophy. *Why use ten words when two will suffice?*

"As you're aware, we've been working on a tender for a new hotel resort opening in Dubai."

I nodded.

"It's time to move forward. The process will take about three months and we'll need you in Dubai to oversee everything."

I cleared my throat in the absence of a glass of water, but he held up his hand and continued talking. "I know what you're going to say. When you signed on we mentioned you would be travelling for short periods of time, but this is a big deal, Aden. If we win this tender, we could gain access to many more opportunities. To compensate you, you'll receive living costs and a substantial bonus if you win the tender."

"What about my family?" I said.

"Three months doesn't warrant uprooting your family, Aden."

"Yeah, good point," I said, squaring my shoulders and sitting up straighter.

"You'll be leaving Friday week," he said. "Plenty of time to get your ducks in a row and talk to the missus." He laughed and stood to signal the end of the meeting.

I stood and reached across the desk to shake his hand. "I won't disappoint you."

He winked. "Good man."

I left his office, closed the door behind me and exhaled like I had been holding my breath the whole time. Instead of going back to my desk, I went to the kitchen and made a coffee. I took my hot mug over to the break room and sat on the red sofa that looked out over the river. I could see the two City Cat Ferries on either side of the riverbank: one at South Bank, heading toward New Farm; the other at Queen Street terminal, heading west to West End and the University of Queensland. I pulled my phone out of my trouser pocket and texted Bronte.

ADEN: How would you feel if I worked away from home for three months?

BRONTE: Why are you asking me—I thought the romance was dead?!

ADEN: I was being a dick, okay.

BRONTE: You weren't being a dick, you have become a dick—period.

ADEN: I have to go to Dubai for three months from Friday.

BRONTE: Time apart will do us both some good.

ADEN: I would like to discuss it with you tonight…if you're not writing.

BRONTE: Whatever, Aden.

I stared at the phone and exhaled through my mouth. I couldn't blame Bronte for not caring if I stayed or left. I had been resentful and hostile since we lost Ghost Gum, and I wasn't sure if it was possible to win back her love and favour. I picked up my coffee cup and thought about Ghost Gum. January was traditionally a vulnerable month in the winemaking calendar with hot, humid weather facilitating a host of pests during the fruit set phase. At this stage, when flowering has ended and berries have formed, it is the winegrowers job to protect their future harvest. Regardless of the agricultural techniques—conventional, organic, biodynamic, or hybrid—intervention was required. And although I no longer had a vulnerable vineyard on my hands, the same could not be said for my marriage. Like a swarm of pests converging on a single grapevine, my relationship with Bronte was calling out for some kind of intervention. I thought about Dubai. Perhaps three months away would be the perfect intervention? Bronte would miss me, and we could make a fresh start when I returned.

CHAPTER 11
Bronte

January

Aden waved goodbye from the back of the taxi at 5 a.m. on a Friday morning. Five minutes earlier I had nodded like a good wife when he shed tears and said he would miss me and the kids. But the only emotion I felt now, as I watched the taxi stop at the end of the road and turn onto the strand, was a tidal wave of relief. *This is going to be a good day*, I thought to myself, *Aden is gone, and I have a day off work.* After school drop-off, I swam my laps in tepid water and dragged the sun lounger into the shade to escape the burning sun. The surround sound of summer was in full height—crickets chirruping, currawongs warbling, toads croaking, kookaburras chuckling, cicadas singing their beauteous song of emergence after being dormant underground for half their lives. I could relate to the cicadas—my true yearnings had been dormant since my family died in the fire. As tragic as losing Ghost Gum was, it was also an emancipation of sorts. My emancipation from Aden's dream life and a new lease of life for the aspirations I had buried in the scorched earth where the ruins of my family home lay. The day I climbed into my mother's car (her vehicle of freedom), I left my writing dream behind, not knowing how, if, or when I was ever going to resurrect it.

The humidity had trespassed into the tree's shade and instead of drying off and cooling down, I looked like I'd emerged from a steam room. I gathered my towel and phone and headed indoors for a cold shower. Dressed in an aqua-marine sundress and thongs, I piled my hair up into bun and strolled down the esplanade toward the quaint little museum where they were displaying historic photos of Sandgate. Inside the museum, a few people milled about—mostly pensioners by the looks of them.

Before I did my rounds of the photos, I read several blurbs about Sandgate's history. Before the British settled in the 1850s, the seashore, creeks and lagoons were inhabited by the Turrbul people, who were a branch of the clan of the Yugarabul speaking people. The Turrbal clan called their coastal land 'Warra', meaning an open sheet of water. After the British settled, the Sandgate suburb was called Cabbage Tree Creek. The Sandgate name was said to derive from the English Kentish town of Sandgate—most likely named by the first English settlers who arrived in the 1850s. In the late 1860s, seaside cottages were listed in newspapers as being available for rent at £3 per week. I thought of our $450 per week rent, which was about $100 cheaper than the going rate. Before the railway line was opened in May of 1882, transport consisted of a horse drawn coach service.

There was something about the smell and colour of old photos—much like a dusty old book—that triggered the writer in me. The faces of people who once stood on this shore—mothers, children, men. All tended their own secrets. All struggled in some way. All laughed and loved. With ideas blossoming in my head like the blue jellyfish blooms Sandgate was known for, I left the museum and headed for a cafe. Seafood cafes and restaurants were a dime a dozen on the main drag, so I picked the nearest one.

A young waitress with tattoos and piercings seated me at a two-seater table with an ocean view and took my order: a cold bottle of San Pellegrino and salt and pepper squid salad. I thanked her, pulled out my laptop and began to type about a woman who is found tangled in the mangroves around Cabbage Tree Creek by a fisherman who has recently lost his wife and daughter in childbirth. Taken with her beauty, though she is as pale as a goose egg, and fearing she is dead, he drags her onto the prawn trawler and tries to resuscitate her. As he is about to give up, she coughs and rolls onto her side, then sits up straight as a broomstick and begins talking in a foreign language at the speed of sound. A dozen thoughts run through the fisherman's head: *Who is she? How did she come to be tangled in the Sandgate mangroves of all places? What happened to her? And how do I get her to stay?*

A mystery novel, I thought when reading back what I'd written. Since preparing my writing room and starting my editing job, I had been daydreaming about writing but hadn't written anything worthwhile. The only real thing I'd experienced was imposter syndrome and a whole lot of doubt; that little mocking voice in my head that said: *You? A writer? Don't be ridiculous. You're too late. You'll never amount to anything, sweetheart.* I closed my laptop and opened Twitter. While I didn't want to believe the voice in my head, I did possess an awful fear it was right. In need of validation, I published a self-deprecating tweet.

BRONTEWRITES: Aspiring or flailing writer? #undecided #word-choice

I wasn't expecting an instantaneous reply, but I got one.

LOL_AUTHOR: Neither, already an amazing writer #just-saying

I couldn't help smiling. Intrigued, I clicked on this user-name to check out his profile pic. His name was Luther and his bio said he was writing the third book in his paranormal series. Look-wise, he came across as a broody, arty type with his mop of dark hair, black-rimmed glasses, and black T-shirt. My wedding ring said *don't encourage him*, but the flirt in me said *go on, what's the harm?*

BRONTEWRITES: You're hired ;-) #flatterywinseverytime

LOL_AUTHOR: will flatter for free haha

BRONTEWRITES: My ego is purring

LOL_AUTHOR: just your ego? #justkidding #seriously

BRONTEWRITES: Sarcasm and flattery

LOL_AUTHOR: marriage made in heaven?

BRONTEWRITES: I'm already married

LOL_AUTHOR: me too

BRONTEWRITES: Thank God! Thought you might be a perve 😅

LOL_AUTHOR: Worst case scenario—stalker #kidding-notkidding

BRONTEWRITES: Moving on…what's with the LOL username, lol?

LOL_AUTHOR: Luther O'Leary

BRONTEWRITES: Aha! Makes perfect sense now.

Luther—even his name drove the writer in me a little wild.

The way it sounded in my mouth made me quiver.

LOL_AUTHOR: What's the time in Australia?

BRONTEWRITES: I checked my phone. It's 11 a.m.

LOL_AUTHOR: On Thursday?

BRONTEWRITES: No, Friday.

LOL_AUTHOR: That's mad. It's 9 p.m. on Thursday in Boston, so you're literally in the future.

BRONTEWRITES: A 14 hour time difference, and yet here we are…

LOL_AUTHOR: Kismet @BronteWrites

BRONTEWRITES: Hmmm, seems so, Luther ;-)

LOL_AUTHOR: Are you at work at the moment?

BRONTEWRITES: No, I have the day off.

LOL_AUTHOR: Special occasion?

BRONTEWRITES: My husband left for Dubai on a business trip.

LOL_AUTHOR: How long?

BRONTEWRITES: Three months.

LOL_AUTHOR: Whoa, three months. That's a long time.

BRONTEWRITES: Yeah, it is.

LOL_AUTHOR: Will you miss him?

BRONTEWRITES: I can't answer that on the grounds that it will incriminate me #kidding #darkhumour #seriously

LOL_AUTHOR: LMAO

BRONTEWRITES: 😼

LOL_AUTHOR: Can I ask you a question @BronteWrites?

BRONTEWRITES: Sure

LOL_AUTHOR: What's your favorite book?

BRONTEWRITES: Aah, too easy. It's been Wuthering Heights since forever. What's yours?

LOL_AUTHOR: Promise not to laugh?

BRONTEWRITES: Pinky swear, Luther

LOL_AUTHOR: Mine is Alice in Wonderland

BRONTEWRITES: For real?

LOL_AUTHOR: For real

BRONTEWRITES: Okay, I'm intrigued enough to move this convo to DMs

LOL_AUTHOR: I thought you'd never ask ;-)

BRONTEWRITES: You make me 😂

LOL_AUTHOR: I aim to please 😜

Luther was an American, part-time writer and poet, who had been widowed then married a second time to a woman who was less soul and more mate. His daughter was the same age as Leyla and Liam.

BRONTEWRITES: What's your daughter's name?

LOL_AUTHOR: Adelaide

BRONTEWRITES: Seriously?

LOL_AUTHOR: Yeah, why?

BRONTEWRITES: I was born and raised in Adelaide.

LOL_AUTHOR: No way

BRONTEWRITES: Way

   While he messaged me, I engaged in a bit of social media snooping on his Facebook page, where I found an unsmiling couple with an obvious gap between them. All of which confirmed Luther's story about being unhappily married to the wrong woman.

BRONTEWRITES: Set the scene for me, Luther. What's the weather like in Boston at the moment?

LOL_AUTHOR: It's minus five degrees. Snow is falling. From my basement (or dungeon if you ask my wife), I can see the oak tree where I made Addy a tire swing.

BRONTEWRITES: Complete opposite here. I'm sitting in a seaside cafe. It's the height of summer and I can hear the cicadas singing their song of resurrection.

LOL_AUTHOR: Mmm, the joy of connecting with a fellow writer.

BRONTEWRITES: Yeah, I know what you mean. The more I work at being a writer, the more I realise that writing is a wonderful, strange, and isolating gift that makes we want to run toward the page and away from the real world.

LOL_AUTHOR: Oh my god, woman, if you keep this up I'm gonna fall head over heels in love with you 😍😘

BRONTEWRITES: haha, I'm assuming you can relate?

LOL_AUTHOR: Um, yeah. I have been publishing books in secret for years. When my wife found out recently, she said, and I quote: "Did the shitty sales of book one and two not give you a hint that you're wasting your time?"

BRONTEWRITES: Oh my God, that's brutal. Sorry, Luther. 😭

LOL_AUTHOR: Does your husband get your writing?

BRONTEWRITES: I haven't been writing long, so I haven't given him a chance. But it's safe to say his passions lie elsewhere.

LOL_AUTHOR: You can call on me anytime to read your work or bounce ideas, Bronte.

BRONTEWRITES: Aww, thanks. I appreciate the offer, and I might take you up on it.

LOL_AUTHOR: Like I said, I'm all yours 😇

BRONTEWRITES: You're gonna be trouble. I can feel it 😅

LOL_AUTHOR: Not all trouble is bad 😏

BRONTEWRITES: Oh, believe me, I wasn't complaining 😍 haha

In the hour we texted, I gave Aden little thought. Luther embodied the kind of broody writer I secretly fantasised about, and his witty repartee and relentless innuendo only exacerbated the itch on my ring finger.

CHAPTER 12
Aden

January

The pilot announced our descent and the fasten seatbelt lights flickered to life. Air stewards took their seats. "For those old-schoolers who have watches, the time in Dubai is 12.51 a.m", said the pilot. I smiled in appreciation and looked at my watch. It was 6.51 a.m. in Queensland. I reset the time, placed the Emirates magazine back into the seat pouch and shifted my body to look out of the window. Against the backdrop of a dark sky, a red light flickered on the right wing that was angled down as the plane began its descent toward Dubai airport. Down below, a sea of lights hinted at the glitz and artifice of modern Dubai. From this vantage, it was impossible to imagine that Dubai had been a small fishing and pearling village at the edge of the desert less than fifty years ago, and I wasn't sure how I felt about living in such a place. I was at home in nature; the concrete jungle held zero allure for a true blue Aussie boy.

Two days later I descended the escalator stairs three at a time to catch the approaching metro and hopped onto the closest carriage.

"This carriage is for women and children," a young Western woman told me promptly. "There's a steep fine if you get caught."

I backed out of the doorway, bobbing my head apologetically, and the doors closed. Sure enough, when I looked at the markings on the floor, it clearly said *Woman and Children Only*. Seconds later, the glass partition doors between metro and platform closed, and the train took off without me. My cheeks flushed with embarrassment as the carriage glided past and I caught the odd glimpse of women chuckling and shaking their heads. I walked further along the platform until I reached the queue for the correct carriage. Luckily, the Dubai metros were regular enough, and it wasn't long before another one arrived to whisk me off to Deira.

As expected, my first few days amidst Dubai's heart of steel, glass, concrete and lights was enough to send me packing. But without the luxury to leave, I did the next best thing and went in search of alternative accommodation. The synonymous advice from several different sources had me narrow my search to Deira, locally referred to as 'The Old Dubai'. A thirty minute metro ride was a small price to pay.

I bought a small bottle of mineral water before I left the metro station and downed it in a few gulps. The dry Dubai heat was different to Brisbane's humid heat and I found myself needing to hydrate far more regularly. Outside, the sound of the distinctive Adhan, or daily call to prayer, met my ears the minute I crossed the bustling main street. I wasn't sure where I was going, but I flowed with the tide of people and allowed fate or whatever to guide me to where I needed to be. The surge ebbed outside the gates of an impressive mosque—the size of Ikea and the colour of Santorini, with its stark whitewashed walls and sapphire blue minarets. I let the crowd of men carry me forward like a wave until I was standing outside the entrance, but stayed behind as they removed their shoes and placed them in a rack before flowing in single file through the main doors.

Once the crowd had disappeared into the mosque hall, I peered around the door. Some men lined up to wash their arms, feet, and heads at a stall of taps that ran along the back of the mosque. Others unrolled their prayer mats and kneeled in preparation for the midday prayers. I had read about the daily prayers on the plane to understand the basics and avoid offending anyone out of sheer ignorance. There were five prayers in total: Fajr, meaning Dawn; Dhuhr, occurring after midday; Asr, meaning afternoon; Maghrib, occurring at sunset; and Isha, occurring at nighttime.

I had never given much reverence to Islam as a religion, but my fascination grew tenfold as I stood outside the mosque and experienced a sense of inner and outer serenity. As I stood there, filled with a kind of divine harmony, I thought about how different the last four months of my life would have been if I had had this daily prayer ritual to depend upon and ground me. Would prayers have kept me connected to the land, to the earth, and my beloved vines? What if I had used those prayers to keep my faith? Might I have changed my perspective and seen the situation through Bronte's eyes—not as a loss, but as an opportunity to fight harder for what I wanted? Why had I given up so easily? Back at Ghost Gum, when I was outside among the vines, I would say my own prayer of thanks. Thanks to the glorious sun that rose each day and injected my vines with life as she moved across the sky. Thanks to the setting sun that would bring a drop in temperature, but no frost. Thanks for the daily rhythm that was so present and appreciated when working on the land.

The sound of prayers echoed around the hall and spilt onto the doorstep where I stood. As a non-Muslim, I wasn't sure if I was allowed inside, so I walked around the exterior instead. In Australia, the closest I had come to a sacred religion was the vibrant Sikh community in Woolgoolga. The Sikh community grew after the Second World War when Punjabi migrants first worked on cane fields in Queensland and later settled around Coffs Harbour to farm bananas. The community grew and thrived to such an extent that the Guru Nanak Sikh Temple was built in the 1970s. I had never been inside because it was another world—one I didn't belong to, but a world that beckoned me all the same.

I remember one afternoon when Mum was at her worst, and cancer had riddled her body; I got in the car and drove. I didn't have a set destination in mind, but I needed to escape and clear my head. I found myself parked outside the Temple, its whitewashed exterior pristine against the blue sky and its numerous arches and gold-trimmed domes godly. I got out of the car and ventured to the entrance. The Temple was closed and deserted, which was both a disappointment and a relief. The prospect of talking to a stranger appealed because I needed to talk about my feelings. But I was also scared shitless in the event my emotions bubbled to the surface. In the absence of a willing human ear, I placed my hands on the cool, white paint and said a silent prayer to any God who was willing to listen to me. *Please don't take my mum. Please don't take my mum.* But either God was listening to someone else in that moment or he had a policy against those who only prayed in desperate times. Whatever the reason, Mum lost the battle a week later.

The sound of silence, following the cessation of prayer, brought me back to reality, and I took a few deep inhales and exhales before I exited the mosque gates. The experience convinced me that I wanted to stay in Deira and nowhere near the Dubai Marina with other western tourists and business people. In the not too far distance I spotted the iconic Deira clock tower that looked like a giant sundial as well as a red *Hotel* sign. Walking towards both landmarks I passed a market—known as a souk to the locals—and made a mental note to return at some point to buy a suitable mosque garment for when I plucked up the courage to visit. The pavements in Deira were mostly made of a reddish brick that had a glossy tinge in the sun. A stark contrast to bog-standard concrete. But the oddest thing I'd noticed about Dubai was the lack of clouds on any given day. Unlike Australia, where cloud-lovers would be spoiled for choice with the array of cumulonimbus, cirrus, and stratus clouds, the Dubai sky was much like the surrounding desert it was built on—a minimalist, blue canvas. While I had been told that January and February would likely yield the city's annual nine millimetres of winter rain, the event remained a case of seeing is believing.

Inside the hotel, the white reception desk looked to be floating above a yellow light. Behind the receptionist, a panel of bamboo slats tempted the eye to the enormous fish tank behind it. Six overhead pendant lights illuminated exotic colours and feathery fins. Clocks set to different time zones were embedded in the desk—New York, London, Paris, Sydney. Judging by the surroundings, I figured the room would be too expensive for my work budget, but I asked for room rates all the same. Surprisingly, the long-term apartment rate came in under budget and after a full tour of the facilities—gym, prayer room, swimming pool, to name a few—and room—with king size bed and kitchenette—I handed over my credit card and checked in with immediate effect.

CHAPTER 13
Luther

January

My birthday was the one day of the year when I didn't mind Tina's propensity for parties. Every year she threw me a big birthday bash. And though the day didn't all work in my favor—Tina would mostly invite her friends—I did get to pick the theme. For three years running, I had picked fancy dress and dressed as the Madhatter each time.

I parked my car in the garage and took out a smoke when Tina, dressed as Maleficent— complete with black horns and cape—swung open the kitchen door.

"When are you going to give up that filthy habit?"

"Hello to you too, Tee."

Before Tina could get going, Addy's comedic timing saved my hide. Dressed as Elsa from Frozen and singing 'Let it Go' at the top of her lungs, she ran toward me. I pocketed my smoke and dropped my bag before extending my arms for Addy to jump into my grasp like a ballerina in Swan Lake.

"Hello Daddy."

"Hello, gorgeous." Addy made me smile. She was the cherry on top of any and all life accomplishments. Although she was the spitting image of her mother with her blue eyes and blonde hair, she had my heart and creativity. We'd started spending our Sunday afternoons writing poems and painting pictures. Addy had a gift for poetry, and she loved reading. She made me proud.

"Luther, you need to hurry up. They'll be arriving in twenty minutes."

I sighed and followed Tina inside. "You're the most beautiful girl in the whole world," I told Addy putting her back on solid ground.

The doorbell rang and Tina doubled down on the drama. "Could you hurry up already, Luther?" She pushed passed me, as I headed for the stairs.

In the bathroom, I applied my Hatter makeup, taking pleasure in the fact that it would irritate Tina enormously. In marriage, it was sometimes the little things that got you through.

My phone buzzed and I reluctantly picked it up thinking it would be Tina harassing me. But the gods were smiling upon me because it was Bronte.

BRONTE: Did you know you have magical powers, Luther O'Leary?

LUTHER: I didn't know they worked long-distances ;-)

BRONTE: Ha, seriously. Poetry wasn't my jam until you came along. Now I can't stop.

LUTHER: You're not a bad muse yourself. I'm also writing more poetry than usual.

BRONTE: Feel free to share.

LUTHER: I'll show you mine if you show me yours, haha.

BRONTE: Haha, Luther.

I saw my chance to woo her with words. Give me a sec, Bront,

I'm gonna send you a poem.

BRONTE: 😎 I'm not going anywhere.

LUTHER: Here goes…

I have never wanted to fly so much

Like a bird,
you make me dream of migration
away from this icy winter
toward your summer solstice

For it is always summer where you are
and it will always be summer in my heart
so long as you are near me

BRONTE: Your words melt my heart.

LUTHER: I'm glad. Your turn…

BRONTE: Okay 😅 but please remember, I'm no poet…

LUTHER: I'll be the judge of that.

BRONTE: Okay, here goes…

You are light years away
in map-speak
A celestial body that will never collide with mine
But our hearts are astronauts—
weightless & floating
Exploring love
in a time-space continuum

LUTHER: You are a poet, Bront.

BRONTE: Thanks. You are fabulous for my ego 😜

LUTHER: There is one thing about your poem…

BRONTE: Eek. What's that?

LUTHER: "A celestial body that will never collide with mine." There's still time 😄

BRONTE: Would that I could…

Tina hammered on the door. I put my phone in my back pocket and opened the door. When she saw me, she rolled her eyes and pursed her lips. "Oh, look, Luther is dressed as the Mad Hatter, again." I bowed dramatically and laughed.

"Hurry up, will you? We're all waiting on you downstairs."

"I'll be down in two minutes."

She opened the timer app on her iPhone and pressed start. "Two minutes starts now."

I rolled my eyes and closed the door. When I heard Tina's footsteps travel downstairs, I pulled out my phone to text Bronte.

LUTHER: Sorry, hun, my wife is literally beating the door down, coz it's my birthday and she's throwing herself a party on my behalf, haha.

BRONTE: Lol, you make me chuckle. Happy birthday, Luther 🙂

LUTHER: Thanks, beautiful xoxo

CHAPTER 14
Bronte

February

I turned my pillow over for the umpteenth time, trying to catch ten seconds of cool cotton before the humidity nuked it. On my back again, I wriggled down the mattress to get closer to the overhead fan, but it was spinning and churning hot air. It didn't help that Leyla and Liam were hogging the bed. With Aden away they'd taken to sneaking into my room, saying they didn't want me to be alone. But the truth is they were still afraid of the dark and preferred to be in the comfort of their mother's room. Having them close eased my mind, to be fair. Without Aden around, my ears were tuned into the slightest sounds—a branch scratching on the window, a possum scuttling across the roof, the flying foxes squealing over space in the fig tree outside the window. Most nights, we all slept peacefully, but on the odd occasion all three, or one of us, tossed and turned.

I edged off the bed and tiptoed out of the room, careful to avoid the creaky floorboards. Upstairs in my office, I grabbed my journal off the desk. Before Luther, I considered the writing of verse to be a special gift bestowed upon famous poets like Plath, Sexton, Levertov and Dickinson but since Luther's entry into my life the poetry wouldn't stop. Poems weren't confined to my burgeoning feelings for Luther mind you, I wrote about my distress over losing Aden too. With distance between us, I finally had the chance to put everything in perspective and breathe again.

I settled into my red armchair and began writing.

There is a forest in my head
an ocean in my heart
and there you are
taken with the desert
Not a drop of wanderlust left

So I wander alone,
tell you I'm alright
I'm alright
I swear it day and night
I. am. alright

Although Aden Facetimed me and the kids every weekend, he didn't talk much about his life in Dubai. Even so, I could tell from his manner and composure that he seemed happier. All of which raised an alarm of doubt within myself. Had I not been supportive enough when we lost the winery? I knew Aden had been a dick, but I was cognisant of his reasons.

I copied my poem into a text and messaged Aden.

ADEN: Everything okay, Bront?

BRONTE: Can't sleep. Thinking about us and wondering what will become of our relationship?

ADEN: I thought you were glad to see the back of me?

BRONTE: I was

ADEN: But?

BRONTE: You weren't always an arsehole, and I need to know what happened. Why did you turn on me the way you did?

I held my breath, half expecting him to bite back with an equally vicious insult.

ADEN: You're right. I have been an arsehole. I was angry and I made mistakes. I took everything out on you and you deserved better.

BRONTE: Maybe I didn't deserve better?

ADEN: Why would you say that? I am to blame. Only me.

I unfurled my legs from under me and peered out of the port-hole window. I could see a few tiny lights scattered across the ocean. Most likely container ships.

ADEN: Bront, you still there?

I sat back in my chair.

BRONTE: Yeah, I'm still here. I don't know what to think. You don't communicate with me anymore. The last time we argued, you told me the romance was dead. I'm in the dark half the time with where you are and what you're thinking.

ADEN: I promise you, if anything, I am keeping to myself and reflecting.

BRONTE: Are you sure you haven't met someone?

ADEN: What? As in romantically?

BRONTE: Yes.

ADEN: No. Nothing could be further from the truth.

BRONTE: I won't hold it against you if you have met some-one.

ADEN: Where's all this coming from? Have you met someone?

I chewed my thumbnail as I weighed up whether or not to tell Aden about Luther.

BRONTE: No, nothing like that. I have an online friend who I talk to about writing. His name is Luther.

ADEN: Just a friend?

BRONTE: Yes, just a friend. He lives in America and he is married with a daughter.

ADEN: Okay

BRONTE: You're not angry?

ADEN: No. I'm happy you have a friend to discuss writing with. You know I don't exactly get it.

BRONTE: I know, Ade. That's why it's important to me. And although we're not talking like we used to at Ghost Gum, I'd prefer not to hide it from you.

ADEN: I know you stopped telling me things to avoid my angry outbursts, and I'm sorry I subjected you and the kids to that. If it's any consolation, I am atoning. Five times a day to be exact.

BRONTE: Five times a day? You mean the daily prayers?

ADEN: Yes

BRONTE: You're not planning to convert to Islam, are you?

ADEN: Nothing that radical. I'm finding the ritual of daily prayers to be incredibly soothing and comforting.

BRONTE: I'm happy you've found something to help centre and balance you.

ADEN: Thanks, Bront. And you'll be glad to know I've stopped drinking alcohol too.

BRONTE: You mean no more chain-drinking beers and kicking my feet off the table? ;-)

ADEN: You've put up with a lot, and I promise to make amends.

BRONTE: I guess we've both been grieving in our own ways.

ADEN: What you said in the poem—*Taken by the desert and not a drop of wanderlust left*—that's not true. I am taken by the desert, but I've still got plenty of wanderlust left for you and for life. Okay?

BRONTE: Okay, Ade.

ADEN: Will I speak to you and the kids on Saturday?

BRONTE: Of course! The kids can't wait.

ADEN: Okay. Speak to you on Saturday xo

BRONTE: Look forward to it xo

CHAPTER 15
Aden

February

Irolled up my prayer mat and placed it in the wardrobe. From my room window, on the tenth floor, I could see the blue and white mosque with dawn's fleeting silhouette behind it. A chevron of tiny birds moved in waves over the clock tower, and flocks of seagulls congregated in and around the Deira creek. I lifted my arms above my head and stretched, grateful that it was Saturday morning.

Having spent the majority of my first month acclimatising to the local customs and culture, as well as finding my groove at work, I had not yet plucked up the courage to visit the mosque and pray with the locals. But it was time to take the next step. All I needed was a traditional garment. After a breakfast of eggs and toast, I visited a Souk, that I had walked past and lingered around outside repeatedly in the weeks since my arrival.

The souk was abuzz with the sounds of birds and people when I entered from the street. Most of the souks had silver roller doors, but the one I was visiting had a weathered wooden door that had Arabic engravings and a decorative brass handle. Inside, the mud-wash effect walls combined with hanging moroccan lanterns and glowing sickle moons were reminiscent of Ali Babas cave, my favourite childhood story. My height always made it difficult for me to keep a low profile, but I tried all the same to surreptitiously flick through the traditional garments that hung on hangers all around the shop, all the while intently watching the shop owner, from the corner of my eye, as he went about wrapping the roots of a tree cutting in a plastic bag. I found my size in white with gold trim, along with a matching head covering, and approached the man at the counter.

The shop owner addressed me with a curious tilt of his head. "I would usually ask a Westerner if they are here for business or pleasure. But I see you pass my shop every day on your way to work."

"You're right," I nodded. "I'm here for three months on business."

"Maa ismuk?"

"Ismii Aden."

He smiled, nodded and held out his hand. "Ismii Rashid. You know some Arabic?"

I pulled a pocket guide out of my back pocket. "Only the basics."

"I am impressed. Most visitors don't try to talk Arabic."

"Arabic is a beautiful language. The way you greet one another—peace be upon you - Asalamu Alaikum—the West could learn a thing or two.

He tilted his head and smiled. "Shukran. Your pronunciation is good."

I bowed my head. "Shukran."

"So, what brings you to my shop today, Aden?"

He pronounced my name Eye-din. I liked how it sounded. It was yet another opportunity to rediscover and reinvent myself.

I gestured to the clothing draped over my arm. "I am planning to attend a daily prayer at the   big mosque down the road. If westerners are allowed. Are they?"

Rashid nodded. "Yes, Eye-din, I can take you there one morning or evening and introduce you to the imam if you like."

"You would do that?"

He nodded and titled his head again. "Of course."

I nodded and smiled. "Shukran."

"Do you know much about Islam?"

I shook my head. "Only a bit—like my Arabic—but I'm interested in learning more."

He asked me to wait while he disappeared behind a gold and white lace curtain at the back of the shop and rifled through some papers. While I waited, I rubbed the glossy leaves of the tree cutting between my thumb and index finger, expecting a fragrance when I brought my fingers to my nose. But the leaves had no scent.

"Mashallah," Rashid said triumphantly when he returned. He handed me a leather-bound book that looked distinctly like a bible. He bowed his head and said, "A Qur'an, for you."

"Shukran," I said, with a slight bow of my head, "but it might take me a few years before I can read a word."

The man shook his head. "You don't need to read. You only need to listen."

I tilted my head as if I didn't fully understand. "Listen?"

He placed his hand over his chest. "Every man has an inner Qu'ran. Like a compass, every man knows what is right and what is wrong, but they don't always listen." He placed the Qu'ran in my hand. "Keep this with you all the time. It will remind you to do the right thing. Inshallah."

I took the holy book from him and looked him in the eye. "What if it's too late?"

He titled his head to the right and closed his eyes. "Asalamu Alaikum. It's never too late."

"Wa Alaikum asalam."

He patted me on the arm.

I pointed to the tree cutting that Rashid had placed on the counter when I approached. "Do you mind if I ask what kind of tree that is?"

"You are interested in trees?"

Under normal circumstances I would never strike up such a personal conversation with a stranger, let alone open my heart the way I was doing with Rashid. But there was something fatherly and safe about him, and I had reached a point in my journey of grief where I needed to talk to someone.

"I had a special tree in Australia. It was called a ghost gum and it had a twin trunk. Unfortunately, it was struck by lightning and split down the middle. After it fell, I chopped it up and stored it in a shed because I couldn't bear to lose it. But seeing you now, wrapping that tree cutting, I wonder if I could have saved a piece and replanted it? I don't know why I never thought of that before?"

Rashid was watching me and listening intently. He

touched the branch and said, "this is a pomegranate tree. It is considered a holy tree for Islam, but that is not why I have it. It is a birthday gift for my wife, Mehrnoosh."

"Mehrnoosh," I repeated. "That is a beautiful name."

Rashid nodded and smiled. "It means immortal sun."

He stopped talking for a few seconds and closed his eyes. I wondered if he was experiencing the same flame of emotion I was at the thought of Bronte.

Rashid swallowed and put his hand over his heart before resuming his story. "Mehrnoosh—she is my immortal sun."

He emphasised the word my, and I nodded, not wanting to interrupt him and eager to hear more.

"She grew up in Persia," Rashid continued. "One of her sweetest childhood memories was celebrating Shab-e-Yalda—an ancient Persian tradition that celebrates the sunrise after the longest night of the year. Mehrnoosh's family would stay up all night, telling stories, reading the poetry of Hafez and Rumi, and eating pomegranates. At dawn, when a light split the sky, they would know that good had conquered evil, and they would give thanks to the pomegranate, that can blossom in the coldest winter."

"Was that before the Iranian Revolution?" I said, curious to learn more.

He nodded and regarded me with interest. "You are not like other Westerners I have met, Eye-din."

"I guess I'm just a lonely soul at the moment, Rashid. My father died last September and we lost our family winery. I have not treated my wife, Bronte, very well since it happened."

A bell tinkled as someone entered the shop. Rashid touched my arm and said, "We will talk more tomorrow. I will meet you at the mosque for Fajr?"

"I would like that very much. Shukran."

He nodded and titled his head. "Aaraka Ghadan."

I consulted my pocket book and when I found the underlined text, I said, "Ma᾽a al-ssalāmah."

Rashid smiled and waved as I exited the shop into the morning sunshine.

There was an uncanny, uncommon dry heat in Dubai. Others who'd been here for years talked about how you didn't tan quite as readily under the sun in the United Arab Emirates. Maybe it was the particles of dust from the desert that had floated into the atmosphere that brought about the strange climate. But as I took a seat on a nearby street bench and leafed through the Qu'ran that Rashid had gifted me with its Arabic script, I began to feel more comfortable in this arid environment.

CHAPTER 16
Luther

Valentine's Eve

With the exception of a pink glow emanating from Addy's night light, the house was dark when I gave up trying to beat insomnia and snuck downstairs to my dungeon to write. I lit a fire and sat on my chesterfield while I waited for the room to warm. Beyond the glass doors, the garden looked like Snow White's palace—fairy lights blinking intermittently. I rubbed my hands together to warm up my fingers. All I could think about, and all I wanted to think about, was Bronte. If my marriage had been laboring before I tumbled down the Twitter rabbit hole, it flatlined afterwards. I could share moments with Bronte that Tina would have considered insignificant. Like the silver fox who visited each night: after I had read Addy a bedtime story; after I had eaten dinner and made zero conversation with Tina; after I left Tina in front of her reality TV shows and retreated into my dungeon to write.

I unlocked my phone and opened my hidden album dedicated to the few images I had of Bronte. In one shot, her green eyes were accentuated by the bamboo forest behind her. In another, her distant expression stirred the traveler in me. Like I had told her before in poetry, she made me want to migrate to her shores more often than not.

LUTHER: Happy Valentine's, beautiful

BRONTE: You still up, Luth? It must be 1 a.m. your time.

LUTHER: I've turned into an insomniac for you, Bront 🖤

BRONTE: Be still my beating heart 🐿

LUTHER: What are you doing? Did I catch you at a bad time?

BRONTE: I'm at the beach with the kids. They're building the most elaborate sandcastle I've ever seen.

The fox stalked past the sliding doors, and I managed to snap and send a pic to Bronte.

BRONTE: Oh my, look at all that snow. It's crazy to think it's as hot as Bangladesh here and cold as the arctic where you are.

LUTHER: Yeah, can't wrap my head around it at times.

BRONTE: The fox looks extra silver against the layer of snow.

LUTHER: I know. Isn't it magnificent?

BRONTE: It is. From what you've told me, it's been visiting you a lot.

LUTHER: Yeah, I see it most nights.

BRONTE: Have you heard about animal messages?

LUTHER: Nope. What are those?

BRONTE: In certain spiritual traditions or cultures, they believe guides or totems can take the form of animals. They also say that if an animal visits you three times or more, it is bringing you a message.

LUTHER: Tell me more.

BRONTE: I've bookmarked a couple of good websites. Give

me a sec to look up fox and text you the gist.

LUTHER: I'm not going anywhere, hun

I turned my icy back to the fire while Bronte did her thing. Unlike Tina, who failed to see the wonder and beauty in a solitary silver fox, Bronte saw an animal guide with a crucial life message. It was these types of moments that consistently convinced me that Bronte and I were meant to be together, and that we complemented each other in ways our existing partners did not. I could envision Bronte being a mother to Addy. I could foresee us having a child together. Unfortunately, the obvious obstacles rendered that fantasy an impossible goal for all intents and purposes. Still, one I couldn't keep my mind from pondering, weighing up, and scheming.

BRONTE: Okay, I've found it. Fox is bringing you the following message. I quote: *A combination of persistence and patience will eventually lead to solving what appears to be an insurmountable problem.*

Bronte didn't realize my marriage was the problem and she was the solution. She didn't realize my persistence in convincing her of my love, and my patience for her to realize she loved me too (or at a minimum, admit it) would eventually lead us into each other's arms.

I texted back.

LUTHER: Insurmountable problem = marriage

BRONTE: I'm sure all married people can relate at some point.

LUTHER: Can you relate?

BRONTE: Of course.

LUTHER: Solution = Bronte

BRONTE: In a parallel universe, maybe…

LUTHER: It could happen

BRONTE: Um, hello Luther, geography, marriage, kids.

LUTHER: Sometimes I've believed as many as 6 impossible things before breakfast

BRONTE: Okay, Luther, a parallel universe OR Alice in Wonderland ;-)

LUTHER: Imagine how perfect our kids would be

BRONTE: How did we get from silver fox to having kids? 😊

LUTHER: I believe your website led us astray. My insurmountable problem is marriage and you're the solution 😊

. . .

The dreaded three dots, I thought. I hated watching those three dots bounce up and down like a juggler with three balls in the air. It usually spelled equivocation, and I could never be sure if it was for or against me.

And what if Wonderland existed…
A parallel world in this dimension
A rabbit hole connecting us
A magic potion holding us together
instead of this mosaic we have constructed with poems and innu-
endo
What then?

Usually, those balls juggled for an excruciatingly long time, only to disappear without warning. But tonight Bronte opened the door a crack and let the light of possibility glow a little. I held the phone to my heart for a few beats before I replied.

LUTHER: Wonderland does exist, and there's no doubt in my mind you're the real Alice. I just need you to believe in the impossible.

BRONTE: Marriage, kids, and geography is as impossible as it gets, Luther. Besides, I'd hate to ruin our writing friendship.

LUTHER: Always the editor…

BRONTE: I'm underlining the reality of our situation, Luth.

LUTHER: I'll believe for both of us.

BRONTE: Sorry. The kids want to swim. We'll have to pick this up later.

LUTHER: I'm not going anywhere, hun 😊

BRONTE: I'll text you later xo

LUTHER: Not if I text you first

BRONTE: 😄

CHAPTER 17
Aden

March

Iknelt alongside Rashid in the main hall of the mosque. The Saturday sunset prayers, or Maghrib Salah as I had come to call them, were drawing to a close. The light from the chandeliers and tens of copper lanterns reflected off the blue painted windows, illuminating the Islamic drawings and Arabic inscriptions that adorned the walls. The hall could accommodate fifteen hundred men, and it looked to be at capacity as I scanned the space and turned my head over my right shoulder, saying "As-salamu 'alaykum wa rahmat-Ullahi wa barakaatuh." Then turned my head over my left shoulder and repeated the same words.

At times it was hard to reconcile my old and new life. When Dad was alive and Ghost Gum still belonged to us, March was a busy month of ripeness and grape tastings before the harvest kicked in. Now, I was living in Dubai as a teetotaller and attending daily prayers. And while I still yearned for my vines and kept a mental journal of the seasonal changes that I was no longer privy to, I did appreciate my new surroundings and the opportunity to lick and heal my wounds. Each time I unrolled my mat and kneeled alongside other men, who had possibly also made terrible mistakes only Allah could absolve, the anger in my heart crumbled and the fog in my mind cleared a little more.

I was always the last to leave the hall. I liked the sound of emptying out, as men filed outside, followed by the music of stillness. It was in these fleeting, post-prayer moments that I felt the shifting snake of emotion uncoiling and rising within me. Addictive moments, if I'm honest. Moments that transported me back to Ghost Gum, to tending my vines, to feeling the pulse of the land, to doing something that gave me purpose and made me happy. A tap on the shoulder prompted my eyes to flicker open.

"Imam," I said. "Sorry, I have stayed too long."

The imam shook his head and held up his hand. "Not at all."

I bowed my head and said, "shukran," not knowing what else to say.

"I am curious," he said. "Although Dubai is full of western businessmen, I don't see them attending mosque. Yet here you are every day, at least once a day. Men who come here are either devout Muslims, or they are seeking something."

The tone of his last statement left no doubt that he was asking a question: *Was I a devout Muslim, or was I seeking something?*

"I have not converted to Islam, imam, but the daily prayers are giving me much-needed solace at this moment in my life."

"Solace is necessary for a man who has spent many days and nights wandering the desert alone without food and water."

"It's interesting you mention a desert," I said. "My wife wrote a poem about a desert last month, and before I came to Dubai, I felt like I'd been stranded in the desert. I didn't know how I was ever going to save myself—or my family."

"Mashallah." The imam bowed his head and gestured to an exit sign that I had not noticed before. "Come, Aye-din. We will find somewhere to talk."

I followed him in silence to the outer wings of the great hall, through a heavy fire door, and up several flights of stairs until we reached a landing. The imam took a key from his pocket and unlocked a small blue door that led into a minaret.

"Wow," I said, my eyes swimming in the sea of Deira's lights and beyond. I took thirty seconds to breathe in the scents of wafting street food, to listen to the sounds of cars, distant music, and bird chatter from the surrounding trees, to admire the sickle moon and her friendly stars. "The view from here must be even more spectacular during daylight."

"Allahu Akbar," he said.

I nodded in agreement and gave him my full attention.

"You were talking about your wife and said you were stranded in the desert," he said. "Tell me more."

I told him the whole story—Dad's heart attack, losing Ghost Gum, moving to Brisbane, my rage, turning on Bronte, and how my time in Dubai had shifted the sands of change within me. He did not interrupt at any point, only rubbed his beard and nodded occasionally.

"Prophet Muhammad (peace be upon him) said in his teachings: *God does not burden any soul beyond its capacity. Any good a soul earns is to its own benefit and any evil a soul earns is to its own loss.*"

I regarded him silently as I considered my answer. "When

I lost my livelihood, I felt like God had burdened my soul beyond its capacity, and I almost let my anger destroy everything I loved."

"Almost," the imam repeated. "This is what God has willed! There is no power except with God!"

I nodded. "Yes, I'm beginning to see that."

The imam rubbed his beard. "How long will you be in Dubai?"

"Three months if all goes well."

"Do you communicate with your family?"

"Yes, every week."

"Are you planning to divorce your wife?"

"No, not if I can help it."

"Then you are still the head of the family, and it is your duty to make this right."

"Shukran, Imam."

He bowed his head and closed his eyes in affirmation. "Inshallah."

Downstairs, Rashid was waiting for me, as he did every week, by the mosque door. "Ready for dinner, Aden?"

I nodded and smiled. "Meals with your family are the highlight of my week, Rashid."

Rashid bowed his head. "Mehrnoosh is cooking a Persian specialty for you. And can you guess the secret ingredient?"

I smiled, knowing exactly what he was referring to. "Could

it be pomegranate?"

He chuckled and nodded. "Mashallah."

CHAPTER 18
Bronte

April

LUTHER: Hi beautiful.

I couldn't suppress the smile when I saw Luther's name. His texts gave me a buzz—gold and yellow honey bees in the hive of my stomach. If I closed my eyes, I could picture him sitting in the red velvet armchair next to my desk. While I told myself our perpetual banter was harmless, I knew that our feelings for each other ran deep. I replied with an emoticon half the time because words would only serve to implicate me in something I was skirting around at best. Emoticons offered the gift of wild abandon. A red heart could easily equal a warm, friendly gesture versus an actual declaration of love. And I consistently hid behind those emoticons. I sent those love hearts because I had real love in my heart. But Luther hid behind nothing.

BRONTE: Wait, isn't it about 5 a.m. your time?

LUTHER: Yeah, I couldn't sleep. Plus, you're like the character in my book—always on my mind.

BRONTE: To what do I owe the pleasure? 😊

LUTHER: Don't get mad. I submitted 1 of your poems.

BRONTE: You what?

LUTHER: Yeah, naughty, I know, but also nice because it's been accepted.

BRONTE: No way?!

LUTHER: Yes, way.

BRONTE: Where did you submit?

LUTHER: An online journal called 'Letters'. It's a play on the word letters—as in written correspondence, letters of the alphabet, etc.

BRONTE: I don't know what to say. I could hug you and never let go.

LUTHER: Just a hug? 😜

BRONTE: Honestly, no. Probably a whole lot more.

LUTHER: Okay, now you're teasing.

BRONTE: You make it difficult to not love you.

LUTHER: Ooh, did Bronte finally admit she loves Luther?

BRONTE: If circumstances were different, my feelings for you would be scary strong.

LUTHER: I'm not scared xoxo

BRONTE: 🖤

LUTHER: I just need one thing from you.

BRONTE: Uh oh, what's that?

LUTHER: A bio, silly.

BRONTE: Ohh, haha. Oh God, I have no idea. I've never written a bio.

LUTHER: What about something like this:

Bronte plans to fall in love with an American writer and live happily ever after, though she doesn't know it yet.
BRONTE: That made me cringe, laugh, and secretly fantasise that it was true.

LUTHER: Ooh, I should submit your poems more often. I'm enjoying this side of you.

BRONTE: Two people with similar interests and mutual affection yet, married and living on opposite sides of the globe. It's times like these that I think meeting you is cosmic cruelty.

LUTHER: Mmm. I hear ya, love!

My phone started buzzing. I looked at the screen and saw Aden's name flashing for a FaceTime call.

BRONTE: Shit, duty calls. Can we pick this up later?

LUTHER: Only if you promise to pick up where we left off?

BRONTE: I promise.

LUTHER: Okay, beautiful xoxo

BRONTE: Luther?

LUTHER: Yeah

BRONTE: Thank you 🖤

LUTHER: That's what future husbands are for, haha.

BRONTE: 🖤

LUTHER: xoxo

I quickly composed myself and hit answer. Aden's face filled the screen and my face popped up into the right hand corner. "This is unexpected," I said.

"I didn't get you at a bad time, did I?"

I waved my hand back and forth. "No, of course not. You don't usually call at this time."

"Yeah, well, I have good news."

"Oh?"

"We won the tender, Bront. I'll be coming home next week."

"Wow, that's amazing news. Congratulations."

"Thanks. My boss is flying out in a few days to wrap things up, and my flight home is booked for next Friday."

"Meaning you'll be home sometime on Saturday?"

"Yes."

"The kids will be excited."

"What about you? Will you be excited?"

I pasted a smile on my face and hoped it didn't look fake. "Of course I'm excited."

"I'm glad to hear that, because I can't wait to see you all."

We talked for a few more minutes about nothing in particular and then said goodbye. As much as I had missed Aden, I had also acclimatised to my new independent-woman-routine and enjoyed a blissful three months without arguments and criticism. Three months that I didn't have to step on broken eggshells and edit everything I said. It had also been three months of Luther. Texting him whenever I wished and replying to his texts at all hours of the day and night. And now I had made it all worse by admitting my feelings for him.

CHAPTER 19
Aden

April

I gave my name to the restaurant host and he scanned the monitor before nodding and saying, "Mike is waiting for you, sir. Follow me."

I was meeting my boss for a celebratory dinner at the Jumeirah Beach Residences—his choice. More than a restaurant, it was a popular nightspot where you could drink alcohol, dine, listen to live music, hang out on the terrace, or sit at the bar. The food was a fusion of Turkish, Lebanese and Moroccan, and I had only heard good reviews about it. With alcohol usually prohibited, it was weirdly confronting to see a flashy bar sporting hundreds of bottles of spirits in the centre of the room. The polished wooden counter and array of hanging glasses sparkled beneath the yellow glowing drop lights, and the hint of gold detail in the dining chairs and on the ceiling reflected and shimmered in the refracted light. The host led me to the dining room, which felt like a step back in time to the Ottoman Empire. Rich fabrics and antique decor—forest green wallpaper with gold undertones, geometric patterned drop lights and upholstery, luxurious Persian carpets throughout, and scatterings of stacked cushions. Soft background music, combined with the laughter and chatter of diners, created a welcoming and vibrant ambience.

Mike was already drinking a beer when I shook his hand and sat down. "What are you drinking, Aden?"

"I'll have a sparkling water while I look at the menu."

Mike's expression left no doubt as to what he would say next. "A sparkling water? Come on, mate."

The waiter looked at me and poised his pen to write. I switched from English to Arabic, telling him that I had not drunk alcohol for three months, that I had no plan to start, but that I did not want to insult my boss. His demeanour changed when he realised I wasn't like all the other expats—it had become my secret weapon in Dubai.

Mike couldn't help but interject. "What the fuck, Aden, you can speak the lingo?"

"Enough to get by," I shot back.

The waiter spoke to me in Arabic, and suggested bringing a glass of something non-alcoholic that looked distinctly alcoholic.

"Shukran," I said, smiling at our little conspiracy.

When the waiter returned with my non-alcoholic beverage, he told us the specials and explained that most dishes were designed for sharing.

"Mind if I order a selection of food, Aden?"

"Not at all. Knock yourself out."

Mike was jovial and chatty for a change—due to the successful tender, no doubt—and I was only too happy to let him monopolise the conversation. Westerners like him had become as foreign to me as the arid desert weather had been when I first arrived. Since then, I had not only acclimatised to the climate, I had become accustomed to and grown fond of my adopted city's customs and culture. No alcohol being one of them.

The waiter arrived with a selection of dips and oven-fresh breads: hommous; taktouka, grilled peppers and oriental spices; Haydari, a strained yogurt infused with garlic, mint and fresh herbs; and zaalouk, smoked aubergine and spices. Mike tucked in and continued to make small talk about the usual subject suspects: work, sport, rinse, repeat.

The main course arrived swiftly after our starter plates were cleared—lamb tagine, a selection of kebabs and a salad of diced tomatoes, green peppers, red onions, parsley, walnuts, ezine cheese and pomegranate molasses—at which point the conversation moved onto Australian current affairs and my thoughts drifted to Bronte. Dubai was my comfort zone— the job, my sole responsibility, combined with the soothing ritual of daily prayers in the mosque—a place where I didn't have to contend with commuting, Bronte, and the kids. A place where I didn't have to see that restless ocean. A place with no reminders of my beloved vines at the foothills of the mountains.

Mike excused himself to go to the bathroom and pay the tab, and I stretched my legs on the outside terrace. The music was as good a partition as any between spaces, with Queen's Bohemian Rhapsody in mid-flow. I leaned over the railing and cast my thoughts into the water like an optimistic fisherman, hoping to hook an answer or two to the uncomfortable questions that lurked below the surface of my marriage.

Aden, is that you?

I turned around to see a smiling elderly man with a red nose and a glass of whiskey in his right hand.

"Aden, it's me, Barry." He held out his hand.

I looked at him for several seconds while attempting to place him.

"Your dad's friend from Coffs Harbour. Although you probably remember me as Bazza— that's what everyone in Australia calls me."

The penny dropped. "Oh, of course. Sorry, Barry, it's been a long time since I've seen you."

"No worries, Aden. Small world, isn't it? What are you doing in Dubai of all places?"

I laughed. "I could ask the same of you?"

He touched his nose. "Touché."

I told him about the tender and that I was having dinner with my boss from Brisbane.

"Are you free for breakfast tomorrow? I would love to catch up."

I thought about my morning prayers and commute to work. "How about a coffee in about twenty minutes? My boss will be heading off shortly."

"That'll work. See you at the bar."

After organising Mike a taxi and wishing him farewell, I met Barry at the bar. Neither of us had a coffee. Barry ordered another whiskey, and I opted for a pot of peppermint tea.

Barry pointed to my tea. "I see you've taken on the local customs."

"Yeah, I needed a detox."

He nodded like he understood, but I doubted that. Barry had one of those red, bumpy, swollen noses that usually gave alcoholics away.

"How is your dad, Aden?"

I sipped my tea before I answered. "Sadly, he passed away last September."

"Oh God, I'm sorry. I didn't know. Me and my big mouth."

I shook my head and waved my hand in a *don't be silly gesture.* "You've obviously been away from Australia for a while."

He nodded. "Yeah, I travel most of the year."

"When was the last time you saw Dad?"

He scratched his head as he reflected. "It was the year your mother passed."

"That long ago?"

"Yeah, your Dad was in a bad way. Trying to keep the farm above water, while paying for your mum's experimental treatment."

I put down my glass teacup. "What experimental treatment?"

"Oh God, have I put my foot in it again?"

I shook my head. "No, Baz, this is something I need to know."

Barry nodded his understanding. "The doctors had given

up by that stage, but your dad was determined to exhaust every avenue. He found an experimental alternative, but it was costly. If memory serves, he had to take out a loan to pay for it."

This new information hit me like a sledgehammer. I knew nothing about Mum's experimental treatment. "How did I not know any of this?" I said.

Barry put his glass down on the polished counter and placed his hand on my forearm. "You were a young lad, Aden. Your dad didn't want to unnecessarily upset or stress you."

"How long did the treatment last?"

"Your dad hoped the treatment would see your mum through to you realising your winery dream, but Rose never finished the course because she passed a quarter of the way through."

I tried to choke back the lump in my throat by resuming to sip my tea.

"Say, what happened to your winery plans?"

I put my glass down with too much force and the bar tender eyeballed me. "Sorry," I said, raising my hand and standing. "Um, Barry, will you excuse me a sec?"

Barry stood and nodded. "Sure, Aden. I'll be right here."

Tears hit the second I closed the bathroom stall door. Was Ghost Gum's debt connected to Mum's treatment? If so, I had nothing to be angry about and everything to apologise for. Dad had tried to save Mum, at any cost. And there was no price on her life.

CHAPTER 20
Luther

May

My mother firmly believed in Mercury Retrograding—an astrological phenomenon in which the planet Mercury appears to move in reverse for a period of time. Note that word *appears*, because Mercury is not technically moving in reverse; it is simply an optical illusion. Semantics aside, the phenomenon gained a bad reputation over the centuries for being a potentially chaotic and volatile period when we experience major disruptions and good old-fashioned bad luck. Like my mother, I became a firm believer in the theory when Lily-Rose died during a retrograde period. And the theory only strengthened the week Bronte rejected me.

I arrived home later than usual on a Monday night, thanks to a juggernaut skidding during rush-hour traffic and plowing into several commuters before it rolled into the oncoming lane. Between gridlock and emergency clean-up services, I added two hours to my commute. I couldn't wait to get inside, kiss Addy's forehead, and chill out with a glass of bourbon.

I caught a glimpse of the silver fox as I pulled into the driveway, and thought of Bronte. We were so near, yet so far. I checked the time on my phone. Tina would probably be watching her reality shows. I had a quick smoke before trying to sneak in the back door. But Tina was not watching television. She sat at the kitchen table with a pile of unopened mail and my new poetry book in her hand.

"What the fuck?" I said. "Did that arrive today?"

She nodded and stared at me with narrowed eyes. Her red lips pursed.

"Since when do you open my mail?" I said, with a sinking feeling.

"Since you're late and you didn't phone."

"A juggernaut caused a massive pile-up on the highway."

"I know that now, Luther, but I had to turn on the radio to hear about it. You could have phoned, or texted."

"I'm sorry, Tina, I didn't think. I have a lot on my mind."

She dropped the book on the table and tapped it with her index finger. "Mm-hmm. I see how much you have on your mind, and it's neither Addy nor me."

"What?" I said, trying to buy time.

"Don't play dumb, Luther." She opened the book to a poem called *Wuthering Heights*. "For Bronte," she read out loud. "Who the fuck is Bronte?"

"She's nobody. It's fiction."

"Do you think I'm stupid?"

"No."

The chair scraped as she pushed it back and stood with her phone clasped tightly in her right hand. Standing next to me, she opened Facebook and navigated to my Friends Page, her red fingernails tapping. "Are you saying your Facebook friend 'Bronte' is a coincidence?"

I stepped away from her and pulled out a chair to sit

down, all the time weighing up the pros and cons in my mind. I had to make a choice: to remain in a miserable, loveless marriage for the sake of my daughter; or save my soul by admitting my unhappiness and moving on. After finding Bronte, I knew I wanted to move on. I also knew Addy would be better off in the long run. "Is that the only poem you've read?" I said.

She sat opposite me and opened the book. "No, Luther, I've read them all. Two sections. The first is obviously about your safe choices— May and me. The second is about the love of your life—this Bronte woman." She put the book down and pointed to Bronte's Facebook picture on her phone. "Judging by your writing, Luther, she obviously is the love of your life."

I crossed my arms, frowned, and leaned back in my chair. "What's that supposed to mean?"

"I've read your books, Luther, and they're mediocre at best." She hammered the book with her index finger like a woodpecker would a birch. "This poetry is your best work by far."

"What do you care, Tina? You're not in love with me any more than I'm in love with you. You tell me every day how I'm not good enough for you or for Addy."

"Stop being dramatic, Luther. Does this Bronte know how dramatic you are?"

"Leave Bronte out of it. I'm talking about us, and I'm not being dramatic. You and I don't love each other. We don't make each other happy."

She stared at me.

"At least admit that we want different things," I said.

"I will admit no such thing. This has been our dynamic from the start. Why the sudden change of heart?"

"It's not sudden. It's been a long time coming, but I've been hanging on for Addy's sake."

She crossed her arms and straightened her spine. "I blame your mother."

I frowned. "What has Mom got to do with this?"

"She filled your head with all that Alice in Wonderland bullshit."

"It's not bullshit."

Her voice rose. "No relationship is perfect."

"I don't want perfect, Tina. I want true love."

She laughed and shook her head. "Do you hear yourself, Luther? You have a wife and child right here, but you're willing to forfeit us for some fantasy woman who lives on another continent."

"I'm not forfeiting Addy."

She leaned across the table. Our faces were inches apart. "You can kiss goodbye to visitation rights, Luther, because I will use this affair against you." Her voice hissed.

I pushed my chair back to get some distance between us. "I'm not having an affair with Bronte. She is a friend, that's all. She's married and lives in Australia. But she has taught me more about myself and about love than you and May combined."

"Addy and I are a package deal, and the courts do not look

favorably on fathers who cheat."

"For fuck's sake, Tina, I haven't cheated, and I *will* fight you with everything I have because Addy is the only thing that matters to me."

She pursed her lips, and tears welled in her blue eyes. "Yeah, that much is clear."

I realized my mistake and walked toward her. "I didn't mean it like that, Tee."

"Fuck you, Luther. You're destined to be a pathetic loser."

I nodded. "That's why we need to end this, Tina. You've always treated me like a loser."

"I'll see you in court."

"Fine." I walked past her to go upstairs, but she grabbed my arm and pulled me back.

"What the fuck do you think you're doing?"

"I'm gonna kiss Addy goodnight and take a shower."

"No you're not. This is my house, and I want you to leave."

"I pay half the mortgage, and Addy is my daughter."

"Tell it to your lawyer. My parents paid the deposit, and I pay half the mortgage. You have less right to be here than I do, and I want you to go."

I stared at her and sighed. "Where do you expect me to go?"

"Go to your mother's. I don't care."

"You know what?"

"What?"

"The old me would have gone, but the new me is saying no—not tonight at least. I will sleep in the basement, speak to Addy in the morning, and I'll take a bag with me when I leave for work. Tonight I am staying."

She threw the book at me and called her mother. At the foot of the stairs, I heard Tina say, "Mom," before turning on the waterworks. I would have taken it all back if I'd believed for a second that her tears were real. But I knew better. Tina was like a Netflix movie; she could cry on demand.

CHAPTER 21
Bronte

May

I woke up at four-thirty on the morning of Aden's home-coming. While the kids slept soundly, my head was louder than the kookaburras, who were chatting and chuckling up a storm. In the bathroom, I shrugged off my pyjamas and pulled on my swimsuit.

Outside, first light was evident on the ocean's horizon, but it hadn't yet reached the swimming pool. I dived in without feeling the temperature, and the grogginess cleared the second my head submerged. After three warm-up laps, I reached for my stopwatch at the poolside, pressed start and lunged straight into my laps.

As my body warmed up and my mind sharpened, I thought about Aden's return. Our virtual communications had been pleasant enough, and although he hadn't clued me in on everything that had happened, he had clearly undergone a profound change. Something good had dismantled the toxic anger and reinstated the old Aden in its place.

The prospect of a third version of Aden gave me pause. If the winery-Aden had been calm and kind, and the post-winery Aden had been angry and cruel, what was Dubai-Aden going to resemble? He had taken to praying five times a day. Had the ritual given him a false sense of stability, or had it genuinely transformed him?

Aden wasn't the only one who had changed. No longer the

dependent housewife and mother he left behind, I was building a career and falling in love with Luther. Luther, who lit a fire inside me and constantly declared his adoration. Luther, who was so close to my heart and yet light years away on the physical plane. I knew an actual relationship wasn't possible, but that knowledge and reality did nothing to dissuade my heart, which fantasised with what-ifs and yearned a little more each day.

Would the new Aden and Bronte still have a marriage? That was the question that needed answering.

The day passed as slowly as a water dragon shedding its skin, though the kids attended a birthday party until midday, and I had an article to edit for a deadline. It didn't help that I hadn't heard from Aden, or what time to expect him. *I'll be back sometime tomorrow,* he had texted the day before. *And don't worry about picking me up. I'll get a cab from there.*

In the afternoon, the kids took advantage of low tide, playing in rock pools and saving stranded blue jellyfish and sea slugs. When Priya rang at 5 p.m., we were eating salted caramel ice creams at the local gelato cafe.

"Hi, Bront. Is Aden home yet?"

"Not yet, Priya. And I don't know what time; it could be in the next hour or later tonight."

"Can the kids come for a sleepover tonight? It will give you some time alone."

"Hang on a sec, I'll ask them."

I put my hand over the phone and asked the question. They both jumped out of their seats with excitement and Liam's ice cream nearly plummeted from its cone to the floor. "What about Daddy?" I said.

"We can see him tomorrow," said Leyla.

I looked at them both with a hint of sadness. Aden had lost his connection with them. I took my hand off the speaker and swallowed the lump in my throat.

"Sure, Priya, they'd love that. I'll pick them up early tomorrow morning if that's okay?"

"We'd love you to come for lunch if you're available. Anura can't wait to see Aden."

"Okay, sounds good. Thanks, Priya. I'll drop the kids off in about half an hour."

"Bye, Bront. See you soon."

On my way home from Priya's, I stopped to buy a bottle of champagne and remembered Aden had stopped drinking. I put the bottle back in the fridge and tried to avoid eye contact with the shop assistant, who was eyeing me suspiciously. I settled on sparkling water from the supermarket and texted Aden when I got to the car:

BRONTE: What time will you be home? Kids are sleeping over at Priya's. We could get a takeaway for dinner?

I stared at the phone until I saw *delivered*. But five minutes passed without a reply. *Maybe he's still in the air*, I thought. He had provided zero flight details, but flights from Dubai to Brisbane were likely limited. I opened Safari and checked the flight times. One flight had landed an hour ago, and the other flight was due at midnight.

I decided to try my luck and dial his number. He answered

in a hushed voice after a few rings.

"Hi Bront, sorry I haven't called. I caught the airport train instead of a taxi."

"Oh, you have arrived? Can I pick you up from the station?"

"Not to worry. I'll get a taxi."

"Do you want me to get the kids? I didn't know what time to expect you."

"No, that's okay. I'm looking forward to spending some time alone with you."

"I'll see you soon."

"You will. Bye, Bront."

"Bye."

At home, I ran up the stairs two at a time and headed to my writing room. I needed a few moments to prepare myself. Aden seemed infinitely better, and the prospect of having my kind, loving, gentle husband back made me temporarily dizzy. My phone buzzed with a notification. I half expected it to be Aden, but it was Luther.

LUTHER: Hi beautiful, whatcha doing?

I sank into my red chair and smiled.

BRONTE: My husband is on his way home from Dubai.

LUTHER: Ohhh!

BRONTE: Yeah. What are you doing?

LUTHER: Addy's with Mom and Tina's out with friends, so I'm all alone.

BRONTE: Wish I could visit you.

LUTHER: Mmm, if only.

I heard the front door open and shut and felt the familiar tug of war that had become Luther versus Aden. "Hi, Bront, I'm home. Are you upstairs?"

I shouted "yes" to Aden and then texted my reply to Luther.

BRONTE: Sorry, Luth. I've gotta go.

LUTHER: Text me later?

BRONTE: I'll try xo

LUTHER: 🖤

I stuffed my phone into my back pocket and turned to find Aden standing in the doorway.

"I forgot how tall you were," I said, grappling for words.

His eyes were moist as he approached me. "I've missed you, Bront. And I'm sorry for everything I've said and done since we lost Ghost Gum."

He pulled me into his arms before I could answer. My voice was muffled as I spoke into his cotton shirt. "I missed you too." He hugged me tighter and began to sob. Tears caught in my throat as I thought about my recent text to Luther; *scary strong feelings.*

"I understand if you haven't missed me. I certainly haven't missed the old me."

"I have missed you, Ade."

We stood that way for the length of time it took for the sun to settle beyond the ocean horizon and for twilight to cast shadows from the mango tree outside the window. Aden, using body language to ask for my forgiveness; and me saying yes with mine. Only, my body was split like the fallen ghost gum, and I didn't know how I was going to escape the mess I'd made.

That night, we ate takeaway Chinese and talked about the future. He told me all about his healing experience in Dubai and his chance encounter with Barry. He sincerely apologised for his behaviour after leaving Ghost Gum and assured me his anger was firmly in the past. I saw a glimmer of the Aden who had invited me to feed the kookaburra, and guilt swooped down like a vulture to pick at my conscience. *I'm the one who should be apologising*, I thought to myself. I had fantasised about a future with another man. I deserved to be stripped of the title Bronte and be re-branded as Jezebel.

In the early hours of the morning, when we made love, I sobbed uncontrollably. I loved Luther in a way I had not loved anyone else, in a way I didn't love Aden, but I was a married woman with two children, and I had no right to flirt with Luther and daydream about some imaginary life. I had to stop for his sake and mine. As soon as Aden fell asleep, I snuck downstairs to the kitchen and texted Luther.

BRONTE: Luther, I'm sorry, but I can't do this. We're both married and we have to respect our other halves.

LUTHER: I'll support whatever decision you make, but I won't lie to myself or you. I love you Bronte.

BRONTE: I don't want to cheat on my husband, Luther. Surely you feel conflicted about Tina?

LUTHER: I'm not conflicted anymore. Tina and I are getting divorced.

BRONTE: What? Since when?

LUTHER: Since Tina found out about you.

BRONTE: Oh my God, Luther. You're getting divorced because of me?

LUTHER: No, Bronte. I'm not getting divorced because I'm unhappily married. I thought your situation was the same.

BRONTE: My marriage is more complicated than that.

LUTHER: Then maybe you should uncomplicate it.

BRONTE: And how do you propose I do that?

LUTHER: You can stop editing your feelings for one.

BRONTE: And then what? Have you thought this through to conclusion?

LUTHER: You could get divorced and come and live with me.

BRONTE: As long as I have children that's impossible.

I switched my phone to silent and sobbed into the tea towel that was folded beside me on the kitchen bench.

CHAPTER 22
Aden

May - Mother's Day Weekend

Our road trip kicked off at 6 a.m. on Friday with Lynyrd Skynyrd's *Free Bird* playing; me in the driver's seat, Bronte in the passenger seat, and the kids in the back. Only I knew the destination, and I wanted to keep it that way for as long as possible, although I knew Bronte would twig the minute she saw the sign for Toowoomba.

Leyla was engrossed in a game on her iPad, and Liam was drawing dinosaurs in his sketch pad.

"Do you mind if I write?" said Bronte.

I disguised my disappointment by patting her knee and saying it was fine. She nodded in acknowledgement and returned to staring out the window as we passed farms with symmetrical rows of purple cabbage and green kale, each tract of land separated by T-shaped machines that irrigated the crops with a fine mist. Since returning from Dubai it was obvious that Bronte had acclimatised to my absence and carved out her writing routine around the kids and work. Most nights she'd last a couple of hours before getting ants in her pants and excusing herself to write. I planned to use the road trip as a way to try and reconnect with her and hopefully reset our marriage.

I turned my attention to the kids. I hit play on an 80s playlist I'd curated and focused on the journey ahead. When we lost Ghost Gum, I vowed to stay away, but my Dubai bonus had helped us make significant savings, and my warm memories were returning.

Driving along the Cunningham Highway, the Flinders Mountain range looked like volcanic peaks in the distance. We passed an old war plane monument, a palm nursery and a red barn before hitting a stretch of dry, expansive land with hay-coloured grass that shone like velvet in the sun. A congregation of cows gathered in the shade of a solitary tree.

A fews later, the kids were restless, and Bronte needed a bathroom break. We stopped at a servo that had a cafe and bathrooms. The parking lot was heaving, so Bronte hopped out with the kids while I drove around and tried to find parking. When I had no luck, I pulled over to the left and put my hazards on, hoping someone would come out soon enough. I opened the windows and turned off the ignition. In Bronte's haste, she had forgotten to take her bag. I reached over to pick it up and put it on the seat. As I did, a family returned to the row of cars where I was stopped and waved for me to take their parking. I dropped the bag on the floor and waved back at them to say *thank you.*

Perfect, shaded spot, I thought to myself as I parked the car, closed the windows and turned off the ignition. Remembering Bronte's bag as I locked the doors, I clicked the alarm and rounded the bonnet to the passenger side. I kneeled on my haunches to gather the contents that had fallen out when I dropped it. Bronte's notebook was among the items. A pen marked her latest entry like a bookmark. I looked up and around me to see if anybody was around. *You shouldn't look at it,* I thought, *but I need to know what's happening with my wife. A quick peek won't hurt anyone,* I told myself. I opened the page and found a poem.

> *My voyeurism is on repeat*
> *but I hunger still for voyage*
> *I wish I was the nearest star*
> *—owned a bunk bed on the moon—*
> *but I am mere mortal;*
> *leather journal, bound*
> *by porcelain skin*
>
> *Oh, how I wish*
> *I could travel*
> *like a bottled message*
> *Or build a raft*
> *and paddle to you every night*
>
> *But this is not*
> *the Night Garden*
> *and I've used up all*
> *my wishes.*

I heard Bronte calling me and snapped the book shut. "You forgot your bag," I said on standing and finding her and the kids looking at me.

"Do you want something to eat?"

I nodded and handed her bag to her. "I'll have a snack, but I have something planned for this lunch so don't eat too much."

She smiled at me, like my old Bronte. But she wasn't my

old Bronte. Something had changed. And I suspected it had something to do with her new writing friend, Luther.

When we arrived at the holiday cottage a few hours later, swimming was first on the kids' agenda, despite the chilly temperature. A green fence enclosed the kidney-shaped pool, and a landscaped rock garden, reminiscent of the Granite Belt boulders, decorated the deep end. On the shallow end side, a mini wooden bridge led to a spa pool. I knelt to activate the jets. "The spa pool is ready to go, kids." But they had already jumped into the pool. I joined Bronte near the deep end and sat on a green plastic pool chair.

"Is it weird being back here?" said Bronte.

"I loved our life here, Bronte, and we lost everything in a heartbeat. I'm not sure time will ever soften the blow."

She sighed and looked over her shoulder toward the garden. "We lost the winery, Aden, but we still have two healthy children, and we still have each other."

"Do we still have each other, Bront, because it doesn't feel like it?"

"What are you talking about? I thought we were getting back on track?"

"Something's changed between us, or maybe something's changed with you. It's as if you have a double life, and your other life is slowly but surely gaining territory."

For a split second, panic sprinted across her features, but she adjusted herself immediately.

"Oh, you mean writing? It's nothing personal, it's an occupational hazard."

"It's not technically an occupation though, is it Bronte? I mean, until you publish something and earn actual money, it's essentially a pipe dream."

She sat back in the pool chair and looked at the sky. "Thanks a lot, Aden. I am having a poem published soon."

"Is that so? When? How?"

She shifted uncomfortably in her seat. "It's all thanks to Luther."

"Luther? Your American writing friend?"

She nodded. "He submitted one of my poems, and it was accepted."

"How did Luther get his hands on your unpublished poems?"

"I sent him some for feedback. After all, I'm not a poet."

"Is he an editor or something?"

She shook her head, and her cheeks flushed. "No, but he's far more experienced than I am. He's published two novels, and he's writing his third."

I nodded as I digested her words. "What does he want in return?"

"What do you mean?"

"People aren't saints, Bronte. Everyone has an angle. The question you should be asking yourself is: what is Luther's angle?"

"I am asking myself a question, but it's not about Luther, it's about you."

"Get it off your chest, why don't you."

"I'm finally doing something I love, Aden. Why can't you be happy for me?"

For a wild nanosecond, I thought about asking her if she had feelings for this Luther but decided against it. After all, I had invaded her privacy and read her journal. And I didn't know if the poem was random or about Luther. Instead, I said, "You're right, Bront. That's fantastic news about the poem and I'm happy for you."

She nodded and smiled weakly. "Yeah, it's a start."

I stood and gathered the kids' towels. "Time to get out, kids. We have a special lunch planned."

"Where are we going?" said Leyla.

"We're going to visit our old neighbours, Fred and Marjorie."

Bronte stood. "You stayed in contact with Fred and Marjorie?"

"Yes. I'm not a complete monster."

"That's not what I meant. I've stayed in touch too. Did you know that they've renovated their house?"

"Um, no, I didn't know."

She smiled and touched my face. "Can we put the animosity behind us and enjoy the weekend?"

I put my hands up as if to surrender. "No more animosity; I promise."

I parked the car in the shade of a poinciana tree and

stepped out to admire the house. They lived in a sprawling Queenslander that differed from ours in Sandgate. Theirs had many heritage features, including slatted screens, stained-glass bay windows, and a fancy lattice gate that led to the front door. The once-orange cladding was vivid white, and the brown painted gutters, handrails, awnings, and gables were iron-grey. Marjorie opened the lattice gate and waved before heading down the flight of stairs to greet us. Fred approached from the converted barn to the left of the house. With carpentry his main hobby, it was where he spent most of his spare time.

Before anyone could speak, Liam belted out a loud "G'day mate" to Fred, which broke the ice and made everyone laugh.

"This is his latest thing," said Bronte. "He rolls down the window when I'm driving them to school, or parking in the lot at Woolworths, and yells out "G'day mate" to anyone who is passing by. It's funny most of the time, but sometimes you get an old grouch with no sense of humour."

Fred chuckled, ruffled Liam's hair, and held out his hand. "G'day, cobber."

Liam shook Fred's hand and beamed from ear to ear. "G'day mate, seen any crocs lately?"

We all laughed, and Fred played along. "No crocs, today, young Liam, but I had to relocate a snake from me shed before you arrived."

Liam's eye widened. "Was it venomous?"

"It could kill you in the blink of an eye," said Fred.

Marjorie slapped Fred's arm affectionately. "Don't scare the boy, Fred."

Liam shook his head. "I'm not scared. I love snakes."

"Me too," said Leyla.

Fred ruffled the hair on both of their heads and laughed. "In that case, I know a little spot where we can find a carpet python."

"But, first, lunch," said Marjorie.

"The kids have been hungry for the last hour," I said.

"Let's go," said Marjorie, ushering us toward the house and up the stairs.

"I love how you've modernised the exterior, Marjorie," said Bronte. "I can't wait to see inside."

Marjorie nodded excitedly. "And I can't wait to show you, Bront."

"Wow," I said the minute I entered the front door. They had removed internal walls to create an open-planned space. The polished floors gleamed and rugs differentiated spaces. A Persian rug in the entrance, a woolly cream and white rug in the formal lounge area, and a brightly coloured hand-woven rug in the dining room. The kitchen, which was Marjorie's favourite place in the house, had been refitted with stainless steel European appliances and whiteware.

I pointed to the freshly baked apple pie on the granite countertop. "One thing hasn't changed."

"She can bake them with her eyes closed," said Fred.

Marjorie chuckled and told Bronte to look around the house. The kids headed straight for the table, eager to eat.

I caught Fred's eye and whispered, "Can I show her after lunch?"

"You bet, mate. It's ready to be unveiled."

"Thanks, Fred."

Marjorie's lunch of roast chicken, new potatoes, onion gravy, and homegrown vegetables did not disappoint. Neither did her renowned apple pie, custard, and vanilla bean ice cream. With our bellies full and dishes cleared away, Marjorie took Leyla and Liam down to the paddock to feed the horses, and Fred took me and Bronte to his workshop.

He opened the door for us and said, "Aden, you can take it from here."

I thanked him and took Bronte's hand. "Close your eyes and come with me."

"What are you up to?"

"You'll see soon enough." I led her across the polished concrete floor. "Fred calls this place his shed," I said, "but it's more like a cathedral with its lofty ceiling and leadlight windows."

"I can smell sawdust," she said.

"That's because it's whirling all around us like glitter."

"Can't you give me a clue?"

I laughed. "No time for clues."

We stopped walking.

"Okay, you can open your eyes now." I stepped aside and watched Bronte's reaction as she took in the desk.

She looked at me with moist eyes and pointed. "Is that…?"

"The wood from the twin ghost gum," I said, finishing her sentence, "yes."

"How did you…what did you…?"

"After we lost the winery, I asked Fred to buy the ghost gum wood in the hopes that we would someday be able to buy it back. But Fred wanted nothing in return. He agreed to store it here in the shed until we were ready to take it back."

"And the desk?"

"That was my idea. I've given you such a hard time since we left Ghost Gum, and I wanted to make it up to you. I had a lot of time to think in Dubai, and I phoned Fred a couple of times to discuss the possibilities. I told him about your dream to become a writer, and that you were actively pursuing it. He suggested the desk."

She hugged me tightly. "I'm speechless, but my emotions are rising like floodwater."

"Your reaction is all I need."

"The colour of the wood and the texture of the grain is stunning," she said, walking around it and examining every inch.

"Fred's done an outstanding job," I said. "Look, it has drawers too."

We both turned around at the sound of the shed door opening and closing. Bronte held out her arms as Fred approached. "Thank you, Fred. Words cannot describe how grateful I am for this thoughtful gift."

"Don't mention it, love."

When Bronte released him from her bear hug, he said, "There's something else. Something that I hope will help you rekindle your love of wine, Aden."

I shook my head and said, "I never stopped loving my wine, Fred."

"Maybe not, but your wife here tells me you killed your passion for it, and you haven't bought a single bottle of wine since you left Ghost Gum." He led us toward an object hidden beneath a white sheet and said, "Go on."

I slowly tugged at the sheet. Fred had carved a wine rack from my beloved ghost gum; a thing of beauty. I closed my eyes and ran my fingers along the smooth wood, admiring every inch. It had eighteen layers with each row holding twelve bottles, fitting a total of two hundred and sixteen bottles. Magnificent didn't begin to describe it.

"Fred. Words are not enough."

"I'm happy you like it, Aden. You deserve a break after everything you've been through."

"Are you happy to store all of this until our circumstances change?" I said.

"Wouldn't have it any other way," said Fred.

"Our circumstances are already changing," said Bronte. "Focus on that, okay?"

"You're right."

"I'll leave you two alone," said Fred. "See you in a few ticks."

We watched him go, then I turned to Bronte. "It would sound crazy to anyone other than you, Bront, but that tree meant more to me than the winery in many respects. It represented us."

"I know how much that tree meant to you, Ade, which is why I appreciate this gesture."

I reached for her hand. "One more thing. Forget what I said about your writing."

She flicked her hand. "Like the backspace on a keyboard, it's gone."

I smiled, hoping that this day would mark the beginning of a new phase.

PART II

6 MONTHS LATER

CHAPTER 23
Luther

November

After Bronte revealed her true feelings, I thought I'd finally broken through the barrier. Then the dust of her husband's homecoming settled, and she withdrew. Much like her dreaded text bubbles, that undulated like the scales of justice, I was in one minute and out the next.   With Tina and I finally settled on visitation rights and a payout for my investment in the family home, I decided to let things cool down before contacting Bronte again. But I had no intention of giving up.

To keep my hands, heart, and mind busy, I threw myself into house hunting. While I was grateful to Mom for putting a roof over my head after Tina threw me out, I was ready to move on. Fortunately, my house hunt was relatively quick and painless. During my first week of visiting open homes, I fell in love with an historic condo in North Andover, designed by Boston architect William G. Preston and built in 1889. Complete with stained glass windows, hardwood floors, high ceilings, and sweeping views of the landscaped grounds, I considered it the perfect place to start my new life and raise Addy. With little more furniture than my desk, I spent alternate weekends visiting antique shops to furnish each room. My best pieces were a bookcase and a framed T.S. Elliott quote from *The Love Song of J. Alfred Prufrock* that dared me to disturb the universe.

Each time I passed it, hanging on the wall above my

writing desk, I thought of Bronte. I also thought of Mom's words—*Your father has conditioned you into playing it safe your whole life.*

My single work colleagues habitually congregated at a bar called *Merchant* after work. I usually used Addy and my commute as an excuse to head straight home, but when they caught wind of my divorce they joined forces and hassled me daily to join them for a drink.

When I walked through Merchant's glass sliding doors, the place was already crowded with young professionals and animated with chatter. It wasn't my scene; it was a place to be seen, and the minimal, brightly lit space was more clinical than convivial. I much preferred intimate gatherings in dimly-lit jazz clubs or an open mic night for poets and comedians.

I scanned the room and spotted Sharon from Payroll, who waved me over to the marbled bar. I narrowly missed a waitress carrying a trio of mezze plates up each arm and had to shoulder my way through a group of brash, stockbroker types, who were comparing the size of their portfolios. When I reached the bar and made eye contact with the dreadlocked barman, I ordered a Bud Light because I had to drive home.

Before my second swig, Sharon announced she was off to the ladies room and Abbey from Marketing swooped in to ask if I knew Laura, seated to my left. Laura held out her hand and introduced herself as a friend of Sharon and Abbey, who was also newly divorced. I glanced at Abbey for an explanation. When she winked and gestured that she too was going to the ladies room, I knew I'd been set up.

Laura had short dirty blonde hair and worked as a paralegal in a top law firm. She reminded me of Tina right off the bat—asking a lot of status-related questions as opposed to human ones. We quickly traveled down the drop-down list of superficial conversation topics—our jobs, our divorces, the weather, our favorite movies. The conversation showed signs of distress when she moved on to TV shows, and I confessed I didn't own a TV but preferred to watch Ted talks and read books. I made my excuses soon after and left—relieved to climb into my car alone and flood it with the sounds of Brontes-playlist. Bronte, Bronte, Bronte. After my tedious and awkward evening, I desperately wanted to reach out to her. But what if she rejected me again? I didn't have the strength for another rejection. Instead, I did what I always did; I wrote a poem and told myself to wait for the perfect moment.

I think of you
        between playlists
Home alone
Untouched by the storm
that tore the roof off my heart

I imagine you
        pacing
between poems
        like a fox before dusk
Thoughts of me

scrunched up,
        like pages of a work in progress

Your new smile
assures me
that your heart is as buoyant
as your tweets
that you're carving your desk
into a masterpiece

Are you writing poems about the girl
from the equator
who fell in love with snow?

or the girl
who cultivated her heart like a rose,
and bled out when she tried to pluck it?

CHAPTER 24
Bronte

November

A billabong is an Australian term for an oxbow lake. During arid periods, when the lake dries up, they are called 'dead rivers'. Before I cut communication with Luther, my mobile phone had been a billabong in which every text and image had represented precious drops of rain. After we cut communication, and I scrubbed our text and social media history for fear that Aden would find evidence of my emotional infidelity, Luther's presence slowly evaporated from my life like water from a drought-stricken billabong. But while erasure helped to ease my guilt, it did nothing to stem the heartbreak that followed, and I quickly began building a new billabong with poems about my secret, forbidden love for Luther. Like a tap jammed open, the poems were so prolific that I created an anonymous Instagram account in an effort to find an outlet.

I called the account *Wonderland*, because I had become Alice in many respects. I also hoped that Luther would discover the account and beg me to give him a second chance. But instead of Luther finding my poetic breadcrumbs, it was an American literary agent that came knocking on the door of my rabbit hole. I'm not sure how it happened—right time, right place, or genuinely puncturing the love vein of the larger population—but my Wonderland insta account exploded from a couple hundred followers to a hundred thousand followers in a matter of three months. It was this rapid growth and large following that attracted the likes of an agent called Katy Stone, who landed me a publishing contract to convert *Wonderland* into a poetry book.

The day I received the proof copy of *Wonderland*, Katy and a journalist skyped me to do an interview for the upcoming book launch. I pulled out all the stops by getting my hair done at a local salon and donning a new black, silky shirt that I'd splashed out on the previous week. Minutes before the call, I set up the laptop on my walnut desk and elevated it with a stack of uber-thick books so the computer screen and ocean view were at eye level. The weather was perfect. No humidity combined with a cool sea breeze ensured that my salon-smooth hair would not turn frizzy.

My stomach knotted when the Skype call chimed. I took two deep breaths, donned a charming smile and hit answer. The journalist was standing when I answered the call. She resembled a rock chick from the cover of Rolling Stone with her dark, glossy hair down to her waist, hazel eyes and hourglass figure. She wore black, skinny jeans, black stiletto ankle boots, a loose black leather waistcoat over a silky lavender blouse. Her glittery nails matched the colour of her blouse and sparkled in the light as she picked up the notes off Katy's desk and settled into her seat.

Katy was just as glamorous. She wore a dusty pink cashmere top with her long dark hair pulled back into a ponytail.

"Right, let's start," said Katy. "Bronte, this is Sasha. Sasha, Bronte."

"Bronte, I love your name," said Sasha. It has literary electricity!"

"Thanks," I said. It was impossible not to smile in her exuberant presence.

"Before we do the Q&A", said Katy, "I thought I'd give Sasha some background."

"Amazing," said Sasha, putting her recorder on the table and focusing on her handwritten notes.

Katy spoke animatedly about the rise of Instapoets and the shift it had caused in the poetry publishing world. She also mentioned the criticism Instapoets were garnering. "My client is a respected poetry publisher, and they see Instapoetry as a type of pop-plagiarism."

Sasha and I chuckled a little and nodded.

"Which brings me to the reason why I contacted Bronte. She has gained the popularity of the instapoets, but her work is truly unique."

I smiled. "Thank you."

"You're welcome, Bronte." She turned her attention to Sasha. "She's all yours."

"Wonderful," said Sasha, turning her attention to me. "What does it feel like to be an overnight success, Bronte?"

"I can hardly believe it," I said, "I mean, I didn't consider myself a poet."

She waved her hand in the air. "The ARC for *Wonderland* says otherwise. Now, tell me how *Wonderland* started. What inspired the title?"

I inhaled before I said, "It's a reference to the book *Alice in*

Wonderland, and the concept is basically impossible love."

She paged through the proof copy. "I see the book is divided into three sections: Part I: Rabbit Holes; Part II: Wonderland; and Part III: Underland."

I nodded and smiled.

"Talk me through the sections, Bronte."

"When Alice falls in love she believes the impossible is possible. But as time ticks away and reality dawns, she realises that love is only possible in Wonderland and entirely impossible in the real world..."

"The real world being Underland?" said Sasha.

"Yes."

"Is there an 'unless' in this impossible love equation?"

I nodded. "Unless she finds a way to live in both worlds."

She leaned forward and chewed the corner of her lip. "And, can she?"

I twirled a strand of my hair. "That remains to be seen, but I'm optimistic."

"What is the magic potion in your version of Wonderland, Bronte?"

"It's polyamory."

She raised her eyebrows. "Polyamory? Now there's a concept that's getting a lot of attention lately."

"In America, maybe," I said, "but the few people I've mentioned it to think I'm referring to *polygamy.*"

"Oh my God," she said and laughed.

"If it wasn't for TV shows like *House of Cards* and…"

"*You Me Her*," Katy chimed in. "Have you seen it?"

"I have," I said, nodding, "although it's a bit too 'sitcom' for my taste."

"Yeah, I know what you mean, but these concepts take time to enter the mainstream, and humour is usually the less confronting way to do it, right?" said Sasha.

"You're right. Humour smooths many paths."

She quoted a snippet from the manuscript:

He called me Alice / stretched my heart into Cheshire's smile / and though my costume fit perfectly / we never escaped the truth about rabbit holes…

I nodded in anticipation of her next question.

"Why do you think *Wonderland* resonates with your insta audience, Bronte?"

"I think there are many people out there who are in unhappy relationships, and finding love in virtual reality is happening more than we realise."

"Hmmm, I think you're onto something, Bronte. Temptation has become but a thumb and slide away, right?!"

I laughed and nodded. "Yes, exactly."

We talked officially for twenty more minutes, and off the record for another ten. After Sasha left the room, Katy and I talked about the book launch as well as my other work in progress—a memoir titled *Flammable*. She said that she had spoken to a few of her contacts and mentioned that there was significant interest.

After we said goodbye, I leaned back in my chair, hardly able to believe what had transpired. *My God*, I thought, *you have an agent, and you're launching a poetry book. Now all you have to do is break the news to Aden.* Amazing as a publishing contract was, it put me in a pickle. My Wonderland insta account was still anonymous. Nobody knew my real identity, and I had planned to keep it that way. For the next thirty minutes I picked at my fingernails, like Deborah Meaden on Dragons' Den, and ran a stream of hypotheticals through my head. If Aden knew I had written enough poems to fill a book about my secret love for Luther, he would likely have a meltdown. If Luther knew I'd written a book of love poems for him, he'd finally have his proof that I wanted him as much as he wanted me. But at the same time, this was a once in a lifetime opportunity.

It was time to tell Aden about the book, and it was time to reconnect with Luther. While I did love Aden, and I didn't want to break up our family unit, I could not suppress my feelings for Luther any longer. It was time to ride or die.

I picked up my phone and absentmindedly opened Facebook. A silly Fortune Cookie quiz popped up, and my curiosity beat me. The answer was uncanny:

Two of your close friends are going to fight for your love.

I closed it without sharing on my feed—a little freaked by its accuracy. I didn't want to break any hearts, but wanting didn't make it so. Before I could talk myself out of it, I texted Luther.

BRONTE: I know you're probably asleep but I miss my friend…

I held the phone in my hands like a magic eight ball and begged him to reply.

LUTHER: Miss you more!

My heart turned into a gymnast, doing a back flip and a somersault.

BRONTE: OMG, you have no idea how happy that makes me. Thought I'd blown it…

LUTHER: I'm imagining you saying the word 'blow' out loud. Haha

BRONTE: Oh, haha, Luther, I see you haven't lost your wicked sense of humour 😄😝

LUTHER: Trying to break the ice, love. Life's been tough without you.

BRONTE: Ice is officially broken. Can we forget about what happened and go back to being superlative writing friends?

LUTHER: Whatever you want. Life is not the same without you.

BRONTE: Ditto 🖤

LUTHER: I was beginning to worry about you.

BRONTE: Why?

LUTHER: You haven't posted anything on your social media

pages for months. What gives?

BRONTE: Can we organise a FaceTime or Skype? The answer is too complicated to text.

LUTHER: Mmmm, you mean I'll finally get to see your face...

BRONTE: God, I miss your humour 😊 Is that a yes?

LUTHER: Yeah

BRONTE: How about next Sunday (your time)?

LUTHER: How about right now?

BRONTE: Really?

LUTHER: No time like the present. Give me a sec to get set up.

My attraction to Luther multiplied the second his face filled my computer screen, and I thought about how weird, wonderful, and fucked up the internet was. He existed in virtual reality, yet he shared a real space in my heart and memory.

He leaned in close. "God, you're even more gorgeous than your picture."

I chuckled and twirled a piece of my hair. "You're not so bad yourself."

"Tell me what's been going on."

"Right, well, here's the thing. After I cut contact with you, I started writing poems."

"U-huh," he nodded.

"So many poems that I opened an anonymous Instagram

account and went on a posting frenzy."

"Hey, no fair, how do you expect me to stalk you properly? Haha."

I laughed and chewed my lip nervously. "It's called *Wonderland* and…"

He held up his hand like a stop sign. "Hold up, hun, let me look it up quick."

I held my breath while he typed *Wonderland* into the insta search bar.

"What the fuck, Bront? A hundred thousand followers, are you fucking kidding me?"

I shook my head. "No, it's ridiculously real, and it's the reason why I needed to FaceTime you."

"I'm listening," he said, scrolling through my insta gallery.

"A literary agent approached me about converting my *Wonderland* content into a book and I've signed a publishing deal."

He looked up from the phone screen. "Oh my God, seriously?"

I nodded.

"I thought you said you weren't a poet."

"I'm not," I smiled, "but I do have an excellent muse."

"Are you saying these poems are about us?"

I blushed and nodded. "You know they are."

He shook his head. "No, I don't know. I was clear about my feelings for you early on, but you have dodged that bullet every time I've shot it your way."

"You want me to be honest, Luther?"

"Yeah, it's time."

"I harbour a deep well of love for you. If you were in the room with me right now, I'd lean across the desk and kiss you. But our situations couldn't be more fucked up if we tried."

"Does your husband know about this?"

"No, you're the first person I've told."

"I don't mean the book. I mean about your feelings for me?"

"Oh." I shook my head. "No, Aden doesn't know."

"Don't you think it's time to tell him?"

I sighed. "Tell him what exactly? That I've written a book of love poems for a man that I haven't met but fantasise about twenty four seven? Tell him that I love him but I'm in love with someone else?"

"I think you need to be honest with yourself and with your husband. If your feelings for me are half as strong as mine are for you, then your only choice will be to tell Aden and decide what or who you want."

"What if I want both of you?"

"I love that you're thinking like Alice, but we both know that you can't have your cake and eat it."

I narrowed my eyes and leaned forward. "If you ask me, the real Alice would find a way."

CHAPTER 25
Aden

November

I must have fallen asleep on the couch because I woke up in front of the TV at 1 a.m. In the master bedroom, whilst fumbling for the ensuite light switch, Bronte's phone lit up with a notification. It piqued my curiosity enough to tiptoe over to her side of the bed and snoop. A string of text messages from Luther.

LUTHER: Miss your face.

LUTHER: When can we FaceTime again?

LUTHER: Have you spoken to your husband yet?

LUTHER: Love you. Sorry, not sorry. Text when you get this.

Luther, I thought, *I knew it*. Unable to let it go this time, I positioned Bronte's thumb just so to unlock her phone.

BRONTE: Hello Luther! What's up, mate?

LUTHER: Lol. That's very Australian of you.

BRONTE: Yeah, well, I am Australian after all.

LUTHER: You're Australian, I'm American… Lol, is this going somewhere, Bront?

BRONTE: Just reminding you that we're worlds apart when all is said and done.

LUTHER: You're acting weird. Are you alone?

BRONTE: I'm just getting bored is all.

LUTHER: Huh?

BRONTE: We're seeing too much of each other on here⊠

LUTHER: You being a bit unfair, no? What's wrong?

BRONTE: JK wit ya.

LUTHER: Ok, now I know something's up. You'd never say JK wit ya. Did I catch you at a bad time?

BRONTE: No. Just yanking your chain.

LUTHER: I'm not convinced.

BRONTE: You respect my marriage though, don't you, Loser?

LUTHER: Who is this? I know it's not Bronte.

BRONTE: You stay the fuck away from my wife or the repurcussions will be massive.

LUTHER: Aden?

BRONTE: Has the penny dropped? Has the little American one-cent coin finally landed?

BRONTE: You still there? Come out and talk, you coward.

LUTHER: All makes sense now. None of this message is in keeping with Bronte's voice. Or intellect, I might add.

BRONTE: You cheeky bugger.

LUTHER: What are you doing with Bronte's phone?

BRONTE: I was getting into bed with my wife when her phone chimed. I reached over to see if it was urgent and your stupid name pops up.

LUTHER: You're probably breaking the law there.

BRONTE: Breaking the law? What about the social norms

involved in a marriage between a man and a woman you can't have, Luther?

LUTHER: Social norms involve being there for your wife, isntead of jetting off overseas when the pressure gets too tough.

LUTHER: *instead

BRONTE: I have to put food on the table, Luther. I'm not a flake like you.

LUTHER: Flake?

BRONTE: my marriage is rock solid.

LUTHER: I'd beg to differ.

BRONTE: So what do you want to tell me? I can just scan your messaging history while I'm here now, and learn what Bronte's been saying about us.

LUTHER: She didn't say much but I can glean from context that you're something of a flake yourself, when it comes to providing emotional support.

BRONTE: I will knock seven kinds of shit out of you ifi I hear of you coming near my wife in an online capacity again. Got it, Loser?

LUTHER: LOL

BRONTE: WTF?? YOUR LAUGHING NOW?

LUTHER: *You're

LUTHER: I'm not scared of you, Aden. I didn't expect this but we'll let Bronte decide if she wants to maintain an online friendship witrh me.

LUTHER: *with

BRONTE: You're not gonna even MENTION this convo to her, mate.

LUTHER: Again, we'll let Bronte decide if she wants to maintain a friendship with me, Aden. I think you're breaking the law even being on her phone, spousal privilege or not.

BRONTE: It's gonna be deleted from this end once I wrap things up with you. She won't know about it.

BRONTE: I'm willing to let bygones be bygones here.

LUTHER: I get that you're upset, but we can be civil to each other.

BRONTE: Fuck. You. Loser.

I was so engrossed in my convo with Luther that I failed to see Bronte sitting up in bed with her arms crossed and her eyes narrowed.

"Oh, hey Bront. What's up?"

She gestured to the phone in my hands. "I could ask you the same thing. Is that my phone you're holding?"

I looked at my feet.

Her voice was but a whisper. "I've been watching you texting angrily. Is it Luther?"

I shrugged. "Yeah, I've been texting loser, and I'm not sorry."

"I don't know what to say. I would never break into your phone and read your text messages."

"You might if you suspected I was having an affair. But I would never cheat on you."

"What did you say to him?"

I handed her the phone. "Here, read it for yourself."

She took the phone from me. We stared at one another for several seconds, speaking no words but communicating with our eyes. She was disappointed. I was seething. "By the way. What conversation is Luther referring to? What do you need to tell me?"

She flung the sheet off and stepped out of bed. "Not here, Aden. Give me a minute to put on a trackie and we'll talk downstairs."

I inhaled sharply in an attempt to hold down the bile of rage that I'd worked so hard to purge in Dubai. She didn't move for a few seconds, just stood and stared at me, uncertainty straining her features, not sure if I was going to revert to angry-Aden. Her phone buzzed. Our eyes communicated what we both knew but didn't need to say—it was Luther. She chewed her lip and narrowed her eyes, then opened the bedside drawer and said, "I'll leave the phone here."

I exhaled and nodded. "I'll meet you at the pool."

The saltwater pump thrummed, and the night light gave the water a cloudy appearance.

Bronte spoke first. "This is not how I wanted you to find out."

"Find out what? That you're having an affair with Luther."

She shook her head. "No, about my poetry book and the publishing contract."

"What poetry book?"

"I planned to explain everything to you in the morning."

"Explain away," I said, fighting to maintain my composure.

She started by admitting that she had feelings for Luther, and had told him as much the week before I returned from Dubai. Then she had cut communication with him because I had finally had a "wake up call" and she felt guilty, only to realise she couldn't stem her love for him. That love quickly manifested itself as a slew of poems that she posted anonymously on Instagram, which miraculously blew up from a couple of hundred followers to over a hundred thousand, and put her on the radar of a literary agent who had signed her as a client and landed her a publishing deal to publish a book and capitalise on her insta popularity. To say she rendered me speechless is an understatement.

"Whoa," I said, waving my hands like an air traffic controller, "let's back up a minute."

She swallowed and scowled.

"Let's go back to Luther for a second. When I spoke to you during our Granite Belt trip you said Luther didn't want anything in return. Were you lying?"

"No, Aden, I wasn't lying."

"But you knew he had feelings for you?"

She swallowed before she spoke. "Yeah, I knew how he felt, but I didn't think it mattered, considering our situation."

"And when you say situation, you mean marriage, geography and children?"

She nodded.

"Help me out, Bront. How did you move from writing

friends to mental lovers?"

"We're hardly mental lovers, Aden. We write each other poems and flirt. There has never been any sexual talk."

"But you are sexually attracted to each other?"

She nodded, pursed her lips, and exhaled. "It's complicated."

"It's not complicated from where I'm sitting, Bronte. You've written a book of love poems for another man, and you've admitted you have feelings for him."

"Yes, and what role do you think you've played in that?"

"Are you kidding me, Bronte? You're turning this on me?"

She shook her head. "I'm not turning anything on you, Aden. I'm asking you to be a grown-up and take responsibility for your part in this."

I laughed out loud. "You're unbelievable."

She shifted her body toward me like a soldier preparing for hand-to-hand combat. "After we lost the winery you were angry, resentful, emotionally absent and withholding. Which I both understood and tolerated because I thought it would be short-lived. But when your anger stretched into four months, our relationship felt more like a prison sentence than a marriage."

"A prison sentence? Give me a break, Bronte."

"You turned into an ogre, Aden. In fact, you were a hair away from crossing the border into domestic violence. I lost count of the days when I pussy-footed around you, and nights when I lay in bed and worried about what you would have done if I had been less responsive to your moods.

Would you have hit me, or worse, the kids?"

Her words hit me with the force of a scythe beheading wheat crops. My jaw dropped open. I blinked and stuttered a few nondescript words before I managed to string a sentence together. "I don't know what to say, Bronte. I had no idea things were this bad between us."

She stood, took two steps away from me, and crossed her arms. "You had no idea because you were completely wrapped up in your own misery."

I rubbed my chin and put my hand over my mouth. "Fair enough, but what about our marriage vows—for better or worse? Didn't I see you through your worst times in the early days of our marriage? Don't I deserve a little bit of slack?"

"I did cut you slack, Aden. But let's be fair. Never did I ever, not even in the midst of my worst times, did I ever mistreat you, belittle you, dismiss you, isolate you…the way you have done with me. I had my low moments when I dipped into depression, but I never took it out on you. Never. If anything, I was grateful to you."

I reached out and touched her shoulder. "Yeah, okay, Bront, I admit that I've handled things badly. But cheating on you? I would never cheat on you."

She pulled away, tears catching in her throat. "I have tried to resist my feelings for Luther. But…"

"But what?"

The sorrow in her eyes was as palpable as the breeze that grazed the palm fronds around the pool. "I'm not killing my heart to save your feelings any longer. I don't know why

Luther came into my life, but I can't deny he has made me happy. The happiest I've been in years."

"It's a fantasy, Bronte. Don't you see that? Luther is not real. Like your social media pages, he curates what he wants you to see and know."

She stood up and crossed her arms. "This happy marriage that you're trying to save is the real fantasy, Aden. Losing Ghost Gum has changed us both in ways we couldn't imagine, and we are not the same people anymore with the same common goal."

She retreated into the house, while I remained dumbstruck and mute.

I unlocked my phone and found Luther's Instagram account by searching Bronte's followers. It didn't help any. I grimaced and gripped my phone as I read one love poem after the next. How did I know they were about Bronte? It was obvious. One poem in particular referenced the same physical features I adored about my wife. The barely visible maroon tear-drop birthmark at the tip of her cleavage. The dimple on her right cheek when she smiled just so. Her emerald eyes and the distant expression that spread across her face when she was immersed in writing. The more I read, the more I stewed over two facts: that another man was writing intimate poetry about my wife; and how unnervingly well he wrote about her. He wrote about Bronte as Shakespeare wrote about love, and I won't deny I envied his ability to write about her that way. *What if this guy was the love of her life?* I thought. *Her writing partner, her perfect match?* I couldn't think about it. But it was all I could think about.

Determining when to harvest can be a tough decision for a winemaker. Dependent on the weather and the size of the vineyard, it involves gathering the healthy, ripe grapes that are free of noble rot. Ripeness checks and grape tastings are nearly constant prior to harvesting. The day after Bronte told me about Luther and read me the riot act, I thought about our marriage in the same vein as the harvest period. There were healthy grapes—like our children, and our history together—but there were also patches of noble rot setting in—Luther and my period of bad behaviour after losing Ghost Gum. If I wanted to save my marriage, I would need to harvest the good grapes and salvage as many as possible before the rot spread any further. I would also need to check in with Bronte on a regular basis to avoid further emotional drifting.

I had been naïve to think my time in Dubai could erase four months of conflict in our marriage, and I hadn't fully appreciated the depth of Bronte's unhappiness where I was concerned. To show her I was serious about atoning for my part to play in the breakdown of our marriage, I phoned Mike to book a few weeks of annual leave and offered Bronte an olive branch by taking over her home duties for a few days.

After school drop-off, I returned to what felt like an empty house. Though I knew Bronte was upstairs in her writing room, I felt the weight of loneliness bearing down on me.

My life revolved around Bronte and the kids, and I did not want to break up our family unit. I picked up the kids' cereal bowls and scraped the remnants into the chrome bin. As I stood there, with my foot on the bin pedal, Bronte's *Rules for Happiness* poster stared back at me. Bronte had made many rules in our house, but not the bad kind. She called them *Rules for Happiness*, and stuck them to the fridge with alphabet magnets.

RULES FOR HAPPINESS

1. When someone sneezes, we say *bless you* and kiss them on the cheek.

2. Whatever happens today, will not be carried forward tomorrow.

3. No arguments or fighting while we're eating a meal.

4. Nobody goes to bed fighting or angry.

5. Nobody goes to bed without a goodnight kiss and cuddle.

6. If you promise to tell the truth, Mummy and Daddy promise to not get angry.

7. Treat others how you want to be treated.

8. Love nature like you love your teddy bear.

9. Your heart never lies. Listen when it speaks.

10. Storms pass and rainbows await.

I was sure the kids would grow out of the first rule as they grew up. But they didn't. Like Pavlov's dogs, they became so accustomed to Bronte kissing their foreheads or cheeks after a sneeze that they would seek her out to claim their kiss. She wrote number two for my benefit. I reminded the kids of their bad deeds from days and weeks gone by. But Bronte preferred a constructive approach. She didn't want to instil guilt or negativity. In retrospect, she probably wrote most of that list for my benefit because she played the role of parent better than me.

I'd never paid much attention to number nine while at Ghost Gum, because I was already living my dream. But the meaning had arrived. Bronte had followed her heart all the way to Luther because I had neglected and mistreated her. The tumble dryer pinged. I'd only been on domestic duty for a few hours and I already felt like Cinderella. In the laundry, I piled the warm clothes into a wicker basket and headed upstairs to sort, fold and put away. But as I reached the upstairs landing I heard a series of chimes coming from Bronte's study.

CHAPTER 26
Bronte

November

Aden's patience with me plunged after school drop-off one morning. Sitting at my walnut desk, typing on my laptop, my chiming phone broke my concentration. On seeing Luther's name, I smiled like a lovestruck schoolgirl and laughed when I read his message. In fact, I was so engrossed with Luther's text that I didn't see Aden standing at the door watching me.

"Am I your favourite mistake, or is Luther?"

I jumped out of my seat and turned my phone over on impulse. "Favourite mistake?" I frowned. "What are you talking about?"

He held up his finger. "This song. Sheryl Crow, isn't it? *My Favourite Mistake.*"

"You make it sound like I deliberately picked that song, Aden. But I was oblivious."

"I can tell." He pointed to my phone. "Is that Luther?"

"I don't check to see who's texting you, Aden, so I don't see how it's any of your business."

He drew a sharp intake of breath before he spoke. "Seriously? My wife and her affair is none of my business?"

The song ended, and Sheryl Crow's *Anything But Down* started. A cloud must have passed across the sun because the room darkened, like a sun lounge at dusk.

"Luther lives in America, Aden, I'm hardly having an affair."

"You haven't had sex with him, Bronte, but you're emotionally invested. It's written all over your face."

I looked down and fiddled with my hands. My cheeks burned.

"How can we work on our marriage if you've got one foot out the door? Don't you care about Leyla and Liam? Do you want us to break up and destroy their lives?"

I stood and walked over to him. "Don't play the double standard, Aden. How many months have I played mother and father while you sulked and shirked your domestic responsibilities? You know how much my children mean to me. Don't you dare suggest otherwise."

"I'm not suggesting otherwise, Bronte, and I know how much slack you've picked up because of me. I know all of that, and I'm sorry. I'm sorry, and I'm trying to make it up to you. The least you can do is stop flirting with Luther and give our marriage and our children a chance."

"Ugh. The male double standard never ceases to amaze me. I'm the one who looked after the kids while you jet-setted to Dubai, but somehow my relationship with someone who lives across the ocean makes me a bad mother."

"I didn't say you were a bad mother."

"No, you implied it."

He pointed to our wedding photo on the wall. "Tell me something. Does this Luther person, whom you've never met before, mean more to you than our history together and our family? Is that what you're telling me?"

"I'm not saying he means more to me, Aden. I'm saying I want to explore the feelings I have for him."

"And how do you intend to do that, considering he lives in America and we are still married?"

"I don't know, but I can't kill my feelings for him."

"Okay, let me ask you this. Do you still love me?"

"Yes, of course I love you. But…"

"But what?"

"I connect with Luther in a way you and I will never connect."

"You mean with writing?"

I nodded.

"What do you want from me, Bronte? You want to have your cake and eat it too?"

I looked over at my computer. "Can I show you something?"

"Please do, Bronte. I'm hanging on by a thread here."

I turned on the wifi, opened Safari, and typed a search into google. I clicked on the Wikipedia page and moved aside. "Here, I need you to read this."

Aden sat in my chair and read aloud: *Polyamory (from Greek, poly, "many, several", and Latin amor, "love") is the practice of or desire for intimate relationships with more than one partner, with the knowledge of all partners. It has been described as "consensual, ethical, and responsible non-monogamy".*

I held my breath, praying the gods would cut me some slack. When he finished reading, he pushed the seat back a few inches and leaned back. "Is this what you want, Bronte? A polyamorous relationship with Luther?"

I walked around him and sat on the desk to face him. "Yes, Aden. I know it's crazy, but that's what I'm asking you."

He didn't speak for twenty seconds or more. A currawong settled on a branch outside the window and began to warble. The dishwasher played its little ditty to signal the end of the wash cycle. A car hooter sounded in the distance. A troop of rainbow lorikeets shot past the porthole window like kamikaze pilots.

"Have you spoken to Luther about this yet?"

I shook my head.

Aden was about to say something when my phone buzzed. My heart dropped into my knees, knowing it was probably Luther. Aden looked at me, and I looked at him. "That's probably Luther right now. Why don't we ask him?"

I shook my head. "No, Aden, not now, not like this."

"Why not? No time like the present, right?"

"Does that mean you'd consider it?"

"I'll consider it because I don't want to lose you, Bronte. That's all I can promise right now."

"Can you give me some time alone to speak to him?"

He stood. "I'll wait for you downstairs."

I picked up my phone and read Luther's text; it was a poem followed by many love hearts. I sat for a minute, not doing anything. I didn't want to ask Luther about polyamory because he probably wouldn't go for it. But if I didn't try, I would lose him forever. And the thought of losing Luther overwhelmed. Perhaps I was acting like a lovesick teenager, or maybe I was genuinely in love. Without polyamory, I would never get a chance to find out. I inhaled and sent the Wikipedia link to Luther.

Read this and tell me what you think.

CHAPTER 27
Luther

November

Mom and I were about to eat a dinner of cajun fish and corn salad in the gazebo when my phone buzzed.

"I can tell from your smile that it's Bronte," she said. "Go ahead, don't mind me."

I pushed my chair back and walked down the three steps from the gazebo into Mom's magical garden. Fairy lights illuminated the statues. Sounds of running water and wind chimes soothed. I sat on a wooden bench and read Bronte's text.

BRONTE: Read this, and tell me what you think.

A hyperlink to polyamory on Wikipedia was underlined. I read with a sinking feeling. I didn't want to share her with Aden. I wanted her all to myself.

LUTHER: I don't know if I want to share you.

BRONTE: Luther, try to think about the big picture for a minute. We live on opposite ends of the world, and our children come first. This could be the only way for us to be together in the short term. Isn't it worth a try?

I thought back to a conversation I'd had with Mom when I first told her about Bronte. We were sitting in Mom's 'reading room', a pile of tarot cards between us, discussing the pros and cons of me and Bronte. Mom had concluded that, and I quote, *If this woman is responsible for the positive changes I've see in you, Luther, she is the real Alice.*

I decided to play along for a while. If the FaceTime call had been such a powerful moment for our relationship, meeting in person could clinch the deal, and I could make her all mine. As long as her husband had his hooks in her, I knew my limitations.

LUTHER: Have you spoken to your husband about this?

BRONTE: Yes

LUTHER: And he's fine with it?

BRONTE: He said he'll consider it.

LUTHER: I need to think about it

BRONTE: Okay. Bye xo

LUTHER: Never goodbye xo

BRONTE: 🖤

I joined Mom in the gazebo.

She forked a chunk of fish and blackened corn. "Bad news?"

I shrugged and pushed my fish around the plate.

"Do you want to talk about it?"

I put my knife and fork together and pushed my plate aside. "Yup, I'm hoping you'll say the words *batshit crazy* and persuade me to leave the whole ugly mess alone."

"Oh dear, what's happened?"

"Bronte is proposing polyamory."

"Polyamory? As in consensual non-monogamy?"

I nodded. "Yeah. Batshit crazy. Right?"

Mom shook her head. "No, I'd call polyamory the perfect solution."

"Are you serious?"

Mom put her fork down and reached for my hands. "How often does this kind of opportunity come along?"

I shifted in my seat. "Define opportunity?"

"Think it through to conclusion, Luther. This woman cannot, in good conscience, leave her husband and children to be with you. Her husband, maybe? Her children? Never. She is not the kind of woman who would do that. And you, my sweet darling…" She let go of my hands and took my chin in her fingers. "You are not going to leave Addy and move to Australia, are you?"

"No, I'm not."

She leaned back and put her hands in her lap. "And, yet, you love each other."

"Allegedly."

"Nonsense, Luther. Don't take that away from her. You can't expect her to drop everything and sacrifice her family for you anymore than she expects you to. Instead, she has come up with a solution that fits your predicament—a solution that will not destroy what you already have."

"But it's ridiculous."

"Why, Luther? Why is it ridiculous?"

"Because love doesn't involve sharing."

"Says who? Who says you can't love more than one person

in a lifetime?"

"All I know is that Bronte is the only woman I have ever felt this strongly about. I don't want anyone else, and I don't want her to have anyone else."

"Luther, don't be like your father and stay in the safe zone your whole life."

"No, don't do that, Mom."

"Fine, I'll leave your father out of it. But imagine how many more Brontes could be out there if you expanded your horizon a little?"

"So you're saying I should walk away and keep looking?"

She shook her head. "No, not at all. I'm saying you should swallow your fear and follow your heart."

"Easier said than done."

"What have you got to lose, Luther? Bronte might be your Alice? But you'll never know unless you do something about it."

"I thought she was my Alice before this polyamory craziness. Now I'm not sure if she's the *right* Alice."

Mom sipped her homemade lemonade. "What do I always tell you when you get lost, Luther?

"I don't know. Humor me."

"Whenever you get lost, retrace your steps and go back to the beginning to find yourself."

"Which beginning? Tina or Bronte?"

"Maybe you should think about both. But as we're discussing Bronte, I suggest starting with her."

I rubbed my goatee and thought about Bronte, who was probably swimming. I closed my eyes for a second and imagined meeting her in the flesh. My skin and senses tingled with excitement. When I returned to the beginning, I was an unhappily married man who had never taken a single risk in his life, other than applying for a mortgage, for God's sake. I was a man who had never properly loved or been loved. I was a man who hid behind Eliot's words—daring to disturb—but dared not disturb a fucking thing. If it wasn't for Bronte I wouldn't have divorced Tina. Well, maybe, eventually. But not when I did. I probably would have suffered for many more years before realizing what I had to do. So, yeah, when I revisited the beginning, Bronte was way more than a friend or a potential lover; she was life-changing. My ego aside, I wasn't ready to lose her.

I looked at Mom, who was eyeing me expectantly. Though she was always right, I didn't see the need to tell her that. I cleared my throat and gave her a measured answer. "If you had told me at the beginning that my trajectory with Bronte would end up at polyamory, I would have ceased and desisted. But that's why we can't time travel, right? We would never take risks if we knew the outcome."

Mom nodded. "Good point. Now let me ask you this: If you could time travel, would you do it all again?"

I leaned back in my chair and tapped the table with my fingers. That was the question, wasn't it? What was my original intention, if any? I had searched for my Alice and found Bronte. The minute we struck the match of our first Twitter conversation, the stick of dynamite had begun its long and fiery course, hissing and crackling all the way until the explosion. Would I take it all back if I had the chance?

Mom waved her hand in front of my face. "Earth to Luther."

"Sorry, I was thinking it through. Yeah, I would do it all again. I can't imagine not knowing Bronte."

"Let's circle back to polyamory, then, shall we?"

I nodded and let her continue.

"This proposal of hers is confirmation that there is something powerful between you. She is asking you to meet her halfway."

"She's asking me to do love timeshare."

"'What would you have her do, Luther? Divorce her husband and drop everything for you? What do you expect of her? The answer will tell you a lot."

"You're right. I do expect her to leave her husband to be with me."

"And what about her children and their father? You are a father now. What if Tina did that?"

"I hadn't thought about that."

"I know, Luther. You rarely think things through to conclusion. Even as a little boy, your imagination promised more excitement than reality. But Bronte is real, and her polyamorous proposal is a desperate attempt to keep you in her life and hold onto you while she figures out what to do with her marriage."

"What do you mean, figure out her marriage?"

"If Bronte was single, do you think she would hesitate to

uproot her life to be with you?"

I shook my head. "No, I think it's more about her kids than her husband."

She smiled triumphantly. "There you go."

"So you think I should do it?"

"I can't tell you what to do, but I will encourage you to remove fear from your decision. I will help you in whatever way I can if you choose to do this."

"We will need to meet in person."

She nodded. "That goes without saying."

I put my elbows on the table and leaned toward Mom. "Pre-planned or grand romantic gesture?"

"Oh, the latter," she said and clapped her hands

CHAPTER 28
Aden

November

I stared at the Wikipedia page:

Polyamory…It has been described as "consensual, ethical, and responsible non-monogamy".

I expected to feel worse after Bronte's proposal, but I could see the upside. If Luther lived down the road, we would have a big problem. But the fact that he lived in America gave me an opportunity to turn things around. If I agreed to polyamory, I would look like the bigger person, and I might hold onto my wife. Worst case scenario, they could visit each other once a year, or every six months at the most. I could live with that. And while I lived with it, the romance would probably wear off.

I was stewing over Luther when Bronte walked into the kitchen.

"I spoke to Luther, and he said he'll think about it."

I closed the laptop and nodded. "While he thinks about it, maybe you can answer a few of my questions."

She raised an eyebrow and pulled out a barstool. "Such as?"

"Did Luther know you were married when you met him online?"

"Yeah, of course. It was one of the first things I told him."

"Did you tell him you were unhappy in your marriage?"

"No, Aden. I never discussed my marriage with him. Give me a little bit of credit, will you?"

"Let me get this straight. Luther knew you were married—maybe happily, maybe not—and he knew you had children and that you lived in Australia. And knowing all of this, he still pursued you, knowing he would be breaking up a family unit. Is that correct?"

"You're making it sound like it was premeditated or something."

"How do you know it wasn't? How do you know he didn't target you? How do you know he's not a player and leading you on? I mean, come on Bronte, do the math will you?"

"I thought you said you would try polyamory?"

"Tell me, Bronte, if Luther lived down the road, would you have fought to save our marriage?"

She shifted her feet and rolled her eyes. "Luther doesn't live down the road, so it's unfair of you to ask."

"Bloody hell, Bronte, stop editing yourself and lying to me."

"I'm not lying, Aden, but you're asking me questions that I'm damned if I do and damned if I don't answer."

"That's bullshit and you know it. You're not answering, because we both know that the answer is no—if Luther lived down the road, we wouldn't be negotiating polyamory, we'd be negotiating a divorce settlement."

She chewed the corner of her lip. She didn't say a word but I could hear her every thought as though they were sailing through a loudspeaker. Her polyamorous proposal was not about keeping me around, it was about buying time until she figured out what to do with me. I brushed past her and headed for the front door. "I'm going to end this right now," I said over my shoulder, "it's either him or me." I fished the keys off the hook on the wall. I wasn't going to leave her; I wanted to call her bluff and pinpoint her position. "What's it gonna be, me or Luther?"

"That's the whole point, Aden, I don't want to run off and leave you. But in the same vein, I cannot kill my feelings for Luther. Which is why I am begging you to agree to polyamory."

"Let me tell you where I'm at, Bronte."

"Fine." She crossed her arms. "Tell me."

"If you want to have a polyamorous relationship sometime in the future, I'll learn to live with it. But what I can't learn to live with is you and Luther."

She threw her hands in the air and sighed. "Why not?"

"Because it's tainted," I shouted. "It's fucking tainted. I don't know why you can't see that and don't get it. You betrayed me with him, and he encouraged you to betray me. You both broke my trust, Bronte, why don't you get that?"

"I'm sorry, Aden. I understand all of that. But what you're not getting is that I didn't plan it. It happened. Call it fate, or whatever, but it happened, and I can't take it back or change it. And to respond to your polyamorous proposal, you need to know this—I don't want anyone else. This is not something I'm planning to do in the future. This is not something I planned to do in the present. It just happened."

She started crying and I couldn't stand to look at her or listen to her another second. I unlocked the front door and stepped outside.

"Where are you going?"

"Out, Bronte. I can't talk about this anymore. I need to go somewhere and think."

"Please, Aden. Don't. I need to know where we stand."

"Where we stand?" I repeated. "I'll tell you where we stand, Bronte. Unless you break off all communication with Luther, I won't be coming back. If Luther stays, I go." I slammed the door behind me.

I drove to the Cleveland Point lighthouse. The restaurant was unusually quiet—probably the calm before the lunch storm—and a few stragglers loitered around the jetty. A warm breeze bounced off the water, and I breathed in and out as the water lapped and slapped against the rocks. My phone buzzed—a text from Bronte.

BRONTE: I don't want to lose you.

I didn't reply. I'd finally patched myself back together when she came swinging at me with a sledgehammer. Goddamn her and Luther. I had to admit that if Luther had lived down the road Bronte would have slept with him. I pondered and weighed up that truth while watching the ships move like snails in the distance. And it did weigh on me. She hadn't been unfaithful in a physical sense, but she had emotionally. I wondered what was worse. Part of me wished she had simply slept with someone and moved on. But this emotional connection she had with Luther went way beyond sex.

I sat at the base of the inactive lighthouse. Compared to most lighthouses, the Cleveland Point light was hexagonal and constructed of timber. It was also a mere twelve feet tall. It had been deactivated in 1976 and replaced with a more modern version. I preferred the original, both for its aesthetics and the parallel with my predicament. Like the Cleveland Point Light, initially powered by kerosene, then a powerful lens before converting to electricity and finally deactivated, I had been powered by Mum, then Ghost Gum and finally Bronte. But whereas the Cleveland Light had no choice in its final deactivation, I did have a choice in fighting for and salvaging my marriage.

I stood, dusted the dirt and grass off my jeans, and fished my car keys out of my pocket. While my ego howled at the thought of a polyamorous relationship with fucking Luther, I knew it was the only card left to play.

CHAPTER 29
Bronte

November

I redefined crying the day Aden gave me an ultimatum. A primal cry unearthed from the belly of civilisation where God borrowed Adam's rib and commanded Eve to be eternally grateful for the gift. I cried in such an awful way that tears came out of my mouth instead of my eyes. My gut clenched so bad that no sound could escape my depths but instead manifested in my heaving shoulders and contorted face. And in between ruptures, I wondered why the universe had been so cruel.

I must have cried myself to sleep because I woke up with a start from a dream. In the dream, my heart was out of my chest and suspended in the stormy sky. Rain, relentless as a monsoon, quickly flooded the garden—green wheelbarrow, silver watering can, terracotta herb pots— hammering the swimming pool that teetered on the edge of overflow. Near the deep end, Aden and Luther sat with their backs to me in yellow wicker chairs. I called their names, but they couldn't or wouldn't hear me. From where I stood, I watched an avalanche of muddy water erode the bank and sweep the yellow chairs into the belly of the pool. I started running but slipped and ended up at the bottom of the pool. When I resurfaced and dragged myself out, the sky had cleared, and my heart had returned to my chest, but the wicker chairs were upturned and Luther and Aden were gone; I had lost them both.

On waking, I checked the time and searched the house. Aden had not returned. I checked my phone, but he had not texted either.

BRONTE: Aden, I know you're angry with me, but let me know that you're okay.

ADEN: Will talk to you later, Bronte. I'm picking up the kids soon and taking them to the beach for a gelato.

BRONTE: Okay.

I dragged myself to the kitchen and crashed ten minutes later in my writing room with a cup of tea for my emotions and a notebook for the unrelenting flow of poems.

Hours later, I heard the back door open and close, followed by the kids running upstairs to see me. I closed my laptop, took a deep breath and stood. Seconds later, they wrapped their arms around my waist, and I kissed the tops of their heads. Aden stood in the doorway with two takeaway coffee cups in his hands. "I thought we could talk by the pool."

I nodded.

"Can we watch TV?" said Liam.

"What about your homework?" I said.

"Already done," said Aden.

"Wow, I'm impressed," I said.

"Can we?" said Liam.

I nodded and laughed. "Yes, you can watch TV."

They ran out of the room like a whirlwind. "Change out of your school clothes first," I shouted. But they were already at the bottom of the stairs.

Aden held out the coffee like a peace offering. "Shall we go to the pool?"

"Lead the way," I said.

We sat on pool chairs and gazed at the water. Aden flicked a green ant that had dropped from the mango tree onto his thigh. I fiddled with the lid of my coffee cup.

"I'm sorry," we both said in unison.

I looked at him. "Wait, why are you sorry?"

"I shouldn't have given you an ultimatum. But you need to understand that I thought I'd lost you. Why are you sorry?"

"I cheated on you, Aden. I cheated on you emotionally, and I didn't have an iota of remorse until today."

Aden put his coffee cup down and inched closer to me. "How about we agree that we've both made mistakes and that neither of us is perfect?"

A kookaburra swooped from a branch to the grass outside the pool area and chugged back an earthworm.

"Remember the kookaburra at Grey Gum?" said Aden.

"I remember the old Ade from Grey Gum; the kookabur-ra-Ade that I mourned because I thought he was dead."

"He's not dead, Bront. He was dying, I'll admit, but he's not dead. Before Dubai I was living on autopilot and taking my anger out on you. But Dubai did change me, and I did a

214

lot of healing. When I realised Dad's debt was in service of Mum's cancer, my anger dissipated, and I naively believed our marriage would resolve itself. I had no idea how unhappy you were."

"I didn't appreciate that before, but I do now. I know that this thing with Luther has been a shock, and I haven't handled it well at all. But at the same time, I can't undo my feelings for him."

"I don't want to lose you."

"You were never going to lose me, Aden. We're parents and partners who will always be in each other's lives."

He tucked my hair behind my ear. "Okay, let me put it another way; I don't want to lose my wife. I still love you. I'm still hopelessly attracted to you. I don't know what we're going to do about this Luther situation, but I am not destroying our family because of him, okay?"

I nodded. "Luther may not even agree to polyamory. But whatever happens, I promise to give our marriage a chance. Okay?"

"That's all I ask."

I held up my coffee cup as if to say *cheers.*

In the weeks following my confession to Aden, I swam every night—when the first star appeared alongside the waxing half-moon, when flying foxes flew west, when lime tree frogs began their nocturnal chorus, when carpet pythons slithered out to hunt, when blue-backed night-spinners wove their sticky webs, and when nuclear families congregated around the dinner table. Unlike my morning swim, when I pushed my lungs and muscles to capacity, that night swim was my escape.

After a few token tumble turns and laps, I would float on my back, watch the night slowly devour the remaining daylight, and fantasise about Luther—a man who desired me as much as I desired him. I would envision Luther and I sitting side by side on pool chairs, like a real couple. I would scheme up ways to surmount our impossible situation: me, married with children in Australia; Luther, married with a child in America. And finally, I would try to wrap my head around the fact that I had fallen in love with a man who I had not yet met in person.

There had been a time when I had secretly managed to love Luther from a distance. A time when the fantasy had been enough to sustain me. A time when Luther and Aden had been separate planets that had orbited safely around me. But that time had passed. Luther and Aden were no longer orbiting; they had both collided into me, into each other, and we were all haemorrhaging equal amounts of love and hate.

I loved my husband, but I was in love with Luther. That night swim was everything.

CHAPTER 30
Luther

Early December

I closed my book—Collected Poems by Edna St Vincent Millay—as the plane began to descend. I had stumbled upon Millay during one of my many internet searches for the term polyamory. Millay and her husband both had lovers during their 26-year marriage. For Millay, one relationship was with the poet George Dillon. It was impossible not to draw parallels with Bronte and Aden. Was I Bronte's George Dillon when all was said and done? While Bronte undoubtedly measured up to Alice—the ideal, but impossible, woman I had built up in my imagination, I also had to admit that the situation we found ourselves in fell way short of the dream. I half-blamed my Capricorn traits. My heart believed with absolute conviction that Bronte was my Alice, but my rational brain questioned if she was the right Alice. As much as I wanted to follow Bronte blindly into the abyss of love, I couldn't deny that to truly consider her polyamorous love triangle proposal was to consider the fact that she was not the right Alice. While Bronte had found a solution to a problem that appeared impossible from the average person's perspective, the Bronte that I'd fantasized about was nothing more than smoke and mirrors.

The Bronte I'd found on Twitter was a fledgling writer. Hell, she hadn't even written a poem. But in six months, she had landed an agent and a publishing contract. My original *why*—to boost her confidence and guide her along the indie publishing track—was null and void. Bronte had surpassed me. She didn't need my help. Which begged the question: What did Bronte need from me? And how could I eventually make her mine?

I wanted everything to be perfect for Bronte. Mom had suggested a grand romantic gesture, and I planned to deliver. Aden could hold onto Bronte with his chest of history and memories, but I had the power to woo her with the things that made her heart skip a beat. I pulled out all the stops. Housekeeping sprinkled the king-size bed with rose petals and placed vanilla blossom-scented candles on each bedside table. The concierge helped me source a bouquet of two dozen long-stemmed Dame de Coeur cherry red roses. Room service delivered a selection of pastries and a pot of coffee. Had it been after midday, I would have ordered champagne.

Once I prepared the room, I focused on the music. I had made a playlist for our relationship; a musical trajectory, if you will. Otis Redding's *I've Been Loving You Too Long*, and *These Arms Of Mine*, Nina Simone's *Feeling Good* and *Wild is the Wind*, to name a few. The pièce de résistance was a personalized gift—a one-off, handmade book of poems written to her, about her, and for her. I had commissioned a local bookmaker to construct it with a hundred percent recycled paper. The red velvet cover was embossed with a white title—*The Real Alice*—and the spine was hand-stitched with hemp twine. I planned to read the poem *She* to her:

She
is the stillness of a lake
on a misty morning
She
is summer feet
warming winter's doorstep
She
is the quickening of a heart
before lovers' kiss
She
is a smiling stranger
to a lost traveller
She
is the lighthouse, sighted
just before the wreckage
She
is the dreamer's dream
I dared dream

So loved, she is
My Alice.

Keeping busy calmed my nerves. The object of my affection was finally coming to see me. We were finally going to meet. I had fantasized about this moment so many times since I first saw her Twitter profile. I imagined her skin smelling like a meadow filled with knee-high lavender, her lips tasting as sweet as summer strawberries, her green eyes as hypnotic as the ocean, and the warmth of her soft cheek next to mine. Her head and long lustrous hair resting on my bare chest. The rhythm of her beating heart against the palm of my hand. Her voice in my ear, conversing like real people and completing full sentences versus condensing everything into text messages. I imagined my anticipation of Bronte in the flesh being akin to Neil Armstrong's anticipation of his moonwalk. Bronte had a lot in common with the moon: mysterious and beautiful; a light in the darkness and always on the move; orbiting around me and keeping my axis tilted just so. She was lovely. She was poetry. She was a moon that promised so much discovery and adventure for a lowly astronaut like me.

CHAPTER 31
Bronte

I was scooping ground coffee into a french press, still dressed in my swimsuit after my morning laps, when my phone buzzed with a text notification.

LUTHER: I'm here

I stared at the words, not knowing what Luther meant.

BRONTE: Lol, are you drunk? Where is here?

LUTHER: Stone-cold sober. I've come to give you my answer in person 🩶

I swallowed hard. My heart and thoughts were simultaneously frozen and alight.

BRONTE: Are you messing with me?

LUTHER: No, I'm staying at the Prestige in Brisbane.

I swallowed hard again. Before I could reply, he texted.

LUTHER: How soon can you get here?

BRONTE: I'll need a few hours—kids, school, etc.

LUTHER: Text me when you're on your way xo

BRONTE: Okay xo

I typed okay before my brain could override my thumb. Then again, what else was I going to do? I had already told Aden, albeit in a roundabout way, that I would see Luther if he ever made a grand gesture. No hesitation or discussion; I would go.

"Do you want me to finish the coffee?"

"Holy shit," I squealed and jumped.

Aden laughed and shook his head.

"You scared the shit out of me," I said, hiding my phone like a lie.

"You're jumpier than usual. What's up?"

I tried to neutralise my expression while my head transmogrified into the hadron collider. I thought about telling Aden, but my insides felt like they were undergoing embalming. I needed time to process Luther's news, so I told a half-truth. "I dreamt that Luther came to Australia," I said, watching for a sign that Aden's hostility toward Luther had mellowed.

"Aah, I see," he said, filling the kettle with water and flicking the switch. "Do you wanna talk about it?"

I sat at the kitchen table. "Maybe?"

He looked at me with a half-grin and sat opposite me. "Better out than in, as Mum always said."

I cleared my throat and shifted in my seat. "I'm curious. What would you do if Luther did visit?"

His face turned serious. "I would kick seven kinds of shit out of him."

My heart and face dropped into the pit of my stomach.

He laughed and playfully poked my shoulder with his hand. "Joking, Bront. Jeez, relax, will you?"

"I'm serious. How would you react?"

The kettle whistled for a few seconds before switching off automatically. Aden stood, poured the boiling water into the french press, and returned to his seat. "Honestly, I'd be relieved."

"Relieved? Why?"

"Because we need to move past this, but that won't be possible until you get him out of your system."

Before I could answer, Leyla and Liam walked in, rubbing their eyes.

"You're both up early," said Aden.

"Are you hungry?" I said.

They both nodded.

"Cereal, toast or fruit?"

They both opted for a combo of toast and fruit. While I made the toast, Aden poured me a coffee. "Did you have any dreams last night?" I said. Leyla rarely remembered her dreams, while Liam frequently shared wild, adventurous dreams about dinosaurs, crocodiles, and snakes. But on this occasion, they both shook their heads and said they couldn't remember. Aden and I drank our coffees and talked to the kids while they ate breakfast, but all I could think about was my predicament. What I once considered a beautiful predicament, I now found gut-wrenching.

I worked through the assembly line of school lunches, school runs, and shifting my work schedule. Before I started the car, I texted Luther.

BRONTE: I'm leaving now.

LUTHER: Mmm, cannot wait to see you.

BRONTE: I cannot believe this!!

LUTHER: Believe it, love. Not giving you up that easy
BRONTE: 🖤

I arrived at the hotel in record-breaking time and rapped on the door with my knuckles. He opened seconds later. Luther. My Luther. The man I had been permitted to imagine in dreams—in a cruel, parallel, suspended fantasy world—but not in reality. He invited me into a candle-lit room with Nina Simone's *Wild Is The Wind* playing in the background. My whole face smiled—bigger than Alice's Cheshire cat, bigger than Wonderland itself. And I hugged him as I had imagined in recurring fantasies. Like I had told him I would. And he held me like he said he would.

Love me, love me, love me, Nina sang.

We stood, embracing, for what seemed like half an hour. He smelt like an American with his foreign cologne and hint of smoke. I stood back and studied his beautiful face and half-smile, desperate to find the answers I had been seeking—all of which I found. Luther and his love were genuine, and he had come to reassure me that our love was real. I hugged him again as Nina sang about leaves clinging to trees, and failed to hold back my tears. The emotion that accompanied meeting Luther in the flesh, and experience his heart pounding against mine, overwhelmed me. Actions that had existed in my imagination were finally manifesting and rendered me breathless. As Nina reached the end of the song, Luther held me at arm's length and said, "You are more magical and beautiful than I ever imagined. And believe me, I imagined a lot."

I touched his face. The roughness of his beard under my thumb, the slant of his cheekbone with my index finger, the hint of life's lines on his forehead, the arch of his nose. "And I love you more than I imagined possible. And believe me, I imagined a lot." Touching Luther in the flesh sent quivers through my body and my cheeks burned at the thought of pleasure with this person whom I had longed for, for so long, but whom I thought I would never touch. I wanted to say so many things and ask so many questions, but I couldn't extract the words from my depths, or rather, they wouldn't come of their own accord. The time for words had passed, and the time for action had arrived.

I waded into the sea of emotion I had been swimming against for months until my shoulders were submerged, and my hair floated around me like a mermaid's crown. His strong arms locked around my waist, and I moved my hips toward his. His mouth covered mine, and my tongue met his. A volcano rumbled in my depths. Magic travelled up my hamstrings and sparkled the length of my spine.

A first kiss held the promise of magic and communicated unspoken sentiment, emotion, and desire. My first kiss with Luther didn't disappoint. The urgency to devour one another was indescribable and undeniable. If I had previously doubted Luther's love, then our first kiss deleted the word doubt like a backspace key on a laptop. All the words I had edited since Luther entered my life were undressed and laid bare when we kissed. All passion, formerly compartmentalised, was unbridled like a wild horse free to roam the prairie. That first kiss turned the word impossible into *I'm possible.*

He led me to the bed strewn with marbled rose petals and undressed me slowly. My blouse, my shoes, my jeans, until I stood in my underwear.

"You are amazing," he said, admiring me like an artist admires his painting.

I lay back on the bed, anticipating the seduction I had fantasised about dozens of times, but he grabbed the condom on the nightstand, tore the wrapper with his teeth, sheathed his cock, and lowered himself through the gap in my thighs.

Putting my fantasies aside, I wrapped my legs around his waist, ran my fingers through his hair, and kissed him as he thrust deeper and deeper, over and over and over again, until our moans took up more space in the room than oxygen. And when he finished, he rolled over and pulled me toward him, one arm wrapped around my shoulder, the other hand clasping mine. "Did you cum, honey?"

Not wanting to hurt his feelings, I lied. "Mmm." The fact that he didn't know the difference gave me pause. It amused me when men assumed that a bit of thrusting was enough to bring a woman to orgasm—probably because it was that easy for them. Still, I banished the thought. Intimacy and familiarity with one another's bodies took time. It certainly didn't happen overnight with Aden and me.

"I have a gift for you."

"You're the only gift I need, Luther."

He told me to close my eyes and open my hands. I did. He

placed something velvety into my open palms.

"Okay, you can open your eyes now."

I gasped when I saw the hand-stitched book with a red velvet cover, and cried when I saw that Luther had written a book of poems for me. There weren't many substitutes for an orgasm, but poetry had to be one of them.

"Will you read one?" I said.

He smiled and nodded. We sat upright. He leaned against the headboard, and I rested my head on his chest. He held the book and read.

Come with me, love
Away from these books of fiction
Away from stories that have to end

Come with me, love
to wonderland
where impossible is not a word
yet
where time is confined
in grandfather's clock
where timing is stitched
inside Hatter's waistcoat

Come with me, love
away with me, love
because you are
the real Alice.

When it came time to leave, I hesitated. The prospect of facing my reality—Aden and the kids—took my breath away. How would I begin to navigate a path of light after my actions with Luther? The anxiety gripped my stomach again, and I bent forward to pump blood to my light head.

"What are we going to do, Luther?"

"We're going to find a way. Now that we know this is real, we have to find a way."

He kissed me long enough to temporarily reassure me, but my head had already begun to anticipate the waves that were sure to approach.

I left him in the hotel room and tried to calm the tempest brewing in my head. I took my mobile out and pulled up Aden's number to text him. My finger paused over the keys.

BRONTE: There's no easy way to say this, so I'll just say it. Luther is in Brisbane. I've just visited him at The Prestige. He's willing to try polyamory if you are. Are you?

I held my breath in anticipation of his reply.

ADEN: I'm leaving work now. We can discuss at home.

CHAPTER 32
Aden

I left work minutes after I received Bronte's message. As I stood at the pedestrian crossing, waiting for the light to change from red to green, a raven cawed from the sprawling fig tree in the square. I tried to scan my memory bank for the meaning of a raven. Were they a bad or good omen? Bronte's message suggested the former. A storm approached from the west. Ominous clouds and that kind of pre-storm wind that warns you to seek cover. I could only see a single raven. All the usual magpies, butcher birds, and ibis had long since disappeared—in advance of the storm, no doubt. That's what birds usually did before a storm; they scattered, dispersed, took to the skies to seek refuge from nature's anger. Was I the raven? The only one with enough courage and stupidity to face the storm head-on. No cover, no umbrella, only my feathers and wits about me. Luther and Bronte were a metaphorical storm poised to reach a crescendo, and I didn't want to run away. I wanted to confront the situation. Face it. Deal with it. Resolve this Luther business once and for all.

I turned my attention away from the omens and toward the fig tree plantation. The triangular reserve consisted of one Banyan Fig and two White Fig trees that sprawled across the intersections of Eagle, Elizabeth and Creek Streets. They were arguably the oldest trees in Brisbane and could have passed for the Tree of Life with their abundant prop roots and sweeping branches. They were the best part of my daily commute into the city and often evoked the image of ghostly

Louisiana Plantations. But their most fascinating feature was their intricate root system. After everything Bronte and I had endured together, I wanted to believe that we were akin to the fig plantation—irrepressible and guaranteed to stand the test of time.

I had to put my ego aside and think of Bronte, our family, and our marriage. If I wanted our marriage to evolve and I wanted my children to continue living with both their parents, I had to respect Bronte's polyamorous core. Bronte loved Luther, and she needed him to fill a void I couldn't. I had to find a way to rise above my wounded ego and allow my relationship with Bronte to evolve. I knew she loved me. I also knew that if the tables had been turned, Bronte would have allowed me to have my dalliance, or see the thing through to its conclusion. She mightn't have been happy about it, but she would have placed my needs first. I knew that with certainty, and I owed her the same kind of unconditional love. Challenging or not, I owed her that much.

CHAPTER 33
Bronte

I exited the underground parking lot into torrential rain. The blue sky that stretched over Brisbane on my arrival had transformed into a bank of murky rain clouds. Visibility was diabolical; I could barely see the other cars on the road. Lightning struck a white van ahead of me at the traffic light and I jumped in my seat. The road quickly looked like a swimming pool, and my anxiety threatened to drown me when I saw the time and realised I would be late to fetch Leyla and Liam from school. I rang Aden, but he didn't answer. I rang Priya next, but her voicemail greeted me. Eventually, I left a message with the school, explaining that I was on my way but negotiating heavy traffic and an unforgiving storm.

The quick change in weather from fine to fucked gave me an impending sense of unease and doom. My gut told me that Aden would react badly to my news, but it was time to own my decision. I had tried to evict Luther from my heart, as a landlord does a tenant, without any luck. Every day, my pain worsened, and my feelings strengthened.

On second thought, I wondered if I had done the right thing by telling Aden. *Goddamn my naïvety*, I thought to myself. *Men do not share their women, no matter how mature or evolved they are. They do not share their women. Period.* What was I thinking? I knew that neither Luther nor Aden were willing to share. Why was I playing a hand that could only end in disaster?

As I dialled Aden's number a third time the truck ahead

of me slammed on brakes, and I swerved and braked to avoid driving into the back of it. I put my head on the steering wheel and closed my eyes. I had to get a grip.

CHAPTER 34
Aden

I fetched the kids from school because I figured Bronte would be stuck in traffic somewhere due to the storm. The windscreen wipers did little to help visibility. Liam wanted his mum. The lightning still scared him, but Bronte had a way of calming and reassuring him. She would sit him down and explain the poetry of weather.

There is nothing to fear, she would say, *storms are like orchestras with lots of instruments. The clouds, wind, rain, thunder, and dazzling lightning all play a part in the breathtaking music of the storm.*

"Your mum has gone to visit a friend," I said, "and I've arranged for you two to have a sleepover with Nishanti and Vidu."

The mere mention of their best friends brought a squeal from the backseat and an end to anxious storm-talk. I knew Priya would drop everything for Bronte if she had asked, so when I phoned ahead and explained that Bronte and I had to go away for a few days, Priya happily obliged. With Priya's house being akin to Leyla's and Liam's home away from home, I knew Bronte would approve.

My phone buzzed in my pocket as I pulled into Priya's driveway, but the wind was whipping around the windows and sheets of rain were pelting the car like mini hailstones. Weather aside, I needed to shield myself a little longer from Bronte and Luther and give my full attention to Leyla and

Liam. Shielding myself with an umbrella that kept turning inside out with every gust, I walked the kids inside one by one. Priya had laid out samosas and glasses of apple juice.

She pressed a paper bag of curried puffs into my hands. "These are Bronte's favourites."

"You're a godsend, Priya. We will look forward to eating those later."

She smiled and hugged me.

With my phone buzzing again and the kids settled, I hugged them goodbye and promised to phone later.

"They're already playing and happy," said Priya.

"Always a good sign," I said and smiled. "Thanks again, Priya."

She nodded her head. "Any time, Aden, say hello to Bronte."

"I will. Thanks for the food," I said, holding up the bag.

She opened the door and I braved the rain without the umbrella. I left feeling easier knowing the kids were out of the equation.

CHAPTER 35
Bronte

When I arrived at the school Leyla and Liam were not there. The teacher said their dad had picked them up. I called his mobile again and got voicemail.

"Goddammit," I said, redialling five more times and getting voicemail each time. I drove home to an empty house. That's when I panicked. I waited ten minutes to be sure before I dialled again and got his voicemail. I texted him a frantic message, begging him to answer me, but he didn't reply. I drove to the supermarket and walked from aisle to aisle to see if they were there, but they weren't. The torrential rain began as I reached the car, and within five seconds of fumbling for my keys, I looked like a drenched poodle. My mind attempted to reach for every branch it could as I searched the tree of our life—of where he could be, what he could be thinking, what his next move could be—and came up blank. I drove home, trying to corral every bone in my body to work for me and not against me, like a giant wishing well, but Aden and the kids weren't there. *Shit*, I thought, as an epiphany dropped. I texted Luther.

BRONTE: Are you okay?

When he didn't answer, I texted again.

BRONTE: Is my husband there?

He didn't answer. Fearing the worst, I broke every speed limit to get to Luther's hotel. While I drove, I told myself Luther could have been in the shower, or asleep for God's sake, but my gut disagreed, and my head ran worst-case scenarios. Lera Lynn blasted her melancholic verdict, about cheating, from the stereo, and the truth rang in my ears like a bell in a boxing ring. *Had I delivered the final blow to my marriage with my taboo love for Luther?* I hoped to God she wasn't right, but Lera kept singing about obliterating lifetimes with wanton kisses. My God, the woman had climbed inside my head and turned my thoughts into lyrics.

Aden had started as the lover and best friend I couldn't live without. We had built a life together as winery owners and parents. Then the bank audit had struck and split us down the middle like the storm that broke the ghost gum. After that, Aden had turned into someone I didn't recognise, and I guess I had turned into someone he didn't recognise. Luther had come along and chased me down a rabbit hole, where I found a little glass bottle that said *drink me*. And once I'd drunk that magic potion, my old identity had shrunk, and a new one had mushroomed.

The traffic came to a standstill as the rain pelted down again. "Shit," I muttered. Like the traffic, my messy love life had brought me to a standstill.

CHAPTER 36
Luther

Imet with sheets of rain when I stepped out onto the balcony to have a cigarette. Earlier in the day, the sun had been a ball of searing white flames, and the scene outside my room was incredible considering I was in the city—a spiky lizard sunned itself by the pool, and a group of cockatoos squawked loudly and clipped off the branches of a yellow-flowering tree with their beaks. Fast forward to late afternoon, the apocalyptic sky was unrelenting in its downpour and thunderous echoes. I turned my back to the wind, lit my Camel and took a long drag.

Considering my time clock was still set to Boston, I didn't feel jet-lagged at all. Bronte's visit had spiked my adrenaline and endorphins were buzzing like a tandem skydiver. Compared to Addy's arrival into the world, no other experience came close to meeting Bronte. Bronte embodied the love that Hollywood depicted to death. The love I once thought fantasy. The love I never expected to find. I pinched myself to ensure I wasn't stuck inside an elaborate dream.

Heathcliff's pain, which I'd been living with for months, turned to ash like the Camel tapering toward its filter. I was no longer haunted by Cathy's spirit, and there was no doubt in my mind Bronte was the real Alice. I finished my smoke and went inside to phone Mom. I owed her the world for pushing me beyond my comfort zone. I also had the urge to shout out loud and declare my love for Bronte from the rooftop. Phoning Mom would draw less attention.

"I made the best move by coming to meet her in person," I said, sitting at the desk and doodling on the hotel notebook. "She is way better than any fictional character I could have dreamt up."

"I had a feeling… Have you got a minute while I draw a tarot?"

"Yeah."

I could hear her shuffling the cards.

"You'll never believe it."

"What is it? Don't tell me *The Devil* or something."

"Now, now, Luther, you know *The Devil* is not a bad card."

"I know, but I'd prefer something sunnier if you know what I mean."

"Funny you should say *sunny*, Luther because the card I picked is *The Sun*."

"No way?"

"Yes, way!" She chuckled.

"Can you read the highlights from the book before you give me your personal thoughts?"

"Of course, my darling Capricorn. The *Basic Meaning* states: *self-determined modeling of our lives in a way that is not regulated by habit or routine, but through our own free choice and free will. This means replacing conformist behavior and conventional thinking with a style of life that is truly our own.*"

"Whoa, that is uncanny."

"Uncanny is a word for non-believers, Luther."

I laughed in spite of myself. "You might convert me, depending on what you say next."

Mom chuckled. "I'm reading from the *Love and Relationships* section next. You ready?"

"Ready."

Mom cleared her throat. I quote: "*A promising sign for partnership—the more, the merrier—this is possible when it has room to develop and each partner gets his or her fair share of the sun.*"

"Seriously, Mom? Are you making this up?"

"Ugh, Luther, you're incorrigible. Of course I'm not making it up."

"Are you sure you picked that card at random?"

"I did."

"And you're reading that straight from the book. Not ad-libbing?"

"No ad-libbing, Luther."

The hotel phone started ringing.

"Hey, Mom, reception is calling, can I call you back later?"

"Of course, my darling."

I ended the mobile call and answered the phone beside the bed. Julie, at reception, told me I had a visitor named Bronte. Figuring she'd forgotten the room number or something, I told Julie to send her up.

"He says it's a surprise and asks that you come down to reception," said Julie.

"Okay, tell her I'll be down in a sec."

It was only when I stepped into the elevator that it dawned on me that Julie had said "he", not "she". I shrugged it off. Maybe I had misheard.

CHAPTER 37
Aden

When I arrived at the hotel, I asked the receptionist to call Luther and tell him that Bronte needed to see him in the lobby. She frowned and nibbled her thumb nail.

"He's an old friend. I want to surprise him," I said.

She scrutinised me a few seconds longer and nodded.

Luther appeared in two ticks, looking eager to see my wife, no doubt, but his face drained of colour when he spotted me. Like Bronte, Luther and I hadn't met before, but I had scoped him out on social media. Judging by his sour expression, he had done the same.

"Luther," I called out his name and walked over to him. Luther didn't move, but he did seem to brace himself for a fistfight or something. I couldn't blame him. My angry web chat would have scared me too if the tables were turned.

"I'm not here to fight," I reassured him, "but we do need to talk."

"I'm pretty jet-lagged."

"I understand that Luther, but this situation calls for a bit of extra stamina, don't you think?"

He scowled for a split second and pointed over his shoulder. "What about the hotel bar?"

"We need to talk privately, Luther. Can we go to your room?"

"I don't think that's a good idea."

I took a step toward him and he stepped back. "Look, Luther, it's time we to act like adults and talk this through. But I am not discussing the intimate details of my marriage and your affair with my wife in a hotel bar."

Luther looked around when I said the words *affair with my wife* to see if anyone had heard. "Okay," he said and led the way to the elevator. We travelled to the fifteenth floor in silence.

Inside his room, I found an unmade bed with wrinkled sheets and rose petals scattered all over the floor. I knew that he and Bronte had probably slept together, and I'd be lying if I said my ego didn't catch fire again and burn my insides. Luther mumbled something about tidying up and straightened the bedding. When he finished he offered me a drink.

I nodded. "Yes, a drink will make this go easier."

He took two beers out of the minibar. "Have you spoken to Bronte?"

I took the beer and swigged. "We've done nothing but talk about you, Luther."

He dropped his head for a second and nodded. "Look, I'm sorry about all this, Aden. It happened unexpectedly."

"Did it? I get the impression you've pursued Bronte from day one."

Luther shifted in his chair and swigged his beer. "I loved Bronte early on."

"I can't say I know anything about love, Luther, but I do know that you have been friends with my wife for a while now. I read your Facebook comments from time to time. I knew who you were, and I assume you knew who I was. Right?"

"Right."

"I assume that you saw the family photos that Bronte occasionally posted. Photos of her husband and children?"

Luther didn't reply, but his grim expression implied that he had spotted the final destination of the conversation.

"I'm not going to lie. What has bothered me most about this emotional affair is that you knew she was married with children all along and yet you pursued her anyway—relentlessly. What kind of person does that?"

"A person who's in love."

"Funny, that's exactly what Bronte said. She argued that if the tables were turned I would have done the same thing. And maybe she's right, but I'd like to think my ethics would hold up a little stronger under Cupid's pressure."

"Love can be a powerful force."

"I know. That's why I'm sitting across the table from you, talking, instead of beating seven kinds of shit out of you in the parking lot."

Luther grimaced and looked away.

"I'm not happy about this, but I love my wife, and I understand you give her something I don't."

"Writing."

I nodded. "You speak her writing language—something I'd like to do but can't."

"Yeah, we have an inexplicable connection. Life has been difficult without her."

"Has it, Luther?"

He looked me in the eye. "Yeah, Aden, it has."

"Do you know how many times Bronte has cried over you since you two cut contact? Don't answer; I'll tell you. She has cried every damn day about you. Sometimes in front of me, sometimes on her own when she thinks I'm not looking."

He swigged his beer and fiddled with his pack of cigarettes.

"And by the way, Bronte hates smoking. Did you know that?"

He picked up the Zippo and flicked it open and closed several times before answering. "No, I didn't know that. We haven't exactly had the time or space to discuss the finer details of each other's likes and dislikes."

"What is it between you two, if you have no idea about the finer details?"

"If I had a logical answer, I would tell you straight, but there seems to be no logic where Bronte is concerned. All I can tell you, and I mean no disrespect, is that I love her deeply and in a way that I have never loved anyone else."

The phone rang.

"That's probably Bronte," I said. "I haven't replied to her texts and she'll be assuming the worst."

Luther nodded and answered the phone. "Thanks, send her up." He hung up and faced me. "You were right. Bronte is on her way up. What are we going to tell her?"

"I'm willing to accommodate you and Bronte in order to save my marriage and keep my family intact."

"How do you propose to do that?"

"Bronte's answer is polyamory."

He nodded and stuck his hands in his pockets. "Yeah, I thought it was a dangerous idea."

"It's not as dangerous as breaking up my family, Luther, or as dangerous as you leaving your daughter and moving here."

"Fair point."

"I don't know how, or if, it will work, Luther, but I'm willing to try if you are."

He looked at me for a long time—weighing up the options like Bronte often did.

"Are you willing, Luther?"

He didn't answer because someone hammered on the door.

"That's probably Bronte," I said.

He looked at me but didn't budge.

CHAPTER 38
Bronte

My nerves were too jumpy to wait for the lift, so I took the stairs. I hammered on his door so hard that the guests in the room opposite opened their doors with expressions of irritation and curiosity. I apologised, hung my head, and tried to breathe. I feared I might lose my sight too, thanks to a sledgehammer of a migraine.

I knocked again. "Luther, please, open up." The door opened. I took a step back. "Aden. What…Why…How… Where are Leyla and Liam? What have you done to Luther?" I stuttered.

"The kids are with Priya for a few days, and Luther's right here." He stepped aside and let me in.

I entered the room like a skittish sheep. Luther sat at the table and chairs. He didn't seem to be bleeding or hurt or distressed. "What's going on?" I looked from Aden to Luther for an answer. "Why didn't you answer my calls?"

Aden spoke first. "Have a seat, Bronte, everything is fine. We were having a private discussion, that's all."

I looked from one to the other. I had no idea what they'd been discussing, but I doubted there were points in my favour. "Will somebody say something?"

Luther cleared his throat. "Your husband has been telling me about what's been going on with you two."

"And? What has been going on?"

"He says you've fixed your marriage, and you're committed to him."

My cheeks reddened. I could read the subtext of his comment. My dream flashed before my eyes like a strike of lightning in the dark sky outside. My worst fears were manifesting, and my foolish heart and unrealistic fantasy was unravelling. I would end up alone, without either of them. I panicked. My heart palpitated. My head spun. I thought of Alice in Wonderland. The room loomed like a giant, and I shrunk within its walls before I hit the floor.

My eyes fluttered open. I lay on the bed that Luther and I had made love in hours earlier. Luther and Aden sat on either side of me. Neither of them smiled or showed any emotion. I swallowed. *Then again, they haven't killed each other, or me,* I thought. Nausea swelled like a wave, but I had to get a grip and face my mess. I wasn't a silly little woman from a Jane Austen novel. If I had to lose both, I'd handle it. This did NOT have to be the end of the world for me.

I inched off the bed and stood to face them. "I can't do this anymore. Tell me straight. I've lost you both, haven't I?"

Aden looked at Luther, and Luther looked at Aden.

"Do you want to tell her, or should I?" said Aden.

"You tell her," said Luther.

I frowned as my eyes darted between them, and pictured myself being led to the gallows to face my victims.

"I explained to Luther that you are my world and I have no intention of breaking up our family."

I looked at Luther and tried to read his expression. His dark eyes gave nothing away. "Okay," I said with faux confidence, "this has gone on long enough, and I can't dance anymore. Here are my cards. I love you both, which is ridiculous, I know, considering Luther and I met for the first time today. Aden, we have triumphed over many trials, but we lost some love after losing Ghost Gum. Luther and I don't know each other that well, but we have an undeniable connection I cannot break. I want you both. I know it's unfair, but it's what I want. Aden, if you have the same urge or desire or unexpected experience in a year or five years' time, I will understand and I won't get in your way. You know why? Because I love you. I don't own or possess you, Aden, I love you. And love shouldn't be a slaveowner. I had no idea polyamory was a thing, or that I was polyamorous, but here I am. I am in love with two men who give me different things, and I don't want to live without either of you." I paused my begging, pleading, suicidal monologue to breathe. "I realise I'll likely lose both of you because you're not polyamorous and you don't understand this, but you need to know where I stand."

"This situation is far from normal," said Aden, "but it's the situation we find ourselves in all the same. I think it's time to stop talking and start negotiating."

"What do you mean?" I said.

"Neither of us wants to lose you," said Aden, "so we've decided to put our egos aside. We will try to be mature about this and do something unconventional—for you, Bronte, only for you. I have no idea how it will work, or if it will work, or if I'll be able to live with it and accept it, but I owe it to you to at least try. I don't want to kill your heart, Bronte; I love you. This situation is madness. Utter madness. But I love you enough to try and understand it."

I closed my eyes; the migraine had returned and threatened to explode. *Did Aden say he would consider the poly thing? I must be dreaming or mid-nightmare or both.*

"The question is, does Luther love you enough to do something this crazy?" said Aden.

"I don't know," said Luther. "All I know is I love this woman, and I owe it to myself to see where it leads."

"Where it leads," said Aden, "that's what I'm worried about. What if it leads to you and Bronte realising that you're soul mates and the long-distance pollyanna set up is not enough for you? That's my real worry."

"Okay," I said, "before anyone says anything else, I need to set you both straight. Luther, you need to know my family comes first. A big part of me realises I am being totally selfish here. At best, I could spend a week with you every three months. Is that what you want? That's the question you need to ask yourself."

"I respect that," said Luther.

I sat next to Aden and held his hand. "Aden, I understand your concern, but none of us knows what the future holds, and we owe it to ourselves to find out. If we let fear rule this decision, we will be delaying regret. I want to say we tried. I want to know I tried. I don't want to look back with regret and resentment because I was scared to buck convention. I believe polyamory is the mature solution in this situation. I could have divorced you, Aden. I could have kept Luther a secret. But I didn't. I want to try and do right by both of you. I believe we can make this work if we are adult enough."

I stood, took each of their hands in mine, and kissed their knuckles.

"I know I'm asking a lot, but I'm asking. Please try this polyamory thing with me. We can set ground rules and take one day at a time. We may decide in a week or month or year that it's ideal or it's a disaster. But, please, be brave enough to try. This had to have happened for a reason, right?! So, let's at least try to learn something new and do something different and dare to disturb the universe."

Luther squeezed my hand. He loved Eliot.

"This is totally fucked up," said Aden, "but I'm willing to try."

My face beamed. "You are?"

"I can't believe I'm saying this," said Luther, "me too."

Aden held out his hand and Luther shook it. Tears rolled down my cheeks.

CHAPTER 39
Aden

The three of us agreed to have dinner in the hotel restaurant to get better acquainted and set some rules and boundaries to govern our polyamorous relationship. I'm not going to lie; it wasn't easy seeing Bronte enamoured with another man—I'd never seen her look more content, and her chemistry with Luther could have lit a chandelier in the ballroom of a Gothic castle. I told myself their relationship was no different to new young love; the novelty would eventually wear off. All I had to do was watch and wait while it ran its course.

The restaurant decor was simple and elegant: a mix of earthy colours, standard square tables with a tea light candle in the centre, and high-backed wooden chairs. But it was the scale of the room and ceiling height, combined with tens of copper-coloured, dome-shaped drop lights that imbued it with drama. The hanging lights, which ranged in size and length, resembled planets in a solar system and reflected in the dark tinted floor to ceiling windows that formed two of the four walls. Mercifully, we were the first to be seated. I chose a table in the far corner—against the luminescent gold and black wallpaper and away from the windows.

We ordered a handful of starter plates to share—salt and pepper squid, long-stemmed broccoli with smoked yoghurt and peanuts, Pacific Oysters with Yuzu and lemon olive oil, beetroot and goats cheese terrine topped with walnuts and herbs, and Hasselback halloumi traybake with flatbreads and green salad. With the food order placed, I cut to the chase and opened the conversation with my non-negotiable ground rules.

"It's important you understand and respect that the primary relationship is between Bronte and me," I said to Luther, "meaning nothing interferes with our family unit. I don't need to be your best friend, Luther, and I don't need to know what happens between you and Bronte when you're together, but I do want to know that I can trust you to have her best interest at heart and not undermine our relationship with any outside agenda."

Luther turned to Bronte when he spoke. "My only agenda is love."

I looked down at the table before I answered so that he and Bronte couldn't see me roll my eyes. "I understand that, Luther. I'm referring to your initial pursuit of Bronte—which was fairly aggressive, despite your knowledge that she was married."

Bronte pursed her lips and tried to make eye contact with me, but I focused my gaze on Luther.

"I was married too," he said.

"Which makes it worse, don't you think?"

"Yes and no," said Luther. "Your relationship with Bronte is completely different from the one I had with my ex-wife. We would never have survived what you and Bronte have gone through. And I didn't before, but I respect that now. So, yeah, I will accept those terms."

I looked over at Bronte, who had an *I told you so* smile on her face. "What about you, Bronte? Any ground rules?"

"I understand what you're saying about the primary relationship, Aden, but I don't want to relegate Luther to third wheel status. If it wasn't for society, taboo, and fragile egos, I would live under the same roof with both of you."

"What were you saying about the crazy train, Luther?" I said and laughed.

Luther laughed. "Make that a convoy."

"Oh, haha, you two. Moving on…"

"Did you know she's also bossy?" I said.

Luther gave an exaggerated nod. "Yeah, I've been on the receiving end of bossy."

Bronte laughed despite herself and relaxed a little.

"Sorry, Bront," I said, "what else did you want to add?"

I think we should keep our private relationships private. For instance, I won't discuss you, Aden, with Luther, and vice versa. Okay?"

Luther and I nodded and said, "Totally agree," in unison.

"What about you, Luther?" I said. "What do you want, need or expect from this?"

Luther turned to Bronte when he spoke. "I'm not going to lie. Meeting you has only strengthened my feelings for you, and it'll be tough leaving you and seeing you infrequently. I'm not yet convinced it will work, or if I'll like it, or if it will last, but I can't imagine my life without you in it anymore. I'm happy to go with the flow and see what happens. I'm okay with talking to you every day and seeing you every three months, or whatever. I want to spend quality time with my daughter before she becomes a teenager with raging hormones and disowns me."

We all laughed and went off-topic for a few minutes discussing our teenage hormones and how awful we were.

"What about our kids?" said Bronte.

"Elaborate," I said.

"Obviously we are all friends as far as our kids are concerned, right? It's way too complicated to explain to adults never mind children. But, would you be against Luther meeting Leyla and Liam? And, Luther, would you want me to meet Adelaide?"

"If a situation arose where Luther came over to our place, that would be fine. But otherwise, I don't see why," I said.

"I have no problems with you meeting Addy."

"Okay, got it," said Bronte. "You know, I thought this would be nightmarish and awkward and not at all doable, but it's not that bad. As long as we keep our individual relationships to ourselves there shouldn't be any major problems or obstacles. Right?"

"In theory," I said. "For the most part, we'll probably have to cross bridges when we get to them. I do have to play devil's advocate for a while, though."

Bronte sighed and rolled her eyes in anticipation of my next question.

"Come on Bronts, it has to be done. We're all adults here."

"Okay, I'm listening."

"What if your feelings for Luther keep growing and you eventually want to spend more time with him than me?"

"I'd like to hear the answer to this," said Luther.

"I'm not going to answer that," she said.

"Why not?" Luther and I said in unison.

"Because there are many variables at play here. Anything could happen. We could move to America, which would facilitate more time, or you could meet someone, Aden. Or Luther could meet someone. Or we might decide this is not for us after a few months. My feelings could get stronger for both of you, or none of you, or one of you. The point is we cannot control the situation. We have agreed to do this, in part, to let nature run its course, right?"

"Right." Luther and I answered in unison again, and both reached out for Bronte's hand at the same time.

"What about situations like this?" She gritted her teeth. "Awkward."

"These sorts of situations are unlikely to happen," I said. "You and Luther will be on your own, and you and I will be on our own."

"We're seriously doing this?" said Bronte.

"Seems so," I said.

"I never thought I'd ever agree to anything like this, but yeah, I'm onboard the crazy train," said Luther.

"Out of interest, what made you decide to come here?" I said.

"My mother."

"I didn't know that," said Bronte.

"She's in your corner on this polyamory thing, which says a lot because she had no time for my ex-wives. Haha."

"Seriously? She's okay with this?" said Bronte.

"She encouraged me all along to do something out of my comfort zone."

"Ha, good woman," said Bronte.

"I would love for you to meet her one day," said Luther, "she's a lot like you—semi-magical, semi-crazy. Haha."

After dinner, Bronte and Luther ordered coffee and dessert, but I was ready to leave. Halfway home, I realised there was nothing to go home to, so I headed toward Mt. Nebo. My mind and thoughts raced ahead of me, like the headlights on the dark, twisty road, and as I drove deeper into the forest, I passed a winery and thought of Ghost Gum. In retrospect, I had lost much more than the winery; I had buried my passion for winemaking because it was too painful to keep the memory of what I'd lost alive. I had gone so far as to stop collecting and drinking wine—ridiculous, I know, but indicative of my state of mind. Bronte's and Luther's passion for writing had sparked something in me over dinner. I wanted what they had—a dream, a passion, a purpose. I wanted more than I had allowed myself to have, be, and do. I wanted my old life back—in some way, shape or form. With Bronte making progress on her dream, it was time to start thinking about resurrecting mine.

When I reached Jollys lookout, I half expected to see a

group of drunk teenagers around a makeshift fire, but the site was empty and dark except for the million stars and three-quarter moon that glowed reassuringly. I parked the car and used my phone torch to light a path to the viewing platform. It was different to the daytime, when lakes, Moreton Bay, mountains and houses were visible. In the dark, crickets chirruped, and tawny frogmouth owls hooted. The clear sky invited me to count stars, but I was more interested in wishing upon a star. I closed my eyes and made two wishes: that Bronte's relationship with Luther would be short-lived; and that I'd find a way to return to winemaking. I thought of Bronte and texted her.

ADEN: I'm at Mt. Nebo if you want to meet me.

When she didn't reply, a twinge of disappointment travelled through me. Or was it resentment? The polyamory thing was clear-cut in theory, but it didn't account for the messy emotions that came into play when put into practice.

CHAPTER 40
Luther

After dinner, Aden left and Bronte stayed for a coffee. I was fed up with our byte-sized text conversations that achieved nothing but endless circles of non-resolution. She agreed.

"Today was amazing," I said.

"It was," she nodded. "I'm glad I didn't disappoint you."

"Ditto. It was a fair bit of pressure, you know. It could have fallen flat."

"I know, but it didn't." She paused and looked into my eyes. "Luther?"

"Yes, Bront?"

"Thank you for coming to see me. It means the world."

I leaned forward and kissed her. "The pleasure is all mine."

"Make love to me before I leave," she whispered in my ear.

I signed for the coffees and led Bronte into the lift with a crowd of other people. Usually, I would have smoked a cigarette straight after food, but Bronte was proving to be more potent than my nicotine addiction. In the room, I lit the vanilla-blossom candle while Bronte wrapped her arms around my waist and unbuckled the belt of my jeans. When I turned around, she had stripped down to her underwear, and her sexual energy sucked me in like a vortex. Sex with my ex-wives had been clumsy on occasion, with a side of going-through-the-motions. But sex with Bronte was intuitive—

like I was responding to her invisible but urgent signals.

I unclasped her bra and moved her backwards toward the bed, like a dancer leading his partner in the tango. She twirled her tongue around mine as if she was knotting a cherry stem and ran her fingers through my hair. "Mmm, I can't wait any longer, get a condom, I want you inside me already." Her phone buzzed on the bedside table. "Shit." She rolled out from under me. "I better check it in case it's the kids."

"Urgent?"

"No." She pulled me close and guided me inside her.

She arched her back and kissed me with the same urgency as my thrusting. Her skin smelt like roses and felt like velvet. And I swear we fit together perfectly—like a hummingbird's beak inside beebalm. As she kissed me, in between moans, in between thrusts, I had never felt so connected to a human being in all my life. Ecstasy overwhelmed my senses. I wanted the moment to last forever.

Bronte was saying something, but I could barely hear her voice—as if it was underwater and muffled.

She pushed her hand against my chest. "Luther, did you use a condom?"

It took me a moment to register her words. "Ssh, it doesn't matter."

She pushed my chest with her palm and tried to wriggle out from beneath me. "Oh my God, Luther, yes it does."

I rolled over and pulled the sheets over my chest. "Yeah, calm down, love."

She scrutinized me before she spoke. "This has to be one

of our rules."

I laughed. "Always wear a rubber?"

"Luther, I'm serious. This is serious. We don't need to add pregnancy to our growing list of impossible problems."

"It wouldn't be that bad, would it? Imagine how perfect our child would be. Haha."

"Haha, Luther. Jokes aside, another child is not something I want."

"Even with me?"

"Not with you, or Aden or Idris Elba."

"I've gotta tell you, that kinda stings."

She cupped my face in her hands. "In an ideal world and situation, I would be honoured to have a child with you. I mean, can you imagine?"

"Um, yeah, I have imagined."

"I have given my all to my kids, and I love them dearly, but I want my life back. Motherhood has been amazing, but it has also sucked the bone marrow from my identity, and I'm ready to move onto the next phase of my life—my writing life."

"I get that. But what if it happened by accident?"

"You mean if the condom split or divine intervention?"

"Yeah, what would you do?"

"At the risk of contradicting myself, I would be ecstatically happy, and we would make it work because I love you."

"So you wouldn't have an abortion?"

She shook her head. "No. I couldn't do that again."

I frowned. "You've had an abortion before?"

She sat up and leaned against the headboard. "There's a lot you don't know about me, Luther, and I will tell you if you want to know. But not tonight because I'm going to have a quick shower and make a move."

"Will I see you tomorrow?"

"Of course. You're only here for a short while. I plan to see you every day, silly."

"Can we go to a forest? I have something special planned."

"Too easy.

CHAPTER 41
Aden

When Bronte arrived home, she hugged me for a long time and apologised for not replying to my text. We sat outside by the pool with cups of ginger tea and discussed the night's events.

"Did you know he was coming?"

She shook her head. "I had no idea."

"But you're happy."

"When he texted, my heart skipped a beat."

I picked up a loose stone and threw it into the deep end. "The opposite of mine. Mine plunged at first."

She squeezed my hand.

"But I caught it when I remembered we are stronger than this."

"I nearly had a meltdown when I couldn't get hold of you, and the kids weren't at school."

"Yeah, sorry about that. I wasn't angry or trying to be a dick. I didn't trust myself to talk to you without getting emotional. I should have texted you, but I was having a moment."

"You don't need to apologise. I'm the one who should probably apologise."

"No more apologising for who you are. I agreed to try this polyamory thing—you didn't force me—so there's no need for guilt. I appreciate it though."

"What did you think about Luther? What's your gut feeling?"

"Honestly?"

"Nothing less."

"He is smitten with you. I'm not sure he'll be happy with having you on a part-time basis."

She nodded. "And what about me? What's your gut feeling about me?"

"I can see you have strong feelings for him, Bronts, but I don't think they will go the distance."

"Meaning?"

"Meaning, I can see you outgrowing him."

She nodded. "Is that why you're okay with this poly thing? Because you suspect it will be short-lived?"

"No, Bronts. I'm agreeing to this poly thing because I recognise it as being an integral part of who you are at your core."

She nodded and sipped her tea.

"Believe it or not, this business with Luther is not all bad. It's stirred up the energy around me and got me thinking about my future."

Her face lit up. "You have no idea how happy that makes me."

I nodded. "Yeah, I drove up to Mt. Nebo after dinner and thought about everything I lost or rather tried to bury when we left the Granite Belt."

"Like your winemaking dream?"

"Yeah," I nodded. "I think I've punished myself enough."

"You have."

"I'm not sure what I want to do or how I plan to resurrect my winemaking career, but I'm going to make a concerted effort to get back into it, one way or another."

She lifted her teacup. "Cheers, I'll drink to that."

I clinked her cup. "You know, Bront, I considered the winemaking process to be a lot like life because of its dependence on timing. From the first stage of harvesting to the final stage of bottling and ageing, timing is paramount. When we met at Ghost Gum, I believed we were destined to mature in oak barrels. But when we lost the winery, I thought we'd been harvested prematurely and hastily bottled."

"But you've reconsidered?"

I nodded. "I think we've been maturing in oak barrels all along, and I know our hard work, effort, angst and tears will eventually pay off and mature into fine wine."

Her eyes were moist. "That's the old Ade I've missed."

CHAPTER 42
Bronte

I drove Luther to the South D'Aguilar National Park the following day. We played Luther's *Bronte Mix*, which brought back memories of the night before and formed new ones as we drove deeper into the forest of ironbarks, bloodwoods, eucalypts and pines.

"Will you read me another poem from *Beloved?* The book is in my bag."

"Do you honestly like it?"

"You're kidding, right? I'm blown away! Nobody has ever written me a book."

He nodded and smiled. "I know which one I'm gonna read."

I sighed a happy sigh and pressed my spine into the driver's seat. "I'm ready when you are."

"Here goes."

My beloved is poetry
you've never read before
and will never read again

She is a poem
She is the poem
She is every poem
ever written, ever sung, ever spoken

My beloved is better
than the Beatniks
And that is as bold as a poet can get

We stopped at a quiet picnic area with a view of the surrounding mountain ranges and the sounds of whip birds and warbling currawongs in the background. I opened the boot to get the picnic basket.

"Here, let me help you with that," said Luther. "Have you got a picnic blanket?"

"Ha, you don't know Australia, do you? There are ants the size of soldiers up here. And they can jump. Nope, we're definitely sitting at the picnic table."

Luther's eyes widened before he looked down and studied the ground. "I temporarily forgot I was down under. Anything else I should be worried about?"

I closed the boot and laughed. "You mean like death adders and funnel-web spiders?"

"Okay, maybe we should stay in the car."

I laughed and hooked my arm through his. "Come on, let's go and find a table."

"Seriously, Bronte, I'm not sure I want to be surrounded by deadly wildlife."

"I can assure you, Luther, the deadly wildlife will not bother you."

Luther placed the picnic basket on the table, and we sat next to each other. "I'm a city boy. Creepy crawlies freak me out."

"Trust me, you would never know that there are probably hundreds of snakes around us right now because they keep to themselves."

"What about when we go for a walk?"

"We won't walk here. I'll drive to another spot."

"Phew."

I laughed. His face had grown a shade paler, and he was clinging to my arm.

I unpacked the food and flask of tea. "I wasn't sure about your diet preferences, so I made sandwiches, raspberry muffins, fruit, cheese and crackers…"

He stopped me mid-sentence. "I'll eat whatever you've made, my love."

I smiled. "Would you like a tea?"

"Please."

I dropped a tea bag into each cup and filled them with hot water from the flask. "I wish you were staying longer. I want to ask so many questions."

"Such as?"

"What was your childhood like? Why is *Alice in Wonderland* your favourite book? How many tattoos do you have?"

"Lol, slow down."

I held his chin in my hands. "It's like I know everything and nothing about you."

"Okay. Easy question first. I have three tattoos—one on

my back and one on either shoulder."

"And what, may I ask, do they symbolise? I wasn't paying much attention to the finer details last night, but I'll be scrutinising you next time, haha."

He shook his head and laughed. "I have a portrait of Addy on my right shoulder, a fox on my left shoulder, and my back is a work in progress—inspired by *Alice in Wonderland*, of course."

"Aah, which brings me to my next question."

"I have a question for you, first."

"I'm all ears."

"Will you tell me about the abortion?"

I scrunched up my face. "Are you sure you want to hear about that?"

I held her hand and nodded.

She inhaled and exhaled before she spoke. "Before I met Aden, I was close to finishing an English post-graduate degree when my family died in a bush fire that destroyed our home and left me destitute."

"Oh, my God."

Over the next thirteen months, I lived hand to mouth while travelling around Australia. I mostly worked in taverns and bars. At one job in rural Victoria, my grief and depression kicked in and I was drinking heavily every night, until one night when a customer spiked my drink and later raped me."

He reached for my hand. "Oh my God, Bront."

"That encounter set me back on the road and sent me spiralling out of control when I missed my period. Long story short, I spent all my money on an abortion and overdosed on pills."

He shook his head and exhaled. "Thank you for telling me."

I fidgeted with my fingers and looked down at my lap. "Thanks for listening. I've only told that story to you and Aden."

He pried my hands from my lap and kissed my knuckles. "You're the bravest person I've ever met."

I nodded and turned my attention to the tea. "Do you take sugar?"

"Two, please."

I squeezed and discarded each tea bag, before spooning in the sugar, pouring in the milk and stirring. "There you go."

He took it and thanked me. "Will you come and visit me in Boston?"

I sipped my tea. "Of course."

"I'm gonna hold you to that."

"I'd be disappointed if you didn't."

"What about your tattoo? I didn't get a chance to read it last night."

I put my tea down, turned my back to him and lifted my shirt for him to read.

He read it aloud: "*She shall never know I love her because she's more myself than I am.*"

I pulled my shirt down and turned around. "It's a quote from *Wuthering Heights*. Well, it's a version of the original quote."

"Hmm. Dare I ask what inspired it?"

My cheeks reddened and I looked away. "I had feelings for a woman once upon a time, but I never told her."

"Pretty sad if you ask me. Why didn't you tell her?"

"We live in a different time now, Luther. In those days, certain love was forbidden or frowned upon."

"So are you bi?"

I shrugged my shoulders. "I don't know. I haven't been attracted to a woman since."

He leaned forward and kissed me. "But you're attracted to me, right?"

I ran my fingers through his hair and kissed him back. "I think I answered that question last night, don't you?"

"Mmm, yes ma'am."

I laughed and pinched his cheek.

He stood and stretched. "Do you mind if I go and have a quick smoke?"

I shook my head. "Not at all. You probably need one after all my confessions."

He winked. "Your confessions only make me love you more."

After lunch, we headed from Mt. Nebo to Mt. Glorious. The two mountains were joined by a single, scenic road that dipped into a deep ravine at the valley of Nebo and rose steeply on the ascent to Glorious. Luther had hinted at a surprise that would require us to walk into the heart of the forest. I suggested Mt. Glorious as it contained untouched tracts of rainforest—specifically the 'Maiala' and 'Boombana' trails. As we drove, I told Luther about the region's logging history as well as some aboriginal background on the sites we were going to visit. "The Kamilaroi Aborigines were the first known inhabitants of the D'Aguilar Range National Parks, and the names 'Maiala' and 'Boombana' are derived from the dialect of the Kamilaroi tribe."

"Do you know what the words mean?"

I nodded. "Maiala means 'quiet place' and Boombana means 'trees in bloom.'"

"Trees in bloom. How poetic is that?"

"I know, right? We can walk at either spot. Contrary to the name, Boombana is the quieter spot, with several forest trails, and Maiala is better known to tourists and local visitors because it has a longer walk that leads to a waterfall."

"Boombana sounds good to me, as long as there are no spiders and snakes."

I chuckled. "There are spiders and snakes, but I know how to avoid them."

He gritted his teeth and inhaled.

"So, what's this surprise?"

"It wouldn't be a surprise if I told you."

I winked and laughed. "Can't blame a girl for trying."

We drove the rest of the way in comfortable silence.

At Boombana, we walked into the heart of the rainforest, where the overarching tree canopies blocked eighty percent of the sunlight, and where fallen trunks and giant boulders were covered in sage lichen.

"I tell Addy that where there is moss, there are fairies."

I squeezed his hand and kissed his cheek. "She's fortunate to have a dad like you."

He pulled me toward him and kissed me. I ran my fingers through his thick, dark hair and kissed him back, wishing I could pause time and stay in the moment a little longer. He pulled two pebble-like stones from his pocket. One, engraved with my name, and the other with his own.

"What are those?" I said.

"Memory Stones."

"What do we do with them?"

He took my hand. "I'll show you."

We walked off the trail and into the forest toward a majestic cypress pine.

"I did this with Addy a few months ago. First, we found a tree. Then we each held a stone and made a wish. Then we kissed the stone and buried them at the trunk of the tree."

"I love it."

We used a fallen twig to shift the soil and dig a little hole. Luther gave me his stone, and he held mine.

"Now what?" I said.

"Now, I want you to make a wish for me, and I will make a wish for you."

"Okay," I nodded. "Can it be about us?"

He nodded.

We both made a wish and kissed our stones. Luther took my stone and gave me his.

"Now we make the same wish for ourselves," he said.

"A-ha."

We repeated the ritual and finally buried the stones at the trunk of the pine tree.

I faced him. "Luther, whatever happens in the future, please promise to never doubt my love for you."

"I promise."

I smiled and hugged him.

"But one thing I can't promise is that I won't try to stuff you in my suitcase and take you home with me."

"Haha."

He shook his head. "Would that I could.

CHAPTER 43
Luther

The day before I left Brisbane, Aden agreed to let Bronte spend the night with me. We spent the evening like an old married couple, ordering room service, talking about writing, and reading poetry. By midnight, we were lying in each other's arms, listening to music and whispering sweet nothings.

"I'm looking forward to dreaming beside you for once, instead of dreaming about you," she said.

"Mmmm, ditto my darling."

Sleep had never been my forte—three or four hours at best after hitting puberty—but the night with Bronte broke that pattern when we slept for seven hours. When we woke, I insisted she stay in bed and relax while I ordered room service. I poured her coffee and served her breakfast in bed.

She squeezed my hand and winked. "I could get used to this royal treatment."

"You are royalty to me."

She smiled and kissed me on the cheek. "Will you tell me more about your life?"

"What do you want to know?"

"I don't know. I told you about my worst experiences yesterday. You must have had some bad experience that tested you?"

I nodded and kissed her on the lips. "Yeah, there is one

experience."

"Tell me."

I told her about Lily-Rose, which prompted her to throw her arms around me and hug me tighter than anyone else ever has in my life.

"I'm sorry. I cannot imagine anything worse."

"It broke my heart, but I made it through it eventually. And I'm relieved that Addy was spared. I don't know what I would have done."

She squeezed my hand and kissed my cheek. "Tell me more. What was your childhood like?"

I filled her in on my parents' divorce and how I had lived with my father but secretly wanted to stay with Mom.

"Why didn't you live with your Mom?"

"Dad fought her with everything he had, and he used her lack of employment history against her."

"What did she do for work?"

"She's a spiritualist, I guess. She reads tarot cards and clears auras and shit."

"Has she mentioned anything about our future?"

"It was uncanny. The day I arrived, and before Aden turned up, she did a tarot reading over the phone."

"And?"

I told her about the *Sun* card and its meaning.

"Oh, wow, that's amazing."

"I know, right?" I squeezed her hand and kissed her palm.

Bronte gazed into my eyes. Much like Mom did when she was trying to read me. "The divorce must have been hard on you."

I nodded. "It was tough. Which is why I stayed with Tina longer than I should have."

Bronte nodded. "Yeah, I get it. You wanted to spare Addy the experience."

"Exactly."

"But something changed?"

"Yeah, the day Addy turned four, I realized Mom was right about Tina. Mom said that her and my dad were like magic and science; each tried to cancel the other out."

"Wow, that's poetic."

"Yeah, I definitely inherited the creative side from Mom."

"Your mom sounds amazing."

"She is. And this thing with you has brought us closer together."

"I'm happy to hear that. Are you sure she doesn't think I'm a lunatic?"

"Lol, amazingly enough, no."

"I don't know how we found each other, but I'm glad we did."

I kissed her. "Promise you'll come to Boston?"

"I promise I'll come and see you.

CHAPTER 44
Bronte

The day I took Luther to the airport tasted bittersweet. In truth, I didn't want him to leave, but knowing that Luther belonged to my future comforted me. I took satisfaction in the fact that somehow, someway, the cruel universe had brought Aden, Luther and me into a space of mutual understanding. I didn't know how long Luther would be in my life, or when he would meet someone else, but none of that mattered. I vowed to find contentment in the moment and follow wherever it may lead.

Luther airdropped the music playlist he'd made for us, and I imagined how Aden would react if he ever stumbled upon it. I hoped polyamory would help me avoid the cheating wife syndrome, but theory and practice were separate planets.

"I hate anticlimaxes," I said to Luther as we walked through the airport terminal.

"Tell me about it."

"Luther." I stopped walking and took his hand. "Promise you won't put your life on hold for me."

"I can't promise you that, Bront."

"Please. You know I love you, but I don't want you to miss out on better opportunities for love and romance."

He leaned forward and whispered in my ear. "I've loved you a long time, and now that I've met you, I couldn't stop loving you if I tried."

I hugged him tightly and breathed in his cologne. The hint of smoke didn't bother me like I thought it would. "I want the best for you, and I'm not that person as long as I'm married with children."

"Don't worry about me. I'm a big boy, and I'm willing to try this as long as you are."

"Okay," I said through tears. "I have loved every second we've spent together, and I will treasure this trip forever."

"Me too."

Luther checked in to get his boarding pass while I ordered coffees and waited for him at a table in the food court. When he returned we tried to stretch time by sipping those coffees until the last minute.

"I have a confession to make."

He frowned. "Uh oh."

I reached inside my handbag and pulled out a book. "Meet my advanced reading copy of Wonderland."

He chuckled. "Jeez, woman, you know how to scare the crap out of me, don't you?"

"Haha, did you think it was something ominous?"

"Uh, yeah."

I watched him intently as he flicked to a random poem. "Okay, you're gonna have to pronounce this title."

I laughed and shook my head. "La Douleur Exquise. It's French for exquisite pain—the self-inflicted pain for wanting someone you can't have."

He nodded and started reading. I saw it as a cue to keep talking. "After I cut contact with you, the poems would not stop. I had a lake of emotion and misplaced love for you, and I knew I would drown if I didn't explore my feelings."

He reached across the table for my hands. "These are heartbreaking, Bront."

"I was heartbroken. But you have made everything okay by coming to see me." I rested my forehead on his hands and swallowed back the tears.

"When is the release date?"

"Next month."

"I would be lying if I said I wasn't a little envious."

"Why? I thought you loved being an indie author?"

"I do like having control of my work, but I'm getting tired of pouring my everything into books that nobody reads."

I took his hands in mine. "I can speak to Katy and ask her for advice if you like?"

He didn't answer immediately. But when he did, he changed the subject. "Will you read a poem to me before I leave?"

"You know, Luther, you can change plans. Nothing is set in stone."

"Meaning?"

"If you wanted to go the traditional route, nothing is stopping you."

"Forget I said anything, Bronte. I am happy being an indie."

I didn't believe him for a minute, but I didn't push the subject any further. Luther was prone to fear and slow to change.

"Will you read to me?" he said.

I squeezed his hand and took the manuscript back. "Sure."

He called me Alice
filled every inch of Wonderland
with love

and when I shrunk
it was my heart
that trapped me;
a palace beating loudly
against my tiny ears
so that it knew
that I knew
how deeply it fell and felt
so it could convince me
to stay

spend every afternoon
with hatter and hare
sipping stories from cups
brewing love in pots
baking words
icing riddles
nonsense and mischief
Felicity

He called me Alice
stretched my brain like Cheshire's smile
and even though my costume fit perfectly
we never escaped the truth
about rabbit holes
couldn't get Wonderland to warp
convention around us

I couldn't stay shrunk forever

He called me Alice
and I always answered
for he dared me
to disturb the universe

He kissed me open-mouthed. "I love you."

A male voice announced Luther's flight over the loud-speaker.

"Oh my God, I'm going to miss you so much."

We kissed like it was our last.

"Speak to you soon, love."

"Bye, Luther."

He placed his finger over my lips. "Never goodbye."

I watched him walk toward the gate and stayed in the same position long after he disappeared. Until I received his final text.

LUTHER: Love you, Bront xoxo

I replied with tears in my eyes and walked with my head

down to the parking lot.

PART III

6 Months Later

CHAPTER 45
Luther

June

I wanted Bronte's first visit to Boston to be more than memorable; I wanted to make headway on my original goal to make her mine, all mine. We had a full week—excluding travel time—and I planned the kind of outings Tina would have hated.

I knew Bronte would love The Harold Parker State Forest in Andover, because she yearned for nature and trees like my ex-wife yearned for new furniture. Located twenty miles north of Boston, the forest consisted of three thousand acres of hardwood, hemlock, and white pine. I smiled inside and out when Bronte showed interest in the history of the area and the trees that grew there. In all the years Tina and I had been married, she had never accompanied me and Addy on our day trips to the forest.

"I've never heard of a hemlock tree," she said. "Which one is a hemlock?"

I pointed to the far side of Berry Pond. "That plantation is hemlock."

"It looks like a pine tree."

"Yeah, it's a type of pine. They call it hemlock because the leaves smell like poison when crushed."

"You have no idea how good this is for my writing. It's not that I don't love gum trees, but I yearn to see different trees."

"Yeah, I experienced the same in Brisbane. I had only seen a caged cockatoo, and it was wild to see them flying free."

She hooked her arm through mine. "I haven't stopped thinking about the white pine forest you mentioned. Can we go and see it?"

"I kinda want to handcuff you to my bed and keep you with me forever. Haha."

"Ooh, handcuffs."

"Why is it that whenever I think of you I imagine devil horns?"

"Ha, that's rich. You want to tie me up and keep me as a sex slave, and I'm the one with devil horns."

I winked. "I didn't say anything about a sex slave." Happiness was effortless in her company; I loved our banter. "I've never met anyone who is interested in these random bits of knowledge I have," I said, "which makes me love you more, of course. Did you know that the white pine is the tallest conifer in North America?"

"No, I did not. But the mere fact you know that is one of the many reasons why I adore you."

"I wondered why I was saving up all of this information, and then you came along."

She smiled. The light caught her green eyes. "Your eyes are emeralds in the forest."

She wrapped her arms around me and sighed. "I love being with a poet."

"And I love you."

"Mmm, your pocket is vibrating."

"Haha." I pulled my phone from my pocket. "Mom is inviting us for dinner."

She laughed. "Does she know I am inexperienced at mother-in-law etiquette?"

"Honey, Mom and I are the same—she loved you before she met you."

"Aah, Luth, you say the sweetest things."

"Is that a yes?"

"Yes," she nodded, "I would love to meet your mom."

We enjoyed a languid picnic at Stearns Pond—a bottle of white wine, cheese, baguettes, and fruit—and talked about everything under the sun.

"Do you know what the S. stands for in T.S. Eliot?"

She raised her right eyebrow and shook her head. "I should, but I don't."

"Stearns…"

"Aah, is that why you brought me to Stearns Pond?" she interjected.

"Perfect place to read my favorite poem out loud."

"The Love Song of J. Alfred Prufrock?"

I nodded.

She lay back on the blanket and looked at the sky. "What a treat."

Midweek, we explored Boston's poetic past, including Bronte's favorites—Anne Sexton, Sylvia Plath, Edgar Allan Poe,
Emily Dickinson, and T.S. Eliot. Bronte shared my love of
books, including the way they smelled, and asked to visit as
many bookshops as we could. She said bookshops were thin
on the ground in Australia, and she yearned to lay her hands
on an old, musty classic. Once we'd exhausted all of my local
haunts, we drove to a neighboring town that had an exquisite
old, independent bookshop that looked and felt more like a
library than a store. Books were stacked from floor to ceiling
on wall to wall shelves, and patrons were encouraged to stay
awhile and read with a bottomless cup of filter coffee or tea.
After hours of browsing, Bronte had found and bought an
armful of books, including every book Anne Sexton had ever
published. Exhausted, but book-sated, we filled two mugs
with coffee and sat in a quiet corner of the shop on a musty,
brown leather sofa that had oversized, colorful cushions and
a little round coffee table—complete with an old-fashioned
bankers lamp. All of which made Bronte squeal in delight.
She said she had only ever seen bankers lamps in the movies.
I wasn't much of a smiler, but I smiled a lot when Bronte was
around. She possessed the same enthusiastic curiosity as my
daughter and eagerly listened to my stories and (for most)
arbitrary knowledge.

"Tell me why you love Wuthering Heights," I said.

"I love the raw, honest, guts of it. Most books of that time
by female authors were so wishy-washy. But Emily broke the

mold. She cut a slice out of real life. And Heathcliff. Oh my God. His character captivated me so—richly complex and dangerous to everyone other than Cathy—the love of his life. I'm not a fan of romance, but I'm a fan of gut-wrenching love stories, and Wuthering Heights is the kind of love story that buries and resurrects you."

"Your passion for books and writing drives me wild."

She leaned back and smiled a seductive smile.

"Don't you think it's amazing that you're named after your favorite author of all time?"

"It is. But the origin story is less literary than you think."

"Do tell."

"The story goes that I was conceived at the beachside Sydney suburb of Bronte."

"And I'd like to know if you inherited your writing gift or if you are a goddess incarnate."

"I'm not sure, but it's the kind of thing I wish I could ask my parents."

"Sorry, hun, didn't mean to bring it up."

"Don't apologize. As I get older, these types of questions pop up." She shrugged. "As far as I know my mother was a winemaker's wife. But who's to say she didn't secretly write romance stories or poetry, hmm?"

I didn't know what to say, so I leaned in to kiss her.

"Luther O'Leary, what do you say we blow this popsicle stand?"

I chuckled. "Say what?"

She bit my lip. "Take me home and make love to me."

"Mmm, yes, ma'am."

We arrived home to a dark apartment. "Two decisions," I said. "Moonlight or candlelight, and jazz or blues?"

"Surprise me." She kissed and nibbled at my neck from behind while unbuckling my belt.

"Jazz and moonlight it is."

We kissed while undressing each other. I lay her on the navy blue duvet she had helped me choose on FaceTime and cupped my hands around her milky breasts. She scissored her legs open and pulled me toward her. "Make love to me."

I paused to admire her wavy hair that fanned out around her shoulders, and a sliver of moonlight illuminated her torso. "It feels like the world stops every time we make love."

She pulled me toward her. "Stop teasing me already."

"I'm not teasing, I'm admiring."

She clasped her hands above her head as I repeatedly thrust deep inside her. The way she closed her eyes and half-whispered, half moaned, my name was as satisfying as the orgasm.

On Bronte's second last day, she wanted to see my childhood neighborhood and school before we had dinner with Mum. Listening to my childhood stories helped calm her nerves about meeting Mom and armed her with lots of conversation threads. She needn't have been nervous. Mom loved her, and they got on like the proverbial house on fire. After dinner, Mom offered to read Bronte's tarot cards. Bronte drew three cards: King of Pentacles; The Tower; and Justice.

While Bronte pored over the cards, I watched Mom's face. A fleeting shadow passed over her expression. The Tower didn't look like a great card—a lighthouse-type tower with violent waves crashing around its base, angry red flames spilling out of the windows, thunderclouds, lightning and startled blackbirds.

"This is an interesting spread," said Mom, which was her way of saying there could be trouble ahead.

Bronte picked up the tower card. "This one looks ominous."

Mom cleared her throat. "Looks can be deceiving in the tarot. Let's start at the beginning and see if we can make sense of it." She pointed to the King of Pentacles. "This is an excellent card that represents career, abundance, security, and ambition. Your hard work will soon pay off, Bronte, and you will reach any lofty goals you've set for yourself."

Bronte nodded. "So far, so good."

Mom tapped on the Tower card. "This one usually depicts an ending of some kind."

I caught her eye when she said *ending*. "It could mean a relationship, or an old habit that doesn't serve you anymore, or a physical move."

Bronte put her elbows on the table and leaned forward.

"So it's not necessarily a bad thing?"

Mom sighed. "Not necessarily; sometimes endings are necessary for new beginnings."

Bronte pointed at the Justice card. "What about this one?"

Mom glanced at me again, which I saw as a bad sign. She was being cautious and not saying what she meant. "On its own, Justice represents making a rational decision as opposed to allowing emotions to be your guide."

"So, again, not the end of the world?" said Bronte.

Mom shook her head in a non-committal way.

I was going to say something when Bronte's phone rang. She stood and excused herself. I looked at Mom. "Be honest, Mom. What do the cards mean?"

She shook her head. "Don't go looking for trouble, Luther."

"I saw your face when she pulled the Tower card. Does it represent the end of our polyamorous love affair?"

"As I said, the outcome is not necessarily negative for you. It could mean an ending to her marriage. I mean, I think you two make a good couple, Luther. I had my suspicions, but I wanted to see you together to confirm."

"And?"

"And, they were confirmed."

"Were confirmed? You mean until you saw the Tower card?"

"I didn't say that, Luther."

"What are you saying, Mom?"

"I think this unconventional set-up is working to your benefit right now, especially as you both have young children. My advice is to simply enjoy this time with her. Don't try and control the outcome. Think of this time with Bronte in the same light as your time with Addy."

"In what sense?"

"You put so much planning and preparation into Addy's weekend visits, and you spend quality time together. Bronte is no different. And you never know what the future will bring. Her husband might meet someone else."

Bronte returned to the room before I could reply. "You will never guess what!"

"What?" We both said in unison.

"Nothing is set in stone as of yet, but my agent has a firm offer from a publisher for my memoir—*Flammable*. And as if that's not enough, there is interest from a movie producer too. She will know more in the next week or two."

I frowned in confusion. "Wait, you wrote a memoir and didn't tell me about it?"

She shrugged her shoulders and looked at me and Mom with an embarrassed smile. "Let me explain," she said, sitting down and placing her hand over mine.

I pulled my hand away and put it in my lap. "I'm supposed to part of your life, Bronte. Which part of that do you not get?"

Mom stood up. "Maybe I should leave you kids alone to talk."

Bronte shook her head. "No, Beth, please, stay."

Mom nodded and sat down.

"Don't be angry, Luther. I didn't tell anyone about the memoir because I wasn't sure if anything would come of it. I wrote it soon after you left Brisbane and sent it to Katy to shop it around. That was six months ago, and I was assuming the worst so I didn't see the point in mentioning it."

I narrowed my eyes. "Did you tell Aden?"

Bronte closed her eyes and sighed.

I tapped the tarot cards with my fingers. "Well, it seems the tarot cards are right on the money, aren't they?"

"I'm sorry, Luther. I screwed up, okay?"

Mom stood up and pulled Bronte into an embrace. "Don't mind Luther, my dear. Luck is a lady tonight, and she has kissed you squarely on the lips."

I had planned to spend our last day in Boston like a lazy Sunday—the kind I had fantasized about a gazillion times. Reading. Making love. Ordering take out. But I was still angry about the fact that Bronte had told Aden about her memoir and not me. So I lied to Bronte and said that Tina needed help with Addy.

CHAPTER 46
Bronte

My last day in Boston was mostly spent with Beth, as Luther had last minute plans with Addy. I didn't mind. To have a maternal figure after losing my own mother, and never meeting my mother-in-law, felt like returning home after a long trip.

As a light rain had descended, Beth directed me toward her sunken conservatory while she made the tea. Built at basement level, the garden-facing section of the room resembled a secret garden with its glass walls and pitched glass roof. A white round table, dressed with a vase of pink chrysanthemums, occupied the central space. Beyond the double french doors, six steps led up into a lush backyard. An established golden elm tree towered over the house and garden like a lighthouse. Luther had clearly inherited his love of literature and creative spirit from Beth. Books lined the walls and imbued the room with that unmistakable scent of nostalgia that permeates spaces where books are stacked. I ran my fingers across the classic spines of crimson, royal blue and gold and thought about Luther. Our shared love of words and books took my breath away at times, and I wondered if it was real or heightened reverie.

Beth entered the room with a bamboo tray which she placed on a low-lying wooden coffee table that sat between two lemon-coloured armchairs. She pointed to an armchair. "Sit, please."

"You have a magical house, Beth."

She poured the tea from a floral-patterned teapot. "Thank you, Bronte. To quote the words of William Morris: *Have nothing in your house that you do not know to be useful, or believe to be beautiful.*"

I smiled. "Luther is fortunate to have a mother like you. He's fortunate to have a mother, period."

"Were you and your mother close, Bronte?"

I shook my head. "Not so much. I'd like to think we would have grown closer if she'd lived long enough to see her grandchildren."

"It must be hard for you, love, having lost so much."

I fiddled with the stitching on my denim jeans. "I've become a master of compartmentalising."

She sank into the armchair alongside me and handed me my tea.

"Thanks, Beth."

"You've had to be strong for yourself as well as your husband and children."

I nodded and sipped my tea. The mention of my husband gave me pause as I sat in the company of my polyamorous lover's mother. "You must think I'm a real flake—holding onto my husband while I test the waters with your son."

I met her eyes. She wore a hint of a smile and seemed to look straight through me. "On the contrary. I think you're a trailblazer."

I tilted my head. "How so?"

"Society has built up this ridiculous notion that one love

fits all. Worse still, we must accept that when we get married, we automatically give up our right to being an individual. Excuse my French, Bronte, but it's utter bullshit."

"You're a woman after my own heart, Beth."

She patted my hand and leaned forward conspiratorially. "You know, Bronte, I have had two daughters-in-law, but you are by far my favourite."

I smiled and squeezed her hand. "By the way, I've been waiting for the right time to thank you."

She cocked her head. "Thank me?"

"Luther wouldn't have flown to Australia if it wasn't for you."

She bowed her head and nodded once. "Luther has never been comfortable outside of his comfort zone. This has been a huge step for him."

I nodded. "Do you think it's too big a step?"

"Why do you ask that?"

"I saw your expressions when I drew the Tower card last night. Is it a bad omen for Luther and me?"

She looked at me for an uncomfortable number of seconds. "Can I ask you something, Bronte?"

I nodded. "Of course."

"Why do you assume it's about you and Luther, and not you and your husband?"

"I love Luther."

"I'm going to be frank with you, and I hope you're not offended."

I nodded and swallowed.

"I don't think Luther will last too long as your second choice. And I don't mean that the way it sounds."

I looked down at my lap. "I know what you mean. Luther wants the nuclear family and a white picket fence. He wants me all to himself, and he's only agreeing to polyamory because he believes I'm buying time to extricate myself from marriage."

She raised her eyebrows. "Are you trying to buy time, Bronte, or do you know deep down that you still haven't found what you're looking for?"

"Honestly, Beth, I wasn't looking for anything. Luther came looking for me. He stalked me on Twitter, don't you know?"

She shook her head. "I didn't know that, but I do know that Luther's heart is in the right place. He's been looking for the real Alice since I read him *Alice in Wonderland*."

"The Real Alice," I repeated. "The problem with this ideal woman is that she is a fantasy and I'm not sure I can live up to her."

"Don't underestimate yourself, Bronte. You more than live up to Alice. The circumstances are the problem."

"Luther said you supported this polyamory experiment."

"I do."

"But?"

"Luther is a sensitive soul, Bronte. He's artistic and melodramatic and romantic."

"I know, Beth. I adore those traits."

She nodded. "I'm his mother, Bronte. I want your relation-ship to work, but I'm painfully aware of his limitations."

"It wasn't a good reading the other night, was it?"

She shook her head. "Your career was positive, Bronte. I can tell you unequivocally that big and better things are ahead of you."

"But the relationship issue is up in the air?"

She met my eyes. "I'm not sure Luther is cut out for the journey you're about to embark on."

"You've seen more than you're letting on, haven't you?"

She nodded.

"Care to elaborate?"

"I see a reversal of fortune, Bronte, and lots of travel. The world and life you have known will undergo an enormous shift, and everything is going to change."

"Why can't Luther be part of it?"

"He can, Bronte, but I'm not sure he will want to. Like you say, Luther wants a simple, quiet life. He isn't overly ambitious, and the main reason his marriage to Tina failed is because she wanted him to be someone different."

"It says a lot that we've made it this far, don't you think?"

"I do. But I also know that he wouldn't have come to you had I not nudged him."

I sat back in my chair and gazed out the window. The rain had picked up momentum and the room had darkened along with the mood. The conversation had taken an unexpected turn and Beth's words had winded me. "Are you going to discuss this with Luther after I leave?"

"Do you want me to?"

"I don't want you to put ideas in either one of our heads should this reversal of fortune never come to fruition."

"It's already happening, Bronte. Your memoir has drawn the attention of a movie producer and your poetry book is a best-seller. Luther is going to quiz me either way about the tarot spread after you leave."

"He didn't have last minute plans with Addy, did he? He's pissed off with me because I didn't tell him about the memoir."

"Try to see it from his perspective, Bronte. Your writing connection is the only ace Luther had up his sleeve. But if you don't need him as a writing partner, and he is essentially your second choice in terms of a romantic relationship, then what is his value?"

I opened my mouth to say something when Luther walked in.

"You're back earlier than I expected," said Beth.

"Yeah, Tina heard about Bronte's visit and wanted to pick a fight."

Beth shook her head. "Not in front of Addy, I hope?"

"No, she was with Tina's mom."

Luther looked at me, realising he'd been caught in a lie.

I put my teacup down and stood up. "Oh, don't mind me. I know you haven't been with Addy today. You just couldn't stand the sight of me."

Luther took my hand. "I'm sorry, Bront. I shouldn't have lied."

I shook my head. "I'm the one who's sorry. I should have told you about the memoir."

"Yeah, you should have. I thought writing was our thing?"

I thought about our conversation at Brisbane airport. How Luther had got annoyed when discussing the traditional versus indie publishing path. But I didn't want to start a fight, so I said, "It is our thing." I forced a smile and excused myself to go to the bathroom. The conversation with Beth and Luther had travelled down a road that I knew existed but hadn't expected to see on the horizon so soon. I felt deflated and hoped that Beth's prediction would prove to be wrong. I also wondered why she had pushed Luther toward me only to pull him back. Had she seen something else in the tarot cards? When I returned to the conservatory, I was relieved to find Luther on his own. "Where's Beth?"

"She's gone to rustle up something for dinner."

I started to protest but swallowed my words. "I was hoping to spend our last night alone. There are things we need to talk about."

"We won't stay long. Promise. Now sit, will you? I want to give you something."

I sat. Luther pulled a brown paper bag out of the inner pocket of his black leather jacket and placed it on the table. "For you, milady."

I stuck my hand inside the bag and pulled out a dog-eared

book. "Luther," I said, inspecting it, "is this what I think it is?"

He smiled and nodded.

"Your mother's copy of *Alice in Wonderland*?"

"One and the same."

I shook my head and handed it back to him. "I can't accept this, Luther. It's too sentimental."

"Open it and read the inscription."

I inhaled and searched his eyes before I opened the cover. "Does your mom know you're giving this to me?"

"Does it matter?"

"Yes," I nodded, "yes, it matters to me. And while we're being honest, I also need to know what prompted your divorce. I know you, Luther, you wouldn't make a drastic decision unless someone forced your hand."

He frowned. I fidgeted in my seat. Neither of us spoke for several seconds.

"Why are you pushing this, Bront?"

"Because I don't want to get between you and Tina if there's a chance to rekindle your relationship."

He pushed the book toward me. "Read the inscription."

I opened the cover and read.

For Bronte

Only the real Alice could make the impossible possible.

Yours, no matter what
Luther xoxo

I lowered my eyes and studied the book to hide my tears. "You are so thoughtful."

"Tina would have thrown it in the garbage, and that should tell you all you need to know about my marriage. Can we drop it now?"

I slid from the chair to my knees and pulled him toward me. "Can you show me your old room?"

He held my face in his hands and studied me before he spoke. "Sure, come on."

I followed him upstairs. His room was the last one on the left. "My brother wanted a view of the street if you'd believe it, so I got the garden."

"You don't talk about your brother much. Does he live nearby?"

"Nah, he lives in New Orleans with his wife and kids. What's with all the questions tonight?"

"It's our last night together. My emotions are getting the better of me."

"Come here." He held me tight. "There will be more nights after this one. Remember, it's never goodbye."

"I do love you, Luther. Please don't ever doubt that." I hugged and held onto him until we heard Beth call us downstairs for dinner.

I forced a smile and conversation during the meal, though I

was neither hungry nor happy. In truth, I wanted to get on the plane and go home to Aden and the kids. While Luther cleared the dinner table and packed the dishwasher, Beth picked up from where we'd left off from our earlier conversation.

"We never finished our conversation, Bronte."

"I disagree, Beth. It seems pretty clear cut to me."

She smiled weakly and sighed. "You know, Bronte, the future changes all the time. Every thought, action, choice, and decision affects the outcome. What was true yesterday, or half an hour ago, might be false tomorrow or thirty minutes from now. Every single moment can change on a dime."

"I agree, Beth, which is why it's dangerous to place too much value in a tarot card spread, don't you think?"

"Bronte. I've been reading tarot for most of my life. Some readings are unequivocal, others leave room for equivocation. Your reading was unequivocal. Rapid change is ahead of you, and I don't see Luther by your side. I'm sorry."

I leaned forward and spoke in a quiet voice so that Luther couldn't hear me. "Tell me this, Beth, why did you push him toward me if you knew it was a fruitless exercise?"

"As I said, the future changes all the time, Bronte, and this has not been a fruitless exercise, I can assure you. You will both find what you're looking for, but the future will be different to the one you both imagined."

I tried to swallow back the tears but failed miserably. Beth stood and wrapped her arms around me from behind. "For what it's worth, I've decided not to tell Luther about any of this. It's best to leave it to fate. The future is always changing."

Beth's parting words failed to cheer me up. Not on the drive home. Not after Luther and I made love. Not while Luther slept soundly and I paced his study. Not at the airport the following day, when I said goodbye and he said what he always said: *Never goodbye.*

CHAPTER 47
Bronte

September

Growing up on a Barossa wine estate meant that the winemaking process was often a family affair. When tutoring my brother and me on seasonal duties, my father would say that the period between disbudding and flowering was especially crucial because activity was speeding up. When I asked him to explain, he said that branches could grow between five and fifteen centimetres a day, and if a burgeoning branch was too heavy for the vine, it could be detrimental to harvest quality. To ensure a good harvest, branches required regular lifting and trellising.

When I returned from Boston, I experienced a similar speeding up of activity, and Beth's prophetic words unravelled before my eyes. One morning, midway through making school lunches, Katy contacted me with news that I would never have imagined in my wildest dreams.

"Hey Bronte, I have phenomenal news."

I chewed on my thumb nail in anticipation. "I'm all ears."

"I've been in touch with a talent agent in Los Angeles called Adam. He liaises with Movie Execs and negotiates deals. He has a client who's very interested in *Flammable* and they want to fly you out for a meeting."

I looked at the kids, who were arguing about who would sit in the front seat on the way to school and pinched myself.

"Are you still there, Bronte?"

"Yeah, sorry, I'm still here. Call me shell-shocked."

"I know. It's absolutely mad. This has never happened to me before either, and I am over the moon for you."

I covered the phone with my hand and told the kids to go and brush their teeth. Then I turned my attention back to Katy. "How do we put this in motion?"

"Adam is keen to chat to you today via Skype. If all goes well, you'll be flying to Los Angeles to meet with the producer."

"Oh my God."

"Tell me about it. What's the best time for Adam to call?"

"Whatever time suits Adam. I will move anything and everything to schedule this call."

She laughed. "Okay, Bronte. I'll let you know as soon as I set it up. But they want to act fast, so be prepared."

"I'll be waiting with bells on."

She laughed again and said goodbye. I stood in the kitchen with my mouth open like a Venus flytrap.

I opened the front door before Aden could get the key in the lock. "You will never guess what happened today."

He kissed me and put his bag down. "You got me; what happened today?"

I led him into the lounge and sat him down on the sofa. "I had a Skype call with an Agent from Los Angeles today, called Adam, and he is organising a meeting with a Hollywood movie producer named Sheryl."

"You're kidding me?"

"Nope. Serious as a snake bit. They're flying me out to LA to meet with her."

"They're flying you out to LA?"

"Yes," I said, unable to tame my smile.

"That is unbelievable! I'm speechless."

"It's not a done deal yet, you understand."

"Don't kid yourself, you're gonna knock their socks off. You're pretty damned bedazzling when you want to be."

"I don't want to jinx anything until it's finalised."

He stood and opened his arms. "Come here, you!"

Two weeks later, I kissed Aden and the kids goodbye at Brisbane airport and boarded a plane to Los Angeles. I had to pinch myself a dozen times before the plane took off and landed nineteen hours later at LAX. I thought of Cinderella, waiting for her carriage to turn into a pumpkin, and worried that I was out of my league. Not in my wildest dreams had I entertained such possibilities, yet I was poised to meet Adam and a big-time Hollywood movie producer.

After catching a cab to my hotel and checking in, I fished out my swimsuit and headed down to the pool to swim laps. Swimming was the North Star that helped me focus and drown out the internal negativity that floated on the periphery of my mind. After fifty laps, my mind was crystal-like, and my exhausted body was primed for sleep. I slid between the cool cotton sheets of the king-size bed and stretched out my legs and arms like a sea star, ready for the Sandman to take me when my phone lit up the room and buzzed. I reached over to the bedside table and picked it up. Luther had texted.

LUTHER: Hey beautiful, how's LA?

I didn't have the bandwidth to manage Luther's emotions, expectations, and questions, so I left him on delivered and rolled over to sleep.

That night I dreamt I was poring over a nature book—like a vivid spread in National Geographic, or an old school Encyclopaedia Britannica. The illustration in the book appeared to be an aerial shot of a dark blue, but crystal clear, expanse of water. Beneath the water, prehistoric kangaroos were swimming. I say prehistoric because they were quadruple the size of modern-day kangaroos. As I studied the picture, the scene came to life as I admired it from the passenger seat of a helicopter. As the chopper hovered in place, the swimming kangaroos emerged from the water and shook off to dry themselves in the sun. I woke up and googled kangaroos then helicopters in association with dreams, and knew it was a good omen when I saw the words *successful, family* and *abundance* crop up multiple times.

I slept for another few hours before I woke up feeling refreshed and ready to meet the challenges of my day head-on. I ordered room service, replied to Luther's text, and chatted to Aden and the kids via FaceTime. I missed them terribly when I was away and doubted if my adventure would be as thrilling and satisfying if I couldn't share the experience with them. After a breakfast of scrambled eggs, sourdough toast, coffee, orange juice and fruit, I showered, dressed, and met Adam in the lobby.

The first thought that popped into my head when I saw Adam was: *he looks like John Cusack*. When he greeted me, his genuine smile and enthusiastic energy were contagious. In the cab, we prepped for the meeting with Sheryl. Adam confirmed the details of my research—Sheryl was a big-time movie Producer who had worked her way up in a misogynistic and male-dominated industry.

"She'll probably ask you about works in progress and upcoming projects," said Adam, "so be prepared to unveil that impressive list of yours like a red carpet."

"Woo her with my work. Got it."

"Exactly! I've worked with Sheryl many times before, and I can assure you that she sees huge potential in you. If today is successful, this will be the start of a long and prosperous professional relationship."

"I will do my best, Adam."

"I don't doubt it for a second, Bronte."

The cab pulled up in front of a driveway and announced our arrival via an intercom. The gate resembled a piece of art or a sculpture made of sheet metal. As it slid open, the leaf-shaped cutouts caught the light and shimmered. The external building was a sprawling split-level structure of glass, steel, and timber, and the lush, landscaped gardens wrapped around the building like a protective, zen womb. Adam paid the cab driver and led me up polished concrete stairs that tapered towards the top. We stood in a light-filled courtyard at the summit, where giant potted plants and desert flowers hugged the walls. I expected a maid to greet us and usher us inside the double glass doors, where we would wait to be seen, but that was not the case. A tall woman in her fifties, with cropped dark hair, opened the door.

"You must be Bronte."

I held out my hand. "And you must be Sheryl."

"The one and only," said Adam.

We followed Sheryl inside. Her pumps clicked as she strode across the polished concrete floors. As we walked, I couldn't help but drink in the scenery from the expansive glass windows. In addition to an enormous lagoon-style pool, there was an infinity lap pool that looked like a slit of water amidst the landscaped gardens and bronze sculptures. Dreamy artwork hung on the white-washed walls, and every room resembled pages in a Home and Garden magazine.

Sheryl led us into an office with a plush ruby carpet. One of the four walls was constructed of glass—a giant window that framed a manicured lawn and flower beds. Another wall was decorated with framed movie posters that Sheryl had produced, and the fourth consisted of a wall-to-wall, floor-to-ceiling, cedar bookcase. Sheryl's desk sat opposite the window and beneath her movie posters, while the sofa chairs were arranged in an arc around the bookcase.

"Sit, please," said Sheryl, gesturing to the three-seated sofa.

I had been nervous beforehand, having witnessed the butchering of eloquent books into popular movie adaptations, but I needn't have worried because Sheryl seemed to have a direct line to my inner dialogue and thoughts.

"Before I tell you about my vision for *Flammable*, I want to hear from you. It is your story after all, and I want to stay true to the original as much as possible. Where were you when you had the idea and wrote the first words? What was it like confronting those painful memories?"

I talked for more than twenty minutes. Much like the day I wrote it, the words and emotion and passion flowed out of me. When I finished, Sheryl weighed in.

"I have a director in mind who is also a screenwriter. My best-case scenario is that you two will hit it off and co-write the screenplay. Assuming you are interested, of course."

I nodded. "I haven't written a screenplay before, but I am a fast learner, and I will do whatever is necessary if the director agrees."

"You might have your chance tonight if you agree to stay for cocktails and dinner."

I looked at Adam for confirmation. He nodded. "Of course we'll stay for dinner. Thanks, Sheryl."

She clapped her hands and stood. "Fantastic."

We followed her into the kitchen, where her chef offered us the choice of three menus—Japanese, Thai Fusion, or

Gourmet Vegan. We chose Gourmet Vegan. While Adam used Sheryl's office to return missed calls and respond to emails, Sheryl and I sat outside in pool chairs alongside the infinity lap pool that overlooked the hills and mountains.

"I'm glad we've got a bit of time alone, Bronte because I'd like to chat to you on a more personal level."

"Oh?"

"I admire you, Bronte, and I adore your writing style. I'd like to work with you on future projects if all goes well with *Flammable*."

"I'd like that too."

"Your memoir only deals with the loss of your family and your subsequent journey. But there's so much more to know about your life. Growing up on a winery in South Australia, then ending up in a winery in Queensland and losing everything. What was that like for you? I can't imagine losing everything and having to start from scratch. Those years alone must have been extremely testing for you."

"I guess I've learned to gloss over it now as unimportant. After all, there are worse things, right?"

"There are always worse things, but I don't know many people who have started their life from scratch once, never mind multiple times. It's admirable."

"Thank you, Sheryl. I admire what you've achieved in your career. In many ways, I think it's harder to achieve what you have than to survive what I did."

"It takes a certain mindset to do both, Bronte, which is how I know your success is close at hand."

After a few minutes, we were talking like old friends. She wanted to know more about Aden and how he had coped with losing the winery, which inevitably led to a conversation about Luther and polyamory.

"Open marriages have long been the norm in Hollywood, but it's only beginning to permeate the mainstream. Have you ever considered writing a play?"

"For the theatre?" I said.

She nodded and kept talking while I concentrated on swatting away feelings of inadequacy like flies. This woman, a complete stranger for all intents and purposes, was speaking to me like I was her creative equal, but, in my mind, I considered my creative skill to be in its infancy.

"You could co-write it with Luther and leave the rest to me." Sheryl winked. "I have connections, you know."

"I'm up for the challenge."

"I'm thinking RomCom."

"Social Liaisons," I said, thinking out loud.

Sheryl clapped her hands. "A title and concept are all I need to make it happen. Float the idea with Luther when you talk next and get back to me."

Adam exited a different door and crossed the stepping stones to where we were sitting. "What are you two scheming?"

Sheryl laughed. "Oh, this and that."

"Will your partner in crime be joining us for dinner?" said Adam.

"Unfortunately not. Avi's in New York this week, but I have someone better in mind." She laughed and stood. "You two stay and enjoy the view. I'll send Maria out with some snacks while I phone Sam."

Her pumps clicked as she crossed the stepping stones and disappeared through the door that Adam had exited.

"Who is Sam?" I said.

"She's the writer/director that Sheryl has in mind for your memoir."

"Aah," I said, trying to catch my breath, "not overwhelming at all."

"Think of it as preparation meeting opportunity, Bronte."

I inhaled and nodded.

"You've got this, and I've got your back. Okay?"

"Okay."

Sam arrived when the sky swirled with tangerine, lilac and rose. Before Sheryl could make introductions, Sam glided over to me and held out her hand.

"Hi, Bronte."

A surge of heat travelled from my toes to my cheeks, and I smiled like a shy school girl standing opposite her first crush. She looked like Shane, from the L-Word, with her blunt haircut, angular features, and bedroom eyes. I shook her hand. "Hi, Shane."

She chuckled and raised her eyebrows.

I covered my face with my hand and laughed. "Oh my

God, I'm sorry. I meant to say, hi Sam."

Her eyes twinkled with amusement. "Do I remind you of someone?"

I nodded, and willed my cheeks and body to stop burning. "Yeah, you remind me of Shane from…"

"Katherine Moennig?"

I nodded.

She smiled. "Yeah, I get that a lot."

I smiled like a fool in love, and no intelligent words came to my rescue. There was something about the way she stared at me like I was the only person in the room that roused the butterflies in my stomach.

"I expected you to be either incredibly beautiful or incredibly photogenic, but I wasn't prepared for both."

I blushed self-consciously and chuckled. "That's not what I expected you to say, but thank you."

"You're talented too. Your memoir blew me away. I've been looking for something raw and exquisite to sink my teeth into, and along came *Flammable*."

"Thank you," I said again, worried that I was teetering on the edge of losing the power of speech in her company.

She hooked her arm through mine and told Sheryl and Adam that we'd be in Sheryl's office discussing the screenplay. My nerves settled once we were alone, and my feelings of inadequacy diminished once Sam starting chatting passionately about my work and the ins and outs of co-writing a screenplay together. By the end of the conversation, I felt like I'd taken a dip in a creative think tank, and I had no doubt Sam would retain the integrity of *Flammable*.

When we returned to the sunken lounge, Sheryl and Adam were drinking cocktails and chatting.

"Everything okay?" said Sheryl.

"Better than okay," said Sam. "Bronte and I have worked out a writing schedule, so it'd be great to get the contracts drawn up and signed before then."

Sheryl held up her glass. "Did you hear that, Adam? Our work here is done."

"Was there ever any doubt?" said Adam.

Time slipped away as fast as the colours in the sky, and we ate dinner in an open-plan dining room lit with ambient LEDs that changed from blue to green to yellow. Beyond the open glass doors, the pool and city lights formed their own star-scape. After the dinner plates had been cleared and we were waiting for dessert, Sam changed the conversation.

"Sheryl and I have a confession to make, Bronte."

I raised my eyebrows. "Oh?"

"We had an ulterior motive for inviting you to dinner."

Sheryl waved her hand like she was swatting away a mosquito. "Don't listen to Sam, it's more a case of serendipity than ulterior motive."

"Sheryl's right," said Sam. "It's a strike-while-the-iron-is-hot sort of thing."

"Sam and I have partnered in a number of investments over the years," said Sheryl. "The arthouse production company that's going to produce *Flammable* is one such investment."

"A mineral water sourced from the Alps is another," said Sam, "and all have been relatively easy to manage and make returns on."

"But we may have bitten off more than we can chew with our latest acquisition," said Sheryl.

I looked from Sam to Sheryl. "I can't imagine what it has to do with me."

"We've bought a boutique winery in Napa," said Sam.

"Congratulations," I said, "but you needn't be over your head if you hang onto the existing staff and treat them well."

"That's precisely the problem," said Sheryl. "We've lost the entire winemaking team."

"Oh, shit," I said.

"Shit was our initial reaction, Bronte, and then your work came across Sheryl's desk, and our scheming little minds went into overdrive."

I raised my eyebrows to mask my expression while my brain moved into overdrive to compute every possible angle.

"Sheryl explained how you and your husband were forced to foreclose on Ghost Gum Winery and start over again. What we want to know is this: Is your husband interested in moving back into winemaking?"

I finally saw where the conversation was heading and nodded. "Aden has mourned Ghost Gum and his winemaking dream like the death of a loved one." I stopped to take a breath. "Now that we are back on our feet, he would like nothing better than to return to his true passion. We've been talking about ways to get back into the industry, but the path forward hasn't yet presented itself."

"Consider it presented," said Sam. "If Aden is keen, then we have a proposition for him."

"Wow," I said, "I am at a loss for words."

"You deserve a break, Bronte," said Sheryl, "and Aden will be helping us achieve something new and exciting with the winery. Do you think he'd be willing to discuss the opportunity with us via FaceTime?"

"Sure," I said, feeling like a leaf could knock me over. "Do you want me to prepare him first, or shall we dive straight in?"

"Let's dive straight in," said Sam.

"Okay," I chuckled.

Sheryl stood. "I'll tell Maria to hold the dessert and coffee a little longer."

Sam took mine and Adam's hands. "Come, we'll set the call up on the big screen."

CHAPTER 48
Aden

September

I was unpacking the kids' school bags and lunch boxes when I received a cryptic text from Bronte.

Ade, I don't know what's going on, but the heavens are answering all of our prayers in one fell swoop. I'm gonna FaceTime you in a minute. Make sure you look decent and put your game face on!!!

I settled the kids in front of the TV and went up to Bronte's study. Sure enough, the phone rang as I sat in her red chair. When I saw Bronte and three other people sitting on an enormous sofa, I chuckled. Nervous reaction, I suppose. After Bronte made the introductions, a woman called Sam took the lead.

"I'm gonna cut to the chase, Aden. Sheryl and I bought a winery in Napa a few months ago, but the winemakers were angry and resigned. While we didn't plan for mass resignations, the upside is an opportunity to start afresh and take the winery in a new direction."

Sheryl stepped in. "What do you think so far, Aden?"

I ran my fingers through my hair. "What direction do you want to take?"

"We absolutely want to go organic," said Sheryl.

"That's a must," said Sam, "but we were hoping to bring a couple of new winemakers on board to help figure it out and lead the way forward."

"Sounds like a dream job."

"Does it sound like your dream job?" said Sam.

"In my wildest dreams, sure, but you know I've been away from winemaking for a few years now?"

"We do," said Sam, "and while that would possibly count as a strike against you with an established winery, Sheryl and I see it as a bonus."

"How so?"

"Much like Bronte, you are passionate and talented, Aden, but you've been dealt a shitty hand. In our experience, those who are hungry and passionate are most likely to succeed."

"I won't argue with that, and I can assure you that I am both ravenous for this opportunity and grateful to be considered."

"We have also approached a French winemaker, called Jacqueline Deschamps, who is already working in Napa temporarily. She is keen but wants to talk to you before she makes any decision."

"Tell me when and where," I said.

"Same time tomorrow?"

"Done."

My FaceTime with Jacqueline, Sheryl, and Sam exceeded my greatest expectations. Jacqueline possessed a passion for grapes and terroir like Bronte had a passion for words, and her vision for Sheryl's and Sam's winery ran parallel to the long-term plans I had envisioned for Ghost Gum. She wanted to grow grapes organically by planting insect-repellant wildflowers and herbs between the vines—lemon balm, rosemary, and lavender. When she said lavender, she used the French word 'lavande', which sounded poetic and made me think of Bronte. We all agreed the winery needed a rebrand to better suit its new direction and philosophy. Our discussions ended with 'Lilac Honey Winery'—symbolic of the adjacent lavender fields and honey bees the flowers attracted, as well as our plan to use lavender as pest control and maintain organic grapes.

It went without saying that Jacqueline would lead the charge, but I made a point of backing the decision. Jacqueline shushed me, and emphasised that we would both bring different ingredients to the recipe of success. Sheryl and Sam mentioned that the winery estate included the main house and a cottage, which were both vacant, and suggested it would be beneficial for at least one of us to live on the property.

"The cottage has a private lane and is completely separate from the house," said Sam.

"Aden has a family, so I am happy to live in ze cottage," said Jacqueline.

"I know from Ghost Gum that it's crucial to either live on or be close to, the property," I said.

"That's settled then," said Sam. "You and Bronte can take the main house, and Jacqueline can have the cottage.

CHAPTER 49
Luther

September

BRONTE: Hold onto your hat, Luth, your quiet life is about to take off.

LUTHER: Uh oh

BRONTE: FaceTime?

LUTHER: For you, always

BRONTE: I'm dialling now…

When her face filled the screen, I smiled. "What's happening in Bronte's Wonderland?"

"Oh my God, it's a whirlwind."

"Tell me."

She told me about her meeting with a movie producer and Aden's opportunity to work at a winery in Napa.

"You're all moving to the States?"

She nodded and smiled. "I sure am, we're slowly but surely closing the gap between impossible and possible."

"So you are willing to move your life—just not for me?"

She raised her eyebrows and then frowned. "Don't be like that, Luther. This is progress; we're down from twenty-four hours to five hours distance between us."

"Okay, we'll agree to disagree then."

"Are you serious, Luther? This is a huge opportunity for

Aden and me. I thought you'd be happy?"

"It's not about you getting closer, it's that your priorities are staying the same. I'm not your priority, and I'm not sure if I ever will be."

"I thought we had covered this ground? Aden and the kids are my priority, much like Adelaide is yours. And you keep flipping the onus onto me like some tired old double standard. Why don't you turn the mirror on yourself? I mean, I doubt you would move to LA for me."

"Okay, Bront, cool your engines. I take your point. Let's start over again. You mentioned some exciting news for you and me. What's that all about?"

She told me about her meeting with the movie producer and the play about our polyamorous relationship. "It'll be a RomCom, and the tentative title is *Social Liaisons.*"

"Who's gonna write this play?"

"You and me, Luth."

"Um, you haven't agreed to anything have you?"

"No. That's why I needed to speak to you...so we can discuss it."

"I don't know what to say."

"Yeah, talk about falling down a rabbit hole." She held up a wad of paper. "This is the contract. I'll read the salient points to you and let you decide if you want to go ahead."

She read out clauses and words like "deadlines" and "rights" and my mind drifted away to the night my mom read Bronte's tarot cards. *Your hard work will soon pay off...the Tower usually depicts an ending of some kind...Justice represents making a rational decision as opposed to allowing emotions to be your guide.* I had been writing longer than Bronte, yet she was already progressing in leaps and bounds. I'd be lying if I said I wasn't a little envious of her talent, but I was mostly overwhelmed. To see her success unfolding in real-time meant I could never measure up to her.

"This whole thing is above my pay grade, Bronte. What do either of us know about writing a play?"

She frowned while she scrutinized me. "Oh my God, Luther, what's got into you today? I mean, are you kidding me or what?"

I shook my head. "No, Bronte, I'm not kidding you."

"What did you know about writing a novel before you wrote one?"

"That's not the same thing."

She crossed her arms. "How so?"

"My novels didn't need to hold up under any public scrutiny."

She rubbed her face and sighed. "How will you ever grow professionally if you don't stretch yourself, Luther?"

I lit a cigarette to irritate her and buy myself time to think about my answer. I pictured a future in which Bronte became a writing superstar while I continued to work in the same office job and write books that nobody read. She had already relegated me to second place as a lover. Did I want to be second as a writer too? It didn't have the glow it had before.

"Maybe I don't want to stretch myself, Bronte."

"Don't you have any ambition, Luther?"

I took a long drag and shook my head on the exhale. "Not like you, no."

She sat back in her seat with her arms still crossed and dropped her head. When she looked up seconds later, she said, "This conversation is not unfolding as I planned."

I flicked the growing ash into an owl ashtray. "That makes two of us."

"Are you saying you won't consider this at all, or are you telling me you need time to think?"

"I'm telling you I won't consider it at all."

She shook her head and laughed incredulously. "I don't know what to say right now, Luther. Are you punking me or something?"

"I don't know what to tell you, Bronte. I'm not like you."

"What does that mean?"

"It means I'm content with what I've got and where I am. You basically get up in the morning because you believe you were born to be and do something extraordinary. And you're right as it turns out. But I'm not comfortable with operating at that level, and I'm not comfortable with selling out my art."

"Oh my God, every time I think this conversation has hit rock bottom, it sinks another rung. I am NOT a sellout, Luther."

"I beg to differ."

She held up her hand like a judges gavel. "I'm gonna stop you right there before we both start saying things we regret. I know it's a lot to take in, Luther, so please sleep on it before you make any rash decisions, and we'll chat again in a few days."

I shook my head and tapped my smoke on the edge of the ashtray. "I don't need to sleep on it, Bronte. I don't want to ride this rollercoaster with you."

"You spoke to Beth about the tarot cards, didn't you?"

"It would have been better coming from you. But you seem to be making a habit of not telling me things lately."

"Luther, they're bloody tarot cards, for God's sake."

"But they're turning out to be pretty accurate, don't you think?"

She sighed loudly and shook her head. "You have rendered me speechless. I don't know what to say."

"Don't say anything." I leaned forward. "Do you appreciate that our polyamory will become a talking point if you go ahead with this play? That it will be the center of discussions in all of the press releases, and the after-show interviews at the stage door? That I'll have to admit to playing second fiddle to a massively successful poetess and memoirist, and her husband, and two kids? You know what the etymology of polyamory is, Bronte?"

"I'd think it's Greek, right? I mean--"

"It's Poly, yammering on about having more than one sexual partner at her fucking Broadway premiere!"

"I can't believe that you feel this way." Her voice had softened.

I sat back again, and inhaled hard on the cigarette. "Let's pretend this never happened."

"Wait, pretend what never happened? This conversation, or you and me?"

"I have to go, Bronte. Tina is letting me take Addy out for dinner, and I need to leave soon to beat the traffic."

I hung up without giving her a chance to speak. Cowardly, maybe, but I couldn't take another second of seeing her look of disappointment. I lit another cigarette with the dying embers of the existing one and then stamped it out in the ashtray. *Fucking Bronte*, I thought to myself. She was like a mirage. Just when you thought you were closing in, she would shimmer, disappear, and reform on the horizon. I had only agreed to the polyamory insanity because I thought it was her ultimate get-out from Aden. I thought she would eventually be mine. But Bronte wasn't closing the distance between us; she was increasing it.

Before Bronte, I had certain expectations for my writing career. No delusions of grandeur. I simply wanted to write my books on my terms and establish a loyal base of fans. But Bronte was heading in a whole other direction, and it scared the crap out of me. Maybe I was letting fear get in the way, or maybe I wanted a simple life. I had already dipped my toe into uncharted waters by following Bronte into complicated love-territory and playing second fiddle to Aden. Now she expected me to trail the dizzy heights of her writing career like a dying star and accept a position where our polyamorous relationship could become public knowledge. No way. If I knew anything with conviction, I knew that I did not want that.

CHAPTER 50
Aden

December

Time moved like a whirlwind after my call with Sam, Sheryl, and Jacqueline. US Immigration approved our family visas in November, and we moved to Napa in December. With Christmas around the corner, Bronte and I had a bit of time to settle into the winery house and enrolled Leyla and Liam in their new school. When Sam had referred to the main house as a 'farmhouse', I had envisioned a ramshackle do-it-upper, but it was clean, modern, and spacious. From the driveway, the house resembled a little cottage, with its sunny yellow weatherboards and neatly trimmed hedges, but the house was much larger beyond the front door. Arches partitioned the open-plan space, creating the illusion of separate rooms without physically separating the rooms. Sam and Sheryl had organised to have the house dressed while Bronte and I settled in and waited for our own furniture to arrive. The master bedroom was the size of a hotel suite and had a grey suede headboard that reached halfway to the ceiling. The kids each had a bedroom, Bronte had an office, and I had a wine cellar. The outdoor area and back garden were no less impressive.

Partitioned by means of pebbles, paving, steps or landscaping, there was an alfresco cooking and dining area, a hot tub, swimming pool, and a mini playground, complete with a treehouse, swing-set and slide, which the kids went nuts for when they saw it. Before the move, Bronte and I worried that the kids would be unsettled and out of sorts, but they treated it like a great big adventure and quickly found their feet. They made friends in the first week and spent afternoons playing at a huge green area a few miles from the winery. The green had a lake at its centre, several different walking tracks, and an adventure playground for older kids.

Grapevines are dormant in winter, but there is still plenty to be done in a winery. Our move to Napa in December was perfectly timed because it afforded Jacqueline and me the time to familiarise ourselves with the winery as well as take stock and plan for the months ahead. When inside the winery, we carried out sulphite and acidity tests. As sulphites are a byproduct of fermentation, they are always present, but most wineries add extra to preserve the wine longer. At Lilac Honey, we needed to keep the natural sulphites at an acceptable level to gain organic accreditation. Time spent outside involved pruning any excessive branches that developed during spring and summer. If we didn't prune, the vines' energy would be spent on developing grapes rather than vegetation.

I had been fortunate in finding Bronte, who had grown up around wine and appreciated everything from planting to bottling. But Bronte's true passion for words eluded me. And while she could certainly speak to the topics of terroir, grape varieties, and the smell of fermenting grape juice, Bronte's true relationship to winemaking had been inherited; she hadn't pursued it by choice.

My first in-depth conversation with Jacqueline took place during our first week working together at Lilac Honey. The mulched grapevine wood was ready to be tilled back into the soil for additional nutrients, and Jacqueline wanted to do it herself. She preferred to be hands-on—a work ethic I admired, respected, and shared. Her philosophy about terroir—that little French word that has no English counter-part and pertains to factors such as the soil, topography, and climate—was that the winemaker was inextricably linked. I couldn't help but smile and listen intently to her when she spoke. Her tongue slipped into French when she spoke of her passions, and she pronounced "the" as "ze". When talking about Lilac Honey, she said: "C'est un rêve d'enfance devenu réalité." And then she looked up, laughed, and said oh, pardon realising that she'd fallen back into her mother tongue. I told her I didn't mind at all and asked her if she could teach me a bit of French every day.

Her face lit up. "Vraiment?".

I nodded. "Oui."

She went on to explain that her parents owned and oper-ated a lavender farm in Provence, while their neighbours had a vineyard. As a teenager, she worked in the winery and learnt everything she could. She was fascinated by the science of soil and how different factors could contribute to the tastes and smells present in the wine. The prospect of leading her own vineyard in Napa's lavender precinct had married her two childhood passions—lavender and vines.

Hoping to surprise and impress Jacqueline in the not too

distant future, I downloaded the DuoLingo app and spent every spare moment learning French.

Bronte and I spent a quiet Christmas together in our new home before Bronte's crazy work schedule kicked off. After we'd eaten a traditional roast lunch, and the kids were ensconced in the family room watching a DVD, Bronte made coffee, and I lit a fire in the fire pit. A few minutes into our conversation, it struck me that Bronte had not mentioned Luther since our move to Napa.

"You haven't mentioned Luther for a while. Did you ask him about writing the play?"

Bronte rolled her eyes and shook her head. "I asked him, and he declined."

"Seriously? When did this happen?"

"Soon after I met with Sheryl and Sam."

"And? What's the story?"

"We argued, he called me a sellout, and hung up on me. I haven't spoken to him since."

"Are you kidding me, Bront? When were you gonna tell me?"

"Honestly, Ade, he pissed me off, and my mind has been elsewhere."

"You know, you could've told me." I downplayed my frustration at Bronte's indifference, but her relationship with

Luther had ramifications for all of us, and she could have told me sooner. "So what now?"

"You mean with writing the play or my relationship with him?"

"Uh, both."

"I told Sheryl the next day. Fortunately, she was happy because she would prefer that I co-write it with Sam."

"So it's still on?"

"Yeah, Sheryl's still keen."

"What about your relationship with Luther?"

"I don't know. I suppose I'll have to be the bigger person and contact him."

"Why bother, Bront? You deserve better than that cowardly little ass hat."

"A cowardly little ass hat," she repeated. I expected her to get all serious and walk out. But she laughed and clinked my glass with hers. "I might steal that line."

I laughed. "I give it freely."

"What about you and Jacqueline?"

"What do you mean?" I said a little too quickly and defensively.

"Ha!" She pointed her finger at me and laughed. "I knew it."

"Knew what?"

She narrowed her eyes at me and smiled. "I heard you repeating a French phrase in the shower this morning. Have you been learning French to impress her?"

I raised my left hand. "Okay, you got me. But I'm not planning to do what you did."

She sipped her wine and then frowned at me. "What did I do?"

"A big whirlwind romance with Luther. I don't want to jeopardise my professional relationship with Jacqueline."

"You have my blessing if you change your mind."

"Wouldn't it give you pause or make you jealous?"

"I wouldn't be much of a wife if I didn't experience a pinch of jealousy, right?"

"Good, I'm glad. I would have worried if you'd said no."

She laughed and shook her head.

"What if things go south with Luther? Would you still be okay with it?"

"Yes, I would never stand in your way."

"For now, Jacqueline and I are friends and colleagues."

"Will you let me know if the situation changes?"

"Will you let me know about Luther?"

She held out her hand. "Pinky swear; you'll be the first to know about Luther."

We locked pinky fingers and kissed.

CHAPTER 51
Bronte

December

S am booked our first writing session for 27 December 2016 at her house in Malibu. In the days leading up to it, my appetite disappeared, and my internal body temperature travelled from dormant to an active volcano. I felt hot twenty-four-seven, and I couldn't sleep more than three hours at a time. The second I woke up, I'd be trying to keep pace with my thoughts as my fingers tap-danced across the keyboard. Luther's negative words plagued my mind like little seeds of doubt—*what do we know about writing a play…public scrutiny…blah blah blah.* Hours before the session, I had a dry throat and sweaty palms, but I refused to hydrate in case I needed to pee. I hadn't felt that powerless and fearful since my suicide attempt—which was ridiculous. After I talked myself down from the proverbial ledge, I sprayed a herbal remedy on my tongue and focused on the advice I'd given Luther—*How will you ever grow professionally if you don't stretch yourself?* After all, as powerful as my over-active imagination and internal assassin were, they were no match for my passion for writing and determination to succeed.

Sam's house on the Malibu coastline was a kaleidoscope of glass and curves. I took deep breaths and focused on the crashing waves as I rang the doorbell and waited for her to answer. When she opened the door and welcomed me inside, I felt like I was submerged in some magical water wonderland. The house and ocean seemed to blur into one, with the floor to ceiling windows filled to the brim with sea and horizon. I forgot all about my nerves the minute I walked inside. I forgot all about Sam too, walking, as if magnetised, to the large dreamy canvases that hung on white walls. All depicted women in surreal, fantasy-like settings.

I stood opposite a painting that depicted a woman's body, submerged in a calm olive sea, only her head visible and cradled in a tree filled with blackbirds and a full moon in the background. Inspiration flooded my body as it had been doing in the days leading up to my visit, and I pulled my notepad and pen out of my bag and scribbled. When I finished, I exited my trance and realised that Sam was staring at me.

I laughed nervously and put my hand over my mouth. "Oh my God, what the hell is wrong with me? Sorry, Sam, you must think I'm incredibly rude, but this painting…" I stopped and gestured to all the paintings. "Every one of these paintings is magical, and I can feel the words throbbing behind my eyes and at the tip of my fingers. Seeing these makes me want to write a book." I stopped talking and took a breath. "Sorry." I shook my head. "I don't know what's got into me."

She put her finger over my lips and shook her head. "Please don't apologise. I'm flattered that you're taken with my work."

"Wait? You did these?"

She nodded.

"Oh, my word. I had no idea you were an artist and a writer slash director." I stopped talking again and frowned while I thought about it. "How come I didn't find anything about your art when I researched you?"

She smiled and chuckled. "I use a pseudonym."

I sighed and shook my head in wondrous disbelief. "Wow. Just wow. These are the most beautiful pieces I've ever seen."

"That might be the most genuine compliment I've ever received."

My cheeks grew hot when she looked at me and through me.

She pointed to my notepad. "Can I see what you wrote?"

I nodded. "Sure. Although I can't imagine my words doing your work any justice."

"I'll be the judge of that." She took the notepad from me and read aloud—much to my embarrassment.

She is buried under moonlight
Mockingbirds for stars
Victorian curls anchored by mangroves

Meanwhile
I dream in shades of lipstick
in a world built on moon rock -

This is not so much a border crossing
as it is a broader crossing
into subconscious iterations

The duality of self
blurred
at the edges

A polaraid of fate
oxidised by time

When she finished reading, she stared into my eyes with an intensity that rivalled our first meeting. "I researched you too, Bronte, and I remember reading an interview you did about *Wonderland* where you said that you weren't a poet."

I smiled wryly and shook my head. "It's true; I'm not a poet."

She tapped the notebook. "I can't do what you just did, and I'm a writer."

I touched my hot cheek with the back of my hand. "And I can't paint like this, so I guess we're even."

"Can I call you B?"

I nodded.

Her expression turned serious. "I don't want to overwhelm you because I know that we already have a lot on our plate with the memoir and the play. But I would love you to write a poem for each of my paintings. We could publish a book together, or organise a gallery exhibition. My art alongside your words. What do you think?"

"I would be honoured." I put my hand on my heart. "Truly honoured."

She smiled. "Good. Now, shall we get started on this screenplay?"

"Absolutely."

I followed her to the airy, light space of the writing room. The ocean was close enough to dive out of the window, and the walls were decorated with more of Sam's breathtaking art.

"I wasn't sure what would suit you best, so I arranged the best of both worlds." She pointed to a large white rectangular desk in the middle of the room. "We can work here when we're brainstorming, and I've set up individual desks for when we need to zone out and write like gangbusters."

"Sounds good to me."

"There's herbal teas, coffee, water and snacks over there, and I've organised caterers to deliver lunch at 1 p.m."

"You've thought of everything."

"Shall we get started?"

I nodded.

CHAPTER 52
Luther

April

After Bronte called me with her big news, I spent a week emptying my anger, pain, and relentless longing into a leather-bound journal. I wrote enough to fill a book, so I transcribed the words into word, formatted for print, designed a cover and published privately, for if and when I decided to contact Bronte. Then I deactivated my social media accounts and went to ground. The thought of Bronte discussing our polyamorous relationship with strangers and possibly speaking about it publicly terrified and angered me. Not that she would do that. But stardom is known to change people. The thought of my workmates finding out filled me with dread.

Mom silently admonished me with a nod of the head here and a shake of the head there when I declined to dish the dirt on my break-up. When I asked her why she had pushed me toward Bronte if she had known the outcome, she gave me her usual oracle-ish reply: *name one thing that can grow without stretching and splitting its skin a little?* I hit back and told her that I wasn't a python or a red balloon, but she only nodded and said she "hoped" I would get it one day in the future. I didn't visit or speak to her for months. Instead, I worked longer hours and devoted the remainder of my time to Addy.

Addy spent every second weekend with me, and I would count the days between like a child anticipating Christmas morning. Our Saturday ritual rarely changed. I woke up before dawn to make her blueberry pancakes, then we spent a few hours at the park and playground before returning home for lunch. Afternoons were spent reading, drawing, and writing poems. Would you believe that her favorite book was *Alice in Wonderland*? Yeah, I couldn't have planned it better myself. The story captivated her enough to ask if we could redecorate her room with an Alice in Wonderland theme. It filled me with joy and changed my perspective on the Alice-Bronte-quandary. Perhaps I had gotten the Alice thing all wrong. Wouldn't Alice better represent my dream daughter than my dream woman? The more I thought about it, the more it made sense.

After that conversation, and between her follow-up visit, I scanned the web for estate sales and planned to visit several antique stores for Wonderland memorabilia, when I stumbled upon a curious classified:

Why is a raven like a writing desk?

Call 988-5011 with your answer.

I stared at the ad for a while and blinked, convinced that I must be imagining it. I checked to ensure I was looking under the estate sale and auction section. I was. I dialled the number, expecting it to be a prank or an error, but a posh sounding man with a British accent answered after one ring and asked how he could help. I introduced myself and said I was inquiring about the ad.

"The raven?" he said.

"That's right."

"Well?" he prompted. "Why is a raven like a writing desk?"

I answered in the words of Hatter. "I haven't the slightest idea."

"Excellent, sir. May I ask about your interest in Alice?"

I told him about Addy and that Alice had been my favorite story since my mother read it to me as a child. He told me it would be best to see the items in person and suggested I visit first thing on Saturday morning.

"May I ask the price range? I'd hate to waste your time and embarrass myself."

"Money will not matter if you are the right buyer, sir."

I wasn't sure what he meant, but I was intrigued, to say the least. I agreed to an appointment on Saturday at 7.30 a.m.

I googled the address as soon as I hung up. The historic home was located in Charlestown—built in the early 1800s and admired for its aesthetics and grand architecture, but infamous for its history of slaves. Similar homes had become museums that were open to public tours. I wondered about the fate of the house I was visiting. Perhaps the death of the last matriarch had prompted her descendants to atone for their past and donate it to the state.

On Saturday morning, I parked on the tree-lined street and made a quiet entrance through the open gate. A sixty-some-thing-year-old butler opened the door before I reached for the brass knocker.

"Good morning, sir. Am I correct to assume that you are Luther?"

"Yes," I said, aware that my accent was far less posh than the help in this house, "you are correct."

He nodded his head. "Follow me, Luther." He gestured for me to walk inside.

I followed him across the heart pine floors and up the cantilevered staircase to the third floor where we took a right, walked to the end of the passage and stopped in front of an impossibly tall door. Instead of turning the handle, he turned to me and said, "This room held great sentimental value to the lady of the house, and nobody has been inside since she passed." I nodded my understanding, even though I had no idea what was going on. He placed a key in the lock and opened the door.

I followed him into the room and stood in awe for several seconds before I said, "Wow, I was not prepared for this."

The butler nodded.

"Do you mind if I have a look around?"

"Not at all, sir. I will wait for you on the landing."

"Thanks," I muttered, nodding and scanning the room like an owl. The space was a time capsule for Alice in Wonderland fans. From the red and white carpet embedded with an illustration of the red and white queens and their court guards, to the black and white tiled bathroom floor. On the walls, alcoves displayed the oversized tapestries that depicted an array of Wonderland characters—Alice holding a flamingo, the white rabbit with an eyeglass, Cheshire in a tree, the blue caterpillar smoking a hookah, the fish footman, and the dodo. A blue dress that looked remarkably like Alice's, hung in the closet, and a first edition of Alice's Adventures in Wonderland sat on the bedside table. Beyond the window, landscaped gardens revealed what looked like a maze and life-size chess set. A single bed in the left corner had a purple velvet headboard, and in the diagonal corner stood a grandfather clock. On closer inspection, the clock face was an image of Hatter. I opened the door and poked my head around the corner to see if the butler was still there. He stood in the same position, much like a Queen's guard.

"Do you mind if I ask what happened here? I mean, it's like I've entered a film set or time warp."

"Yes, sir, it's a sad story, sir." He joined me in the room and recounted the story of a woman whose first daughter had loved the story of Wonderland so much that they had recreated the magic for her at home. Sadly, the little girl had died of pneumonia at age six, and the mother had mourned her every day since. I thought of Lily-Rose and Addy, and understood.

"She locked the room and forbade anyone to enter, remove, or change anything," said the Butler. "Before the last matriarch's death, she bequeathed the contents of the child's room and her collection of books to me, for fear that her family would only sell her beloved items to the highest bidder."

"She obviously trusted you to do the right thing."

"Precisely, sir."

I told the butler the story about my mother reading Alice in Wonderland to me as a child, and how magical statues graced her garden.

He smiled and bowed his head. "There's more to see in the garden."

I followed him downstairs and out into the garden. In addition to the maze and the giant chessboard, Hatter's cottage had been recreated into a child's playhouse. Much like the mad hatter's tea party, teacups and cake trays adorned a child-sized table.

"I don't know what to say. This is the most magical place I have ever seen. It's a shame it's been hidden away all these years."

"My instructions are to organise a delivery for the right person. Will you be taking the lot, sir?"

"Wait, what? I couldn't possibly afford or house all of this."

"Like I said on the phone, money matters not for the right person. Sir."

"Are you telling me that you are giving this away?"

He nodded. "To the right person, sir, which you have assured me you are."

I shook my head. "I don't know what to say."

"You will be granting your daughter a wish, sir, and that is all the lady of the house wanted."

"I won't be able to take the outdoor items as I live in a condo."

"Does your mother have space, sir? I can arrange as many deliveries as you need."

I nodded. "I would need to speak to her first."

"I understand, sir. I'll take your address for the first delivery, and you can confirm the other details later."

"Okay, thank you."

"Follow me, sir."

I followed him inside and gave him my details. "It's not right to take all this without giving you something," I said. "You mentioned inheriting books too?"

"Yes, sir, a library full of books. Would sir like to buy some?"

I nodded. "Most definitely."

I followed him to the library, where he left me to browse. Floor to floor and wall to wall shelves were stacked with old books. Out of reach books were accessed with a sliding ladder. I started on the far left and worked my way around. The books were grouped by category—reference, fiction, non-fiction—and shelved alphabetically. The smell of books reminded me of Bronte. She would have loved this room. I thought of the day we spent book hunting in Boston. I had never been happier, and then I threw it all away. I moved to the B section and ran my fingers along the spines until I found what I was looking for: Brontë, Emily - Wuthering Heights. There were two copies: a pocket-size book with a blue hardcover; and a slightly larger edition with a red hardcover. Both titles were embossed in gold text. The thin, delicate paper was browned at the edges, unlike stiff, modern-day paper. I held each one to my nose and inhaled the scent of a bygone era, where polyamory had not tainted love. The truth is I had loved Bronte enough to try, but I loved her too much to continue. I closed my eyes and clutched the books against my heart. I had tried to shut out all the memories after our last conversation. That exquisite moment when she had walked into the hotel room in Brisbane. Nina singing about the wild wind in the background. Love surged like an electric current between us. Everything about her took my breath away. I opened my eyes again. The room was quiet, but my head had grown loud with guilty voices. I had been a coward and she deserved an explanation, but I wasn't sure if I'd ever be ready to admit that to her, never mind doing anything about it. I would buy the books for her, and maybe, one day in the future, I could use them to atone.

CHAPTER 53
Bronte

April

S am and I quickly fell into a comfortable writing rhythm after our first session in Malibu, reaching the final draft stage for both the screen and stage plays ahead of schedule. For our final editing session and optimal focus, Sam booked a three-night stay at an isolated lake cabin where there was little chance of interruption.

On the second night, after a day of writing, the full moon illuminated the lake like a wireless chandelier. We sat on the deck in recliners cradling steaming mugs of hibiscus tea between our palms and talked about life, love, and writing.

"Are you enjoying screenwriting, B?"

"I'm loving it so much that I don't want it to end."

"I thought as much. What about winemaking? Do you miss it?"

I shot her a look and shook my head.

"Tell me."

I looked into the distance and sighed. "Though I grew up on a winery, I never had any intention to become a winemaker's wife. Writing was my dream."

"Until the fire?"

I looked at her and nodded. "Yeah. I was exhausted by the time I met Aden." I stopped talking to swallow the lump in the throat, but my repressed emotions had finally broken the seal of denial and I started to sob. Sam squeezed my hand. "I'm sorry," I said.

"Don't be sorry. You've obviously been holding this in for too long. And if it's any consolation, you were destined to be more than a winemaker's wife."

I laughed and cried at the same time. Sam passed me a box of tissues. "Once upon a time I was single-minded about my dream to write, and I sometimes struggle with the fact that I settled for everything I never wanted." I turned to face her. "Don't get me wrong—I love my children—but in the process of marriage and motherhood, I lost my identity."

Sam's eyes were locked on mine, and she nodded for me to continue.

"When we lost Ghost Gum and Aden turned on me, the kindle of my old self started to rise from the ashes." My breath shuddered in the aftermath of tears, and I sipped the tea that had cooled.

"Enter Luther."

I sighed loudly. "Yeah. Now Luther is AWOL, and Aden's attraction to Jacqueline is growing by the day."

"Wait, what?"

"Nothing has happened yet, but it's definitely heading in that direction."

"How do you feel about that?"

"It's a strange sensation. One I'm not entirely comfortable saying out loud because of how I look."

"I'm not here to judge you."

I nodded. "I know, and I'm grateful to have someone to talk to." I stopped talking and sighed loudly. "I never had anyone to talk to about my marriage. I had a good friend, Priya, in Brisbane, but in-depth conversations were difficult due to the language barrier."

"I understand. Although I have a lot of a colleagues and acquaintances, I wouldn't trust them with my intimate secrets."

"Would you trust me?"

"I do trust you, B. From the moment I met you at Sheryl's, I had this weird sensation that I knew you from somewhere."

"I know what you mean."

"Tell me about Aden."

"I'm happy for him and relieved for myself."

She frowned. "Why relief?"

I fiddled with the handle of my teacup. "I think that Jacqueline is better suited to Aden than I am."

She nodded while computing my words. "I think I understand. Is that the real reason you persuaded him and Luther to try polyamory?"

I swallowed and nodded. "When I met Luther online and we connected so powerfully over our shared writing passion, I realised that Aden and I were more like partners and parents."

"Luther woke you up."

I nodded. "Exactly."

"And part of you started scheming up ways to dismantle

your conventional marriage."

I nodded again. "Yes. My God, that feels good to finally say out loud, but it doesn't do anything to lighten my guilt."

She swung her legs off the chair, stood and held her arms out to me. "Come here."

I stood. We hugged for a long time. Not wanting to cry, I focused on the owl hooting in the distance and tried to identify the exquisite scent that I had grown to love and expect from Sam. *A heady combination of hyacinth and rose water.*

She released me and held me at arm's length. "It's okay to cry, you know? It's unhealthy to keep all this inside and invalidate your feelings. Nobody expects you to be a saint or a martyr."

I nodded, and we sat. "Marriage expects it of me," I said, "and maybe that's the real reason why I've been scheming up ways to dismantle its power structure."

"Playing devil's advocate for a minute. What if Jacqueline wants more of Aden than polyamory allows?"

"I think you already know the answer to that question."

She nodded. "As we've waded into personal territory, I have another question for you. That tattoo on your lower back?"

"You've seen my tattoo?"

"I've glimpsed part of it. *She shall never know I love her...* what does the rest say?"

"*She shall never know I love her because she's more myself than I am.* It's a quote from *Wuthering Heights*."

"Hm-hmm, I'm familiar. If I recall, it's Catherine talking to Nelly about her feelings for Heathcliff."

"You know Wuthering Heights," I said. "One more thing to love about you."

Sam smiled. "Is the quote about someone you loved but couldn't love out in the open?"

I made eye contact with her and nodded. "I met her—Claudia—while I was studying my English degree. She was a foreign exchange student from Italy, and we hit it off. It was the first time that I'd ever experienced sexual attraction towards a woman. I don't know what it was like for you growing up in LA, but I grew up in a time and place where two women was not an option. Hetero was the gold standard that few deviated from. And those who did deviate were considered sick or perverted."

"I would imagine that Australia would have been worse than LA, but it still wasn't easy for me growing up. We live in a much more progressive time now. Thank the goddess."

"Amen to that!"

"What happened with Claudia? Did you ever tell her how you felt? Did you stay in touch?"

"No and no. I was planning to visit her in Italy after my graduate degree, but the fire interrupted my plans."

"And the tattoo?"

"I couldn't tell her how I felt at the time because I lacked social courage. The tattoo is my way of saying it and owning it after the fact, I guess."

"What are your thoughts on same-sex attraction now? If

you don't mind my asking."

"I'm not sure that I see people according to their sex, if you know what I mean?"

"I think I do. Tell me more."

"I think that I'm attracted to the person—their mind and their essence." I chuckled nervously. "I don't know—it probably sounds woo-woo, right?"

"I don't think it's woo-woo at all. I'm hanging on your every word at this point."

I smiled and blushed.

"Assuming I'm not misreading the signals..."

I interjected. "You're not misreading the signals, Sammy. I was attracted to you the minute you walked through Sheryl's door, but..."

"But what?"

"I wouldn't want romance to jeopardise my professional relationship with either you or Sheryl. The pair of you have moved mountains for me."

"I wouldn't want to jeopardise that either. What else?"

"I betrayed Aden by having an emotional affair with Luther behind his back, and I never want to do that again. If you're serious about this, I ask you to give me some time to discuss it with Aden and resolve things with Luther."

She reached for my hand and placed it over her heart. "I am serious, and I will give you as much time as you need."

We both leaned back in our chairs and watched the moonlight spill across the lake like skimming stones.

Hours later, after tossing and turning, I decided to text Luther. I put on my puffer jacket and fluffy socks and tiptoed outside to the porch. The thought of contacting him filled me with dread, but a bigger part of me needed to resolve the situation.

BRONTE: Remember me?

LUTHER: This is not a great time

BRONTE: I should have guessed. If not now, when?

LUTHER: Why now?

BRONTE: What do you mean, why now??!!

LUTHER: You've gone this long without texting

BRONTE: Oh, I see, we're back to playing that tired old game.

LUTHER: What do you want from me, Bronte?

BRONTE: I'd like to have a mature discussion (on the phone or FaceTime at the least) to talk about where we're at.

LUTHER: I think we said it all last time

BRONTE: Do you mean when I offered you an amazing opportunity to co-write a play with me and you said no and hung up? Are you so emotionally immature that you consider that conversation in some way ends or ties up the loose ends of our relationship?

LUTHER: As I said, I'm not like you. I made a mistake going along with your polyamory craziness. And btw, I'd appreciate it if you leave my name out of any public declarations you make in the future.

BRONTE: Public declarations? I would never do that, Luther! Do you not know me at all??!!

LUTHER: No, I don't know you, Bronte. I thought I did, but I didn't.

BRONTE: Polyamory aside, what about our friendship? How can you turn on me after everything we went through? I don't get it.

LUTHER: Just move on, Bronte. I have.

BRONTE: I can't bloody believe you, Luther.

I stared at the phone. He didn't reply. I half-wanted to smash the phone, and half wanted to text him every expletive in my vocabulary. But he wasn't worth it. Sam touched my shoulder.

"Is everything okay?"

I turned around to face her. Tears spilt onto my cheeks.

She held my face in her hands and pulled me into an embrace. "Luther?" she whispered in my ear.

I cleared my throat and sniffled. "It was like texting a child."

She held me at arm's length. "You mean he didn't talk to you on the phone?"

I pulled a tissue out of my pocket and blew my nose. "Nope, he said he'd already moved on and that I should do the same."

"You deserve better than that cowardly little fuck, my sweet."

My tears turned to laughter, and she took my hands in hers.

CHAPTER 54
Aden

April

Bronte and I were ships in the night for the first four months while we juggled our work schedules and shared parenting duties. Bronte spent three days a week in LA co-writing with Sam. When she was away, I took responsibility for the kids, and when she was in Napa, she would take over parenting duties. I didn't mind. After all, parenting had previously fallen squarely on Bronte's shoulders.

I spent a lot of time in Bronte's shoes during those months. Where I had struggled before to wrap my head around Bronte's intense physical and emotional attraction to Luther, I started to understand how she had connected with someone other than me. Someone who had fulfilled a need I couldn't. On the one hand, Jacqueline reminded me of Bronte—long dark hair, intellectual, open-minded, passionate. But beyond those similarities, she was different. Jacqueline was content to simply be. Bronte's head reminded me of an old grandfather clock that steadily ticked and tocked. She was always writing, even when she wasn't. Jacqueline was a hundred percent present, a hundred percent of the time. Like I had once had a calming effect on Bronte, Jacqueline had the same calming effect on me.

The weekend before Bronte started filming, our furniture arrived from Australia, and we had some much needed time together. We helped the kids unpack their boxes first. There was much oohing and aahing, having forgotten most of what they had packed. Tired and hungry by late Saturday afternoon, we ordered pizzas and called it a day. With the kids watching a DVD, Bronte and I sank into the hot tub with glasses of wine.

"I'd forgotten all about the ghost gum furniture. Thanks again for organising the shipment."

"You're welcome."

"Tell me all your news. We haven't had a proper conversation since Christmas."

"I know, it's been hectic."

"I don't know how you do it. You have a lot on your plate. Are you feeling the pressure or taking it in your stride?"

"The latter. The truth is I prefer to be busy."

"I'm proud of you, Bront."

"Thanks. I'm proud of you too. Is it divine to be back amongst the vines?"

"Dream come true. I am blessed."

She raised her glass. "Cheers to us."

I clinked her glass. "Cheers."

She sipped her wine and leaned over to restart the jets. "I finally contacted Luther, and we are officially over."

"You spoke to him?"

"Well, technically, I texted him because he refused to

phone or FaceTime."

"Seriously? After everything we've been through?"

"Sam says he's a coward."

"She's not wrong there. Are you upset?"

"I'm disappointed with him. I mean, how does someone do a one-eighty so quickly?"

"I don't know. The guy's never made much sense to me."

"M-hmm."

We both fell silent for a moment.

"How are things with Jacqueline?"

"I'm not sure. I'm not good at reading the signals."

"But you like her?"

My smile answered her question.

"Have you told her about our agreement?"

"Not yet."

"Then I would start there and see where it leads."

I was going to voice my doubts about continuing on the polyamorous path, but she spoke first.

"And while we're being honest, I find myself in a similar situation with Sam, but nothing has happened."

"Bronte, Bronte, Bronte. What am I going to do with you?!"

"I don't know. All I know is that the world and her infinite possibilities are finally opening up for both of us, and I don't want the unnatural restrictions of some antiquated institution hindering us from pursuing our own paths and desires."

I nodded and tried to make light of it. "Between you and me, I'd much rather share you with Sam, haha."

"If you have reservations, speak now or forever hold your peace."

"I will say one thing."

"What?"

"Does it give you pause that I'm attracted to another woman?"

"If Luther hadn't happened, definitely. But we agreed to give each other leeway when our individual paths demanded it."

"I hope you know I still love and adore you?"

She leaned over and kissed me. "I love you too."

After Bronte went to bed, I took a few moments to stargaze while her news washed over me. *The end of Luther,* I thought and smiled. Beyond their writing connection, I had never understood what Bronte had seen in him. On the other hand, I was grateful to him because he had been a huge catalyst for change in my relationship with Bronte and our lives in general. The fact that he couldn't, or didn't want to, embrace change told me all I needed to know about him. There was a time when I had hoped Bronte would outgrow him and simultaneously feared she would eventually leave me for him. I was relieved to finally put both scenarios to bed and contemplate a future without him. If Bronte was ultimately seeking a challenging and rewarding writing partnership, Sam was far more qualified for the job. *But what if she is seeking more?*

I thought to myself. I didn't know how to feel, and I wasn't ready to seriously entertain the thought.

CHAPTER 55
Luther

May

The Alice consignment arrived before Addy's weekend stay. Fortunately, my condo had high ceilings, so the scale of the tapestries made the room look more grand than overcrowded. When Addy saw her room, she held her breath so long I had to remind her to breathe. To say she was enthralled would be the understatement of the decade. She said she never wanted to leave and would rather live with me than Tina, which broke my heart and tore the fabric of my world. In those moments, I considered making amends with Tina to be with Addy all the time. I thought about Bronte. She had found a way to have her cake and eat it. I don't know how she did it. Tina would never have agreed to what Aden did. In many ways, I wished Tina had agreed to it. Like Bronte, I would have been able to stay with my daughter during the years she needed me most.

With the outdoor Alice furniture at Mom's, I took Addy and her BFF around on Saturday afternoon to have a Mad Hatter tea party. The girls played chess as soon as we arrived, and Mom laid out strawberry cupcakes, sandwiches, and glasses of milk for them inside the playhouse. While they chatted and ate, Mom and I sat in the garden and drank tea.

"Are you going to tell me what happened with you and Bronte?"

"I thought you already knew, oh wise one."

"Don't be snarky, Luther."

"She was talking about movie producers and contracts, and she asked me to co-write a stage play with her about polyamory."

She put down her teacup and held up her hand. "Wait, she asked you to co-write a play with her? As in a Broadway play?"

"Yeah, it was the movie producer's idea."

"And you said no?"

"Yeah, I took the advice of her Justice card and defaulted to my rational Capricorn self."

"You mean you chickened out?"

"Pfft." I lit a cigarette.

"Did Bronte walk away, or did you?"

"I did."

"Why?"

"Because I freaked out, okay, Mom?! I was envious of her success and her talent. I realized I'd never be her priority, and I decided I'd had enough."

"Did you tell Bronte any of what you've just told me, or did you shut her down and shut her out like you do everybody else?"

I took a long drag of my cigarette, then flicked the ash into the ashtray, and exhaled smoke rings. "I'm your son, Mom, and you should be standing up for me, not her."

She nodded and furrowed her brows but didn't speak immediately. She looked like she was chewing on something.

"Are you gonna say anything?"

"Do you think you were envious of more than her success, Luther?"

"Meaning?"

"Are you envious of the relationship with her husband?"

"Are you a mind reader now too?"

"Is that a yes?"

"I can't get one person to love me as much as Aden loves her. But somehow Bronte manages to find two people to love her like no other."

Mom sighed loudly. "She did love you that much, Luther. Much more than Tina ever did or ever could. But you punished her for her circumstances."

"So it's all my fault, is what you're saying?"

"No, Luther, that's not what I'm saying. I'm trying to help you see that you're not the victim you make yourself out to be. Aden's love for Bronte is a testament to real love. When the going got tough, he didn't give up and run away. He stood his ground and fought. You could have done the same, but you chose not to."

"Love shouldn't be that complicated, Mom."

"Like you and Tina?"

"Can we just drop it, Mom?"

"Okay, Luther, I won't mention Bronte again." She stood. "Tell the girls I have a surprise for them."

I watched her walk away like a cloud, much like the day of Addy's fourth birthday party, feeling the same way I did then and thinking the same thought—*Mom is right; when are you going to listen to her advice?*

CHAPTER 56
Bronte

May

After five months of intensive co-writing sessions sitting opposite Sam, our words were jumping off the page in the quiet wings of a film set. We were wrapping up the last scene of the day, during our first week of filming, and meeting up with the cast for drinks later in the evening. Sam squeezed my hand before she said the words: *And, action.* As the actress spoke words from my life, I thought back to when I was travelling around Australia with little more than a weak sense of adventure and wondering how my life would ever come together. If someone had told me I would end up here, on a Hollywood film set, sharing professional space with an amazingly creative and talented woman like Sam, I would have thought it impossible—more impossible than the situation with Luther. Yet, here I was; screen and stage plays in the bag, starting a six-month film shoot for *Flammable,* writing poems to accompany Sam's paintings for an upcoming exhibition, shopping around my murder mystery book series as well as writing my second poetry book.

And, cut.

Sam's voice brought me back to the scene at hand. While our relationship had remained purely professional after our conversation at the cabin, my attraction to her had grown.

"Wanna grab dinner before we meet everyone for drinks?"

I nodded. "Sounds good, but I need to phone Aden and

the kids first."

She looked at her phone. "Is two hours enough?"

"Plenty."

"Okay, I'll pick you up at 8."

"Okay."

She turned to leave.

"Sam?"

"Yes, my sweet?"

"Thank you for changing my life."

She winked and blew a kiss. "See you soon."

Back in my hotel room, I ran a hot bubble bath and phoned Aden.

"Hey, Bront, how's it going?"

"It's good to hear your voice, Ade."

"Work going alright?"

"Oh, yeah, work couldn't be better. The first week of filming is done and dusted, which is amazing and surreal. I still have to pinch myself most days."

"I know what you mean. Are you still coming home tomorrow?"

"Yeah, of course."

"Listen, Bront, I don't want to be rude, but I'm over at

Jacqueline's for dinner."

"Oh, right. Shit, sorry for interrupting. Are the kids with you?"

"No, they're at that movie marathon birthday party. I'll pick them up later."

"Oh, yeah, I forgot all about that. You better get back to Jacqueline. What's for dinner?"

"Coq au vin."

"Aah, your favourite!"

"You know me so well."

"Have you had the talk with her yet?"

"No, but I think tonight might be the night. What about you and Sam? Anything to report?"

"No, nothing yet."

"Are you still sure about this?"

"Yes, Ade, go and enjoy yourself, and I look forward to having a long talk tomorrow."

"Love you."

"Love you too."

Sam knocked on the door of my hotel suite at eight sharp. Her blunt haircut looked freshly styled, and she wore dark blue jeans and a sheer black top with a lacy black bra underneath.

I kissed her on each cheek. "Mmm, you smell like hyacinth and rose."

"It's called *Live in Love* by Oscar de la Renta."

Her sultry smile never failed to stir the butterflies in my stomach. "Come in," I said, stepping aside. "Do you want a drink before we go? I have champagne."

"I never turn down a glass of bubbly."

I winked at her. "A woman after my own heart."

"Did you enjoy your first week of filming?"

I hit play on a newly curated acoustic playlist and handed her the glass of bubbly. "Enjoy is a huge understatement." We sat next to each other on the turquoise chaise at the foot of the four-poster bed.

She sipped her champagne and grinned. "There's something on your mind, I can tell."

I kept eye contact with her while I took a sip. "Did you mean what you said at the cabin?"

"Every word. Did you?"

I took her glass and put it on the table with mine. "I did," I said, kneeling in front of her. She opened her legs, and I leaned in to kiss her. Gently at first, my lips brushing against hers, my fingers caressing her thighs. She pulled the butterfly clip from my hair, and my curls cascaded around my shoulders and down my back. Our lips parted, and our tongues joined like serpents. She tasted like spearmint and honey. Pheromones flooded every inch of my body. Our tongues grew more urgent, twisting together like vines and licking each other like flames in a fire pit. She inched off the chair

and tried to take the lead by unbuttoning my jeans and strad-
dling me on the floor, but I manoeuvred myself to straddle
her instead.

"You said you would wait for me," I said, between kisses,
"and I want to show you that I'm happy you did."

She pressed her palms into mine and clasped my fingers.
"Only if you promise to let me have my way with you afterwards."

I answered her with a kiss before moving onto my haunches and standing up. She took my outstretched hand, and I
pulled her up and toward me into another passionate embrace. Before we reached the bed, I clasped both of her hands
in mine and pressed her against the wall. "Mmm, I've been
dreaming of kissing you since the day we met," I murmured.
"Mmmm, Me too." I slipped my hands under her top and
explored her creamy skin until I reached the clasp of her bra
and unhooked it. She lifted her arms to let me pull off her
shirt and bra. My lips moved from her mouth to her neck
and lingered on her beautiful collarbone before they found
her breasts. While I licked and gently sucked her nipples, my
hands unbuttoned her jeans and pulled them under her hips.
I slid my right hand inside her black lace panties; her pussy
was so wet. She lifted my chin. Our lips locked once again—
tongues dancing and intertwining like stringed instruments
in a climactic piece of music. In between breaths, we moved
to the bed. I pulled her jeans off and stroked her inner thighs
at first, followed by the curve of her bum and around to her
pussy. While I stroked and rubbed her clit with my fingers,
I kissed a slow path down her ribcage, torso, tip of her hip
bones, until my mouth found her pussy, and my tongue took

over from my fingers. And instead of feeling like I had a load-ed gun in my mouth, like every blow job from my past, Sam's pussy felt like home—the petals of a beautiful flower opening like a river daisy at first light. She gripped a lock of my hair and pulled as her back arched, and she gasped in pleasure and moaned my name.

I left her on the bed to fetch our champagne flutes. When I turned around, Sam stood behind me.

"You're still fully dressed. We're gonna have to remedy that."

I handed her the bubbly. "Drink first."

We both sipped. Sam placed the glasses on the coffee table and led me to the bed with her hand. With my spine pressed against the bed poster, she began to undress me, slow and seductive, one item at a time. When I stood naked before her, she held my hips and kissed me with a hungry urgency, while leading me backwards. On the bed, she opened my legs and gripped my hips to pull me closer to her. My bum was close to the edge of the bed, and my feet were on her shoulders while she kissed my pussy like no man ever had. I didn't need to give her instruction or draw her a map, she instinctively knew where and when to touch, caress, kiss, suck, and lick me. I'd had orgasms before, all with Aden after years of ex-perimenting, but not like this. This was something else—an altered state with senses heightened; connected to Sam like a plug in an electric socket. I knew that sex would never be the same again.

Hours later, with our limbs intertwined beneath Egyptian cotton sheets in the four-poster bed, my cheeks burned hot from pleasure, and my body felt the most satisfied it had ever been.

"I'm glad I waited."

"If I died right now, it would be in pure contentment."

She leaned on her elbow and kissed me. "Don't die yet, my sweet. I want to do this again and again and again with you."

CHAPTER 57
Aden

May

One Friday evening, when Bronte was on set in LA, and the kids were at a movie-marathon party with their friends, Jacqueline invited me to her home for a French meal. When I walked through her picket-fenced entrance, I was met with the heady smell of lavender and rosemary. When she opened the door, the house smelled like a French Bistro.

I handed her a bottle of Granite Belt Shiraz. "Bonsoir."

She kissed me on one cheek and then the next. "Salut chéri. J'espère que tu aimes le coq au vin and l'escargots?"

I nodded. "Bien sur. Coq au vin is my favourite."

"Merveilleux." She clapped her hands and turned her attention to pouring two glasses of chilled Sancerre.

I took my glass. "Merci."

"On y va," she said with a wave of her hand, "we look at ze vines before the sky gets dark."

I followed her outside into the back garden, where she had planted neat rows of young Petite Sirah and Cabernet Franc grapevines.

"Have you stashed barrels somewhere?" I said.

"Mais oui. I have oak barrels in my basement."

I smiled. "Of course you do."

While she talked about her plans to experiment with the

vines, I didn't take in much of what she said because her passion for wine and grapes rendered me lightheaded. Ever since our arrival at Napa, Jacqueline and I had spent long days outside, beneath the Californian sun, our fingers alive in the rich, loamy soil, enjoying lengthy conversations about winemaking and Top Ten regions we wanted to visit.

We were about to go inside for dinner when my phone buzzed.

"Sorry, Jacqueline, I better take this quickly, it's Bronte."

She waved her hand. "Pas de probléme, chéri. Take your time."

Jacqueline was pouring two glasses of Veuve Cliquot when I joined her at the dining room table.

"Sorry, Jacqueline."

She handed me the glass of bubbles. "Pas de probléme." She cocked her head to one side and eyed me. "You look different? Something has made you happy?"

Her blue eyes shimmered like water in the candlelight. The twinge I'd felt between the vines turned into an urge of longing and unbridled passion for a woman other than my wife. A woman who shared my passion for wine. A woman who could tap into an integral part of my soul and heart in a way that Bronte wasn't able to. And at that moment I understood what had happened between Bronte and Luther. And I felt overwhelming love for Bronte, for bringing me to a place of openness and love. And I felt pain for letting my ego stop her from following her heart. If it wasn't for Bronte, I might never have reached the place where I found myself with Jacqueline. A place where I could love without borders, and without the chains of jealous possession or ownership.

"Come, sit and tell me while we eat dinner."

"Sounds good." I sat opposite her at the round table. The setting took me back to a little French bistro that mum and dad took me to when I was a child. The white tablecloth, a small vase containing a bunch of wild flowers from Jacqs' garden, and a long red candle set with wax inside an old wine bottle. In the background, French music drifted through the cottage like a gentle breeze.

We talked while we ate. I told her the whole story about losing the winery, about Bronte and Luther and our poly-amorous arrangement. When I moved on to the latest news about Luther and Sam, she listened without judgement and shared her thoughts about relationships, which was quint-essentially French—laissez-faire. After we'd talked our way through dinner and dessert, Jacqueline took my hand and led me outside to the edge of the vines, where she had laid out a king-size picnic blanket made of green silk and embossed with a golden tree.

She pointed to the gramophone handle. "Can you, how do you say?" She gestured a winding motion with her hand?"

"Wind up the gramophone?" I said.

"Aah, oui, wind up, s'il te plâit, chéri."

"What a beaut. Did you bring this with you from France?"

"Oui, it was a gift from Papa when I was a girl."

I waited for Jacqueline to place the vinyl onto the turntable before I cranked the handle. The record slowly started to spin. Jacqueline unfurled and readied the needle and then voilá, the upbeat sound of *When Summer is Gone* travelled up into the night sky and echoed through the vines. I took Jacqueline's hand and asked her to dance. She was less than an inch shorter than me, and her cheek was warm against mine. She smelled like cherry blossoms and hummed along to the music as our feet moved in sync. When the track finished, Jacqueline played something slower and more romantic—the sound of a French accordion changing the mood, like a car switching gears. I touched Jacqueline's face; we French kissed, and as our kisses grew more urgent, we sank to our knees. I cradled her head beneath my arm; her dark hair cascaded all around. The way she looked at me was intoxicating. I wasn't sure if Bronte had ever looked at me that way before; she certainly hadn't looked at me that way after we lost the winery. My previous belief that a relationship's history was the bee-all-and-end-all came under scrutiny; it seemed that a clean slate held as much, if not more, power. Had Bronte experienced the same with Luther? He saw her as a writer; I had seen her as a wife and mother. None of it made me love Bronte any less. I appreciated her more. Not many wives, if any, would have given me the gift that Bronte had given me. Most couples faced with questions of infidelity ended up in divorce. I lost myself after that, surrendering like a wave in the Pacific Ocean, and only resurfaced after our bodies climaxed and the gramophone needle went thump, thump, thump.

CHAPTER 58
Bronte

May

Ireturned to an empty home the following day and found a note addressed to me on the fridge.

Dear Bront,

I've had an emergency at work and had to leave the kids with Jacqueline. Please don't be angry. I couldn't organise anything else at such short notice. I told Jacqs you would pick them up as soon as you got in.

I love you and look forward to having a good old chat when I see you tonight.

All my love,
Ade xoxo

I put my bags in the bedroom and drove straight to Jacqueline's house, where I met with the enchanting sound of French music, animated talk, and laughter. Faced with a closed front door, I tiptoed past to the window, not wanting to disturb them and with a teeny desire to eavesdrop. The adjacent floor to ceiling window offered a clear view through the open-plan cottage into the kitchen where Jacqueline was baking with the kids. Jacqueline looked like a snow queen, with a wooden spoon in one hand and flour-dusted hair. She spoke in broken English as she read out the English recipe—for chocolate cake, I gathered. Every so often, she paused and repeated a word as if it was a question, and either Leyla or Liam would correct her. After which, the three of them would peal with laughter. I watched them, for a few minutes, with a smile on my face and in my heart. For years I had mothered those kids—or smothered them—and wished my mother had been around to help out during my moments of emotional exhaustion. To see Jacqueline interacting with Leyla and Liam, and vice versa, filled my heart with so much joy I couldn't contain the tears. I moved away from the window and leaned up against the white wall. After Aden's dad died and Aden withdrew into his angry shell, I had struggled with the burden that Liam and Leyla had no extended family. We had no proverbial village to help us raise our children, which is why Priya was such a godsend in so many ways. I wiped my eyes and peeped in the window again. Emotional relief washed over me as I watched Leyla and Liam with Jacqueline. Polyamory had given us much more than romantic partners; it had helped us form our own village.

Lost in my own world, I fished in my bag and took out a tissue to blow my nose. Jacqueline caught a glimpse of me through the window. She must have misinterpreted my expression as anger, upset, or jealousy because a look of concern replaced her smile, and she straightened her spine as if she were a teacher who had been caught by the headmistress teaching unconventional methods.

She opened the door. "Oh lo lo. Je m'excuse Bronte."

"Non, non, Jacqueline, these are happy tears." I wrapped my arms around her and embraced her until Leyla and Liam joined us.

"Don't worry about my mum," said Leyla, "she is happy crying."

I let go of Jacqueline and smiled at her. "Merci for being kind to Leyla and Liam."

"Aah, c'est mon plaisir. You promise you are okay?"

She stepped back and studied me. She was about an inch taller than me without heels, which could have triggered an inferiority complex, but it didn't. Jacqueline was like a tree of love—not a single leaf of agenda or branch of ulterior motive.

"I promise I'm okay."

"Can I make you a tea, Bronte? We can sit and talk while ze cake bakes, and ze kids can play in ze garden."

I nodded. "Yes, please. I'd like that."

CHAPTER 59
Aden

June

When Bronte worked in LA, she stayed in hotels or with Sam and often complained that Leyla and Liam couldn't go with her. So, when she approached me about buying a house in LA as an early birthday present for herself, I supported her all the way. With Sam's help and connections, we narrowed down the area to West Hollywood and organised a day out together to view several properties. Bronte fell in love with the third house—a 1920s Spanish beauty in Beverly Grove. In addition to being vacant and ready for immediate occupancy, it had everything on Bronte's wish list—bedrooms for Leyla and Liam, security, vaulted French doors, built-in bookcases, decorative staircase rails, chandeliers, private courtyard, landscaped garden, alfresco dining area, and a lap pool. She made an offer above the asking price, and the owner accepted later that day.

I left the winery in Jacqueline's capable hands when Bronte moved in the following weekend to spend quality time with her and the kids. In the morning, we went on a wild furniture shopping spree. For the first time in both our lives, we shopped without looking at price tags and let the kids choose whatever they wanted for their bedrooms. Exhausted on Saturday night, after placing each piece of furniture, unpacking every box, shelving every book, and hanging every piece of artwork, we ordered pizzas for the kids and Chinese takeout for ourselves. The kids had barely finished dinner when they crashed on the sofa. Bronte carried Liam, and I carried Leyla up to bed.

Outside in the courtyard, we lit an array of candles and poured glasses of port.

"What a week," said Bronte, "I still have to pinch myself every day to make sure this is all real."

I swirled the port in my glass and nodded. "Same here, Bront, our lives were predictable after we lost Ghost Gum. Now, look at us."

"It's been ages since we had a proper conversation."

"Let's make up for it tonight. Have you heard any more from Luther?"

"Nope."

"You don't sound particularly sad about it?"

"I think he's a coward and I've grown indifferent about the whole affair."

"Maybe you've outgrown him?"

"Not maybe; definitely."

"Will you contact him again?"

She shook her head. "There's no need. If love is a drug, consider Luther purged from my system."

"Wow. I never thought I'd see the day."

"Me neither. But here we are." She downed her port. "Want a refill?"

I handed her my glass. "Please."

She popped the lid from the glass decanter and topped

our glasses.

"Have you changed your mind about polyamory?"

She settled back down on the sofa and faced me. "In what sense?"

"We don't have sex anymore, for one. We've become ships in the night, only meeting and talking to discuss the kids."

"I didn't think you wanted to have sex with me anymore. This may sound weird, but I didn't want to get between you and Jacqueline."

I met her gaze and sighed. "Okay, let me rephrase. Would you still want to have sex with me if Jacqueline wasn't in the picture?"

She took her feet off the table, stood and faced me. I looked up at her. She slipped the spaghetti straps off her shoulders and let her dress fall to her feet. "I could ask you the same thing."

She unzipped my jeans, pulled them off and straddled me on the sofa. "Stop being polite and take me already." She kissed me with a passion I'd never experienced before, biting my lip and digging her nails into my back as I thrust into her like a wolf driven wild by the full moon.

The kids woke us up in the morning by opening the blinds and squeezing in between us. Bronte propped up her pillows and sat up. "Good morning, my darlings. Did you sleep well?"

"Yes, Mum," said Leyla. "Did you?"

"I did, thank you."

"What are we doing today?" said Liam.

"You tell us," I said. "What do you really, really, really want to do today?"

"I want to get my ears pierced," said Leyla. "My friend Ruby said it stings for a second but then it's fine."

Bronte kissed Leyla on the top of her head. "Earrings it is."

"Thanks, Mum."

I ruffled Liam's hair. "What about you, buddy?"

"I want to go to a Justin Bieber concert."

I looked at Bronte, and we both laughed. "Liam, honey, Justin doesn't have a concert on today, but we will book tickets for the next one, okay?"

He pulled a face and said, "Okay," followed by a huge sigh.

"What's number two on your list?" I said.

"What about mini-golf and ice cream?"

"Mini golf and ice creams it is." I put my hand up in the air and we high fived.

Bronte got out of bed. "First, Mummy needs a shower and coffee."

I stood too. "How about you have a shower and let me make the coffee?"

"No arguments from me," she said.

"What time are we going, Mum?"

"As soon as we're all dressed, Ley."

Leyla stood and pulled Liam's pyjama top. "Come on,

Liam, the sooner we get dressed, the sooner we can go."

Bronte chuckled and said, "Don't forget to brush your teeth," as they left the room.

"We won't," they chimed.

Bronte laughed and joined me at the foot of the bed. "Justin Bieber and ear-piercing; our children are growing up."

I was about to reach for her hand when her phone buzzed on the dresser. She walked over and picked it up. I saw her expression in the mirror. Her face lit up.

"Who is it?" I said.

"Text from Sam," she said, reading the message with a smile.

"Good news?"

"Hmmm?" She said absentmindedly while typing a reply.

"Good news, Bront?"

She looked up from her phone, and for a second she seemed light years away. "Oh," she said, realising she'd checked out on me. "She's sent an invite for my birthday at an undisclosed location and wants to know who and what my favourite music artist/album is at the moment?"

"Sounds intriguing."

She raised her eyebrows and nodded.

"Out of curiosity, what is your favourite album at the moment?"

"Halsey's *Room 93* and *Badlands*."

"I used to know those things."

She walked back over to me. "How about we pick up the conversation we left off last night when this busy day is over?"

"Sounds good."

She stood on her tiptoes, held my shoulders, and kissed me once on each cheek. "Me too."

After a long day out, followed by dinner and a Netflix movie, the kids crashed in their beds while Bronte and I claimed our new favourite spot outside in the courtyard. An L-shaped midnight blue sofa hugged the white wall, and a gothic-looking chandelier lit the space. Beyond the arches of the covered alcove, the courtyard space resembled a secret garden with its tall hedges, creeping ivy, and potted palms. Bronte had lit a rose-scented candle and picked an acoustic playlist from Apple Music. The ambient vocals and instrumental sounds danced in rhythm with the flickering flame. Light and shadow on the bare walls created a textured wallpaper effect.

I sipped my wine. "I can picture you sitting out here writing."

Bronte nodded and smiled. "Mmm, it's dreamy out here."

"It's your birthday soon, and I have no idea what to buy the woman who has everything."

Bronte sipped her port. "You don't need to buy me anything."

"But I want to treat you."

"How about I think about it and get back to you?"

I nodded. "Fair enough. But don't take too long."

We sat in comfortable silence for a several seconds before I spoke again. "Do you think we've broken our marriage, Bront?"

She met my gaze and frowned while she thought about it. "I don't think we've broken marriage, I think marriage is broken. Like the school system and the government, marriage is an antiquated institution."

I shook my head. "Maybe. I'm not convinced."

"Tell me what's on your mind? We're supposed to be honest, remember?"

I nodded. "Are you sleeping with Sam?"

The first song had ended, and the next began. The sad notes of an acoustic guitar and the gentle sound of lapping waves ebbed between us. She nodded. "I never said anything because I assumed you knew."

"I suspected. But I wanted to hear it from you."

"Does it bother you?"

"Not like Luther."

"Because she's a woman?"

"Not at all. You forget that I never liked or approved of how you and Luther got together."

"I'm sorry, Ade."

"You don't have to apologise. You asked, I answered."

She nodded.

"What's it like?"

She frowned in confusion. "What's what like?"

"Sex with Sam."

"Oh!" she chuckled. "Let's just say I'm experiencing something of a sexual renaissance."

"I had a glimpse last night."

"Haha. How are things going with you and Jacqs?"

I nodded and took a sip of my drink. "Well, I think."

"You think? Why? Has something happened?"

"I'm not sure. Something feels off, but I don't know what it is."

"I take it you haven't discussed it with her?"

I shook my head.

"Why not? What's holding you back?"

"Do you want me to be honest with you, Bront?"

"I expect nothing less."

"If I had known things were going south with Luther, I might not have let myself go with Jacqs. But now that I have, I think she wants more than polyamory can give her."

She shifted in her seat. "Wasn't that the point of polyamory all along? To let ourselves go and allow love to be what it is—free of borders and outdated religious rules?"

"You and I both know that the reality of love and emotion is far more complicated than your romanticised theory."

She had a faraway expression while she twirled a strand of hair.

"We aren't a married couple anymore. We're like divorced

parents. I'm in Napa, you spend most of your time in LA, and the kids come and go between us. Spending time together as a family this weekend and making love to you last night gave me a glimpse into how much I miss normality. There was a moment this morning when I was going to propose that we try again as a normal married couple, but..."

"But?"

"I saw your face when Sam texted. It took me back to the day in Sandgate when I saw you texting Luther. I knew then that I'd have to decide—one way or another."

She put her head in her hands and shook it from side to side. "I don't think I can apologise again without sounding trite, but I am sorry, my God, I'm sorry."

I swallowed back the lump in my throat and put my arms around her shoulders. "I don't want you to apologise; I want you to love me one hundred percent or release me to someone who can."

Her shoulders heaved and shook as she began to cry and then sob into her hands. I patted her back. "Bront, it's okay." But the tears kept coming. She bent over and buried her face between her knees. I put my arms around her and held her tight while her emotions ran their course. I don't know what I was expecting, but it wasn't this reaction. Again, I had a flashback to the night of my homecoming from Dubai when she sobbed mid-orgasm. I couldn't understand why she was so sad. It was only later when I put the pieces together that I realised it was due to Luther. She had lost Luther because she was married to me, and she didn't want to be. The knowledge that I had grown to accumulate since that night had taught me something about Bronte that I had wanted to bury instead of confront—it wasn't that Bronte was unhappy with marriage; Bronte was unhappy with me. The text from Sam that morning had forced me to confront that truth.

"I need to know something, Bront."

She tried to compose herself before she looked at me. "What's that?"

"Were you happy before we lost Ghost Gum? Did you ever truly love me?"

She put her arms around me and cried again. "I'm so sad, Ade. Sad that I am responsible for all of this. Of course, I was happy. Of course, I loved you. But you need to understand that I buried a part of myself after the fire, and after we lost Ghost Gum that buried fragment started to rise up like a phoenix and wouldn't let go."

I could have been angry with Bronte. Maybe I should have been angry. But I wasn't. She had allowed me to reach that moment of understanding in my own time. In retrospect, I was the one who had insisted on it.

"Don't be sad, Bront. We did everything we could, let nature take its course, and ended up here—in a place of more loving openness than I ever thought possible. And for what it's worth, I think that Sam will be a far better partner to you in the long run."

She released me from the hug and leaned back in her seat. "I haven't discussed the future with Sam."

I held her hand. "Maybe now you can."

She nodded and cried again. "What about the kids?"

I hugged her again. "The kids will be fine. We've raised them to be balanced and confident, and we won't be fighting over them or forcing them to split their time between us. We'll talk to them, and do what's best. Okay?"

She pulled away and blew her nose. "What about their school? The dust of our move has barely settled and they've made friends. I don't want to disrupt them again."

"The kids are resilient, Bront, and judging by their answers this morning—a Justin Bieber concert and ear-piercing—you may find that they are happy to live with you in LA."

Bronte laughed despite herself and held my hands in hers. "Promise me that our friendship will survive."

I turned over her palms and kissed each one. "My love for you is eternal. You are the mother of my children and the best friend I've ever had. Nothing can change that unless you choose."

Her face contorted and she broke down again.

CHAPTER 60
Bronte

July

I thought I would miss the southern hemisphere, having spent all my life there. And while I did miss seeing the moon and its bunny ears right side up and hearing the contagious laughter of kookaburras, the northern hemisphere blessed me with a summer birthday and summer holidays with Leyla and Liam.

With Sam planning to take me out on the night of my birthday, Aden agreed to babysit. Before he arrived in the afternoon, the kids and I spent the morning baking a triple layer chocolate cake. We were seated on bar stools at the kitchen counter and measuring out ingredients when the intercom buzzed. "Hang on a sec, you two. Somebody is at the door."

The courier showed me where to sign and handed me a luxurious looking black box.

"Is it fragile?" I said.

He shrugged and said, "Don't think so."

I closed the door, placed the box in my study, and returned to the kitchen, hoping the kids hadn't started a food fight or worse. Alas, the air was snowing with flour, and a layer of raw sugar coated the marble bench top.

Hours later, with baking complete, cake slices consumed, and a clean kitchen, I took a knife and dragged it along the edges of the box. Inside, I found a black silk evening dress, a blind-fold, and a card from Sam.

Wear this tonight xoxo

The doorbell sounded again. Aden stood in the doorway holding a bunch of balloons and a gift the size of a painting. He leaned down and kissed me on the cheek. "Happy birth-day, Bront."

I stepped aside to let him in. "Thanks, Ade." I peered out-side, expecting to see Jacqueline smelling the hanging potted flowers or admiring the architecture. But she was nowhere in sight. I closed the door and searched for Aden. He had tied the balloons to a kitchen barstool and leaned the gift against the island. Leyla and Liam were talking a thousand miles a second, so I sat on a barstool and waited until they had exhausted themselves of every story and update they could think of. When they finally came up for air, Aden spoke before I could.

"Hey kids, why don't we let Mum open her present?"

They both grabbed a side and lifted it off the ground.

"Careful not to drop it," said Aden. "It's fragile."

"I never followed up about the present," I said.

"Not to worry. I thought of something on my own." He took the gift from Leyla and Liam and placed it on the floor in front of me. "Open it."

"Shall we open it for you," Leyla and Liam said in sync.

I laughed. "Thanks, kids, but I can handle it."

They all watched as I tore the gift paper and wiped a tear from the corner of my eye. It was a family photo, blown up to poster size, and framed in an ornate gold frame.

"Do you like it, Bront?"

I stood and hugged him. "I love it. I couldn't ask for anything better than this."

He hugged me back. "I'm glad."

"Will you help me find a place to hang it up?" I said.

"Of course."

Liam tapped Aden on the leg. "Daddy, will you come and jump on the trampoline with us when you're finished?"

"You bet. Give me ten minutes, okay?"

"Okay." He took Leyla's hand and ran out of the kitchen.

Aden picked up the photo. "Any ideas where you wanna hang it?"

I stood, "Yeah, there's a spot out here in the entrance hall."

"Have you got any hooks and a hammer?"

"I do." I crossed the kitchen and pulled out a box of hooks, a mini hammer, and a pencil.

"Lead the way."

He followed me to the hall and I showed him where I wanted to hang it. "I was expecting you to bring Jacqueline."

Aden was marking the spot with a pencil. "Yeah, sorry about that. Jacqs is resting in the hotel room."

"Is she okay?"

He nodded while hammering in the hook. "Everything's

fine."

"Did you get to the bottom of what was bothering her?"

He smiled like a Cheshire cat and nodded. "I did, and it's all working out for the best."

He picked up one side of the frame. "Can you help me hang it?"

I nodded and grabbed the other side. When we'd successfully hooked the string onto the hook, we both stood back to see if it was straight. Aden moved the frame a tad to the left. "There, perfect."

"It's beautiful. Thank you."

"Don't mention it, Bront. Now, why don't you go upstairs and relax in the bath with a glass of bubbly while I spend some time with the kids?"

"You sure?"

"I am."

I stood on my tippy toes and kissed his cheek. "Thanks, Ade."

"It's my pleasure."

I'd been soaking in steam and bubble bath for ten minutes when my phone buzzed. I dried my hands on the towel and turned my phone over; Sam had texted.

SAM: Did you get the dress?

BRONTE: Yes! And the blindfold 🐺

SAM: Nice pussy, haha

BRONTE: I thought you'd like it, lol

SAM: What are you doing right now?

BRONTE: Relaxing in the bath with a glass of bubbles

SAM: Mmmm, wish I was there

BRONTE: What time are you arriving?

SAM: An hour?

BRONTE: Okay, see you soon, mwah mwah

SAM: Mwah

Sam blindfolded me in the limo so I couldn't see where we were going. When we reached our destination six songs later, Sam led me, blindfolded still, up many steps and along corridors. Wherever we were, the delicate, warm breath of the night air wafted around my neckline and bare shoulders. The acoustics were pristine; every little sound was magnified and illuminated—a cricket, a frog, a night bird, the heels and soles of our shoes as we walked.

"Okay, that's far enough for now," said Sam.

We stopped walking, and she guided me into a chair. It was lower than a dining chair and felt more like one of those cinema seats that flick closed when you stand up. Her thigh brushed against mine as she sat. It was silent for a few seconds; I could only hear my own breathing. Then, a voice broke out.

The words seemed to drift upwards as well as being

perfectly suspended in the space around me. Sam removed my blindfold. I blinked to adjust my eyes, but I already knew what was waiting for me. Halsey. *Trouble.* The lyrics and music I knew by heart after months of listening on repeat play. But I still had no idea where we were. I looked around.

"Oh my God, Sam, the Hollywood Bowl! The whole Hollywood Bowl and Halsey all to myself?"

"Happy birthday, my sweet."

"This is the most thoughtful thing anyone has ever done for me, Sam."

"Nobody deserves it more, my sweet." She kissed my hand and my cheek. "Enjoy."

The lump in my throat was stronger than my will to appear stoic, and my face contorted like Claire Danes when she ugly cries. But I didn't care. I squeezed Sam's hand. My shoulders trembled with tears of joy and disbelief.

When Halsey finished the first song, she said, "Happy birthday, Bronte. I hope you enjoy the private show." Then she sang one of my favourite songs from the album—Coming Down.

Sam whispered in my ear. "I can see why you like her. She's a brilliant songwriter."

"She really is. If I could write songs, I would write songs like this."

She squeezed my hand and said, "Enjoy, my sweet B."

Halsey saved the best for last—Hurricane. After the final

note, she blew a kiss and wished me happy birthday again before exiting the stage with the other musicians. Sam and I stayed seated. The bowl felt like a cradle, and I didn't want to leave.

"There's a hurricane building in my heart for you, Sammy."

"The sea level is rising in mine too, Bront."

She slipped off her chair, kneeled opposite me, and leaned in to kiss me. I opened my legs to pull her in closer and kiss her back. Every kiss was as explosive as our first. Kissing Sam was different to kissing Aden and Luther. Kissing for them was a prelude to sex. Kissing Sam was to partake in the pleasure of kissing. And while our kisses inevitably led to sex, the unspoken pressure of progressing to the sexual act was absent or suspended—like Halsey's beautiful musical notes in the Hollywood Bowl. We could have been kissing for ten minutes or thirty, I had no idea, but I do know that in that moment and on that night in that cradle of love, my feelings for Sam reached new heights.

Sam's head had moved beneath my silk dress, her tongue between my thighs.

Sex with Sam blew my mind. She wasn't afraid to experiment, and the level of intimacy I was able to achieve with her rivalled anything I'd experienced with both Aden and Luther. It wasn't just physically different between women; it was spiritual. My sexual experiences with men had involved an unspoken hierarchy and undercurrent of aggression; domination and control versus the pleasure of sex and the celebration of love.

I threw my head back and gasped. Sam was rubbing my

g-spot and licking my clit. Orgasms with Sam were endless. I used to have three or four with Aden, but Sam wielded her fingers and tongue in such a way that ten times or more was not unusual. I adored her like no other. We were best friends, writing partners, and lovers. She made me laugh all the time, and I never fought with her as I had with Aden or Luther. When friction did arise on the odd occasion, it rapidly fizzled. And with none of the resentment and anger that had plagued the last few years of my marriage with Aden. I guess we were better suited when all was said and done, and my polyamorous yearnings went from a raging fire to burnt-out ash.

One Year Later

CHAPTER 61
Bronte

July

The host introduced their next guest speaker, but I only heard bits and pieces—*best-selling author, award-winning memoir*—and all the shiny labels I had accumulated since moving to LA. I didn't hear my name, but Sam nudged me forward. "Break a leg, my sweet."

I walked out onto the stage, temporarily blinded by the white lights of the auditorium. My nerves were in my stomach, and my shallow breaths weren't helping any. The lights dimmed as I reached the podium, and I glimpsed the packed auditorium. I saw Aden, Sheryl, Adam, Katy, and Daphne in the front row. Sam's face beamed from the backstage wings. I took a small sip of water unfolded the paper, and began my speech.

"Social media is full of people who label themselves survivors," I said, looking out at the audience, "but I never considered myself one of them." I made eye contact with Aden briefly before continuing. "For a long time, I viewed surviving as the ultimate failure. Surviving my family's death, for instance, was more of a curse than an achievement. Then came my suicide attempt." I shook my head and exhaled. "Despite my best efforts, death also rejected me. And, while I gave thanks in the aftermath for the second chance, and my rational mind finally settled on rejecting death as an option, my subconscious formed its own negative associations about what I did and didn't deserve."

I looked up from my speech and glanced at Sam, who smiled and gave me two thumbs up. "Among those things I didn't deserve, love and creative success claimed the top two spots. By the time I eventually gave myself permission to pick up a pen and chase my long-held dream, the trauma of loss had manifested itself in my life like a trope in a dystopian novel. At times it seemed all effort was wasted. Fruition, constantly one step ahead of me. Even so, I hung onto that dream, like the beloved fictional character, Heathcliff, who held onto his love for Catherine—a lover-obsessed, tethered to limerence, la douleur exquise, refusing to accept the possibility that we (me and writing) were not meant to be. But…"

I held up my finger for effect.

"But the more words I allowed to escape my crowded head, the more my psychology shifted, and the more I sensed an unshackling. The creation of space in a once crowded room. A space that facilitated my creative breakthrough with my memoir, *Flammable*."

I stopped to take a sip of water and looked out at the sea of faces. All eyes were on me, with everyone listening intently. I felt the internal butterflies calm and continued my talk.

After my speech, I stayed behind to sign books while the others waited for me to meet them in a restaurant down the street. Feeling like I needed a few quiet moments to myself, I stole into the dressing room and collapsed in an armchair. It hadn't been thirty seconds when I heard the door click open. I turned around, expecting to see Sam or Aden, but it was neither one of them. He wore his usual black t-shirt and jeans, but he had gained a couple of tattoos on his forearms.

"Luther? What are you doing here?"

"I came to see your speech. And to apologise. And to bring a peace offering."

He handed me a gift; it felt like a book. I pointed to a plastic chair. "Do you want to sit down?"

He nodded and pulled the chair opposite me. "Your speech was amazing. You are amazing."

"Thanks, Luther. It's been a wild ride."

"I can't wait for you to see what I bought you." He perched on the edge of his seat and pointed to the gift in my hand. "Open it. You won't believe the story when I tell you."

I nodded and turned it over to slip my fingers beneath the tape. "Oh, my," I said, "this might be the most exquisite thing I've ever seen. Where on earth did you find this?"

His face beamed. "I thought you'd like it. I found it in an estate sale when I was looking for *Alice* memorabilia for Addy."

"How is Adelaide? And Beth? I miss her."

"Beth wouldn't speak to me for a while after we broke up."

I cocked my head. "I'm sorry to hear that, Luther. I hope

you're talking now?"

He nodded.

"Did Beth persuade you to come here today?"

"Yeah."

I pursed my lips and looked at the book. "You shouldn't do things you don't want to do, Luther."

"What? Oh. No, that's not what I meant. I chose to come here today because I owed you that much."

"Why now?"

"I'm not like you, Bronte."

"Yeah, I know. You've already counted the ways we're unalike."

He shook his head. "No, I mean I'm not decisive and certain like you are, and I don't have your talent. When you asked me to co-write the play, I wasn't up to it. The idea scared the shit out of me, and I knew it would only be a matter of time before you became a hotshot in your own right, and you wouldn't have time for me."

I nodded my head and looked at my feet. "I guess we'll never know."

"No, I guess not."

"So, what now?" I said, making eye contact with him again.

He shrugged. "I know we can't go back to the way things were, but I miss my friend."

I sighed and nodded my head. My world had expanded exponentially, and yet it felt far too small to accommodate Luther. I could hardly reconcile the fact that I had been lovesick over him once upon a time, for I wasn't sure I liked him anymore. I knew in my heart there was no going back and no real possibility of friendship. Not because of what had happened between us, but because I was not the same woman Luther had stalked on Twitter and projected his *Alice in Wonderland* fantasy onto. That woman who lived in Australia like a mouse stuck in a trap had indeed drunk a magic potion and permanently shrunk her former self. My former self was no longer recognisable. The people in the auditorium had proven that to me tonight. Yet Luther had, once again, made an effort to make amends, and I owed him more than a few stilted words to say my goodbyes. "How long are you in LA for?"

"I fly back tomorrow night."

"Okay, how about we meet for breakfast tomorrow and have the talk we never had last time?"

He nodded. "I've missed you, Bront."

I stood and forced a smile. "You'll need my new number."

"Yeah, of course." He pulled out his phone and punched in the number as I read it out.

"Text me the name of your hotel, and I'll meet you there for breakfast at nine."

"Okay."

"Bye, Luther."

"Bye, Bront."

I watched him walk away and exhaled a deep breath. My phone vibrated on the table where I'd left it with two texts from Aden and Sam.

ADEN: You should be here by now. If you don't text back, we're coming to find you.

SAM: I'm hoping you haven't been cornered by a stalker! Aden and I are coming to get you.

I texted them both back.

BRONTE: Everything is fine. I'm on my way xoxo

CHAPTER 62
Luther

July

I waited in a darkened doorway in the building opposite the auditorium hall after seeing Bronte. The meeting did not go as I had hoped. All the warmth she had previously held for me in her emerald eyes and tight embraces had frozen over like a winter lake. I knew she'd be surprised to see me, but I wasn't expecting her to look displeased. She didn't hug me or say anything more about the book.

I pressed my back against the wall and stayed dead still when I saw her reach the bottom of the staircase and exit the revolving door. She was about to cross the road when a woman approached her, and they exchanged a few words. The woman handed Bronte three books and a pen. She obviously wanted an autograph. While Bronte was signing the books, a woman I had seen sitting with Aden earlier in the evening approached from across the street. I knew who she was because I had followed Bronte's every move on the internet. Bronte's face lit up when she saw Sam. She returned the signed copies and said goodbye to her fan.

Sam touched Bronte's face and said something. Bronte smiled, took her hand, and they crossed the street. I held my breath, anxious they would walk past me, but they didn't. I counted thirty seconds before I peeked out from the doorway. Then I wished I hadn't. Bronte and Sam were a couple of feet away, oblivious to the world as they passionately kissed. Sam had Bronte pinned against the wall of a Japanese kimono shop—the salmon wall paint curling and peeling, like discarded pencil shavings. Sam's right hand was buried beneath Bronte's black dress. Bronte moaned in ecstasy.

I put my head down, dug my hands deep into my pockets and walked as fast as I could in the opposite direction. I stumbled into the first bar I saw and ordered shot after shot of bourbon. I was a fool to think Bronte and I would pick up where we left off. She had moved on. She didn't need me anymore. Hours later, I was in my hotel room with a woman called Angela. While I unscrewed the caps off mini bar booze bottles, she picked up a book from my bedside table and read the inscription.

For my darling Bronte...

"Put that down," I said, taking the book and handing her a bottle of vodka.

"What is it?"

"It's a stupid book of poems."

"Who's Bronte?"

"An ex."

"Were you hoping to get back together or something?"

"Or something."

She put down the bottle and pulled me toward her. "I'm gonna make you forget all about Bronte," she said. "Pfft. Bronte. Dumb name if you ask me."

I closed my eyes and let her go down on me, hoping it

would erase the image of Bronte and Sam together.

The following morning my phone woke me, but I let it go to voicemail when I saw Bronte's name flash on the caller ID. I rolled over in annoyance, forgetting all about Angela and bashed her hand. "Shit, sorry," I said, but she rolled onto her back and started snoring. My head pounded like a nightclub speaker when I stepped off the bed and stood. A wave of nausea propelled me toward the bathroom and I chucked up until there was only bile left. I listened to Bronte's voicemail while I brushed my teeth.

She was all business-like, much like the night before.

BRONTE: Hi Luther. Tried to phone. Still on for breakfast at 9?

I turned on the shower and let the hot water massage my pounding head. *Should I meet her, or should I not?* I said the words over and over like a foolish teenager would pluck flower petals and chant: *she loves me, she loves me not.* When Angela came in to pee a few minutes later, I decided to meet Bronte as planned.

LUTHER: Tell me where to meet you

BRONTE: Oh. Not your hotel as planned?

LUTHER: Nah

BRONTE: Okay. I'll text you an address.

LUTHER: Got it. See you soon.

Angela washed her hands and glugged some of my mouthwash.

"I've gotta check out now, Angela. Sorry. Thanks for the company last night."

"Oh, right." She scribbled something on the hotel notepad and handed it to me. "Call me."

"Sure," I said. "Sorry to rush you out like this."

I packed my bag while she dressed in the bathroom and said goodbye to her five minutes later.

The restaurant was like a suspended birdcage filled with light. I kept my sunglasses on to see without being blinded. I spotted Bronte waving me over to a table in the corner. This time she stood and hugged me stiffly before she sat back down.

"Rough night?" She chuckled.

"Huh?"

She pointed to my glasses. "Oh, yeah, sorry." I took them off, slipped them into my jacket pocket, and hung the jacket over the back of my chair.

She handed me a menu. "What did you get up to last night?"

"It pales in comparison to yours, I'm sure."

She frowned. "Meaning?"

"Never mind," I said, waving it off and burying my nose in the menu. "Are you gonna eat?"

"That's what we usually do at breakfast, isn't it?"

I looked up from my menu; she was still frowning at me. "I saw you and Sam last night, okay?"

She shrugged her shoulders. "And?"

"I mean, I literally *saw* you two together, on the street outside the auditorium."

Her cheeks flushed, and her frown deepened. "What were you doing? Stalking me?"

"Pfft." I shook my head and looked away.

"Why did you come here, Luther? What do you want from me?"

I met her narrowed eyes. "I told you. I wanted to make amends."

"Okay, Luther, I'm going to level with you. I did love you, once upon a time, but I don't anymore, and I can't see a future where you and I can ever rekindle the friendship we once had because I'm not the…"

"The real Alice," I interjected.

She rolled her eyes. "Oh, for all that is holy, Luther, would you drop the Alice bullshit already."

I looked around the restaurant. "Keep your voice down, Bronte, people are looking at us."

She crossed her arms and leaned back in her seat. "You know, Luther, I hoped we could have a mature conversation about what happened and walk away with some sort of resolution."

"We can."

"Then talk. Tell me what happened that day on the phone when you turned down the opportunity of a lifetime and never spoke to me again."

The waitress came to take our order. Bronte ordered two coffees and asked the waitress to come back in five minutes.

"I told you. It was all above my pay grade."

"And what about our relationship, Luther? After everything we went through, you simply cut contact with me with no explanation. If I hadn't sent a follow-up text months later, you probably would have continued saying and doing nothing."

"Okay, I fucked up. Is that what you want me to say?"

"I wanted an explanation at the time, Luther. It's called communication, and it's what adults do when they're in a relationship."

The waitress delivered our coffees and prompted us to order.

"I need a few more minutes," said Bronte.

"I'll have the big breakfast," I said.

The waitress nodded and left.

"Have you been writing much, Luther?"

I reached into my jacket pocket and handed her the book. "I wrote this in the days after our last call, but not a drop since."

She sighed. "What's this?"

"It's a poetry book. I wrote it for you."

She skimmed the crema from the top of her coffee and

then dropped the teaspoon into the cup. "I can't, Luther. Words and poetry is not enough this time."

"But it was before."

"A lot has changed. In fact, everything has changed."

"Tell me about it. You're a lesbian now."

She rolled her eyes and shook her head. "Love is fluid to me. I don't see it in terms of gender."

"Yeah, okay, Bronte, let's not get all intellectual about it. The point is you've changed, and I haven't."

She smiled weakly. "Exactly, Luther. You haven't changed. And if our experience was not enough to change you, then I doubt anything will."

"I thought love was about accepting someone, not changing them?"

"I'm not talking about changing your personality, Luther. I'm talking about the kind of change that comes from experiences that offer us the chance to either grow or stay the same. You resist change at all costs, and you are happiest when things stay the same."

The waitress placed my breakfast plate in front of me and asked Bronte if she was ready to order. Bronte shook her head. The waitress sighed and walked away.

Bronte reached into her bag and pulled out a small paper bag. "Here." She pushed it across the table. "I think you should have this back."

I picked it up and looked inside. It was the copy of *Alice in Wonderland* I'd given to her at Mom's. "Why are you punishing me, Bronte?"

She shook her head. "No, I'm not punishing you."

"Then, what?"

"I'm releasing you, Luther. You will find your real Alice someday; a woman who is willing to commit to you a hundred percent. Just ensure you don't let her slip through your fingers next time." She stood and hooked her bag over her arm, leaving my poetry book on the table.

People were looking at us again, so I stood too. "Bronte, please don't go yet."

"Sorry, Luther. I don't see what else there is to say."

I swallowed and nodded.

"Give my regards to Beth, and call me if you ever need a professional hand up. Okay?"

I didn't reply.

She kissed me on the cheek and whispered *Bye, Luther* in my ear. She smelled like coconut and raspberry.

"Never goodbye," I said. But she was already gone.

I arrived at the airport early and boarded the plane as soon as the gate opened. Once I'd stowed my bag in the overhead luggage compartment, I settled into my window seat and hung my jacket over my knee. I watched the steady stream of people flow in for a few minutes before turning my attention to the copy of Alice in Wonderland that Bronte had returned to me. A piece of folded paper with handwriting slipped out and fell into my lap. I opened it; it was blue on one side and pink on the other. The blue side was dated weeks after our last phone call.

I have deleted you
from my life
but your words live on

like ghosts
they will haunt my head
until exorcised

and I say haunt, darling
because you have left me
like a loved one leaves
the living

and all I have left
is the loose change of words

regrets, what ifs, if onlys
and the exhausting sense of
not knowing-
who you were
how you felt
or if you even loved me, the way I loved you

Enough loose change
to fill a shelf of glass jars—
this is all I have left of you
and it devastates

like a hole in the ground
where a church once stood

I looked out of the window, trying to focus on something other than the lump in my throat. A boy, of Addy's age, and his mother took the seats next to me. She had a colorful sleeve tattoo of a Mexican Day of the Dead skull, a clump of chains around her neck, and purple streaks in her hair. She smiled at me and stuffed her two bags into the overhead compartment. Her crop top revealed more tattoos on her torso.

"Do you want some help with the bags?" I said.

"That would be awesome, thanks!"

I slipped the paper back into the book and placed it on top of my jacket on the seat. It only took a bit of rearranging to fit her two bags in, and when I finished the boy had taken my seat. His mother noticed at the same time and apologized profusely. I told her it was fine, as long as she didn't mind me taking the aisle seat. She didn't. Once we were all seated again, she gave the boy a tablet and focused on her mobile phone. I pulled the piece of paper out of the book and read the pink side. It was dated a month after the blue one.

I can't see your face anymore
not like I used to
It's an old photo
kept too long in the back pocket of my jeans
The ones I wear everyday
The ones I never want to wash

And the memories we made
are also fading
As if they never happened at all

And I guess this is called moving on
and letting go
The last wisp of sadness
The remaining drops of loss
Before you disappear
as enigmatically as you appeared

I held the piece of paper and stared at it through moist eyes. Physically, it was as light as a leaf. Emotionally, it was as heavy as a paperweight.

"Oh my God, is that *Alice in Wonderland?*"

The woman had her chin over my shoulder and pointed to the book.

"Yeah," I said. "Are you a fan?"

"Am I ever?! *Why, sometimes I've believed as many as six impossible things before breakfast.*"

I smiled and pointed to her son. "It's been my favorite since I was his age."

She held out her hand. "I'm Skye."

I shook her hand. "I'm Luther."

"Luther? Oh, I love that name!"

"Are you from Boston, Skye?"

She nodded. "U-huh. You?"

I nodded. "Whereabouts?"

"Near Salem."

"Me too."

"No way. You married?"

"Divorced."

"Yeah, me too. Kids?"

"A daughter, Adelaide—Addy for short."

"Have you got a picture?"

"Yeah," I said, pulling out my phone and flicking to the photo app.

"Aww, she is gorgeous."

I nodded. "She's my life."

She patted her son's knee and said, "Yeah, Jasper's my life too."

I smiled and pointed to her tattoo. "I like your tattoo, by the way. It's a Day of the Dead skull, right?"

She nodded. "Have you read the literary Calaveras?"

I shook my head. "No, what are those?"

"They're satirical poems in which Death visits the land of the living to take someone to the land of the dead."

"You like poetry?"

"No, I looove poetry." She leaned in conspiratorially and whispered: "Don't tell anyone, but I'm writing my first poetry book."

"I'm a poet too," I said. "I can help you if you like."

She looked at me and smiled. "You know, Luther, I am usually the unluckiest person in the world, but I'm thinking today is my lucky day."

The flight crew announced we would take off in five minutes and reminded everyone to turn off their mobile phones and fasten their seatbelts. While Skye turned her attention to Jasper, I tried to mine conversation topics in my head. When she put her phone in her bag and buckled her seat belt, I tried to engage her in conversation again.

"What brought you to LA, Skye?"

She pulled a book out of her bag and held it up. It was Bronte's poetry book—*Wonderland*. She pulled out two more of Bronte's books—*Flammable* and *Social Liaisons*. "I came for her. I have a major writer-crush, and I wanted to hear her talk. Have you heard of her?"

I took the books from her and nodded. "Yeah."

She opened the covers of each to reveal Bronte's autograph. "I caught her on the street last night after her talk and asked her if she would sign them for me. She was super lovely..."

I tuned out temporarily as I remembered the night before. The woman I had seen talking to Bronte was Skye. It couldn't have been a coincidence. I thought back to my parting conversation with Bronte at breakfast. *You will find your real Alice someday; a woman who is willing to commit to you a hundred percent. Just ensure you don't let her slip through your fingers next time.*

"I knew her before she was famous," I said.

"Whoa! You're kidding me?"

I shook my head.

"Is that why you're in LA? Did you come to see her talk?"

"Yeah, I did."

"What's she like?"

"Complicated. Smart. Totally out of my league."

She nudged me with her elbow. "Don't say that about yourself, Luther. You look like a pretty good catch to me."

"Have you dated since your divorce?"

"Nope, and not for a lack of trying."

"I would date you. For what it's worth."

She smiled at me. "Give me your phone."

I fished it out of my jacket pocket and handed it to her. She punched in a number, typed her name, and handed it back to me and winked. "That's what it's worth."

The plane started to taxi down the runway. I rested my head and watched the terminal building and planes slide past slowly. I heard Mom's words echo from the not so distant past. *Whenever you get lost, retrace your steps and go back to the beginning to find yourself.* Before Bronte, I labelled myself a committed Capricorn—a rational thinker who rarely let emotion creep into my decisions. And look where it had gotten me. Mom and Bronte were right. It was time to change, and change would never have been possible without Bronte.

over
own
that
nd
ies. I
back
e
nd
it
l my
me.
un-
ht

HAPTER 63
Bronte

September

: table with love in my heart; Aden and
-laws—Sylvie and Augustin—Jacqueline,
and her husband Avi. Daphne Dalloway,
Aaron; and even Fred, Marjorie, Priya,
d Vidu had made the trip. We were
ne's family's sprawling lavender farm
n's and Jacqueline's wedding. A bronze
an oak bureau and played a jovial samba.
ren laughing and playing outside on the
Liam and Vidu hung upside down, like
pranch of an oddly shaped tree, while Leyla
between two slender cypress trees, talking
nd watching Amélie—Leyla's and Liam's
—crawl back and forth.

ned by the need to breathe in solitude and
flood of miracles and blessings, I quietly slipped
om and made my escape through the kitchen
d hear the buzzing of fat bumblebees as I walked
usty clay tennis court whose rusted fence was
ed in flowering jasmine and creeping ivy. I stopped
my face at the stone fountain, and took my sandals
a the gravel footpath met the wild grass that crept up
ing hill. The elevated pool overlooked neat rows of
fields and golden wheat beyond.

ad swum my daily laps here since arriving at the farm a

few days before. To meet the sun each morning as it rose
the mountain and illuminated the lavender fields held it:
sense of wonder and bliss. The potted flowers and herbs
hugged the pool's perimeter filled the air with fragrance
attracted an array of visitors, including bees and dragonf
lay on a pool chair with the sun behind me and thought
to my summer night swims and my fantasy involving thr
pool chairs. Back then, it had all been a dreamy fantasy, a
while I had hoped to manifest the impossible, I doubted
would materialise. I opened my eyes, sat upright, remove
sunglasses, and looked at the pool chairs on either side o
While things hadn't worked out with Luther, Luther had
doubtedly been the catalyst for a string of events that mi
not have happened otherwise. Disbelief and relief swelle
inside me, and I surrendered to the tears.

"Bront?" I heard Aden's voice behind me. "You okay?"
massaged my shoulders.

I squeezed his hands and nodded. "I'm having a mom

He walked around, sat on the adjacent pool chair, and
took my hand in his. "Our reversal of fortune is overwhel
ing when you stop and think, right?"

I nodded and blinked the remaining tears from my ey
lashes. "Thank you for taking this journey with me."

"Thank you for inviting me. Who would've thought tha
after losing the winery, and nearly each other, we would ev
tually end up here—living out our wildest dreams with ne
partners."

I smiled and nodded. "I say it all the time, but I still pir
myself every day."

"We haven't had a proper chance to speak since your talk. What's been happening in the exciting world of Bronte?"

"I had a surprise visit from Luther the night of my talk."

He frowned and scoffed. "Oh, boy. How did that go?"

I shook my head. "Bizarre. I mean, I wasn't expecting to see him again. But apart from that, it was like an out of body experience—like I was seeing him for the first time, or with different eyes, and I couldn't understand what I'd ever seen in him."

"Hmm, that's kinda how I felt after you told me about your feelings for him."

I scoffed and rubbed my face. "I agreed to meet him in the morning for breakfast, but the only emotion I experienced was overwhelming indifference, and I left after ten minutes."

Aden chuckled. "Ouch. That bad, huh?"

I let out a huge sigh and nodded. "I shouldn't criticise him, or myself, but I would have made a monumental mistake if I had stayed the course with him."

"I doubt it would have gone that far, Bront."

I turned serious and searched Aden's eyes while I weighed up the words I wanted to say but probably shouldn't.

"Uh-oh. What's going on in that head of yours?"

I shook my head, thinking better of it. "Nothing. Let's change the subject, shall we? You and Jacqs are getting married tomorrow! Any wedding jitters?"

He chuckled and shook his head. "None whatsoever."

I nodded and smiled. "I'm glad you've found happiness. You deserve it after everything I put you through."

"Now, now, don't be silly. If you hadn't gone poly on me, we might not be sitting here today."

"True."

"What about you and Sam? Any plans to tie the knot?"

The mention of Sam's name induced a smile, but I shook my head all the same. "You and I both know that I am not the marrying kind."

He held both my hands and searched my eyes. "Listen to me. Our marriage had its ups and downs, but don't throw out the good parts with the bad, okay?"

"Okay."

"Marriage is not the villain you keep portraying it to be."

I smiled weakly, sighed, and looked away.

He held my chin in his fingers and turned my face so that I was looking at him again. "Can you do something for me, Bront?"

I nodded. "Of course."

"Forgive yourself."

I looked down and willed the lump in my throat to go away.

He squeezed my hands. "I hold no resentment toward you. None, whatsoever. If anything, I'm grateful for what happened. Grateful for Luther, grateful for the poly adventure, grateful for Jacqueline and Amélie, grateful…"

I started to laugh, but it only served to release the lump in my throat, and the tears spilt like a waterfall.

Aden continued. "Do you remember when I asked you to release me?"

I nodded and cried some more.

Aden pulled a tissue out of his pocket and gave it to me. "I need you to release yourself from the guilt. Please. For your sake and mine. Forgive yourself and let Sam into your heart and your life a hundred percent."

"I have let her in," I said mid-sob.

Aden shook his head. "Not completely. As long as you wage this war against marriage, you are partitioning off a piece of yourself. Surely you see that?"

"I don't think I can trust myself again. When I saw Luther recently, my coldness toward him scared me. What if I'm incapable of love? What if I end up disappointing Sam too?"

He stood and pulled me toward him. "If anything, you're capable of too much love, and what happened with Luther has nothing to do with your ability to love, it's a matter of personal growth. Luther was fucking groundhog day. You're a bird of prey. You need to be up there." He held me at arm's length and pointed to the sky. "You belong in the sky, Bront, and you've found the perfect partner who belongs up there alongside you."

I couldn't hear anything through my tears and sniffling, and my face buried in Aden's chest. When the tears finally subsided, and I relaxed my body enough for Aden to release me from his arms, I realised Sam was standing next to me.

"How long have you been standing there?" I said.

"Hmm, let me see: incapable of love, disappointing Sam, birds of prey."

I rubbed my face and sighed.

"Close your eyes."

I frowned in confusion but did it anyway.

She placed something into my right hand. I opened my eyes. There were two chains. Each had a pendant with a crown and a heart. One was engraved with an *S* and the other with a *B*.

Sam picked one up and explained. "This symbol is a Claddagh. It has three components: a crown, for loyalty, two hands, for bonded friendship, and a heart, that denotes love." She picked up the S-pendant and placed it around my neck, then placed the B-pendant around her own. "To fear anything, be it disappointment or something else, is to live the life of a caged bird, and I don't want that for either of us, my sweet. I wanted you from the moment I saw you, and I have grown to love you every day since. We don't have to sign a piece of paper or exchange rings. Just know that my heart is fully committed to yours."

"Rings are so twentieth century," I said, trying to lighten the previous mood I had created. "No offence, Ade."

He shook his head and smiled. "None taken."

Sam smiled and took my face in her hands. "I love you, B. That is all. And Aden's right; an eagle does not belong in a cage."

"I love you too, Sammy."

"I'm glad we sorted that out," said Aden. "Now, what do

you say we rejoin the others!"

"Okay," I said, looping one arm through Aden's and the other with Sam's.

CHAPTER 64
Aden

September

Jacqs and I exchanged vows the following day in the local chapel. Although, the word local did not have the same meaning in France as in Australia or America. The local chapel was an historic building built of stone sometime in the fourteenth century. As it was in walking distance to the family's lavender farm, we made our journey on foot—a procession of people who had once been strangers but had grown into friends and family. Jacqs's parents, Sylvie and Augustin, married for forty years already, led the way, with Sheryl and Avi in tow. Close behind them was Bronte, who carried Amélie on her hip, and Sam, who held hands with Leyla and Liam. Anura, Priya, Nishanti and Vidu were behind them. Jacqs didn't believe in wedding-day superstitions, so we walked hand in hand.

With the lavender harvest weeks away, the surrounding fields were a spectacular sight. Seeing Jacqs's Provence home made me wonder if she was trying to replicate a little piece of it at Lavender Honey, and I made a mental note to talk to her when the wedding celebrations were over about offering Sam and Sheryl a buy-out of some sort. When we reached the chapel ten minutes later, the guests were already seated and waiting. Our little procession took their places in the front row while I waited at the altar for Jacqs and Augustin to make their entrance. Jacqs carried a bouquet of wild lavender, and she seemed to glide down the aisle in her creamy, satin dress.

While she made her slow approach, I looked over at Leyla

and Liam, and Bronte, who was still holding Amélie, and said a quiet prayer of thanks for all my blessings. When Bronte uttered those words, *I'm in love with Luther*, I thought love had broken us, and we had broken love. I spent months in a constant state of fear. Fear of loss. Fear of being inferior. Fear of scarcity. Fear of love itself. But, when I eventually wrapped my head around the concept of Bronte's polyamorous nature and needs, the fear subsided, and my perspective shifted. With a little bit of time, I realised that surrendering to love was the antithesis of our fears. Only when I stopped trying to control, and allowed nature to run its course, did love blossom for both of us. If I hadn't come to terms with Bronte and Luther, Bronte and I might have divorced, I wouldn't have met Jacqs, or moved to Napa, or had Amélie, and Bronte and Sam might never have written their play or made the movie together. In the end, love did not ruin us, as I had feared. It made us stronger and ushered in more love than we could ever have imagined.

Jacqs stood beside me, radiant and present as the rainbow of light streaming through the stained glass windows. The thing I loved and appreciated most was how I felt like the only person in the world when we were together. As much as I had loved Bronte, I had never felt that way with her because she seemed miles away, even when she was in the room with you.

The service began. The same pastor who had christened and baptised Jacqs was now marrying us. After we exchanged the vows we had written for each other, we sealed them with a kiss and then the wave of people and well-wishes began. Leyla, Liam, and Amélie joined Jacqs and me for photos, and I didn't see Bronte until later in the evening.

Back at the house, Jacqueline's friends, family and neighbours joined us for a celebration dinner. After many introductions and well-wishes, toasts and dances, Bronte managed to corner me alone.

"Can you spare a minute for me, Ade? I'd like to give you your wedding gift."

I grabbed two glasses of champagne and followed her outside. We found a quiet spot and sat on a stone wall. The music sounded muffled, like when you're underwater.

"It was a beautiful wedding. In fact, it's been a beautiful day. Who would have thought, after losing Ghost Gum, we'd end up here."

"I thought all was lost, Bront. But life has a way of regenerating."

"It certainly does." She handed me an envelope. "Congratulations, Ade, from the bottom of my heart."

I balanced the champagne glass on the wall next to me and took the envelope from her. "Thanks, Bront. Do I open it now?"

She nodded.

I slid my finger beneath the flap and tore it open. Inside was a wad of paper—it looked like a contract or a deed. I looked at her enquiringly.

"Open it."

I unfolded the document and began to read. "You've bought the winery in Napa?"

"I bought it for you, Jacqs, and Amélie."

"Is this legit?"

She nodded and laughed. "Of course. All you have to do is sign the deed."

"How did you? You shouldn't have. Oh my God."

"When we lost Ghost Gum, I was powerless to do anything about it. But I have the power to do something now. I have more money than I know what to do with right now." She laughed. "A situation I never thought I'd find myself in. And what's the point of money if you can't spend it on those you love the most?"

"I don't know what to say?"

"You don't have to say anything. You and Jacqs are building Lavender Honey with love, much like you and I tried to build Ghost Gum together with love." She choked on her last few words, and a tear rolled down her cheek. "Just know I adore you and Jacqs and Amélie, and I want Lavender Honey to be yours."

I embraced her for a long time. Possibly for the length of the song that played in the distance. When I eventually let her go, I held her at arm's length. "You were destined to be more than a winemaker's wife, Bront."

She nodded. Her eyes were moist. "I'm happy you think so."

I nodded and reached for her hand. "I do, Bront, and I'm incredibly proud of what you've achieved."

She picked up the champagne glasses and handed me one. "Thanks, Ade. I'm proud of you too."

I raised my glass. "To l'amour."

She smiled and raised hers. "To l'amour.

-THE END-

Bianca Bowers

Love Paradigm

Where does love come from?
Where does it go?

That crackling birth and monotone death
Are we nothing more than lithium-
batteries
with an expiration

And if this is true
then we misunderstand love

for it shouldn't be imprisoned
obsessed over, smothered, possessed
does not belong to us

love has a birthday and a death
an inevitable denouement after a glorious climax
destined for reincarnation

Perhaps it's our thoughts about love
that cause its downfall

> *we think too little*
> *and feel too much*
> *in the beginning*

> *think too much*
> *and feel too little*

in the end

What if our brains are slaveowners
and love was never meant to be imprisoned?

—Bianca Bowers, Love is a song she sang from a cage (Paperfields
Press, 2016)

Glossary

Maa ismuk? WHAT IS YOUR NAME?

Ismii MY NAME IS

Shukran THANK YOU

Mashallah WHAT GOD HAS WILLED HAS HAP-
PENED

Inshallah GOD-WILLING

naäam YES

Asalamu Alaikum PEACE BE UPON YOU

Wa Alaikum asalam UPON YOU BE PEACE

Allahu Akbar GOD IS GREAT

Afwan YOU'RE WELCOME

Aaraka Ghadan GOODBYE

Ma' a al-ssalāmah PEACE BE WITH YOU

As-salamu 'alaykum wa rahmat-Ullahi wa barakaatuh   MAY
PEACE, THE MERCY OF ALLAH AND HIS BLESS-
INGS BE UPON YOU

Credits

I gratefully acknowledge the following sources and quotes:

www.goodreads.com. (n.d.). A quote by Lewis Carroll. [online] Available at: https://www.goodreads.com/quotes/9467-alice-laughed-there-s-no-use-trying-she-said-one-can-t.

www.goodreads.com. (n.d.). A quote from Wuthering Heights, Emily Brontë [online] Available at: https://www.goodreads.com/quotes/344016-he-shall-never-know-i-love-him-and-that-not [Accessed 18 Jun. 2023].

www.goodreads.com. (n.d.). A quote by William Morris. [online] Available at: https://www.goodreads.com/quotes/408415-have-nothing-in-your-house-that-you-do-not-know.

Mount Glorious History: https://www.mountglorious.com.au/about-mt-glorious/history/

Barossa. Be consumed. Advertisement: https://vimeo.com/89979667

Sandgate history, State Library of Queensland: https://www.slq.qld.gov.au/blog/sandgate

Sandgate history, Wikipedia: https://en.wikipedia.org/wiki/
Sandgate,_Queensland

Tarot quotes: Fiebig, J & Burger, E 2015, The Ultimate Guide
to the Rider Waite Tarot, Llewellyn Worldwide.

Quran quote: 2:286

Edna St Vincent Millay: https://en.wikipedia.org/wiki/Edna_
St._Vincent_Millay

Acknowledgements

The Idea

This, my second novel, has been in the works since I penned the first draft in 2017. It was spawned after my third poetry book—Love is a song she sang from a cage—in which I toyed with the one-love-til-death-do-us-part ideology, but wanted to explore further than poetry would allow me. By nature, a long-term union is demanding and punctuated with compromise. But at what personal cost? If the needs of the union are always placed above the needs of the individuals, then isn't it more of a dictatorship than a democracy?

This revolutionary idea of dictatorship versus democracy became the seed of this novel, Till Marriage Do Us Part, an idea that I hope you, the reader, will meet with an open mind and heart.

The Writing Process

This novel has had a number of working titles—Three Hearts; The Real Alice; The Winemaker's Wife; Till Marriage Do Us Part—and it has taken me in excess of 50 drafts to reach a point in which I can say that I have exhausted every avenue in terms of revisions, rewrites, alternative beginnings and endings and everything in between.

Looking back over the last several years, it is satisfying as a writer (and independent author) to know that I have been patient with this book and placed craft ahead of the race to publish. This element of time is an indie's greatest strength and weakness—we have the freedom to publish whenever we think we are ready, but too often we think we're ready when we're not. In the traditional publishing world a team of people are assigned to a book to ensure it is fit for publication. As such, a book passes many hands and falls under the scrutiny of many eyes before it goes to print. An independent author does not have the same resources or assistance, and, if my decade of independent publishing has taught me anything, it is to be patient. In the absence of a team, time is tantamount, it is your best friend. Be patient with yourself, with your book. Learn to be an objective critic of your own work. Writing is a craft, and craft can always be improved.

Seeking external assistance

There have been many times over the last 7 years when I have decided that the novel is finished and ready to publish. But, after setting it aside for a few or several months, I have returned to find that it can and should be improved. On a few of these occasions, I have sought outside help.

The first was Julie Christine Johnson, who gave an invaluable critique on the first twenty pages of an earlier draft, which in turn sent me back to the beginning to rethink the starting point, simplify the timeline, strip out the unnecessary exposition from each chapter and instead write amidst the heart of the action.

Fast forward a few years, when I deemed the novel finished again, and sent copies to a group of beta readers—Tommy, Danielle, Laura, and Merrill—who helped me identify the strengths and weaknesses. Thank you, ladies. Your feedback was so helpful.

Last year, when I deemed the novel finished yet again, I sought the help of Richard Gibney, who provided editorial feedback and offered valuable insights and additions.

Alas, my inner critique was not fully satisfied and insisted that I could push myself a little more and make further improvements. So, I put it aside and returned several months later. This time, I made brutal changes, deleting 20 chapters, trimming the word count by 10k and simplifying the timeline again.

Sufficed to say, any mistakes in the final draft are my own.

Research

A special thanks to @Subbo (Twitter) who shared his valuable knowledge and experience about the Australian winemaking industry.

Final Thanks

Thank you to my husband, daughter, son and hound for your love, encouragement and support. You are all my light when I am lost in the darkness of self doubt.

About the Author

Bianca Bowers is an immigrant, best-selling poetry author, novelist and award-winning poetry editor. She holds a BA in English and Film/TV/Media Studies and has authored several books through her imprints Paperfields Press and Auteur Books.

She is known for her deeply personal writing style that seamlessly weaves cultural and literary references into work that is informed by life experience and inspired by love, relationships, personal evolution, and the human condition.

Bianca's first poems were published in 1999, in the esteemed New Zealand poetry anthology, Tongue in your Ear. Since then, Bianca's poems have appeared in various print anthologies, online journals and a trailer for a short film.

www.biancabowers.com

https://www.amazon.com/author/biancabowers

https://www.goodreads.com/BiancaBowersAuthor

https://www.instagram.com/BiancaBowers_Author